# Empires Of The Crab

Dale Cathell

Bloomington, IN

Milton Keynes, UK

*AuthorHouse™*
*1663 Liberty Drive, Suite 200*
*Bloomington, IN 47403*
*www.authorhouse.com*
*Phone: 1-800-839-8640*

*AuthorHouse™ UK Ltd.*
*500 Avebury Boulevard*
*Central Milton Keynes, MK9 2BE*
*www.authorhouse.co.uk*
*Phone: 08001974150*



*First published by AuthorHouse 4/18/2006*

*ISBN: 1-4259-1320-2 (sc)*
*ISBN: 1-4259-1321-0 (dj)*

*Library of Congress Control Number: 2006902188*

*Printed in the United States of America*
*Bloomington, Indiana*

*This book is printed on acid-free paper.*

# Author's note

In the summer of 2004 I developed the idea of writing a book based upon what I perceived was a great love story - the relationship of Brice and Shirley Phillips of Hoopers Island and Ocean City, Maryland. I was inspired by what I knew about their contributions to the communities and my original plan was that it would be a limited edition type of book that I could create just as a memory for the Phillips and their friends.

I met with Shirley and Brice in their office at the Crab House in Ocean City. They were surprised and initially made light of the idea that anyone might want to write a book about them or their family, and if it was written, that anyone would want to read it. But, after considerable effort on my part to convince them, they finally authorized me to undertake the writing of their family's story. Once they agreed to allow me to try to put together this project they cooperated in every way, except for one area. Shirley and Brice steadfastly declined to furnish me with any information about the family's charitable and civic contributions, on the basis that the issue is between them and God. In other words, God knows and that's enough for them. Steve, their son, later expressed similar feelings. Accordingly, almost all of the information included in the book about the Phillips' charitable and civic contributions to their communities was obtained from other sources, including my own personal knowledge. None was obtained directly or first from Phillips family members, although, on occasion, one of them might confirm what I discovered from other sources.

From that first meeting, the project grew in scope as I uncovered more and more about the Phillips and Flowers families (Shirley was a Flowers.)

Early in the project, Shirley remembered that she had saved every letter that Brice had written her when they were engaged and first married - and he wrote several letters a week. There were literally hundreds of letters dated in the mid-1940s. She very graciously made them available to me and, among those letters, I discovered a series that Brice wrote Shirley from various countries in Europe when he was stationed with a combat unit during World War II.

I knew that, in addition to a great love story between Brice and Shirley, there was much more - a story of how the enlisted G. I. s in that War felt about it, about VE day, about the upcoming invasion of the home islands of Japan, about what the American fighting men who were going to be involved in that invasion thought about the dropping of the atomic bombs on Hiroshima and Nagasaki. There were books out there that had included letters from different soldiers about the war, but I couldn't (and still don't) recall reading any books that contained chronologically ordered letter after letter containing one intelligent soldier's musings on the progress and outcome of World War II.

I had more than a love story on my hands. An odyssey had begun to tell itself, to tell me what to write.

I began to do research on the early days on Hoopers Island, Maryland, and in the process discovered a unique place and was able to feel how it was, in the days of the Great Depression, to grow up on one of the islands at the center of the Chesapeake Bay's crabbing industry. One thing led to another, and eventually the book took my mind to that other Empire of the Crab halfway around the world.

In the process I have gone from the aft-cabin of the Schooner *McCready* in 1920, to outrigger boats in the Visayan Sea in the Philippine Islands in the present decade. That trip through time with the Phillips family and their friends, has enabled me to address some of the practices and problems within the seafood industry, past and present. It has also allowed the sharing with me, and through me to the public, thoughts of very learned people on possible solutions to the consistent problems of shortages within the Chesapeake Basin. Ultimately this book became the story of an American family and its century-long relationship with a complex creature - the crab.

Most of all, it allowed me to paint a picture of an extraordinary American family. The Phillips of Hoopers Island.

# Acknowledgments

The book is based largely on numerous interviews with many people. I acknowledge the persons who have not asked to remain anonymous. Of course, of primary importance were Brice and Shirley Phillips and their two sons, Steve and Jeffrey. My interview with the various members of the immediate family consisted of more than 35 hours of taped sessions. An extensive interview with the late Dr. Tom Flowers of Cambridge was especially helpful not only in respect to the immediate Phillips and Flowers families but also in respect to the culture of Hoopers Island in the early days. Likewise, his book, *Shore Folklore,* helped me to immerse myself into that culture and hopefully write a better book. Semore Dofflemyer, Paul Wall, Jay Newcomb, and Dr. Geoffrey Robbins provided important insights into the Phillips family from very different viewpoints. Bernice and Harry Murphy (her son,) Jane Groff, and Joyce Flowers all provided hours and hours of information I could not have obtained elsewhere. Lil Townsend and Ann Showell were especially helpful in developing the Ocean City years. The Nabb Center at Salisbury University was very useful in developing some of the early history of the families, especially Shirley's family - the Flowers. Additionally, I was able to draw extensively from numerous newspaper articles over the years that were kept by Mrs. Jane Groff, Brice's sister, who graciously gave them to me, along with the picture of Miss Leone and Captain Ellie on their wedding night in 1919. The newspaper articles kept by Mrs. Groff contained information dating back to the sale of the schooner *McCready* in 1920.

I used several volumes of the Phillips Crab House yearbook and certain biographical information contained in a forward to a cook book that Shirley had contemplated writing several years ago. Steve Phillips and Phillips Foods made numerous papers and documents available, especially those relating to the overseas operations. There were numerous articles in various publications about members of the family or their businesses, or their history, or the history of Hoopers Island, that were made available from the collections of various family members.

I was able to extract much information on the status of the crab and rockfish populations in the Maryland portion of the Chesapeake Bay throughout the years from various records maintained by the Maryland Department of Natural Resources. From them, and from the expertise of the Phillips family, and from Jay Newcomb, I was able to extrapolate the average Maryland commercial production of picked crab meat and compare the State's production with the Phillips' needs as they moved into the present century.

A short description of the way in which I have structured the book may be helpful to the reader in identifying the speaker at any particular part of the book. All statements of persons other than the writer that are contained within paragraphs are book-ended by quotation marks. When a quotation by one of the persons I have interviewed comprises fifty words or more, it is generally set off in a separate paragraph, indented additional spaces, and the speaker is identified just before the beginning of the quoted material or just after the ending. On occasion, the speaker may not be identified specifically, but the identity is clear from the context. On some occasions there may be no attribution to the source of a quote. In most such cases the speaker has declined to be identified about that particular quote. However, those particular comments should be contained in tapes that I have maintained.

Generally, unless a different speaker is clearly identified, italicized material at the very beginning of a section or chapter of the book is a result of the writer taking literary license with the known facts. As an example, at the very beginning of the first part of the book there is an italicized narrative of a voyage of the *McCready.* No one now alive knows whether that particular voyage took place or whether Captain Augustus Elsworth Phillips Jr., ever raced to Cape Hatteras against his uncle, Captain Warren Simmon's 'pines'[1] and banana bugeye schooner, the *Morning Star.* But, considering the Phillips family's genes, had the two captains met off Charleston, South Carolina, on the same course which, considering that they sailed the same limited areas of the sea,

[1] 'Pines' was the name given to pineapples by Hoopers Islanders involved in what they referred to as the 'fruit' trade - coastal cargo schooners carrying pineapples and bananas from the Caribbean to the cities along the coast. The 'pines' trade along the Atlantic coast continued until the major growers in Hawaii began to take over the pineapple market.

they very likely did, it would probably have resulted in the race I describe. So I created how it might have been. There are several other such instances throughout the book.

In some parts of the book there will be what might appear to landlubbers to be serious grammatical mistakes. The grammar may be wrong, but, generally, it is not a mistake. I have, on occasion, used the language of the water. I grew up around it, as did the Phillips. For instance, in many places in the the book I refer to fisherman or watermen 'catching crab.' Crab is in the singular when most people might think the correct phrase is 'catching crabs,' with the plural use of the word. But commercial watermen catch crab, perch (not perches) rock (not rocks), or to use the other term for that great Maryland fish, watermen catch striped bass not striped basses.

Additionally, throughout the book I often refer to the efforts of watermen to catch crab, as 'fishing'. When so used, it is a generic term for harvesting creatures of all kinds, including crab, from the sea (a term, itself, which often also includes bays and creeks that are attached to the seas and oceans.) Other similar uses of language may appear throughout the book. I make no apologies. It is the way it really is. Also, Hoopers Island is spelled without an apostrophe in official documents and is spelled that way by Hoopers Islanders (in spite of the fact that it is named after the Hooper family.) And that is how it is spelled throughout the book.

The reader should also keep in mind that some of the people to whom I attribute happenings have been dead for half a century or more, and at least seven of the persons interviewed were in their eighties or nineties. The longer one lives the more there is to remember and, thus, the more there is to forget. The saying that memories dim with time is accurate. I have filled in the blanks in the various memories as best I can. I have created for those that were not available to interview, what I think they might have said or done, based upon what my research and interviews with others indicate would probably have happened or been said had they been here to talk to me. In all such instances, I've tried to be kind.

I want to acknowledge the assistance of four women: Gail Whaley, Janet Cherrix, Phyllis Mitchell and Nancy McElgunn. They have taken the time to read a preliminary draft of the book and have proffered several changes and suggested many corrections. Without their advice the book would be of lesser literary and grammatical quality.

As always, my wife, Charlotte, has supported my efforts as a writer and I am very grateful for that support. I also want to especially thank all the members of the Phillips family and their friends for helping to make this book possible.

# Dedication

The Empires of the Crab is dedicated, as all of the Phillips would want it to be, to two wonderful islands, Hoopers Island and Ocean City, and to island people everywhere.

# TABLE OF CONTENTS

## **BOOK ONE** - Hoopers Island

*The boy - Brice*

Chapters

## **BOOK FOUR** - Living and giving

**The Crab**

*The Crab, the Crab*
*with its pointy little body*
*six little legs*
*and two powerful claws.*

*Its beady marble eyes,*
*stereo-typically red,*
*Sebastian, Chadwick,*
*and the Great Captain Phil.*

*The Crab, the Crab*
*not just a crustacean*
*living its simple life*
*in the wondrous Chesapeake.*

*To me it is a symbol*
*of family and home,*
*good, happy times*
*on the old Eastern Shore.*

*The Crab, the Crab*
*on which we feast in summer.*
*More crackers! More vinegar!*
*In the backyard at dusk.*

*The pounding of mallets*
*accompanied with laughter,*
*with family, with love,*
*just soaking up good feeling.*

*The Crab, the Honorable Crab,*
*for where would my family be,*
*if nothing of your sort*
*inhabited the salty waters?*

*You've brought us fame and fortune.*
*Ha! It makes me laugh*
*that a tiny creature like you has given me so much.*

Carmen Phillips at age 12. Reprinted with permission of the poet.

# BOOK ONE

---

## *Hoopers Island*

## *The boy - Brice*

*The schooner "McCready" was beating to windward on a starboard tack out of Charleston Harbor, trying to head due east to catch the engine of the Gulf Stream and its four knots of push to the north'ard. The wind was blowing ten to fifteen knots out of the northeast and Captain Ellie knew that when he made the turn to the north he would have to work her hard to maintain enough sea room to round Cape Hatteras. They'd then head for the Chesapeake, and on to Baltimore with the cargo of cypress shingles he'd loaded at the docks in Charleston. Next would be a side trip home to the islands of the crab that themselves hung below Taylors and Dunnock Islands. The three islands, Honga/Fishing Creek, Hoopersville, and Applegarth, collectively called Hoopers Island. The year was 1920.*

*He had bought the schooner several years before, when he was only 18, and manned her with a crew of three. She was one of the largest remaining Maryland cargo schooners, boats working under sail. Vessels that hauled cargo up and down the east coast. He'd been young when he'd managed to borrow enough money to buy her. Too young, some thought. But on the islands of the crab, boyhood was but a brief interlude. Work began no later than age twelve, sometimes as early as their fourth year, as the boys followed their fathers on the water. Not where he was sailing now with the "McCready", but big enough water - the Honga River, Tar Bay, and the Chesapeake.*

*As the sea began to take on the deep blue of the stream, he noticed another schooner offshore on a converging course, a schooner with masts raked aft, a bugeye rig. She was heading inshore some, but still northing, working the stream. She was familiar as she got closer. It was his uncle, Captain Warren Simmons, heading to New York from the islands on the pineapple and banana run, hauling the fruit to the city in his schooner, the Morning Star.*

*She was closing fast; the combined speed of two of the fastest working schooners still in service making short work of the distance between them. Captain Ellie turned the wheel to port, bringing the McCready more into the wind, still keeping as much way on her as he could, and his uncle did likewise, turning to port also. Jibing down the wind the Morning Star kept her speed better. Soon the boats were passing, port to port, and Captain Ellie yelled over:*

*"Race you to Hatteras Light."*
*"Done."*

*Captain Simmons put his wheel over to starboard, bringing the Morning Star's head to starboard, up into the wind, then crossing the point of the wind, with the main boom crossing to starboard, and she began to regain her speed some, now heading east on a parallel course with, but now a quarter-mile north and west of the McCready. To the east Captain Ellie had kept the head of the McCready close to the wind to slow her until his uncle could come up with him.*

*Soon Captain Simmons was close abeam and with a wave to his uncle, Captain Ellie let the McCready fall off to the wind, just a little though, just to get her up to enough speed to avoid the covering efforts of his uncle, his uncle's attempt to steal the wind by placing his sails between it and the McCready. They continued offshore, almost side by side, but with the McCready gradually inching forward as Captain Ellie knew she would. She was the faster ship; but barely so. After several miles on an easterly course, the McCready was ten boat lengths east of Captain Simmons' schooner when Captain Ellie quickly brought the McCready's head into the wind, then put her on a tack to the north-west. His crew working vigorously to switch the lines. Soon he crossed his uncle's bow.*

*As his uncle passed, now hard astern, Captain Ellie saw him shaking his fist at the McCready, good- naturely though, and then over the whoshing of the wind and the sound of the schooners' passages through the water, Captain Ellie heard his uncle yell over, "Tell my mom , tell 'Ringie', I plan to be home by Thanksgiving." "I'll tell her," Captain Ellie responded as the vessels passed.*

*As the Morning Star became smaller, Captain Ellie felt hands around his waist, and a forehead pressed gently into the small place between his shoulder blades. They had gotten married just a year before, in 1919. Leone Elizabeth Simmons was the most beautiful woman on an island of beautiful women. From a family that had been on the islands since the 1600s.*

*Their honeymoon had been a trip to Baltimore for cargo and a voyage to Savannah. The only home he had to offer her then was the aft cabin on the*

*"McCready."And she'd come aboard, willingly. They had made their home in the year since on the schooner. She had agreed to the arrangement before she'd married him. She loved him as he loved her. Home was where they were. But, she'd asked only one thing, that their family, when it started, would begin ashore. He had agreed.*

*He didn't turn to face her right away. Where he came from, public displays of affection weren't frequent. They were saved for the quiet times when lovers were alone. That was more so at sea. Especially when the Captain brought his wife aboard to live. On the islands of the crab, a women aboard a vessel was considered bad luck. But he'd had nothing but good luck since they'd married. He'd gotten top money for the cargos they'd carried. Been able to save a considerable sum in the small chest he kept hidden in their cabin. At first he'd thought it was the generosity of the shippers-a wedding present so to speak. But the luck had held past the honeymoon, or what normally passed for a honeymoon period.*

*The crew was on deck, the three of them sprucing up the lines now that she was heading northwest. They'd stay on deck as he tacked back and forth to beat north into the wind and they'd stay there at least until after he rounded Hatteras sometime tonight or early tomorrow morning. In heavy weather, she would come on deck to help with the lines, with the bow plunging into the seas throwing spray down the length of the vessel, sometimes seas mounting and washing over the beam of the boat, putting his wife up to her waist in the sea. He'd been frightened then, when she'd go on the deck, especially when the coming seas were hidden in the darkness of the night. But, when he'd told her to stay below, she'd refused. Said the schooner was her home, all of it. Besides she liked it. The excitement of it. Now though, it was different.*

*She moved to his side, placed her hand on his right arm as he kept the McCready on the line he had chosen. As tight to the wind as she could make way to the north. His wife said then, "Remember what we agreed upon when we married?" He remembered immediately. There had only been the one agreement. He looked at her with a question in his blue eyes. "We're going to have a baby," she answered. It would be a boy.*

*They would name him Brice.*

# CHAPTER ONE

*Captain Augustus Elsworth Phillips, Jr. (Captain 'Ellie')*

The story of our particular Phillips family began almost a hundred years ago on Hoopers Island, with the two Captains, Augustus Elsworth Phillips, Senior, and Augustus Elsworth Phillips, Junior, Brice's father, both of whom at one time or another were apparently called Captain Ellie. Although early records of Hoopers Island contain references to Phillips living there as long ago as the mid-1860s, not much more than their presence appears in the available records. As relevant to the present story, not much is recorded, or now remembered of this particular Phillips family prior to the time of the two Captains Augustus Phillips. Brice's sister, Mrs. Dunbar (Jane) Groff, states that it wasn't known "where our Phillips family came from before my grandfather." They were just there on Hoopers Island at the turn of the 20th Century or a little before.

Augustus Elsworth Phillips, Sr. is remembered by most chroniclers of the time as a former waterman (or schooner captain - or both) and later the operator of a country store at Honga[2]/Fishing Creek. Early sailing records indicate that there was a Captain Ellie Phillips who was the captain of the schooner, *Annie Hodges,* that sailed in Chesapeake

[2] Honga, as a neighborhood name, reflects its relationship with the Honga River that is situate to the east of Hoopers Island. The Honga River was known as the Hunger River in the pre-Revolutionary era.

waters as early as 1901. She was a cargo schooner, but, according to the records at the Nabb Center,[3] she was also used in oystering on the Chesapeake. Mr. William Hooper in his memoirs "My Years Before the Mast,"[4] recalled that he had worked on the *Annie Hodges* in that time period and that two of Captain Phillips' sons, Amos and Goldsborough worked on that schooner with him. In Captain Augustus Ellsworth Phillips Jr.'s obituary it was noted that he was survived by several brothers, one of whom was named Goldsborough. Augustus Ellsworth Phillips, Sr. was also known on Hoopers Island as Capt. Ellie, so the Captain Ellie Phillips of the *Annie Hodges* was very probably the grandfather of Brice Phillips, and Brice's father probably inherited the nickname, Captain Ellie, from his father.[5]

Additionally, Jane Groff remembers that when she was a young girl, she was told that her grandfather had been the captain of some type of vessel in the past, but she doesn't remember what type of boat or what exactly it was that her grandfather did. There are also remembrances that the elder Captain Augustus Phillips had interests on, or in relation to, the water prior to his son's return from the sea in 1920. Moreover, it is universally agreed that the grandfather was also referred to as a "Captain." That title is reserved on Hoopers Island for those who made their living on the water, or from the water, at some point in their lives.

[3] The Nabb Center is affiliated with Salisbury University in Salisbury Maryland. It contains numerous private collections donated to the center relating to the history of the Eastern Shore of Maryland as well as collections relating to Delaware and the tidewater part of Virginia's Eastern Shore. It also contains numerous reference works relating to the same area.
In researching the records and collections at the Nabb Center I reviewed *Chesapeake Bay Schooners,* by Quenton Snediker, *Letters to the Little Ones,* by Gorden Evans Wood, Jr., *Schooners in the Pocomoke,* Collection of Charles Robert and Virgal Hall, and numerous other documents contained in various collections.

[4] *My Years Before the Mast, Memoirs of William Hooper,* compiled with the help of Gladys Hooper. In the collections of the Nabb Center-on line at http://freepages.genealogy.rootsweb.com/fassitt/hooper_21.html.

[5] Additionally, in *My Years Before the Mast,* Mr. Hooper notes that the 'Captain Ellie's" (Captain Augustus Ellsworth Phillips, Sr.) father was Captain Gus [presumably an abbreviation of Augustus] Phillips, who also "was a captain of a vessel in the coastal trade." In all likelihood this Captain Phillips would have captained a schooner as most descriptions of those days indicate that the coastal trade on sailing vessels was primarily on schooners of whatever rig. Accordingly, it is reasonable to assume that Brice Phillips' father, grand-father and great grand-father all captained schooners in the coastal trade. The schooner cargo trade gradually diminished as steam powered vessels took over the trade.

Mrs Groff also remembers being told that her grandmother Phillips would run the store while her grandfather was on the water. So it is fairly certain that Captain Augustus Phillips, Sr. was the captain of the *Annie Hodges* sailing from Hoopers Island at certain points during his lifetime. If so, both Brice's father and grandfather (and perhaps his great grand-father) were captains of schooners.

There was also another Captain Phillips, Charles A. Phillips, who was the master of the schooner *George May.* There may be a connection between him and our Phillips family. I have been unable to find out his complete middle name. It may have been, Augustus. If so, there might be a connection.

Senior's wife was Dorinda Travers Simmons, whose nickname was 'Ringie'. Her father had been the operator of a store at Hoopersville. Her brother was believed to be Captain Warren Simmons, of the large bugeye schooner, *Morning Star.*

There is some confusion about when the A. E. Phillips and Son packing plant on Hoopers Island actually began. Dates as early as 1914 and as late as 1921 are mentioned in various published materials. The explanation that appears most accurate may be that Captain Phillips, Sr., in addition to operating the country store, had begun some activity with processing crab or oysters at least as early as 1914,[6] but that the 'and Son' part was added in 1921 shortly after Captain Phillips Jr., 'Captain Ellie', left the sea and became involved in the business.

Mrs. Dunbar (Jane) Groff recalls her mother telling her that she and Brice's father had come ashore because her mother did not believe that a family should be raised on a schooner. According to Mrs. Groff, when her father sold the schooner, *McCready,* he was in the process of building a home at Fishing Creek, but it was not yet finished. As she was told, her father and mother lived with a brother of Captain Phillips, Sr., Arthur Phillips, for no more than two months, before moving into the house in very early 1921. Later, Arthur Phillips would work for the

[6] It is believed by some that the first commercial packing plant built on Hoopers Island may have been the packing plant of John M. Clayton built in 1890 in Hoopersville. It was followed in 1904 by the Henry I. Phillips' packing plant in Fishing Creek. *300 Years - Hoopers Island, A brief history of Hoopers Island compiled from the written and oral accounts of the people who have lived there,* by Anne Stinson, printed by the Easton Publishing Co. in 1975. From the collection of Jane Phillips Groff.

Phillips and was in the original packing plant when it was destroyed during the 1933 hurricane.

It was upon this move ashore in early 1921 that Captain Augustus Elsworth Phillips, Jr. probably began to work in the crabbing business started by his father. Mrs Groff vaguely remembers hearing that Senior had begun some business relating to the water several years before her father sold the schooner and came ashore on Hoopers Island. It seems reasonable to speculate that Senior, a former waterman, had begun a crab and/or oystering processing business of some type prior to 1921, in 1914, and that it became A. E. Phillips and Son when Junior left the schooner in late 1920 and joined his father in early 1921. Until that time available records do not indicate that there was a son involved in the business. Mrs Bernice Murphy, Shirley's sister, who was born in 1914 and is over 91 years old, and by the mid-1920s was working in the Phillips' plant, recalls that the plant was started by Captain Phillips, Sr., which supports, to some degree, that the packing plant was started before Brice's father joined the operation (probably in 1921.)

Brice Phillips was born in the house at Fishing Creek on Hoopers Island on January 15th, 1921, very shortly after the house was finished. I have read newspaper articles that state that Captain Augustus Elsworth Phillips, Jr. sold the *McCready* in 1920 to a Hollywood film studio where for years it was used in the filming of pirate movies.[7] If the move ashore was occasioned by the knowledge that a child was coming, as indicated by Mrs. Groff's recollections of conversations with her mother, and the move was made at the time of the schooner's sale, and Brice was born in the house in very early 1921, on January 15th, as the records indicate, Brice was very probably conceived in the aft cabin of the schooner, *McCready.* A fitting beginning for the future patriarch of a family bound to the sea.

[7] From an obituary published at the time of Captain Ellie's death in 1954. The obituary is from the collection of Mrs. Dunbar (Jane) Phillips Groff. There is no indication in the obituary notice as to the newspaper in which it was printed. Another obituary in the collection of Jane Groff, published in 1979 at the time of the death of Mrs. Leone Simmons Phillips, Brice's mother, indicated that she had served as the first mate on Captain Ellie's schooner after their marriage and before they moved ashore.

# CHAPTER TWO

## *The early business*

A. E. Phillips and Son entered a seafood processing industry that, in relative terms, was still in its infancy. Most observers and historians generally set the beginning of the organized industry on Hoopers Island at around 1890 to 1900. Of course, the islanders had always crabbed, fished and 'oystered'; but, for the most part, it had been for local subsistence and on a smaller unorganized scale.

They were relatively isolated. The nearest town of any size was Cambridge, 25 miles or more away over dirt, oyster shell, and punch-log roads (trees felled across the course of the road, then split and left there as the road foundation.) There were no governmentally maintained roads down the islands until the late 1930s and no macadam or paved roads to the islands or down the island chain until almost the 1950s.

As late as 1921, when Captain 'Ellie' joined his father's business, there were still memories, or rumors at least, of the practice of shanghaiing pickers and shuckers that had existed ten years or more before. Then, as now, it was difficult to find sufficient pickers in the summer and shuckers in the winter to process the oysters and crab. It was particularly critical in respect to crab because in the heat of summer crab could not be held over for very long.

The packers, when delivering oysters or crab meat to the markets in Baltimore, would sometimes solve their labor problems by frequenting bars in the harbor area, and, to put it kindly, actively encourage persons that were wasting away their lives drinking and having fun to come work in the plants on Hoopers Island. Often, the new employees would not remember their commitments to the packers upon awakening aboard a boat out on the bay in route to the packing houses. Once at Hoopers Island, they were vigorously aided in maintaining gainful employment by new found acquaintances. They were housed in special buildings in a compound on House Point where their activities could be observed. House Point was at the very 'beginning' of a narrow neck between Back Creek and the Honga River (Hoopers Islanders do not consider the point of land nearest the water to be the end of the land, but the beginning, pointing out accurately that the settlement of the land began, not ended, where water and land met.) House Point was almost surrounded by water. From old maps in the Nabb Center, it appears that there was only one road off the small peninsula, and that one easily watched. From time to time, the new employees were actively encouraged not to leave before the picking or the shucking seasons were over. The matter of the shanghaiing practice of the early time is not often discussed in the present time. William Hooper in his memoirs discounts the rumors of shanghaied watermen, saying ". . . .much folklore has been built up about. . . how they shanghaied their crewman, worked them all season, then paid them off by having them knocked overboard by the boom to drown. I'm inclined to believe these tales were fabrications."

While Brice can remember the compound, House Point, being at the end (or beginning) of a neck of land to the east across Back Creek from his childhood home and remembers hearing stories of the practice, if it had ever existed, it had long disappeared before he became active in the packing plant. If it had existed, it probably was occurring in the days of Captain Phillips Sr., and perhaps even in the early days of Captain Ellie, although there is no record of A. .E. Phillips and Son having participated in that method of recruitment.

The advent of bay travel on steamship routes opened up the increasingly urban markets in Baltimore and along the coast. As the demand for oysters and crab meat increased, local entrepreneurs throughout the Chesapeake began to build packing plants and to develop the beginnings of the industry as we know it today. It was not less so, and perhaps even more so, on Hoopers Island.

Even before World War I, packing plants began to be established on the island. In addition to the Phillips' operation, there were operations by Rollie Creighton, the Ruarks, Nelson, Tolly, Applegarth, and others. The seafood processing industry transformed the area from a subsistence to a manufacturing (albeit on a small scale) economy. At the same time, it created something of a class division in the local society. Because no one had much, there was little resentment of those that had just a little bit more. Generally it came to be believed, probably accurately, that the packers had just a little more than the watermen, were just a little better off. But, any resentment of those days was mellowed by the coming of the depression when everyone learned to survive together. In the society of Hoopers Island of the 20s and the 30s, to the extent there was a difference, Brice's family was less poor than some. Less poor, certainly, than the family of his future wife.

# CHAPTER THREE

## *Trot-lining*

The early days of the industry, particularly the crabbing operations, were much different than they are today. Until just after World War II, crab pots were not extensively used in the Hoopers Island crabbing industry.[8] Crabbing, for the most part, was done by trot-lining, a process that was much more conserving of the crab population than the use of pots. Pots take crab twenty-four hours a day; trot-lines only take crab when the line is being 'fished'.

Trot-lining was an art. It took much more skill than does potting crabs, including peeler-potting. Trot-lines were long lines (sometimes hundreds of yards long) made of separate strips of twine, twisted together with numerous baits attached along the long line (some watermen baited directly to the trot line, others used short stringers.) Each end of the trot-line would be weighted down, normally with a piece of chain. Each chain end would have a float attached so that the trot-liners could more easily find an end of the trot-line. The line would be extended across, or along, whichever body of water the crabber wanted to 'fish' and it would be permitted to sink to the bottom, where it would attract crabs that would commence to feed on the bait. After a sufficient period of

[8] Ms. Anne Stinson in *300 Years - Hoopers Island* noted "About 1938, a new-fangled invention was introduced to the island from Virginia watermen. It was the wire cage crab pot . . . ."

time had passed since the trot-line had been laid on the bottom, the crabber would 'fish' it.

The crabbing boats were usually equipped with a roller, pole, or similar apparatus, extending from the side of the boat, usually forward of mid-ships. One end of the trot-line was pulled to the surface, leaving the chain anchors on the bottom. The end was placed over the roller and, as the boat would be propelled up or down the line, it would slowly emerge from the depths riding on the roller and approach the surface. If done properly, the crabs feeding on the baits would hang on to the bait until almost at the surface and the crabber would net (dip) them from the rear. If the boat was propelled too fast, the crabs would drop off. Most of the better trot-liners 'fished' the trot-lines from upwind. Trot-lining could be very dangerous work. In the old days when trot-lines were fished from boats under sail, and one supposes even later when power was used, if a waterman running his boat down the trot-line happened to fall overboard the boat would continue on. Ms. Stinson notes in *300 Years- Hoopers Island,* that

> Crabs were trot-lined from moving sailskiffs; like the dredgeboats, they made a man aware of the hazards of his livelihood. A man overboard was in dire peril. Once in the water, the wind took no notice of his plight and moved the boat away from him. Drowning was a fact of life; in fact, it was a fact of death for many of those brave men.[9]

Such an incident was described in *My Years Before the Mast,* where Mr. Hooper describes his ordeal when he fell overboard from a sail powered boat while trot-lining.

> When running trot-line out at this new location, I sat on the stern . . . . When the line was about halfway out, suddenly the head of the rudder gave way . . . and caused me to tumble into the water. The skiff quickly sailed away from

[9] Shirley Phillips' mother's first husband, Hilbert Simmons, died in just this way. He fell overboard while crabbing, couldn't swim, and drowned.

> me. . . . Encumbered with boots and oil skins I was unable to swim fast enough to catch up with her. I. . . quickly became exhausted.
>
> Meanwhile, my plight had been observed by other crabbers. Brady Dean . . . was closest to me and started to push his skiff as fast as he could to the rescue. . . .
>
> I saw Brady coming, but by that time I was in deep trouble. Exhausted, lungs waterlogged, and spending increasingly longer periods submerged. . . . As consciousness faded, my vision could no longer discern the surroundings. First, a twilight-like dimness, then ever deepening darkness seemed to engulf me - - as though I was passing through a thick dark wilderness.
>
> Brady saw me surface briefly, when he was almost there, but by the time he reached the spot I was again submerged – probably for the last time. He reached [down in the water] past his shoulder and just managed to grasp my thick black hair. Unconscious by that time, I have no idea how he alone managed to haul me . . . into his small skiff . . .

There was an art to dipping crabs from trot-lines and those that were better at it were almost legends. It is generally believed that Donald Pritchett was the greatest trot-line netter or dipper of all time. He could get three times the catch of the average Hoopers Island trot-liner of his day.

As the crabs were brought aboard, they were culled. In the early days before the 1950s, only peelers were culled. Ripe peelers were crabs that would shed out in two or three days. Green peelers would take longer. Anytime there were doublers[10](one crab mounting another crab) in the hard crab stage, one would be a female peeler.

During that period, size made little difference since all of the crabs were going to be utilized in producing packaged crab meat. After World War II, when the Phillips and others began to create the market for live crab, the crabs began to be culled as to size as well as shedding status. Once the market for live crab was developed, the crabbers were paid considerably more for large (mostly male) crabs to be sold as live crabs,

[10] Doublers won't go into crab pots. Watermen say that "doublers don't pot."

than for the smaller females left over for processing crab meat in the plants. In the beginning of the live crab market, before the advent of wide-scale potting, the trot-liners were paid more for the large jimmies, probably 70 to 80% more than were paid for female crabs. Just after the War, the large jimmies would retail for as much as $2.00 a dozen in the restaurants. Today the same large crabs can retail in restaurants for more than $70.00 the dozen.Generally, however, the pre-war price to the trot-liners was around a cent and a half per pound for all hard crabs - or less, depending on the price paid by the distributors for the meat.

As the sun rose, generally by ten to eleven in the morning in mid-summer, the light of the sun would cause the crabs to begin to let go of the baits attached to the trot-lines before they could be dipped. Thus most trot-lining was over before noon. The crabber would then sail, motor, or row to the packing plant of whatever packer he was working with at that time and deliver the crabs. The peelers were kept separate and their price determined separately. In the early days, the other hard crabs of all sizes were put into barrels and the crabs and the barrel were weighed together, then the crabs were emptied from the barrel and the barrel was weighted. The difference was the poundage of crabs that the packer would be obliged to pay for once the price was determined at the end of the week after the packers had been paid by the distributors in the markets in Baltimore. In more modern times, the prices are determined at the packing plants' docks at the time of the landing of the crab catch. In either case there was a difference in the price paid for peelers and hard-crabs.

In the afternoon the trot-liners would re-bait the trot-line in preparation for the next day. Generally, the preferred baits were eels or tripe. Sometimes when eels and tripe were hard to obtain, chicken necks or 'bull noses' or 'bull lips' discarded from slaughter houses were used. A brine would be created so thick that it would float an egg. The trot-line, with the baits, was then soaked in the brine to toughen the bait to make it more difficult for the next day's crabs to pull it from the line. After the trot-line was baited, the crabbers would often go in the packing plants if their wives were still picking and 'clean' crabs for their wives. The cleaning would entail removing the outer top shell ('de-backing',) removing the dead man's fingers (the gills,) and cutting the crab in half for their wives to pick. Later the crabbers would go home, eat, sleep, and head out on the water at 3 or 4 o'clock the next morning - day after day, all summer long (except Sundays.)

Those crabber families who had sons put them to work as early as four years of age. At that age they, as well as some of the young daughters, might be taken by their mothers to the packing plants where they would 'crack claws' and pick the claw meat for packing. Some children could pick as much as 20 pounds of claw meat a day for which their mothers were paid 2 ½ cents a pound (up to 5 cents per pound as the World War II years approached.)

As they got older, generally around ten or eleven years of age, the sons might start trot-lining on their own. The crabbers (with sons) would leave around 3 in the morning towing small skiffs behind the larger boat. The sons were left off in the skiffs, usually on the shallower waters of the Barren Island flats. Some of the skiffs had live wells in them so that the boys could keep the 'busters' (crabs almost ready to 'bust' out of their hard shells and become soft crabs) in the water. The sons would 'fish' their own trot-lines in the shallower waters, while their fathers worked the deeper, more productive waters of Tar Bay or other areas. Around mid-morning the fathers would return, retrieve their sons, and tow the son's skiffs to the packing house. In the afternoon the sons would help prepare the lines for the next day's 'fishing.'

During the early and late part of the crabbing season, when the children were still in school, they were required to go with their mothers to the packing plants in the early morning hours where they would pick crabs until it was time to go to school, then they'd go off to school smelling of steamed crabs. In the winter when there was no crabbing, the boys were expected to pick up odd jobs, often delivering copies of the *Grit, a* newspaper that is still published today. Back then it sold for five cents.

Soft crabbing was accomplished in two ways. First, the culled peelers were 'floated' or penned in areas in the water, and were tended around the clock by people assigned that task by the packers. When a peeler shed its hard shell, the resulting soft crab was immediately taken from the water so that the soft shell wouldn't harden, placed in a container with moist bay grasses and put in coolers to await transportation to the markets. In addition to this process, another much less efficient method of producing soft crabs was used. It was called 'dipping' and was done in relatively shallow, clear water. A boat would be propelled slowly across the water, with the crabber poised near the bow, looking at the bottom. He would be looking for two crabs side by side. When he would see them on the bottom, he would quickly dip both shells bringing them into the boat. Usually, one would be a soft crab and the other the discarded hard shell of that crab. There was also some scraping for soft crabs. A crabber would drag a scrape through bay grasses, bring it aboard and cull the soft crabs from the grasses, throwing the grasses back overboard.

The younger children of the island also got involved in the catching of soft crabs. They would wade the shallows, especially grassy shallows, looking for soft crabs. They would then sell them to the packers. Up into the late thirties the children were paid between two cents to five cents per soft crab, less if it was small.

# CHAPTER FOUR

## *'Arsterin'*

'Arsterin or oysterin' (depending upon the particular accent of the Eastern Shore speaker) was, for the most part, conducted then as it is now, with the exception of patent tonging (which generally wasn't a Hoopers Island practice.) The Hoopers Islanders hand tonged or used sailing craft, usually skipjacks and bugeyes, to dredge for oysters. There are at least two references in the literature of schooners being used in 'oysterin'.

The sailing craft would pull scrapes across the oyster bars, by sail, and later by power. Around the turn of the 20th Century, oysters tonged in Chesapeake waters would often be put upon cargo schooners for transport to other states. The *Annie Hodges* was used at least on one occasion to transport oysters up the Chesapeake, through the Chesapeake and Delaware Canal, down the Delaware Bay to the back bays behind New Jersey's barrier islands, where they were then offloaded overboard where, after a sufficient period of time, they would be re-harvested and sold as New Jersey 'salts'.[11] Today power push boats are used to push

[11] William Hooper, *Two Years Before the Mast.*
A 'salt' is an oyster that grows along the seaside in the 'back bays' behind the barrier islands of the Atlantic coast. It is saltier than it's Chesapeake kin. If it grows its entire life in the 'back bays', it also has a distinctive shell, in that it is sharper and much rougher with more pronounced points. 'Chincoteagues', and 'Blue Points' from Long Island Sound are 'salts'. Natural 'salts' are much more desired by true oyster connoisseurs.

the skipjacks across the bar on days when it is permitted. From about 1940 on, dredging under sail has been more a Cambridge practice rather than a practice much used by Hoopers Island watermen.

Generally, the watermen who had been crabbing in the crabbing season, would set their boats up for hand tonging when the crabbing season was over and the oyster season opened. Again they would usually align themselves with one packer.

The boats would be anchored or fastened to a long pole driven into the muddy bottom. In waters up to ten or more feet, the waterman would stand on the gunwale of his boat and operate the giant scissor-like apparatus to open and close the mouth of the claw end on the oyster bar below, until a sufficient load was felt by the tonger. The claw would be closed and the tongs hand over handed to the surface. There the stuff in the tongs, hopefully a bunch of oysters, would be culled for legal sized oysters. The small oysters and the debris would be returned overboard. Dr. Tom Flowers noted that the first day of the tonging season would almost kill the watermen. The tong handles would rub against the chests of the waterman until their chests were so sensitive they couldn't bear to be touched. It usually took several days for them to get used to it.

Often tonging was a two man operation. One man tonging and one man culling, switching the process when a tonger got tired. When school was out for the various holidays, the men might take their sons with them to do the culling. However, some watermen worked alone, preferring to tong a while, then rest while they were culling. In the very early days tongers normally received around ten to twelve cents a bushel at the packing plants and averaged around ten bushels a day. Sometimes it was a dollar a day work. Mr. William Hooper comments

As natural seaside oysters became rarer in the 1900s, it became a practice to 'move' adult Chesapeake oysters to the seaside where they would be put overboard for at least three tides to 'salt up'. They would then be taken up and sold to the fancy restaurants in the cities as the higher priced 'salts'. The restaurants were none the wiser. In later years, some purveyors on the seaside dispensed with the putting over of Chesapeake oysters to 'salt up', and merely shucked Chesapeake oysters into gallon tins, added salt, and sold them as 'Chincoteagues' or 'Blue Points'.

Around the late 1950s and early 1960s, Brice Phillips and some Worcester County watermen would bring oyster spat from the Chesapeake to the seaside and plant them on leased bottom where they would spend their entire growing period. When oysters were 'planted' on the seaside as spat, they would, in essence, become natural 'salts'.

in his memoirs, "My father told me he had run oysters up to the steam houses when he was paid as little as 12 cents a bushel"

When the tonged oysters reached the packing houses, they would be placed in piles outside until they were shucked. Unlike processing crabs, which had to be done fairly swiftly because of the heat, oysters could be kept stored in their shells for days when it was cool. There were more men that shucked oysters than picked crabs, but shucking was still primarily done by women.

In addition to the tongs used in the deeper water, watermen of the early days also had what they called 'nippers' that would be used in shallow water when they could see the bottom. They were much shorter and lighter than the tongs. The boats would be poled in the shallower water, and when an oyster was seen on the bottom, a much smaller claw like apparatus on the end of the 'nippers' would be used to pick up the oysters, one by one.

Buy boats would sometimes go right out in the middle of the tonging fleet. Many of the packers had their own buy boats and would buy oysters from the tongers out on the oyster bars for use in their plants and there were also independent buy boat operators who would buy oysters and sail them directly to Baltimore or Annapolis. Sometimes the buy boats of a Hoopers Island packer would go to other areas to buy oysters if the local supply got scarce.

# CHAPTER FIVE

## *Marketing*

In the early days, before a reliable road transportation system was built, crab meat (or oysters) was shipped daily by steamship from a steamship wharf on Hickory Cove in Hoopersville[12] to the Baltimore distributors. Shirley Phillips describes the process:

> There was another island [other than Fishing Creek] named Hoopersville Island, where a steamer would come in every day. The watermen would come into the processors around three o'clock in the day and sell their catch. The pickers or shuckers would come to the processors in the evening or the early morning hours and work for six or seven hours picking and shucking until time to go home and get breakfast for the children and get them off to school. The processors would deliver the cans of shucked oysters or containers of crab meat and the un-shucked oysters to Hoopersville Island. There were very few vehicles on the island at the time. They were mostly limited to the packers' trucks.

[12] Anne Stinson notes that passengers paid five dollars for a round trip to Baltimore, plus another two dollars if they wanted a stateroom. On the steamships route around the bay, Hoopers Island was the last stop on the way to Baltimore and the first stop upon leaving Baltimore. The packers would go up one day; return the next. *300 Years-Hoopers Island.*

> The processors would ship their seafood on the steamers to Baltimore where it was transported to distributors at Lexington Market, or other markets, where it would be sold. Once a week, usually on a Saturday, the processors would take the steamer to Baltimore, walk to the markets where they would settle up on what had been delivered.

Accordingly, as Shirley indicates, the packers, including Brice's father, first by steamship and later by vehicle, would go to Baltimore to settle up with the distributors. The price to be paid by the distributors for the previous week's supply would be negotiated at that time (after the fact.) It was only after that price was negotiated with the distributors, that the packers would determine how much per pound of crab or bushel of oysters would be paid to the watermen for the previous week's catch. Each packer paid about the same amount. Accordingly, the loyalty of a waterman to a packer depended upon things other than price-personal things sometimes, family ties, the extension of credit by packers. This old practice of after the fact pricing no longer exists and would probably be illegal if it did. But in those days, it was done that way because it always had been. As Brice puts it, it worked back then because "People were honest in those days and generally wouldn't try to beat you out of what they owed you." Brice further described the process of pricing in the early days:

> The packers established the prices for how much you would pay the watermen for the raw product. The packers still had to pay the shuckers and pickers. The packers' profit, if any, was what they could get when they in turn got the prices from the wholesalers and retailers - the amount over what they paid the watermen, the shuckers and the pickers and the other overhead, coal, tins, and such. The prices for the watermen in the early days were established at the end of each week and the watermen wouldn't know how much they would be paid for the prior week's catch until the packers got the sales price from the distributors at the end of the week. Looking back, it wasn't the fairest process for either the packer or the waterman, but it was just the way it had always been done.

> Now, the pricing is different. Each packer posts the price he will pay in advance so the watermen know how much they are going to get each day when they bring their catch to the packers. That's the way it should be. I'm glad we changed. It's fairer this way.
>
> There were no binding contracts with the watermen, but usually a waterman would stay with a particular packer as long as the waterman thought the packer was treating him right.
>
> It was kind of customary in those days for the packers to extend credit to the watermen so they could get needed materials and equipment. Payment would be over an extended period of time, usually a season.

The life span of the crabs out of water, especially as the season progressed into summer, dictated, and still to some extent dictates, the timing of the processing of the crabs. Because, especially in the days before refrigeration, they couldn't be kept alive very long, the practice began of picking crabs in the early hours of the morning when it was cooler. The watermen would arrive at the packing plants in the early afternoon to off-load crabs. They would be steamed in the late afternoon or in the evening and the pickers would start early the next morning, the exact time depending on the number of crabs landed at the packing house the previous afternoon. Usually, the picking would be finished before the next afternoon, but occasionally would extend into that afternoon, especially during the school year when the women would have to interrupt their picking and temporarily leave the plant to get the younger children ready for classes.

Over time a system evolved on Hoopers Island that was used to summons crab-pickers. The packers agreed among themselves on the timing of the process, which was conveyed to the various pickers. Each packer would have an assigned time in the late afternoon to signal its pickers. After each packer had figured out how much time it would take its pickers to process the number of crabs available for picking, the packer would blow his steam whistle at his assigned time. The respective pickers would know when to listen for the appropriate whistle. If the packer blew his whistle two times, that packer's pickers would know what time the packer's bus would pick them up the next morning - two o'clock. If the packer blew the steam whistle three times, he'd pick them up at three o'clock, and so on.

Shirley remembers the picking and shucking processes. She was a picker, albeit not as proficient as her sister Bernice.

> During the crab picking season, there were long tables, steel tables, long enough to seat eight women, four on each side. The pickers sat on benches with a basket beside them for the crab shells and debris. In front of each pair of women would be a bushel of steamed crab for picking. The women would have a pan sitting in their laps that contained two empty cans. In one can the back-fin lumps were placed; in the other, regular crab meat. The claws would go into a basket to be cracked and picked later. All the crab meat would be weighed in order that each can would contain the exact amount of crab meat required - no more, no less.
>
> The crab picking is still done the same way as 50 years ago, but today, we have only 20 to 25 pickers, rather than the 60 we once had. . . . I have done some picking in my life and am able to get up to 40 pounds a day; however, I am not a fast picker. When really stretching, a fast picker could get a 100 pounds if the crabs were big.

# CHAPTER SIX

*Government regulation*

Especially remembered is the islanders' attitude towards officialdom in most of its versions, but especially regarding inspectors of all kinds. The people of the islands were blessed with a geography that would enable them to pass word of the arrival of inspectors, including game wardens and child labor inspectors, down the length of the three islands by the time the inspector had gotten to the first island - Fishing Creek. Brice remembers vividly what would occur when the child labor inspectors would start down the island looking for children working with their parents in the packing plants. When word came, all the children working in the plants would run and hide in the empty wooden shipping crates used to transport crab meat tins. The crates were about the size of caskets and the children would get in them and close the lids. The inspectors would walk in a plant, look around, see no underage pickers, and leave. They never thought to look in the discarded crates. Mrs. Bernice Murphy, Shirley's half-sister, was an under-age picker at the Phillips' plant in the twenties. She remembers: "A lot of the crab pickers were under-age. When the inspectors came to the islands, a signal would be relayed down the three islands and the under-age pickers would hide."

There was also an almost constant contest to avoid the game and fish people who would try to find crabbers and packers keeping undersized crabs and oysters or operating out of season.Game wardens were treated with the same general disdain. The islanders were used to doing things the way their ancestors had done them, and didn't need "them from the other side[13] (the western shore) telling 'usens' what to do."

The late Dr. Tom Flowers, Shirley's cousin, told of a story involving flickers. In the early days, flickers were much sought after to eat by the islanders for their very tasty breast meat. They were shot, plucked and cleaned and then used in meat pies. They were often sold among the islanders. A particular game warden knew of the illegal practice on Hoopers Island and was intent on stopping it, but could never catch anybody. On one occasion he was at a house of a suspected outlaw hunter when the parents were away, but the young son was home. The warden struck up a conversation with the boy, deriding the boy's father's ability as a hunter. He told the boy that he'd heard that his father was a lousy shot. Finally, the boy got angry and began to argue with the warden about his father's abilities. In order to prove his point, the boy took the warden to an outbuilding where flickers were hanging, awaiting plucking and cleaning. The boy's father was charged and paid a fine of twenty-five dollars.

Even more recently, in the 1950's, the Hoopers Islanders looked upon the ducks and geese as just another cash crop.[14] It was just a business. As a 1950's resident of Hoopers Island describes it:

> When I was growing up, waterfowl provided a pretty big vocation in the wintertime. You could hear guns going off at all hours of the night or day. You would see pick-ups pull up at designated places with hundreds of ducks. At the place would be an assembly line process. One person was the dipper who dipped the ducks in boiling water to loosen their feathers, the next person would be the plucker who would pick the feathers from the ducks, the next person would be the cutter who would slit the breast and stomach of the duck, and another person would remove the visceral and dress the duck and the final person would pack the duck. They sold

[13] According to a prominent Eastern Shore attorney, Russell C. Dashiell, Jr., "God has favored the Eastern Shore with a few original thinkers (something He has denied to the dark region to our west.")

[14] At one time in the 1900s, hawks were considered a 'cash crop'. The State had a bounty on hawks and they were slaughtered by the thousands for the bounty money.

> for $2.50 the pair of black ducks which was considered good money in those days [the 50s]. Most of the Hoopers Island ducks ended up in country clubs and other private clubs in the Philadelphia area. Of course that's all gone now. No one on Hoopers Island would ever participate in illegal gunning in this day and age.

When Brice was asked about whether people on Hoopers Island would always comply with bag limits on waterfowl in the old days, he responded with a question, "Were there limits?" All in all, the inspectors, as Dr. Tom Flowers commented, "Lived a lonely life."

# CHAPTER SEVEN

*Growing up*

While both of Brice's grandfathers had run country stores on different islands in the Hoopers Island chain-grandfather Phillips' store had been on Fishing Creek and Grandfather Simmons' on Hoopersville - they had also been watermen at times. By the time Brice was born, neither his father nor either of his grandfathers still worked directly on the water (buy-boats excepted.) His father and paternal grandfather had become established seafood packers by the time he reached his teenage years - processing crabs during the crabbing season, oysters in the winter. Accordingly, growing up time for Brice (as it later would be for his sons Steve and Jeffrey) was almost always water and seafood related. As a very young child Brice soft crabbed, as did most of the children of the islands.

> We had little push boats and we'd go out with crab nets to catch peelers and soft crabs. We'd sell them for two cents, sometimes one cent for peelers, and if they were small the packers would 'double' you up, only give you the price of one for the two small peelers. When I first started, we only got about a quarter for a dozen soft crabs.

Brice began regular employment as a laborer, a goffer, at the A. E. Phillips and Son packing plant at an early age, although not as early as the children of watermen and the women who picked the crabs in the plants.

> I first went to work when I was around twelve. . . . In those days the packing plants were built quite a distance out over the water in order to be in deep enough water that the boats could land crabs and oysters directly at the plant. They didn't have the means to dredge channels into the shore in those days, so the packer built out to deep water. The end of our packing plant was maybe fifty yards from shore with a narrow, two or three plank walkway to it. Everything going from shore to the plant, or coming ashore from the plant, came over that walkway. That's how I was first put to work. I used a handcart and a wheelbarrow to carry containers of cans and any other materials out to the plant.
>
> We steamed the crabs using a boiler out at the plant. I was responsible for wheel-barrowing loads of coal to the plant from shore to keep the boiler running, and it ran most of the time. It was a dirty and dusty job. You were almost black by the end of the day.

From that time on, Brice stayed involved in the plant (s). In addition to working, there was time for other things.

> The first boat I had was one I built myself when I was ten years old. It was about twelve feet long and was a sailing scow with a mast, with outrigger extensions that I operated as sideboards. . . . In those days, the cans that were being used to pack crab meat came in large wooden containers. After the cans were removed, I took the crate wood and built the sailing scow. She had a mast and a sail, but leaked a lot. I had to handle the sail with one hand while I continuously bailed with the other just to keep her from sinking. I called her the "no name boat." I was too busy bailing to name her. I sailed it on the Honga River side of the island and never tried to take it out into the open Chesapeake. We lived on Back Creek,

which leads to the Honga River and it was easier and safer to sail it there.

Brice remembers being a very happy child. His mother constantly pushed him to improve himself, however, which didn't always meet with his approval. At one point when he was probably in the fourth or fifth grade, a musical instrument salesman found his way down to Hoopers Island and sold Brice's mother a violin for Brice's younger sister, Jane, and a banjo for Brice. His mother signed him up for banjo lessons with a person further down the island, dressed him in knickers which he hated, and for two years, with his banjo hung over his shoulder, he'd have to walk down the center of the island to the house where the lessons were given. He would pass Shirley's house on the way. Although he took lessons, he "never got any good at it."

He recalls, sometimes fondly, sometimes not, growing up on the islands.

> All the boys wore knickers in those days and all of us hated them. We also dreaded the coming of winter because we had to wear woolen underwear and it itched like the dickens. We scratched all winter. Compared to today, we weren't very clean either. Especially in the winter when we couldn't go swimming. In the spring, fall and winter, we'd have maybe one bath a week. The girls might bathe twice a week. Most of the children also worked in the plants cracking claws or picking crabs as they got older. They'd work in the morning before they went to school, and then go directly to school. The smell of steamed crabs went with us. But, because everybody smelled but all smelled the same, mostly, no one noticed anyone else's smell. Our own smell masked the rest.
>
> I was a normal child, a little bit bad and hopefully a little more good than bad. I got "switched" when I did something that wasn't nice and I didn't get "switched" as often as I deserved. Didn't get caught as much as I should of, either.

Brice recalls the normal boyhood pursuits:

When we were kids, recreation was mostly outdoor stuff, except for Sundays when everybody went to church. In the summer, when we weren't working, we'd mess with our boats, go swimming. We boys had a skinny dipping swimming hole up the island. [According to Tom Flowers their mothers could always tell when they had been skinny dipping - their ears would be clean.] Sometimes we'd be swimming as early as April even though the water might be bone cold. Later, as we became interested in girls, (that was actually pretty early for me,) the boys and girls would go swimming together, in appropriate attire of course.

In the winter, as soon as the ice came, all the kids would go ice skating. Ice skating was a big sport on Hoopersville. Shirley and her sister, Bernice, were great skaters. We'd skate almost anywhere there was ice, in the creek, in the harbor, sometimes in the River. We'd even skate on the ice across Tar Bay to Barren Island. Usually, though we'd try to find a sheltered pond where the ice was smoother. Bonfires would be built on the shore. It was a good time.

The men also built ice boats and, under sail with a good wind, could almost fly over the ice. The ice brought other memories as well.

In real severe winters when times were bad and on top of that, all the rivers and bays would ice over, people would go on the ice and saw two big holes in the ice and between the holes, saw an open trench. Then they'd bring an old car out on the ice, lower an oyster dredge through one hole, attach it to the rear of the old car, and run the car on the ice alongside the trench to the other hole. There they'd pull the dredge up, remove the oysters it had scraped up, and repeat the process. They'd cut new holes and trenches as they needed them, and keep pulling the dredge between the holes with the car. This was the only way they could get any oysters for market, or even to eat, when the 'ice over', the freeze, was hard and long. I don't remember anyone ever losing a car through the ice. The men knew what they were doing. It was dangerous work, but

> the men had no choice. It was the only way to put food on the table in the bad times. I suppose before cars they'd used horses, but I don't remember seeing horses pulling dredges through the ice.
>
> They'd do it most everywhere it was frozen hard. They did it on the river and on Tar Bay on the west side of Hoopers Island. In those days Tar Bay was protected to the west by Barren Island. Now Barren Island is mostly gone. Ten years ago the hunting club washed into the bay. Tar Bay probably has ceased to exist as a separate bay.

The house on Back Creek on the east side of the island of Fishing Creek had no indoor plumbing until he was twelve years old. None of the houses on the island did. Everyone had outhouses 'out' behind the main house. In the evening they would use chamber pots. As remembered by Brice, the outhouses were snaky places in the summer time. In that season they were approached with apprehension, and examined closely, before being used.

A Halloween pastime of the young boys was to go around turning over outhouses. If one were particularly lucky, the outhouse would be in use at the time. As Brice recalls, "I don't remember turning them over with someone in them, *specifically*. But, I'm sure it happened." His sister-in-law, Bernice Murphy, notes "Brice turning over privies on Halloween rings a bell."

Before electricity came to the island, ice boxes were in general use. Brice notes:

> We had iceboxes on Hoopers Island. The ice man had a delivery route and would come every day and put a 25 pound block of ice in your ice box. That block was chipped from a larger 300 pound block he had picked up at an ice plant. He carried the block into the house in a scissor-like device with sharp tongs on one end and handles on the other. The ice went in one side of the top of the box in the kitchen, and most of the contents were kept in the other side, except that some items such as milk were kept below the ice so that as it melted it dripped over the containers below and kept them cooler.

The melted water would gather below in a container that was emptied when needed.

Almost all the families kept hogs. The day of the first heavy frost was 'hog killing' because it was generally cold enough to draw the body heat out of the hogs after they were slaughtered. The hogs were killed, hung from a limb of a tree, or the edge of a barn, their entrails removed (but saved.) Then they were dipped in scalding hot water in huge cast iron black kettles suspended from tri-pods over open fires in order to remove the hair. After they had been hanging long enough for the body heat to have escaped, they would be butchered with the various cuts, shoulders, hams, etc., packaged and preserved for the winter.

Sausages were then made. The intestine casings had been saved, and the odd parts of the hog were ground up and, along with spices, were stuffed into the intestine casings to make the sausages. Part of what was left over was mixed with corn meal and turned into scrapple. The rest was mixed with a gelatin mixture and turned into meat souse. Brice noted that very little of the hog was wasted. Pork, an occasional chicken from the chicken house, wild game, and oysters were the 'winter meat' on the islands.

People would sometimes gather at his parent's house after they had the Delco system installed (a power generating system) to listen to the radio. They had a floor model with a big megaphone on top (an Atwater Kent radio.) One of the favorite early programs was "Amos and Andy." There were also quilting parties, where the ladies would gather at someone's house and sew quilts from spare pieces of material. The men would show up later after the work was done and socialize. There were also card parties and dominos.

In Brice's youth there were eleven school grades on Hoopers Island, as was also the case on most of the Eastern Shore. All of the persons from that era remember that they had great teachers. Both Brice and Shirley especially remember, Lottie Stoker, Alta Hage, Bob Smith, Otis Prince, and Raymond Simmons. The curriculum was limited to basic courses. And there was the occasional fight.

Steve Phillips remembers that in his youth, a Hoopers Island boy's fight was different than in the more urban areas.

> The first hard fight I ever saw was two boys fighting in a rest room. They weren't fighting over a girl like city boys would have been fighting, they were fighting over whose dog was the best dog. It's a difference in country boys and city boys. Different watermen's villages would fight among themselves, but let boys from Cambridge or Salisbury mess with somebody from Hoopers Island and all the boys from all the islands would join in against the city boys.

Other Hoopers Islanders have confirmed that when they were teenagers there was a special relationship between the Hoopers Island boys and the boys from Cambridge and, especially, from Salisbury. They didn't like each other. Fighting occurred with some frequency. If the Hoopers Island boys found out that someone from Salisbury or Cambridge was coming down to pick up a girl for a date, and find out in time, they'd notify the bridge keeper (there used to be a draw bridge.) He'd open the bridge right before the Salisbury boy arrived and wouldn't let him on the island. If they didn't find out in time to keep the boy off the island, they'd get the bridge keeper to open the bridge after he was on the island so he couldn't get off. If fighting started, the opening and closing of the bridge was determined by who was winning the fight. Brice remembers the problems between the city boys and the Hoopers Islanders in his generation. "When we went dancing, which wasn't often, we'd go into Cambridge on a Saturday night. I don't remember ever getting in a fight but there were fights between the boys from Hoopers Island and the townees from Cambridge."

All of the families were god-fearing and church-going. Brice's family first attended the Methodist Church and later the Holiness Church.

Electricity didn't come to the islands until the mid-1930s. The packing house and Brice's home each had its own system of electricity before that. It was called the Delco system, and it generated electricity for the plant's lighting, and the house. The local hall that would occasionally show movies used a Delco system to generate electricity to power the projector, and the sewing factories on the islands also used the Delco system.

There was a Doctor Meade on the island when Brice and his sister Jane were growing up. He is remembered fondly. He was called on to make house calls when anything was felt to be serious. The watermen were always getting hurt and Dr. Meade would regularly sew them up. On occasion he'd perform major surgery on the island, set broken bones, help deliver babies in the islander's homes. At one point Jane came down with scarlet fever and Dr. Meade sent Brice to his grandfather's house until his sister was no longer contagious.

Many of the illnesses of childhood were treated with home remedies. Drinking cod liver oil was a common remedy and sometimes they'd be given a formula that had castor oil in it. They were constantly being rubbed down with odorous substances. At other times, they would be made to swallow Vick's Salve at the first sign of illness. Sometimes the thought of eating Vick's was enough to make them feel better. According to Tom Flowers, if a boy (or girl) were to cut his hand and the bleeding wouldn't stop, and it wasn't thought sufficiently serious to summons Dr. Meade, the child would be walked into the nearest barn or shed where there were cobwebs. His hand would be put into the cobwebs and that would stop the bleeding. If a person received a puncture wound, animal fat would be placed on the wound to draw out the infection and heat. Sometimes, they would be made to eat coal oil mixed with sugar as a remedy for one illness or the other. They had several remedies for warts.

There were, of course, unusual injuries, snake bites and the like. One of Shirley's uncles stepped on a sting ray when he was young, and the barb of the sting ray was injected into his leg. He struggled with the resulting problems the rest of his life. Shirley remembers him limping until he died. But, sting rays were part of life.

Home remedies were the order of the day, except for the most serious problems.

## *The girl - Shirley*

*He was swimming now. He'd waded out on the Barren Island flats as far as he could into Tar Bay. But, then it had gotten too deep to wade. He'd been swimming for ten minutes. He figured ten minutes. Couldn't have been much longer. He wasn't tiring yet.*

*When he'd break stroke to look ahead he could see Hoopers Island in the distance, much closer now though, than when he'd started. It was June and a new moon was rising in the darkness of the late night. The lights from the lanterns at Fishing Creek were like beacons, tiny lighthouses showing the way.*

*His parents didn't know he was swimming to Fishing Creek, the northernmost island that made up Hoopers Island. Her parents didn't know he was coming, either. But, she was waiting. The girl, the beautiful girl.*

*He'd slipped out of his room through the window a half-hour before. He'd been wading and swimming since. In another ten minutes he should feel the shallows under his feet. It would be easier then. He'd be able to walk to her.*

*His family had lived on Barren Island for a half-century, or more. Since the days when his grandfather had fought the Indian chief. He was dead now, the grandfather. Dead and buried. The settlement on the island had begun to diminish some, being abandoned little by little. People moving off the island, looking for an easier life. The Barren Creek settlement still had twenty to thirty families, even had a school. But the village was finished. It was just a matter of time. It was too isolated in these modern times. And the island itself was vanishing, eroding, leaving just as surely as were its people.*

*He broke his stroke for a moment to get his bearings from the lantern lights on the shore ahead. He noticed that the tide had carried him to the south'ard, he'd have to adjust. Have to remember the southerly current before he set out on the swim home. Now, adjusting to the north, he began to swim again. In five minutes he paused to check his course. As he started to tread water, his feet touched bottom. He'd come to Tar Bay's Hoopers Island shallows. Sliding his feet along the bottom to avoid stepping on sting rays, he walked towards the shore, just south of where a small dock extended a short distance into the bay. When the water was about thigh high, he saw her. She was waiting for him. He approached her, took her hand in his. That was all. It would go no further than holding hands. It was enough. Puppy love is what it was. Childhood infatuation. He was fourteen, she was twelve. She had snuck out of her house in the hours of the night just to touch his hand. He'd swum a half-mile to touch hers. A half-mile each way.*

*As their hands touched, Ivy and Lillie became two lives that, except for a short period that included The Great War, would be entwined forever as one. That initial relationship would be revived in time, the right time. The time for their daughter.*

*They would name her Shirley.*

# CHAPTER EIGHT

## *The Flowers*

The colonists boarded the three vessels, *Susan Constant, Godspeed,* and *Discovery* at Blackwall, England, on the Thames just downstream from London on December 19th and 20th of the year 1606. They sailed to the new world by way of the Canary Islands and the West Indies, arriving at the site of what would be called Jamestown in 1607.

Among the members of the all male expedition were those known, generally, as gentlemen and those not so known. The term gentlemen had nothing to do with manners. It merely denoted those men related by wealth or other status to the financiers and organizers of the expedition or otherwise claiming status as a result of birth. The remainder of the men of the expedition, in order to be selected had generally made commitments to labor for the colony for a period of seven years - a form of indentured servitude.

The Flowers family thinks that their ancestors arrived in the new world by way of the Jamestown Colony and were of the latter class. Much of information about the early days and origins of the Jamestown Colony may be gleaned from *Love and Hate in Jamestown,* by David A. Price. He writes that a George Flowres (presumably the old English spelling) died shortly after the *Susan Constant* and the *Godspeed* left on the return trip to England to resupply the expedition. He was reported to have died of swelling which was believed to have been caused by drinking of salt and brackish water.

In any event, the Flowers family is one of the Eastern Shore's most interesting families. Certainly, it is one of the oldest families in Maryland. This has since been confirmed according to the late Dr. Tom Flowers, Shirley Flowers Phillips' cousin, and a noted educator, local historian, and author of *SHORE FOLKLORE - Growing Up With Ghosts, 'n Legends, 'n Tales, 'n Home Remedies,* itself an excellent source of information about the islands (which this writer extensively used to learn of island lore.) That the Flowers may have been very early settlers, is certainly supported by the reference to the death of George Flowres in Mr. Price's examination of the Jamestown Colony.

There is also some level of support for the early appearance of Jamestown colonists in the area of Hoopers Island. One of Captain John Smith's exploration vessels, with crew members from the colony, was blown ashore in a storm at Hoopers Straits in 1608, losing all of its sails. After a short stay, Captain Smith was able to make new sails and continued with his voyage.[15] Hoopers Strait is situated to the south and east of Hoopers Island and joins Tangier Sound with the Honga River and the Chesapeake Bay just north of Bloodsworth Island. Whether he had aboard a 'Flowres' from Jamestown is conjecture, but, if he did, it is very likely that a 'Flowres' would have been exposed very early to the area. In any event the early appearance of the Flowers family in the Hoopers Island region is also supported by existing records in the historical collections maintained in the Nabb Center of Salisbury University.

Those records indicate that in 1669 a Thomas Flowers, and others, from the vicinity of the island were rewarded for taking into custody and transporting to Annapolis, Anatchcain, an Indian who was alleged to have murdered a settler's family. Mr. Flowers was rewarded with two hundred pounds for his services. Anatchcain was executed the day after his arrival in Annapolis. Later, in 1674, the same Thomas Flowers was paid another 200 pounds for his services fighting in the Nanticoke Indian war.

The Flowers' more modern history, as told to Shirley Phillips, has her family in her great-grandfather's (or her great-great-grandfather's) time, moving to Barren Island, then an island west of Hoopers Island across Tar Bay. Barren Island was originally 6500 acres and was patented

[15] *Love and Hate in Jamestown,* Price.

to Richard Preston by Lord Baltimore and/or his successors. One of Richard Preston's daughters married a man by the name of Ford and they took up residence on Barren Island. Eventually, Shirley Flowers' great, great grandfather married into the Ford family and also took up residence on that island. From there Flowers would eventually spread across Tar Bay to Hooper's Island. Barren Island has now mostly, if not completely, eroded away.

When the Flowers, and other families, moved to Barren Island it was already inhabited by a sub-tribe of the Nanticoke Indians, believed to be called the Yaocomicoe.[16] At first the two groups lived peacefully with few problems. Mr. Flowers and the chief of the tribe became good friends. They had agreed, so the story goes, that if irreconcilable differences ever developed between the two groups, Mr. Flowers, representing the settlers, and the chief, representing the Indians, would wrestle. Whichever group's representative lost, that group would move off Barren Island to a nearby island to the north called Punch Island.

After a period of time, a dispute erupted over a missing hog. It couldn't be resolved any other way, so great-grandfather Flowers and the Indian chief began to wrestle in the morning. The match lasted all day and into the evening before the chief capitulated. The tribe then moved from Barren Island and the settlers became its only residents. Later, when great-grandfather Flowers died the Indian chief showed up at his grave site as he was being buried and placed a clay pipe in the grave as a sign of respect.

From that time on, until the island became uninhabitable, Flowers were prominent in that island's life. As the emphasized forward to this part of the biography indicates, the boys of Barren Island would swim to Hoopers Island to go a 'a courting'. Mr. Ivy Flowers, Shirley's father, told Shirley when she was young, that he swam from Barren Island to court Shirley's mother when a boy- before the time he would have had a skiff of his own.

[16] Anne Stinson in *300 Years-Hoopers Island,* notes: "A more likely case can be made for the Yaocomicoes, a tribe identified with the western shore. Their hunting grounds were in Calvert County. . . . The same narrow stretch of the Bay at that point would make it as plausible for Indians to have moved across the Bay as it was for the Englishmen to fan out from the settlement at St. Marys on the opposite shore." In Shirley Phillips family, the family lore is that the Indians on Barren Island were the Yaocomicoes.

Not much is recorded, or now remembered, about the early days of Capt. Ivy (as Shirley's father was called,) or of the early days of Miss Lillie (as Shirley's mother was called.) It is known that Mr. Ivy left the Hoopers Island area before or at the time of WWI. He fought in that war, and there is some recollection that he may have fought in the battle of the Argonne Forest, one of the major battles. Nothing else is remembered of his war-time service.

While he was gone, Miss Lillie first married Hilbert Simmons, a waterman. She became pregnant, later bearing a son, also named Hilbert, a half-brother of Shirley's. While Miss Lillie was pregnant with Hilbert, her husband, while working on the water, fell overboard and drowned alongside his boat. Like most of the watermen of that era, he couldn't swim.

After the drowning of her first husband, the newly widowed Miss Lillie married another waterman, Freddie Parker. In 1914, Bernice Parker (Shirley's half-sister of whom we will hear more later,) was born to the couple. During the winter of the great flue epidemic of 1918, a bitterly cold winter when the rivers and the bays froze over, Miss Lillie caught the flue. She was put to bed in the family home. While she was abed, gravely ill, Mr. Parker, who is recalled as a particularly stalwart man, was called upon to lead the effort to break up the ice in the harbor so that the watermen could make it to the oyster bars. While he was leading the break out effort, he fell through the ice. He was able to crawl back out on the ice, but was drenched. The weather was well below freezing, the winter wind blowing, but he kept on with his efforts. Later, in the afternoon he developed a chill, went home, and soon was in bed in another bedroom, with either the influenza or pneumonia.

By this time Miss Lillie was delirious, sinking in and out of consciousness from her own sickness. She remained unaware that her husband was sick in the next bedroom. Mr. Parker died shortly afterwards, while Miss Lillie was still sick. She wasn't told that her husband had died and been buried until several days later, when she recovered. He'd been there when she'd gotten sick, he was gone by the time she got well.

Bernice Parker ( Mrs. Harry Murphy, Sr.,) now 91 years of age, was only four years old when her father died. She doesn't remember his particular funeral services, but recalls the general practice of the early 1900s on Hoopers Island.

> If someone died in the old days they were laid out on a table in their home for several days attended by several people before they were buried. I remember being told that ice, or dry ice, was kept in containers under the tables in order to keep the bodies cool, but I don't have any specific recollection of the ice. After two or three days they were then taken to the church where a service was held and they were buried. Mama (Miss Lily) and Mr. Ivy were buried in Cambridge, not on Hoopers Island, because during storms and times of high water, caskets on Hoopers Island would float up out of the ground and travel around the island in the current. Mama didn't want her and Mr. Ivy to go floating around after they were dead.

According to Dr. Tom Flowers, in the days before embalming became common, one of the reasons deceased persons were laid out in the homes was so that they could be watched to make sure they were really dead. There is a story told by Dr. Flowers in his excellent book on island life mentioned above, that on at least one occasion a woman, thought to be dead, woke up on the table, and lived for several years afterwards. As Dr. Flowers states, it can't be confirmed, but it is part of island lore.

In the meantime, Mr. Ivy Flowers was finishing his duties as a World War I soldier in Europe. That war concluded in November of 1918 and he was shipped back to the United States and mustered out of the Army in Baltimore. There he found work for a short time as a conductor on a train (Tom Flower's father, known as Captain Flowers, was a conductor on a train in Baltimore for a while, as well.) Then he and Captain Flowers took care of a wealthy man's boat up on Gibson Island for a short period.

While the sequence of events is not completely clear, shortly thereafter Captain Ivy was back on Hoopers Island working on the water. There he renewed his interest in Miss Lillie. Eventually, they were married, and Mr. Ivy, or Captain Ivy (as Mr. Flowers was sometimes called,) took over as father to all of Miss Lillie's children. Bernice

Parker Murphy(Mrs. Harry Murphy Sr.,) still remembers him with fondness, saying of him, "Mr. Ivy was a great man, a great man. He treated me just like I was one of his own children. Even though I wasn't his own daughter, he treated me wonderful. Just wonderful." Later Captain Ivy died widowing Miss Lillie once again. She had loved all of her husbands. Many, many years later when she was in her nineties, Miss Lillie told one of the Phillips' Ocean City friends, Ann Showell, "I'd take another one in a minute, if I could find another man as good as any of them."

Shirley was born to Captain Ivy and Miss Lillie on May the $5^{th}$, 1922.

# CHAPTER NINE

*Growing up*

With Shirley Phillips, it is as if there is a life after Brice, every second of which she remembers, and a life before Brice which has been sent to a less memorable place in her mind. She recalls many of the same activities as does Brice. But, in many respects, both before and after Brice, she recalls them, in some respects, differently - from the viewpoint of a waterman's daughter and not a packer's son.

In my first interview with her, I think she portrayed the time and the place of her girlhood, very accurately, when she told me, "Down in Hoopers Island when I was a young girl, we didn't have movie theaters or televisions. We didn't have much of anything, except time, but, we knew what to do with time." She described it:

> When the men came in from the water, their suppers were ready. They'd eat and go down to the country store. In the isolated fishing communities the country store was the newspaper of the day. The men would go there to learn what they needed to know from the gossip - see how many bushels of oysters, or pounds of crabs, depending on the season, the other watermen had caught. There they could find out the prices, or the prices they thought they'd get. They would hope to pick up enough information from the watermen who had

the better catches, to help them find the best places to 'fish' on the next day.

My father would leave the country store and be home around seven-thirty. He'd always bring all of us children a sweet. Children had to be in bed by eight o'clock. That meant we'd eaten our supper, done our homework by that time. Everybody would go to bed early. Life was like that at Hoopers Island. Sundays the whole family would go to church three times. Sunday school, afternoon services, and evening services. The men didn't crab, fish or oyster on Sundays.

At some point, my father had a skipjack and in the winter we'd go out with the sails billowing, and he'd take us over to Barren Island where he was born. There aren't any houses on Barren Island now, and there weren't any when I was young. But when he was born there were twenty-five, or so, houses there and they even had a school.

Miss Lillie Flowers was one of the pre-eminent ladies of the island. She was a self-taught pianist and organist. She played the organ in church for over forty-five years. Shirley remembers that when children would complain about school teachers, which was rare in the first instance, Miss Lillie would say, "Don't come home with any tales about your teachers. What I want to know is what you did wrong. They are there for you to learn." Shirley still remembers that the parents in those days "stood up for teachers because they wanted their children to learn. When children would come home and complain about teachers, the first thing the parents would do is to march the children right back to the teachers. Soon there weren't any complaints. We had great teachers and got a great education." Miss Lillie wouldn't have far to go to march her children back to school to be confronted by the teachers. Shirley's home was right next to the school house. As with so many of the people of that time, Shirley held all of the teachers in high regard.

Shirley's remembrances of the depression years are still vivid. They are memories without rancor, without bitterness.

I grew up in the depression. There were only 800 people on all three islands in those days and we supported each other any way we could. There was a great lady who ran a country store on the islands whose name was Miss Myrtle Phillips. During the depression years whenever there was a big freeze or ice over and they couldn't get out to go fishing or oystering, she would carry any of the watermen and their families on credit. When they got some money they'd pay down the bill. No one ever tried to beat Miss Myrtle out of anything. She was the matriarch of the island and its unofficial mayor.

In the depression no one that we knew went hungry. The islanders were self sufficient. There was never any money in our house. No one had a lot of money. But, it still worked out fine for us.

My mother always had a great garden. She raised chickens and swine. She was an excellent seamstress and made all of our clothes in those years. In addition she hung wallpaper, played the piano and organ in church, and organized many events on the island. She stayed busy.

Even in the winters when everything was frozen over and my father couldn't get oysters, we never really wanted for anything, because there was always something on the shelves. She put up vegetables from her garden. In the summers, Bernice and I would have to pick the bugs off the garden plants. There were no pesticides in those days. We were it. We had to pick bugs for an hour every day in the summer. She would can the vegetables. She had a couple of fruit trees and she'd make preserves. We'd have to do the picking of the fruit from the trees. She also raised watermelon and cantaloupes. . . . There were always mason jars full of stuff that would last the winter. There was always a chicken from Miss Lillie's chicken coop. A pork roast from her hogs. When it wasn't iced over, there'd be oysters and fresh fish. Even when it was iced over we'd have salted fish.

The Hoopers Islanders would also go out into the rivers and bays at low tide and dig for manteos. They were considered a delicacy. They were usually called 'piss clams' because of the way they were prepared. When first dug up they were sandy so they'd be soaked in containers of water for a period of time, during which they would forcibly (and visibly) expel the sand, earning themselves the nickname. Tom Flowers noted that it was common in those days for every family to salt down a barrel of fish in the late fall for the winter, and that in the winter salted fish was considered the proper food item for breakfast. The women would often make 'light bread' - yeast cake bread. Usually, when 'light bread' wasn't on the table, pone bread or biscuits were.

Dr. Flowers shared the memory: "There was a lot of pound fishing in the old days, and haul seining and gill netting. . . . Shirley's mother, Miss Lillie, always had a huge garden. She raised a lot of collard greens and cabbages; in the winter they'd 'mound' cabbages. She also grew string beans. Miss Lillie also had fig and pear trees, and would make preserves."

Shirley remembers that because there was already a large dependence on gardens and raising chickens and hogs on the island, and because, depending on the seasons, there was always seafood of one kind or another, the Great Depression probably made less of an impact on Hoopers Island than other places. They had never had much; they still didn't during the depression years. According to Shirley, there wasn't much difference. They just kept on living the way they had always lived. Besides, as she remembers, everybody was in the same boat. There weren't families that had much more. While the packers' families might have been a little more affluent, they were just marginally so. Everyone was poor. As Brice puts it, "We just self-helped ourselves out of the depression." Shirley's sister Bernice remembers that: "We had it bad in those days but didn't really know it because everybody was having it bad. We just lived off the land and the water. Brice's family had a little more then most families on Hoopers Island, but still didn't have much. Nobody had a lot."

In those days, before the advent of washing and drying machines (and the electricity needed for their operation) clothes washing was a very hands on operation. Shirley, and cousin Tom Flowers, remember that ". . . clothes were washed in large wash tubs using lye soap made from animal fat. Then the clothes would be boiled in water, then washed again in soapy water, and if the clothes were white, bluing was added. Then the clothes were put into rinse water. If they were to be starched and ironed, they were then placed into additional solution, one of flour and water, rolled up damp and later hand ironed. The other clothes would be hung up to dry."

Shirley's very early years were like those of poor country girls everywhere. She had dolls and can remember bicycles. She remembers, as does Bernice, the great love that Miss Lillie and Captain Ivy showered on the children. It was, in her view, just growing up normally.

Rural people were attempting to live off the land, or the water, as much as possible. Gardens were almost a necessity, and Miss Lillie's garden had a reputation as one of the best. Shirley would join millions of children throughout rural America, and those from the island in obtaining fertilizer the only way available. Shirley recalls;

> In those days there were no commercial fertilizers available on the islands. No one had any money anyway. But, there were cows that everyone let roam freely throughout the islands. Everyone was familiar with all the cows and their respective owners.
>
> My mother realized the importance of another product of these free roaming cows. It was there, all over the island, for the picking up.
>
> It was one of my chores to scrounge across the island looking for cow pies. There was a ready supply of cow pies for the picking up. Billy and I would take a bushel basket and go looking for this natural fertilizer. Miss Lillie ground up and spread around the cow pies I and my brother Billy got for her, and that was one of the reasons that my mother had the best garden around.

Shirley became a part of the cash economy when she was six or seven years old` and began wading the bay grasses for soft crabs. She'd sell them to Brice's father for pennies a crab. Then later, when she was twelve or thirteen, she went to work picking crabs in the new Phillips' packing plant, the company her sister Bernice had worked for. Bernice had already left for college, had saved enough money from picking crabs to finance her education. Bernice (now ninety-one years old) explains the crab picking process that the children of the islands grew up with in those days.

> I picked crabs on Hoopers Island. That's how I made my money for college. I got five cents a pound. Five cents. I made about $15.00 a week. I used to go to work picking crabs at two-thirty in the morning before I went to school. A truck would come along and gather the pickers and take them to the packing plants. I picked at Captain Ellie's, which was then right across the street from our house. I aimed to get 40 pounds picked by the time I had to leave to go to school. And that would get me $2.00. Every day I would get $2.00. On Saturday, I'd pick a hundred pounds and I'd make $5.00. That way I'd make $15.00 a week, and that was big money for a school girl in that time. How I loved to get that money. I would save every cent. I wouldn't even buy an ice cream cone because I was saving to go to college. Picking crabs is what put me through Towson College. It gave me an education.

Shirley says that she was not the picker her sister was. She was a forty pounds a day picker.

A year or so before she began picking, the year before Bernice left for college, a major event occurred. An event that would, in time, link islands together in the Empires of the Crab.

# CHAPTER TEN

*August 22nd, 1933*

At sea a great storm had been brewing for several days. On the seaside, huge seas had been building, successive tides getting higher and higher, spilling water into the back bays behind the Town of Ocean City on the North Beach part of Assateague Island. The railway bridge had been closed and the only access to the barrier island was by boat across the bay. The wind had been increasing, coming to an apex. On the August morning of the twenty-second, the Great Hurricane of 1933 threw its full fury at the land. It would transform the island, cut an inlet to the sea, destroy the railroad bridge, but set the stage for the building of a tourist industry that twenty-six years later would nurture the Crab House and the beginnings of the Phillips' worldwide enterprises.

Much has been written of that storm's impact upon the seaside, how it changed the ocean commercial fishing industry, how it gave rise to the sport-fishing business, how it spurred additional tourist development on the eastern beaches of Maryland. Less has been written, and less is generally known, of the storm's impact on the islands of the great bay to the west.

Arthur Phillips, Captain Ellie's uncle, was working in the packing plant in the early morning hours of the 22nd, assisting the ladies picking the crabs that had been landed the day before. He was making sure they had enough crabs, tins and such, keeping them supplied.

Captain Ellie had gone to work the previous day at eight in the morning and worked until after seven in the evening as he always did, making the deliveries to the steamship, arranging for supplies, receiving the crabs from the watermen, steaming, whatever needed to be done. He was scheduled back at the plant at eight in the morning of the 22nd.

It was in the time before formal advance warnings of storms were commonplace. The islanders had noticed that the wind had been up, especially brisk the previous afternoon. But windy conditions on islands were a constant, at some level. Yesterday the wind had been hard, but not that hard. It might be stormy, the tide might be up, but that was part of island life everywhere. The watermen had 'fished' their trot-lines, hadn't complained too much when they had delivered the crabs to the packing plants the afternoon before. The steam whistles had sounded as they always did, telling the pickers when the picking would start at the various plants.

When Captain Ellie got up to go to the plant on the morning of the 22nd, the wind was blowing more than a gale and the water was so high he couldn't leave the house. Boats were floating by between his house and the houses next door. He, Leone, Brice and Jane found themselves marooned at home. They began lifting furniture and other belongings on top of tables, trying to save them from the rising water.

The water had risen so fast that throughout the island people had been trapped in their homes. Some quickly got their chickens, even their hogs, into the houses to save them from the rising water. The few cows that were kept close by families were brought onto porches and tied to porch railings.

At the plant the ladies had been working hard, picking as fast as they could since shortly after the midnight before. As soon as all the crabs were picked, the work would be over and they could go home. The wind had been blowing when they came to work, been blowing for days. It had gotten harder as they picked, howling at times. Like all islanders, they hadn't been overly worried. Wind was always with them.

They had been picking for several hours when someone noticed water coming up through the floor of the plant. They went to the door and saw that the walkway to shore was under water, impassible. The 'fast' land was much further away than it had been just hours before. The wind was beginning to gust now, harder than they could ever remember. The water was rising fast. In just minutes the whole building began to rock on its support pilings, pilings whose tops were already two feet underwater. They were stranded.

Then they felt the building rise. It was breaking loose from the pilings, being blown out into the river. Then it began to break up, the boiler and steamer falling into the river, sinking, the walls of the building beginning to disintegrate. The plant was coming apart with them in it as it floated to the east further out in the river. Someone said, "The roof. We need to get on the roof." It is not remembered exactly how it was done, but soon there was a hole. As the water rose around them, they, one by one, struggled through the hole onto the roof. Staying as low as they could to avoid being blown away, the ladies and Arthur crawled to the crown, and straddling it, drove their picking knives into the shingles, creating a handhold to help them fight the wind.

They were on a roof in hurricane force winds, floating in the rising water out into the river, the shoreline of Hoopers Island receding in the distance. There remain no clear memories of how long they floated with the wind howling around them. But, after a while, the wind changed and slowly they were blown back to The island. The roof hung up twenty or thirty yards from the high land they could see. But it was close enough. The first woman slid into the water. It was neck deep on her at first, than shoulder deep, and then waist deep as she waded to shore. The others followed her to safety.[17]

There was widespread damage. The storm destroyed the last commercial turtling operation on the island. Mr. Applegarth maintained a turtle pound and processing operation before the storm. He had built a turtle pound - an enclosure made up of closely abutting boards set vertically into the bottom out in the water and extending back into the land - so that the pound enclosed both water and land. He would buy terrapin and snapping turtles from the watermen, or from turtle catchers, and hold them in the pound until he had enough to warrant taking them to market in Baltimore, primarily the old Emerson Hotel, whose turtle soup was considered a great delicacy. The terrapins were

[17] The recanting of the destruction of the A. E. Phillips and Son plant in the hurricane of 1933 is based, roughly, on an interview in the summer of 2005 with Bernice Parker Murphy, Shirley's half-sister, who, as a teen-age girl, rode out the storm on the roof of the plant. I have discovered no other persons still alive who survived the ordeal on the roof of the A. E. Phillips and Son plant.

especially prized because they had seven kinds of edible meat in them. Both species were difficult to clean properly. It was a time-consuming process. So many were accumulated before they were processed. When the water receded after the storm, the pound and all of the impounded turtles were gone. The business was never started up again.

The storm is also remembered because many of the caskets in the graves on the island were 'floated'. They came up out of the ground and floated around the islands, along with the boats. It is doubted that all of them were recovered, or, if recovered, found their way back into the same piece of ground. This is why Miss Lillie, more than a half-century later, ordered that she and her husband be buried in Cambridge.

Both of the bridges (one was called Narrows Ferry Bridge)between the respective islands that made up Hoopers Island were also washed away by the storm. Several packing plants were destroyed. The Applegarth packing plant was washed over to the opposite side of the Honga River. And of course the Phillips' plant was gone.

Before the next season the Phillips had purchased a plant that had survived the storm.[18] It was located where the present plant is situated. It was in this plant that Shirley began her career as a crab picker.

[18] Believed to be the H. I. Phillips Crab & Oyster House at Fishing Creek. A 1914 picture of that plant is in the photograph section. The shoreline shown behind the H. I. Phillips plant of 1914 closely resembles the shoreline at the same location in relation to the present plant. Eventually, the plant purchased after the 1933 hurricane was demolished and the present facility built on the same location. Mr. Charles Shockley of Fishing Creek and a friend of Brice and Shirley from their childhoods, in an October 2005 telephone interview with the author confirmed that A. E. Phillips & Son acquired the H. I. Phillips plant after the 1933 storm. Mr. Schockley was the manager of the A. E. Phillips & Son plant for over 20 years and his son, Tony, managed the plant afterwards.

# CHAPTER ELEVEN

*Brice and Shirley*

*Shirley: Miss Lillie's house bordered on the only road leading up and down the island. It had a white fence around the front yard. One day when I was in the second grade, I was playing in the yard. I don't remember exactly what I was doing, but I looked up. There was this older boy walking down the road by the fence. He had knickers on and a banjo hung on a strap over his shoulder. He was the best looking boy I had ever seen. I can still remember shivers going up and down my spine. I fell for him that instant. Knew I wanted him. Wanted to marry him. I was only seven or eight. Fell in love right there as he walked by with that doggone banjo. Been in love with him every day since. It took him a little longer.*

*My mother wouldn't let me even invite boys to our house until I was in the tenth grade. And then when I began dating Brice, even though she liked him, she didn't really approve of our dating. Brice had a reputation as a fast driver, and mother said that when I left with Brice on a date, she never drew an easy breath until I was back in the house.*

*Brice was a real rascal. Teased me with other girls. Sometimes, I thought my heart would break.*

*The first time I kissed a boy, it was Brice. I was in the tenth grade. That was it. A shock went through us and I knew I had him. All I ever wanted out of life was to marry Brice. When he went off to Baltimore to study at a business school, my heart was broken. I just knew some city girl would steal him from me. But, that didn't happen.*

*When he proposed to me, my heart was racing and it's racing now.*

*Brice: I don't especially remember any other girls from my youth. I've been Shirley's all my life. There was this nice young lady whose name I shouldn't mention that I dated for a short while when I was a teenager, but just to attract Shirley's attention. . . . Hoopers Island was always known for the beauty of its women. Still is. Its just a fact. And Shirley was the prettiest of them all. She was beautiful then, she is beautiful now. She and I got together in the 6th or 7th grade. It was about that time that I really got interested in her. Of course she was a little younger. I knew I was in love with her from about the 8th or 9th grade on. My heart would skip a beat whenever I saw her after that. Still does. I never considered myself a lady's man. I was Shirley's man. I've never loved any woman but her. I didn't miss anything. We, the two of us, did pretty well by having each other. We're lucky. That doesn't happen too often.*

In a year after that first kiss, Brice went off to Baltimore to attend Strayer Business School, then took a job with the Owens Yacht building company, and later was hired by Bethlehem Steel. That Shirley had him firmly tangled in her net is soon evident by the letters the homesick boy in Baltimore wrote his girl back home. Shirley saved many of his letters.

In an undated letter while he was still attending Strayer, he wrote:

> Dearest 'Simone' -
>
> Just got home from school. Got your letter this morning and I am answering it before doing anything else.
>
> You don't know how much I missed being home this weekend, but I'll probably be coming home soon to spend a couple of months or so. Just think of all the good times we can have: Fishing trips without fishing lines; walking on the ferry road in the moonlight and the wind blowing in off the bay. . . .
>
> Each minute will seem like an hour until the weekend when I come home.
>
> Love, Brice

He writes in his next letter:

Dearest Sweetie: Thursday night

Just one month ago today since I left my little baby. It has seemed like years. We won't be able to stand it another whole month like this, will we? You just have to be with me.

No letter from you again today. . . . .I couldn't stay up here - away from you – if you didn't write to me, so be sure I get a letter every day. . . .

Love you more and more each and every day.

Forever yours, Brice

She didn't respond as fast as Brice would have wished. He writes again,

Dear Shirley, Friday 10/14/38

I didn't receive a letter from you today. That's two days this week that I haven't gotten a letter from you. What's wrong honey? Forgetting me? I'm writing you every day! . . .

I'm going to stay in every night over the weekend and BE GOOD. . . .

It's going to seem funny Saturday and Sunday - without you. There will be nothing to do to help me forget you.

Be sure to write every day. Brice

He writes on a Sunday evening in November of 1938, getting even more serious.

My Dearest Darling,

. . . . I miss you. I just have to come home to see you this weekend. Friday is Armistice Day, if we get Friday off (which is very doubtful,) I will be home Thursday night.

If I could only be with you tonight, Darling. It's been so lonesome up here this weekend. . . . I never enjoy being with anyone except you. I only hope you feel the same way. You do, don't you honey?

There's only one thing that I have to look forward to darling. That's when you and I can be together always. That won't be long, Will it, honey?

With all my love, Brice

Brice is summonsed to help his father who has gotten ill in Philadelphia, and writes, explaining the situation.

Dearest.

Thursday night and I will be seeing My Sweetie - that's all I know now - tomorrow night [Then he gets a call while he is in the middle of writing the letter].

My father just called and wants me to come to Phila. tomorrow nite. He is sick and says he doesn't feel like driving home. He wants me to come up and drive him down - so Butchie, I guess I'll be going there, and have I been looking forward to Friday nite and all day Sat. with you. We get the toughest breaks, don't we. But I'll be home as soon as I possibly can Saturday, and we'll spend every minute together. Won't we?

. . . I'll see you then - if I can only wait.

Forever yours, Brice

Brice finishes school, works for a short time at the Owen's Yacht facility, then takes a job with Bethlehem Steel. He then writes

> Just got home from work and I'm writing my 'ittle baby right away. All I do every night is stay in and think of you. Think of you - That's all I can do all the time.
>
> . . . . If I don't come home this weekend, I will have something wonderful to look forward to next week end. But, it will seem like years until then. Don't know whether I can wait or not, but I guess I'll just have to find out.
>
> Don't forget that I love you. Brice

When I asked Shirley what she and Brice would do when they were courting, she said they did a lot of things, especially outdoor things like swimming, fishing, boating, ice skating in the winter. When she was asked, "Sometimes you went fishing without fishing lines?" She laughed, "There's a letter that says that?" I answered, "Yes." She responded "Really," cutting her eyes at Brice as she must have done 60 years ago. I accused her then of laying a trap for him, drawing him in, playing hard to get. She admitted to it all, saying

> All I ever wanted out of life was to marry Brice. When he proposed to me my heart was racing and it's racing now [Brice was sitting next to her]. When Brice was in college, I may have visited him twice. There just wasn't enough money to travel from Hoopers Island to Baltimore on any frequent basis. The most our family would ever travel is that we might go into Cambridge (the nearest town) on a Saturday night. We'd all walk up one side of the street, then cross over and walk down the other side, up and down, really a promenade.

I accused her again of playing hard to get with Brice. She laughed, said,

> Well, we had to be hard to get in those days. Times are different now. In those days you were scared to death about getting pregnant. So you knew where you couldn't let a boy go. And, where he could go wasn't very far. The biggest disgrace in the world for a girl or an unmarried woman in those days was to get pregnant.
>
> I'm not saying I was perfect but I had my head on straight. Never wanted anyone but Brice, and he respected me - so we were good kids. We're still good kids.[19]
>
> I still love the boy that I fell in love with in the second grade. And I get to go to bed with him every night. And there's

[19] Sometime in early February of 1945, Shirley's father had apparently taken her to a place called *Fred's* in order to cheer her up. In a letter dated "Sunday Feb. 4 - 45" from Captain Ivy, the emphasis on reputation is reinforced: "Hello Shirley. How do you like it at the Hotel. You're surely having bad luck with the pipes. Guess you will go back when the weather gets warmer. Shirley I believe I was wrong to take you to Fred's. Lillie has been giving me the devil ever since last night. I have been worrying ever since.. . . . There is nothing better than a good name. . . . Well Shirley take care of yourself and be a good girl. Love, Daddy." She was 23 years old at the time.

> been lots of nights. I've still got the man I caught sixty years ago. There was never anybody else.

By the time Brice took over management of the Hoppers Island plant after the war, Shirley finally had enough confidence in her man, that she decorated his home office with Playboy centerfolds.

Brice's job at Bethlehem Steel was in procurement for materials to be used in making items for the military. As war neared, his job became more important and it became difficult to take time off. Their separations from each other became unbearable. Soon Brice was back in Hoopers Island for a short, but important, visit.

He walked up the lane to Mr. Ivy's house. He was asked inside. There he asked Mr. Ivy's permission to marry Shirley. Brice remembers that Mr. Ivy's response was, prophetically, "Good Luck." With Captain Ivy's and Miss Lillie's permission Brice later proposed to Shirley. He remembers it was in her house, he got down on one knee and asked her to marry him. Shirley remembers it.

> Even though we knew we were going to get married, he did the traditional thing because in those days that's what you did. He asked my father for permission to ask me. It was considered the romantic thing to do. Worked, too. Then he proposed. Got right down on his knees and did it! I didn't keep him waiting for an answer.

Bernice recalls, "Miss Lillie liked Brice very much. But, it wouldn't have made much difference to Shirley if she hadn't." The rest, as they say, is history. They were married in 1941 in Miss Lillie's and Mr. Ivy's house, the house where she had been raised. She was eighteen, he was twenty. Brice remembers that Shirley was beautiful and that he was nervous.

Then on December the 7th, 1941 Japan attacked Pearl Harbor and the Second World War began for the United States.

There is little of non-romantic significance remembered of the years between 1941 and 1944 as war raged in the world. They lived in Baltimore. Brice continued to work for Bethlehem Steel, expediting material for the war effort; Shirley got a job with the telephone company.

They were young and in love and did all those things that young married couples did.

Then, in early 1944 Brice received his draft notice. His superiors at Bethlehem Steel obtained a deferment for him because of the nature of his job, but he refused to accept it. He felt he had a duty to go when called. He was inducted into the army.

He was first assigned to Camp Blanding near St. Augustine, Florida for thirteen weeks of basic infantry training. Shirley followed him and got another job with the telephone company. She would follow Brice around the states to his various duty assignments. In the war days the telephone company attempted to accommodate the needs of the soldiers and would try to find jobs for the soldier's wives when the wives followed the husbands. At each of the duty stations Shirley worked for the telephone company. After Camp Blanding, Brice was assigned to the Air Corps and transferred to a post near Houston, Texas. Shirley followed. He was then assigned to Lowery Field just outside of Denver, Colorado for more training. Again she followed him. Then he was sent to a Camp Robinson just outside of Little Rock, Arkansas. By now Shirley was an experienced 'camp follower'.

His next assignment was at Camp Rucker in Alabama. Just before the Normandy invasion, with no reason given, he was transferred out of the Air Corps, reassigned to Army Intelligence and sent to Camp Ritchie, which today is part of the Camp David complex, the Presidential Retreat. After being trained in intelligence matters, including the interpretation of aerial photographs, he was sent back to Camp Rucker. During this process he was offered a commission as a Warrant Officer but declined the commission, choosing to remain in his regular rank. At the end of the war he had advanced to Technical Sergeant. Shirley followed him to each station.

From Camp Rucker he was ordered to go overseas, via Fort Dix in New Jersey. Shirley returned to Dorchester County to be with their families while Brice went off to war. Again the telephone company gave her a job in Cambridge, where she roomed with a friend, also named Shirley.

# CHAPTER TWELVE

*War*

Brice shipped out for Europe through New York harbor aboard the liner *Britannica* which had been converted to a troop ship. The troops were jammed into hammocks and bunk beds in the various staterooms on the former liner. Brice was lucky enough to be assigned a porthole bunk, but he spent as much time on deck as he could. Seasickness was prevalent, but, being from Hoopers Island, he was never afflicted. He recalls that the *Britannica*, a British ship, was sailed according to British traditions. When music was played over the public address system it would be British style music (and the Beatles were yet to be born.) In the middle of the Atlantic, one of the escorting American destroyers came along side the *Britannica*, turned its loud speakers to their highest volume, and as a special treat for the American troops, sent over an hour of contemporary songs and American jazz as the ships headed on to England. They arrived several months after the invasion at Normandy.

Upon his arrival in England Brice was initially assigned to the 66th Infantry "Panther" Division and underwent additional training, both in intelligence and combat. One weekend he was given a three day pass to go to London, and while he was there, the German Army made its break-out in the Ardennes Forest and began the battle that would become known as the Battle of the Bulge. His division was immediately put aboard every available ship and rushed across the

English Channel to reinforce the front line troops in the Ardennes. Two thousand members of the Division, including members of his particular unit, shipped out during the weekend aboard an old liner known as the *Leopoldville.* Brice missed the ship because he was in London and couldn't get back in time.

The *Leopoldville* was torpedoed in the Channel by a German U-Boat and sank. The *Leopoldville* sank so fast that 400 men went down with the ship and over 400 more drowned in the disaster. For years the loss of the *Leopoldville* was kept under cover, only coming to light many years after the war.[20]

Brice was reassigned to a military intelligence unit attached to a combat division, the 66th, upon his subsequent arrival in France. Twice during his time in Europe he was sent to front line duty. Later he would spend the last winter of the war at the front. He can still remember the artillery rounds coming in, hearing the machine guns going off all around him. He notes

> When we first got in France we were assigned to attack the submarine pens at St. Lasaur and St. Lorient on the coast near Bordeaux. The Germans had a railroad car with a 16 inch naval gun mounted on it well within range of our position. They were shooting at us all the time, but were shooting high and the shells were passing overhead, landing to our rear. You could hear the shells coming. We could hear them go overhead. It sounded like locomotives going by in the sky above us at high speed. I was at the front several other times, but I don't really remember the other times and places. Don't remember the circumstances. I can't really say I was ducking bullets. I was just ducking. Mostly it was incoming artillery, sometimes machine guns, but I can't say they were shooting at me.

Brice's division was assigned to contain 60,000 first line German soldiers that had been left behind in German redoubts along the Atlantic

[20] For more information about the Leopoldville sinking the reader is directed to three books: *The Leopoldville Trilogy,* and *Survivors of the Leopoldville Disaster,* both by Raymond Roberts and *From Tragedy to Triumph,* by Carol Coffee,

Wall. His unit's combat function was described in two commendations. The first is a commendation by way of an "Order of the Day" from the Division's commanding officer, Major General H. F. Kramer.

> Our mission of caging up 60,000 battlewise and toughened Jerries in their Atlantic Wall may not seem to be a spectacular or glamorous job, but neither is any tough job in war. We have an arduous mission here and you may be sure that history will record it as an important one in the defeat of Germany.
>
> Those of you on the front line are well aware now of the caliber of your opponent. He is the same fanatical, hard, and adroit fighter who stands with his back to the wall in other German strongholds and who will stay there until he is destroyed. You have been engaged with him for two months now in combat as bitter and as uncompromising as can be found on any battlefront, and you have proved your individual superiority.
>
> The magnificent spirit with which each one of you has endured hardships, and the courage and tenacity with which you have carried on in the past two months, has filled everyone with confidence and self-assurance. Some of you have seen your friends die. You have suffered wounds and pain. You have felt the miseries of cold and hunger and you have experienced the terror and drudgery of war.
>
> . . . .
>
> . . . . Here in France in a little more than two months you have grown wise in the ways of war, you have outsmarted an enemy more experienced and numerically superior, you have won the admiration of our French Allies, and you have gained the abiding respect of your fellow soldiers, your commanders and myself.

The second commendation was from Lieutenant General John C. H. Lee. It describes the service of Brice's division the winter when Brice spent most of his time at the front.

. . . . In this respect I would make special reference to the splendid 66th Infantry Division which . . . we have known and admired from our initial contacts. We have seen it overcome great handicaps - victoriously. We have every confidence that, assisted by such a dependable combat division, we shall be able to achieve the otherwise impossible task that faces us in redeploying and re-shipping troops destined to the Pacific Theater at the earliest possible date.. . .

. . .

The first great test of the Division came in December shortly after it had embarked to the Continent. On Christmas Eve the 14,000 ton Leopoldville, carrying approximately 2,500 troops . . . was torpedoed and sunk five miles from Cherbourg. Fourteen officers, including two battalion commanders and 784 enlisted men were killed or missing. . . .

. . .

Combat, ambush and reconnaissance patrols were sent out daily. . . . .An average 450 rounds of artillery per day were fired against such targets as strong points, gun emplacements and patrols. . . . Later when enemy activity increased, over 1,000 rounds per day were fired. . . .

Approximately, 53,000 enemy troops were contained in the two pockets. . . .

. . . .Enemy action although defensive in nature, included aggressive patrolling. Enemy artillery fire ranged in caliber from 75mm to 340mm. . . . .

Several truces with the enemy were arranged to facilitate evacuation of civilians caught in the pocketed areas, and on one occasion 5,800 civilians were evacuated. The truces were discontinued . . . when the Germans failed to live up to the terms.

. . . .

On midnight of 7 May, enemy forces in the Lorient Sector surrendered unconditionally, while some units in the St. Nazaire Sector continued their resistance for an additional 24 hours.. . .

. . . .

> Total battle casualties of the 66th Infantry Division for their 4 ½ months in the European Theater of operations were 78 officers and 2,170 enlisted men.

When Brice wasn't at the front or performing intelligence duties, he was primarily assigned to headquarters where he was in charge of keeping the situation map for the Division. He helped analyze aerial photographs and intelligence received at headquarters. Maps were marked with enemy positions and sent to the troops at the front. Later in the war, he was assigned to a position in Eisenhower's headquarters in the IG Farben building in Frankford, Germany. He remembers Patton, with his twin pearl handled revolvers and spit shined helmet marching up the steps into the building to be admonished by General Eisenhower. "Our particular unit moved around a lot, and on VE (Victory in Europe) Day, I was billeted in the Hotel Noi on the Rue de Canterbear in Chateaubriand, France." By that time his unit had won several battle stars. He then became part of the occupation army.

# CHAPTER THIRTEEN

*Waiting*

Shirley kept all of the letters that Brice wrote to her during the Second World War and gave the author unlimited access to them. They begin with one in September of 1944, after Brice had been posted to Fort Dix for processing overseas. Shirley was not permitted to accompany him to that facility. Many of the letters are censored, and there are holes where text is deleted. Brice was forbidden from providing his exact location until after VE-Day.

This wartime correspondence, in many ways, is very personal to Brice and Shirley, and their willingness to share them tells a lot about the kind of persons they are - people willing to share their wartime experiences with newer generations, so that they too can experience, vicariously, the fear of being separated in war time. The letters tell a story of love in another age; they are instructive in understanding the feelings of young lovers who were parted by a war now beginning to be forgotten; they emphasize the uncertainties that the war, and every war, brings to the lives of those separated by conflict, and they furnish, as well, an awareness of the feelings of the American GI in that long ago conflict. It is obvious that in some of them Brice is responding to those he has received from Shirley. The letters best tell this part of their story.[21]

[21] The recitation of portions of the letters in this book, so far as the writer is aware, is the first time that their children and grandchildren have seen the letters.

"Somewhere on the East Coast"

28 Sept. 44

"Dearest.

I finally received some mail today, to hear from you. . . . - now my morale is much, much better.

. . . . I understand that you can't send Christmas packages to APO numbers after December one - so don't worry about sending cookies and cake and there isn't a thing that I need. . . . . I hope that I will have the opportunity to shop around for a present for you for Christmas.

Let me know if your father has come home from the hospital yet - If not, I sure do want to write, or make a call.

No, I haven't forgotten about the ring. I haven't moved it since you put it on - and it will stay there until you take it off.

Mac [a fellow soldier] is still walking around in circles, biting his nails and waiting for the blessed event. It was supposed to happen yesterday. I believe he is hoping for a boy. . . .

I got a short haircut today. You should see it - or maybe you shouldn't - about a quarter-inch long - and now I can throw my comb away.

Thinking of you every minute.

All my love. Brice

He apparently had received a short hours-long furlough just before Thanksgiving but it had not been long enough for him to make it to Hoopers Island.

[Deleted by censor]

Dearest:

I guess you have been wondering why I haven't written a long letter since I returned from furlough, but this is really the first spare moment that I have had and now there isn't much that I can say [because of the censor].

Arrived here yesterday just in time for Thanksgiving dinner - turkey - and it was one of the best I have had since being in the army . . . .I remembered the Thanksgiving two years ago - but without the memories this one was just another day - how I would like to go back to that Thanksgiving day two years ago and the two years since. I know the living conditions [in the Army camps] for you haven't been too good, but I have enjoyed every minute of it.

I guess Jane [Brice's sister] is home now and you all had Thanksgiving dinner together. I would have liked to be there - but next year I am sure we can all be together again. . . . .

I still have hope that I may get leave to see you soon.

All my love, Brice

He later writes,

Dearest:

Just another 'blue Monday' - raining most of the day.

. . .

I miss you more every day - especially days like this when it is raining - but it shouldn't be for long - all the news is good [this was before the Battle of the Bulge] - the war will soon be over and we will take that long postponed honeymoon.

All my love, Hubby

# CHAPTER FOURTEEN

*Across the Atlantic to England*

Because of censoring we have no dates on the next letters. They are obviously written while Brice is on *Britannica*. They become different in tone from the ones before.

> "Somewhere in the [removed by censor]
> Dearest:
>
> I guess this will be the first letter for sometime and you are wondering where I am, what I have been doing and why I have not written. This is my first opportunity to write. I had high hopes that I would be able to see you before I left, but it didn't work out as I had expected.
>
> We have been having a pretty nice time since we have been out at sea. It makes a lot of difference being with all the fellows that you know. I have a cabin with some of the other fellows from the unit. We were very fortunate in being assigned very nice quarters - of course everything is crowded as transports always are. I have always wondered how I would feel in a ship when there is a chance of submarine attack at any time - but you just don't think about it - you even forget that you are on a ship until it starts to roll a little and pretty soon you don't even notice that. One of the days was pretty rough - and I was really surprised at the beating a ship takes in the sea - they roll

worse than a rowboat. I enjoyed the stormy day most of all. Spent most of the time out on deck. Quite a number of the fellows were sea- sick. I have been lucky so far, but I guess it isn't too late yet.

Went to church on the ship Sunday. It was quite impressive, with the ship rolling from side to side and the Chaplin shifting from foot to foot to maintain his balance as he led his life preserver-garbed congregation thru a hymn that seemed so different from the contrasting surroundings. Other than the church services, Sunday was just another day.

The last few days the weather has been good - like summertime on the bay back home. We have a porthole in our cabin and have had it open most of the time. Maybe you and I can take a trip together like this when the war is over - I'm sure you would like it.

I didn't have a chance to get Christmas presents before I left - except for those two little things I picked up in the PX. The PX didn't have much to choose from. . . . . .

I have received only one letter from you since I left Ruckers, but I am sure you have been writing every day. I will probably get them all at my new destination - which as yet is unknown to us.

Today they were playing "White Christmas" and "Girl With a Hole in her Sock" over the public address system - songs which bring back lots of memories - they shouldn't play them. I miss you more every day - I hate the sound of the engine on the boat, each new revolution taking us farther and farther apart. How different that sound will be when the ship is going the opposite direction and each revolution will bring us closer and closer.

All my love, Hubby

Another letter was written while Brice was en route across the Atlantic.

"Somewhere at Sea"

Dearest:

Another day on ship - the weather is warm and the sun is out. The sea looks calm - but there are larger waves that really toss the ship around. It seems funny to see the water breaking over the [removed by censor] in what seems to be a calm sea.

Today has been set aside as wash day, and since washing doesn't particularly appeal to me, I have had most of the day free. Tom and I were just up on deck for awhile. He was fortunate in being able to see Fran before he left. It was just impossible for me.

The food here on ship has been very poor and we are served only two meals per day. Have been satisfying my appetite with about a half-dozen candy bars each day.

We received the first of our free cigarettes yesterday, being seven packs. Cigarettes sell for only five cents per pack here on the ship and they have a fairly good selection of cigars, but they are at no reduction.

We have seven in our cabin which is overcrowded, but not too bad. We are fortunate in having a cabin with a port hole, electric fan and a sink. The cabin is about the size of our bedroom in Ozark. I am in the top bunk and every time I attempt to sit up, I bang my head on the ceilings. Since I have been here writing this, my ambitious roommates have strung ropes all over the room to hang their washing on. I don't know how I will get down from my bunk.

They just came down and gave each man a bag from the Red Cross containing soap, cigarettes, cards, sewing kit, shoe strings, pencil, shoe-shine rag, and a soap container. Very nice.

I miss you more and more every day. Hope the time will soon pass and we can be together again. Something happens each day to remind me of something we have done together and I only hope that we can be doing things together again - soon.

All my love, Brice

Eventually, the ship arrived. On a prepared form called a "V - Mail," he wrote from somewhere in England. Portions of the letter were removed by a censor,

> Dearest:
>
> . . . . It seems funny to be sitting by an open fire place in a large room where the velvet curtains rise to the ceiling - which must be eighteen feet above the floor - all by myself. How I wish you were here. Already it seems so long.
>
> Today I walked thru town for the first time. It is a quaint little town - so different from the ones at home. The stores don't advertize at all. It is hard to distinguish a drug store (which is called a "chemist") from a hardware store. A few of the clothing stores do display their wares in the windows. I was trying to figure out some of the prices, but as yet I am not too familiar with the English system. Civilians aren't very plentiful on the streets, they seem to spend most of their time at home. They move around at a very slow pace. It seems unusual to see the vehicles driving on the left side of the street and passing on the right. . . . Most of the English men-folks go to the "Pub" at night which takes the place of our nite-clubs at home, but on a smaller scale. [Pubs] are looked upon much as a club or community organization would be looked upon at home. . . . . They are very rarely patronized by women. . . . . It is impossible to get a good meal at a restaurant since food is under a very strict rationing [system]. . . .
>
> Everything is dark at night and it is hard to find your way from one place to another. The street lights are very dim, just enough light to barely show the outlines of building.
>
> Its hard to realize we are in another country, and I am so far away from you. Everything in the past month has been so different and so interesting and happened so quick, that it seems like a [removed by censor] - It is hard to convince yourself that you haven't just moved from one camp in the states to another. Sometimes I find myself thinking that you will be here soon, as you always were when I was moving between different camps, but, I guess we should consider

ourselves very lucky in having so much time together since I have been in the army and although our living conditions were nothing to brag about at times - I enjoyed every minute of it. I wish I had the last thirteen months to go thru again.

Remember, I love you, Brice

# CHAPTER FIFTEEN

*On to the Continent*

Then it was on to France. Because the disaster of the sinking of the Leopoldville and the loss of over eight hundred lives was suppressed, presumably for security or morale reasons, and those with knowledge were forbidden to speak of it, there is no direct mention in any of Brice's wartime letters of that tragedy. One of his first letters from the continent, was written on the eighth of January, 1945.

> "Somewhere in France"
>
> Dearest.
>
> Another day of routine. Nothing new.
>
> No news about any of the fellows in the division that you know - as I haven't seen them for sometime. . . . I had high hopes of meeting you in New York, but I had only one five hour pass and I didn't know that I was going to be granted that until the pass was in effect - so it was just impossible to see you. . . . I know that you will understand - and you know as much as I would liked to have seen you and didn't - it must have been impossible.
>
> We are issued a combat ration here which includes most of the things that we need such as candy, toothpaste, soap, and cigarettes. . . .

All my love, Brice

By February Brice was at, or near the front. He writes,

"Somewhere in France"
2 February 1944
Dearest:

Rec'd two V-mails from you today. One letter was written on my birthday

- thanks for the greetings. As to your inquiry, spent a very quiet routine day - no celebration like we used to have - I believe. Hays and I did open a can of 'C' rations and had a little wine as a midnight snack in our shack. . . .

. . .

Everything is quiet except occasional chatter of a machine gun in the distance and the sound of artillery. We are always arguing as to whether the artillery is coming in or going out. It is hard to distinguish by the sound unless a round lands nearby. . . . . .

My mother says you have gained weight. How much? Have you gained back all the weight lost while you were in Ozark. Jr. Nelson was lucky to get back home. Next war I will enlist in the Navy.

Let me hear all the news. Remember, I am thinking of you every minute.

All my love, Brice

In a letter on the 14th of February 1945, he fills Shirley in on living conditions at the front.

"Somewhere in France"
Dearest:

Another day - another day in which I missed you more and more. This time passes so slow - I wonder when the war will ever end.

. . . .

"Did I tell you that we had converted our old wood stove in our shack into a gas stove. We have a 5 gallon can on the roof, a pipe with a valve running down to a burner inside the stove. Open the valve, light a match and the stove takes off just like city gas - no more wood no more coal - which was always a big problem. A Sgt. from the French army who moved in with me a few days ago made the whole unit and installed it and it works much better than either of us had expected. He made the burner from a shell casing and the pipe came from a wrecked German vehicle. Our next improvement is going to be hot running water - all the comforts of home. I wish you could drop in some evening. . . . "

All my love, Brice

During this period Shirley is apparently corresponding with the wives of other servicemen she and Brice had met as they went from camp to camp before he went overseas. The women are worried about their men and try to ease each other's worries. She receives a letter from Pee Wee Beauregard of Louisiana dated February 5th, 1945.

Hello Dolly (Ha)

How're you? I'm fine.

Honey, do you hear from Brice. I hear from my baby often. He's in France and from the way he talked in his last letter, he must be in action. He said everything was plenty hot there (he meant the War of course.) I hear from Skip very often. Wish you could have gone down with us- we had more fun. . . .

I'm working at a produce place - mostly answering the telephone ($22.50 wk.) 6 days-off Sundays. I think it's a pretty good deal. Jobs are hard to find making $18.00 on up. . . .

Write me soon. Say hello to Brice for me. Did you receive the '66' book [apparently a book of the 66th Division]. They took the cutest picture of Brice. Let me hear from you.

Lots of love, Pee Wee

Brice writes again on the 25th of February, 1945, apparently having returned from the front.

"Somewhere in France"

Dearest:

After three days at last I have found time to write a few lines. I am now back with Division Headquarters and believe me it seems good to once again be back in civilization where everything is quiet - no chatter of machine guns or sounds of bursting artillery, no living and working in fox holes. I sure was glad to see all the fellows - we had a little party my first nite back. Everyone asked me the same question - "what was it like up on the front" and that is a hard question to answer, it just can't be described and I can now see how you can become immune to anything. You just find yourself forgetting all about civilization and what it was like. Back here [at Headquarters] it is wonderful, in comparison.

. . . .

Shirley receives another letter from the wife of a fellow soldier.

Dearest Shirley:

Honey, I hope you are in better spirits by now. Bob too, sent me the clippings from the Stars & Stripes, but I think they are just guarding them just in case some of them try to break out. As for Brice, I think he maybe was sent out for scouting work. And honey please try to think the best - cause it will just make an old lady of you, if you worry too much.

Honey, I will never forget our last few moments with the boys. . . .

The news from Europe sounds good tonight and I feel that the Germans can't hold out much longer. I think our babies can come home soon after the collapse of Germany.

Honey, I have double worries. My brother has been in the Iwo Jima invasion and we have had no word from him, They have really had a rough time, but we only hope and pray he is safe and unharmed.

When this terrible ordeal is over everyone can relax and begin to live once again.

Bob [the writer's husband] asked me to write my uncle in Hollywood for some pin-up snap shots of the stars. He wants to pass them out to the boys. He says they really go for pictures of this kind. Honey you have a few of yourself that could answer the purpose. Why don't you give the boys a morale boost? . . . .

. . . . Don't do anything that will get you in trouble, tho, honey if you do I can count on you to talk yourself clear. You really can convince anyone.

Until later sugar, Goodnite, Shorty

Brice writes on March 14th about the difficulty he is having buying a present for Shirley in a nearby French town, then adds a poem.

Dearest:

. . . . You should see the trouble we have when we go in a store to buy something. We don't know what to ask for, so we just have to look around until we find it - and sometimes its rather embarrassing after you have looked for 10 or 15 minutes and all the clerks are staring at you and wondering what you want.

Very few of the fellows here have picked up any French. We have little contact with the civilians. Very few of the French in this area speak any English at all.

The days are getting longer now. . . . The weather is much warmer - like late spring at home - our favorite time of the year - why do we have to be so far apart.

All my love, Brice

Enclosed was a poem. (Author unknown.)

*I Bequeath . . .*

*To you, my darling, I would give*
*Whatever things I own;*
*The cozy house wherein I live,*
*My chair, my telephone.*

*I would present you with food*
*And all I have to drink,*
*My energy, my slightest nod*
*And everything I think.*

*Oh, I would offer all I know,*
*Each word, each written line;*
*I would bestow the rain and snow*
*If they were only mine.*

*For you are everything to me*
*My hope, my dream, my song,*
*My future and the memory*
*Of what has passed and gone.*

*To you, my darling, I would send*
*A letter penned in gold,*
*And happily I would extend*
*My heart for you to hold.*

He anticipates the ending of the war in a letter on the 31st of March while still stationed in France. He writes Shirley: ". . . This coming month, in my opinion, will see the end of the war in Europe and then what – that's the $64 question. Everyone has a different answer, but everyone hopes for the same thing - a fast boat to the States."

Then in mid-April 1945 he writes,

> We were sure surprised a few days ago to learn that the President had passed away. It's a terrific loss, especially at this time. He had been planning for years for the day that is just around the corner and I am sure that no one else can carry out the plans as effectively as he could have.
>
> We were awarded a battle star - which means a few more points - which means that I will be seeing you sooner - and that will be the day - if only it will be shortly after V-E.
>
> All my love, always, Brice

After briefly discussing that his brother-in-law is coming home for a visit, he begins to talk about the economy after the War in a letter from France on the 22nd of April.

> Dearest:
>
> Surprised to hear that Dunbar was coming home. I know Jane must be glad. Hope that he will have sufficient time to be around for the big event [Brice's sister Jane is expecting]. He may be lucky, but I understand the first time the date is very uncertain. Is that right? . . .
>
> . . . .I think that bonds are a very good investment and I am proud of you for wanting to save the money, but are you sure you don't need it. Probably after the war the dollar will have less purchasing power than now. Someone has to pay for the cost of the war and it isn't hard to see what group of people that will be. The war news continues to be good day by day and it seems as tho the end is just around the corner, but we shouldn't be too optimistic - although it does help the morale it's worse to be disappointed.

Several days later, Brice writes, "So it was a boy - just what I had hoped for and I believe what Jane and Dunbar wanted. So glad to hear that Jane is getting along fine. . . . Well she did beat you after all, but we'll catch up."

This was to be the last letter that he wrote before V-E Day.[22]

[22] Shirley now recalls the fears at home during the European campaign leading up to VE-Day.

We would anxiously read about the advancing or retreating German troops and about what was occurring in Europe or the Pacific. We huddled around an old Motorola radio as we listened to Edward R. Murrow giving us the latest war news from Europe, hoping to hear good news about our husband's and son's units.

# CHAPTER SIXTEEN

*Victory in Europe*

An immediate concern of the troops in Europe after VE Day was the continuing war with Japan and whether they would be sent to fight in that campaign. The first saved letter that Brice writes home after V-E Day was to his mother, father and sister. They probably shared it with Shirley. It was found among Shirley's letters. It was dated the 14th of May, 1945.

> Mom, Pop and Jane:
>
> . . . .
>
> It is wonderful that the war here in Europe has finally ended - now I wonder what? Probably be one of two things - the Pacific or occupation in Germany. I understand that most of the combat troops if selected to go to the Pacific will go thru the States. I have no idea whatsoever in which category we may fall, but if I had my choice it would probably be the former if we were assured of going thru the States.
>
> At last the point system was announced but no help at all to me, in fact, I know of no one that will be affected by it with the exception of the boys that spent a great deal of time in England. I have only 36 of the required points (85,) 5 of them for the battle star. It seems to me that the present plan is

to hold the bulk of the army until the defeat of Japan - which could be a very long time.

V-E Day was celebrated here, but I realize that this was only another step, however a big one, of the many still ahead before we can return home. The day that I am released from the army and start living again the way that I choose is the one and only day that I care to really celebrate. May it be soon,

The French celebrated V-E day for a full week. They started a day or so before it was officially announced. . . .

I guess Jane is feeling fine now and you are all having a big time with "Junior." I understand Mom, that you don't let him sleep for a moment. I am glad everything worked out well. Dunbar planned his furlough perfect. . . .

Everything is going fine, Brice

In a post V-E Day letter to Shirley, he discusses the possible next steps for them. In the letter he seems to express the general thoughts of the soldiers that had fought in the European phase of the War, noting at one point their hope for "some chance of good fortune" that would save them from the Pacific campaign. That chance of good fortune would come - for them.

Dearest:

. . .

V-E Day was a day we had all been looking forward to, but it remains to be seen how it will change the future for us. It seems that most of the combat units will go thru the States if they are selected to go to the Pacific and probably the ones that remain here for occupation will be here for some time. I have no idea into which category we will fall, but if I had my choice of a furlough in the States and then the Pacific, it would probably be my choice. It would mean so much if only I could see you again soon, even if for a short time. Unless the general plan is changed considerably, I don't think the army will be reduced sufficiently in size to enable me to obtain a discharge until the war with Japan is over and that is estimated from 1 ½ years to 2 years from now and that is a heck of a long time

- much longer than I hope to spend in the army. Maybe some chance of good fortune will come my way [It would be called the atomic bomb].

. . . . I brought back a German pistol for Tom. First time that I had seen him in a month or so. He was down-hearted. Had received word about a week ago that his brother John (his favorite brother I believe) had died - such a short time after his mother's death. I know how he must feel.

I hope to find time to write your mother soon. Please explain for me.

All my love, Brice

With the war in Europe over, much of the censorship was removed, and Brice was finally able to tell Shirley where he had been during the winter of 1945. In a letter on the 17th of May he first discusses the possibility of being assigned to the occupation army.

I guess you have been wondering in what town I was stationed, but you should have had an idea of the general location by me frequently mentioning the trips to Rennes and Angers. Rennes and Angers are approximately 60 miles from here respectively. Chateaubriand is a rather nice little town, being possibly a little larger than Cambridge - you can find it on the map. It was named for the family, Briand, whose tremendous chateau still remains about two blocks from our [present] quarters. We are living and have the offices in what was once a girl's college and it is very nice.

Division headquarters has been here since we arrived in France . . . . We were in the Twelfth Army until recently (as you guessed - how?) when we were transferred to the new Fifteenth Army. Your guess that the Fifteenth Army will be occupation - may be a good one. . . . I will be in Germany very soon - but this does not necessarily mean occupation.

When I arrived in France, I stayed in Chateaubriand for only two days. Those two days we slept on the ground in zero weather and I nearly froze. After staying here for two days, I

> was sent to the front in Lorient for what was originally planned to be only a few days. I went up with Major Parr to set up a G-2 outfit near the front that would be turned over to personnel from the regiments once everything was in order - but as time went on the [G-2] work kept increasing and it was impossible for me to be relieved, consequently I remained up on the front all winter. We were living in our CP [Command Post] and it was in a dugout for protection against the constant shelling of enemy artillery. Luckily our CP was never quite zeroed in by the enemy's artillery. I returned to Chateaubriand, I believe, in March.

Among the letters that Shirley saved, is one she mailed to Brice right after V-E Day. I believe it is in response to the letter above that is among the ones she has just received from Brice. She has no recollection of why it was with the letters from Brice. One can surmise that Brice must have kept it with him during the occupation and when he returned home, Shirley saw it and saved it. I include it here, because I see in it the relief that her husband had made it through the war in Europe alive. It expresses the relief that all waiting on the home front must have felt, and mirrors, perhaps, the anguish felt by the loved ones of the men who did not return.

> My Darling,
>
> I guess right now I am one of the happiest girls in the world. I couldn't be any happier at the present under the prevailing circumstances. Darling, you're the sweetest 'hunk' of a hubby in the world. And why shouldn't I be excited. I got 10 letters from you . . . . And to think I actually thought that maybe you had forgotten me a little bit . . . . had forgotten a little just how much we mean to each other. Please, I pray to God that you will never stop loving me. Without you I barely exist. [The letters] were the first ones in over six months that you've said endearing things. Was it due to the censors? Why? Why? I know its because you've been through so much "hell" over there. Excuse me darling, but I had no idea you had been through so much. I wish I were a writer so I could

word this letter as beautiful as it should be. No words I can think of can quite express my appreciation of thanks to you for loving me.

Please don't think of your wife as a sentimental fool but even now as I write my eyes are filled with tears. I can hardly see. . . . I feel like crying out my heart to these wonderful letters. Darling, you must believe me, this is the happiest I've been since you left. Its almost as if you were here. I'm crying, I love you so much Darling. It's the first big cry I've let myself have since you left. I've been holding so much in, now I'm so happy that you love me, that I can't help but cry like a baby. I'm glad you can't see me. I probably look a sight, but I'm here all alone and no one can see me, so I can cry all I want.

. . .

Dearest, I really had your points figured right to the point, didn't I. Darling, you frighten me when you say that you might be used as a replacement in the Pacific. Oh no, honey, I hope not. I hope and pray you will stay "put." Anything but the [Japanese war]. . . .

Remember I love you always and always.

Just Yours Forever, Wife

# CHAPTER SEVENTEEN

## *Occupation*

Brice responds to Shirley's letter on June 7th, first indicating on the top of the letter "(just noticed the date. I believe I have been using May instead of June,) "

Dearest:

Last two days my morale has jumped high - I received 15 letters - most of my back mail. . . .

When we [his unit] move now it is quite a problem. You should see all the German equipment everyone has picked up. Our convoy from East France to Germany after St. Nazaire and Lorient fell, looked like a gypsy caravan. Everyone tried to hold on to everything they had taken from the Germans. On the trucks were tied beds, mattresses, large mirrors, stuffed chairs, bicycles and everything you could imagine. A lot of units have cars and trucks that were taken from the Germans, some of them were American, English and French cars originally taken by the Germans in their advances through France and Africa. One German general in St. Nazaire had a large Packard conv. sedan, really a beaut, now being used by one of the colonels in Div. Hq. There were numerous Cheves and Fords. Our section has a large German conv sedan. Although most of the

European cars are small, they top the average American car as far as lines.

Due to the gas shortage, most of the French cars have been converted into coal burners. They have two large boilers on the back about 6 feet in height and the driver has to get out to stoke up the stove and shovel in the coal, periodically. I still don't quite understand how these cars work. . . .

. . . One of the most impressive things that I have seen on the roads of France are the thousands of German [vehicles], burned and wrecked just off the side of the road. Sometimes you drive for miles and miles and burned out wrecked cars are lined bumper to bumper on either side of the road. These were usually German convoys fleeing from France and caught by our Air Force. It seems impossible to believe a country could have lost so much and still continue to fight. The answer to this is that the Germans looted every thing of value from every other country in Europe and, combined with these tremendous resources and the slave labor imported from the conquered countries, had organized a production machine probably greater than any other country's - with the exception of the U.S.

They exchanged our money today. The French gov't has called in all the money and it is being replaced by a new issue. This is probably to dispose of the large percentage of counterfeit money and also to bring to light the large sums of money accumulated by some of the soldiers that have been dealing in the black market. Soldiers are allowed to exchange only $150. Some of them have . . . [been] dealing in the black market on a large scale. I do disapprove of the GI s that have made a wholesale money making business out of the black market, but I believe the cases are rare. But, I don't blame the ones that have sold a few items of soap and cigarettes to justify for the ½ pay exchange rate that the Army is giving us [The authorized Army rate of exchange was only half as much as the official exchange rate in New York. GI s were forced to accept the Army's rate]. It is hard enough for a GI to get along on the small wage he receives in a country where everything is sky high, and then when the government cuts the value in half, the purchasing power is practically nil. . . .

Later, after having spent some time in Germany, he comments in another letter on the attitude of the French towards the American troops.

I would like to buy a little something for you, but it is just impossible here. I wonder if they will ever make an adjustment on our exchange rate? Everyone complains, even the high officers - but no one seems to do anything about it. . . . And then on top of that the civilians take advantage of us at every opportunity. It's obvious that our presence in France is no longer desired. It isn't hard to understand why most of the fellows want to go back to Germany. The exchange rate is one of the most important factors contributing towards the friction between the GI s and the French. It is hard to convince the average GI that it is not the individual French merchant that is responsible for our paying four times the price for anything we attempt to buy. . . . Maybe I shouldn't express my view on these prohibited subjects, anyway, this is only a shadow of my real opinion.

He next writes from the Hotel Denoailles in Marseille.

. . . . Dorothy McGuire's troop was in the office this morning (She played in 'Tree Grows in Brooklyn'.) Maybe you have seen the picture, although I believe it is rather new. They were waiting for a train to the Riviera at noon and sat around the office cracking jokes all morning. They had just come from Paris and were staying here at the hotel all night. Those USO show folks don't have a hard life.

The Stars and Stripes announced 8 more divisions going to the Pacific today, but the $66^{th}$ will not go to the Pacific as a unit, but it is very possible that we could go as replacements later.

Forever yours, Hubby

There was a series of letters that followed during June, in which the apprehension of being sent to the Pacific was evident. It is clear that the GI s in Europe wished the war with Japan over quickly regardless of the price to be paid by that country. In the next few letters, Brice comments on that issue and makes stark references to the sacrifices already paid by friends in the war. He writes,

> We had a POW working for us today, just a young fellow, but he could speak English fairly well. POWs are put to very good use here, doing KP and all the details. They seem glad to be in American hands instead of the French. Was surprised at the great number that can speak English. . . .
>
> . . . .When we were in convoy coming overseas we had a lifeboat drill every morning and while everyone was on deck, a little destroyer would pull up near our ship. It had an excellent PA system and you could hear it a mile or so away. They were always playing either, "Don't Fence Me In" or "When the Yanks Go Marching in Berlin." Whenever I hear either of those numbers, I will always remember that little destroyer beside our large liner, tossing in the waves with its decks awash, always its PA system blasting out with jazz. It was a great boost to everyone.
>
> . . .
>
> You seem to be [worried] that the 15$^{th}$ had been announced as going to the Pacific. Doesn't affect us. We are no longer a part of the 15$^{th}$. My opinion is that the 66$^{th}$ will not go to the Pacific as a unit, however, it is very probable, as I have told you before, that sometime in the near future, I will be assigned to an outfit that is destined for the Pacific. The chances are, under present plans, that we will be routed thru the States. I am in favor of that. A month with you would be worth all the hardships possible to be encountered in the Pacific.
>
> . . .
>
> I received a package from Mom and Jane yesterday with a carton of cigarettes, tins of shrimp, *crab meat,* cakes.

. . . .We were all sure we were going directly to the Pacific when we first arrived here, and believe me morale was darn low. That would have been a tough break - and we were just lucky that we didn't.

. . . We all hope that the war with Japan will end soon, but this is just being [optimistic]. The fighting on the islands still continues to be as bitter as ever. I don't believe the Japs will surrender, they are even more fanatical than the Germans, and the Germans fought to the very end. Unconditional surrender is necessary, but I believe it is given too much publicity.

Have you been in bathing much this summer. I haven't been once. We were issued bathing suits captured from the Germans, but they are all large sizes.

Won't we have a big time making up for all of this 'lost time.'

. . .

Maybe you will have the opportunity to see [Europe] after the war, or should we spend the rest of our lives in some quiet corner, just you and I and a Joe - or two?

If only the war with Japan would end soon. They should realize that it is hopeless for them to continue to fight. . . .

. . .

You remember Russ Gee, don't you? I hear he was killed while in France. His brother was killed in the Pacific just before he came overseas and another brother was missing. So many of the fellows that I knew have been killed in this war. I see by the Cambridge paper, a lot of fellows there have been wounded, killed, or missing.

Where is Leroy? Earl, Don, Junior Nelson, Thomas, Gene and all the other boys from home now? Any of the boys from the 24$^{th}$ Division arrive in Cambridge yet?

. . .

The war in the Pacific seems to be progressing rather well. Possible that we can all be surprised as to its length, but I still think it will be at least a year.

. . .

Another coincidence. Johnie [Pee Wee's husband] and his Captain drove up. I talked with him for sometime, said he was receiving mail from Pee Wee in four or five days. . . .

Glad to hear that Johny [apparently a different John] had gotten a discharge. I had suspected that he had Malaria. Maybe it won't bother him if he can live in a cool climate - anyway the cure for Malaria is now in its advanced stages. . . . . This is the worse dread should I go to the Pacific, but most of the fighting in Pacific is now out of the Malaria zone. We are in the Malaria zone here (just on the edge) and have to take precautionary measures. . . .

So Eugene is still in Germany - he should be in the same category as I. It is my opinion that the odds are in favor of us eventually going to the Pacific - if the Pacific campaign continues to be a long-drawn-out affair.

. . .

The war in the Pacific seems to be going much better than anticipated, but I doubt if there will be surrender before invasion. The Air Force and Navy are doing a wonderful job there now.

. . .

Planes and ships still seem to be blasting Japan more than ever. I wonder what effect this will have. If they are smart they would give in, but I doubt we will see that before an invasion. If we could bomb them out, it may take much longer, but would be a tremendous saving in the number of lives.

Still nothing definite as to our chance of going through the States, but I believe there is a 50-50 chance that we may be redeployed through the States eventually, but we shouldn't build up our hopes for that, because there is always a chance of going directly to the Pacific. If only I could see you for a few days it would mean so much. It seems so long. Maybe next summer we can be together to enjoy all the summers again. Have I missed it. You can never imagine how much I have missed you. The war seems so long and the time passes so slowly and I love you more and more every day.

. . .

When the war [in Europe] was going on it wasn't so bad, we were all so very busy, things were always happening and the time slipped by rather fast. Now there is nothing to do but wait [for possible assignment to the Pacific], and keep thinking . . . How much longer? How much longer?

The answer isn't long in coming.

# CHAPTER EIGHTEEN

*The Atomic Bomb*

Brice writes in a letter dated the 7th of August 1945.

Everyone wants to go home, but it is probably better that we with low points remain here for a while less we go to the Pacific. I would still take redeployment to the Pacific thru the States for a 30 day furlough if I had the choice. It would be impossible to turn down that 30 days with you. *Maybe this new atomic bomb will change the attitude of the Japs - it sounds great.* If only the war would end soon.

He writes again about the atomic bomb in a letter the next day.

Seems as if this new atomic bomb will be very effective. At least if it proves practical it will shorten the war. If they are really able to control the atom it will be the greatest invention of all time and will completely revolutionize the post-war world. But it is my opinion that it is slightly advanced of the experimental stage. Probably the papers at home have gone into great detail.

He writes the next day.

We were surprised to learn last nite that the Russians had declared war on Japan and Stars and Stripes carried head lines this morning even larger than V-E Day. Everyone had expected it to come off during the Potsdam Conference, but since this went off with little mention we had sorta lost hope. It is a big event and [will] definitely shorten the war by many months. This together with the announcement of the new atomic bomb has given everyone a boost in morale and more optimistic outlook. We all wonder just how far advanced they are in the new bomb - very little information seems to have leaked out so far. Many people here seem to think the Jap will surrender. I am still inclined to doubt it. Hope I'm wrong.

On the eleventh of August, he starts his letter to Shirley by speculating.

Is the war with Japan over or not - that is the only discussion now everyplace, but as yet we haven't heard any official word. The radio hasn't confirmed it as being official, although the French papers have been running extras for two days claiming that the war is finished and even quoting Pres. Truman as saying it is all over. The French always get the jump. Gee, how I hope they are right. I will be pretty sick if it doesn't work out. I know it will. The French were celebrating V-E day here two days before it was officially acknowledged. I hope they are right again.

The first indication that anyone had as to the Japs quitting was put out in a French extra two nights ago claiming that the war was over and naturally everyone thought it was true. The boys in the staging area waiting for ships to the Pacific went wild, they brought all the bands out, shooting flares and guns everywhere. Several of the boys were hurt. They had to send in riot squads to help break it up. When they were told that there was no official word from the States their morale went back to the usual low. But, everyone still has hope. I am sure by the time you receive this it will all be over.

> . . . Anyway, if it's true, just has to be, it will mean that you and I can be together again soon and live as we please. This waiting won't seem so long
>
> I bet everyone at home is in suspense about the end of the war too - it was the same thing VE Day, rumor after rumor, but no confirmation, really starts you to bite your nails. If only we can be together soon - we just have to. I love you.

While over the intervening years the use of the atomic bomb during World War II, has been ethically and morally questioned, such questions were not an issue in 1945. Hundreds of thousands of GI s who had fought through the European campaign to be victorious on VE Day, but were then to participate in the invasion of Japan, never had any ethical or moral doubts. They realized, immediately, that many of their lives had just been saved. Even now, fifty years later, in an interview conducted prior to any knowledge that the letters he had sent home had been saved by Shirley, Brice still vividly remembered the attitudes of the soldiers in Europe.

> The [European] infantrymen were very concerned about invading Japan. I was in Marseille when the news of the dropping of the atomic bomb became known. I was in a headquarters building when I heard a commotion out on the street. When I went to check on what was going on, the troops were celebrating and one of them told me about the bomb. Everyone was yelling and a newspaper was being held up and there was big print announcing the bomb. I forget exactly what the headline said, but it was announcing the dropping of the bomb on Hiroshima. None of us realized what the atomic bomb was at first. We just knew something big had happened. It was a happy day for us, because we realized that there would probably be a trimming back on the number of troops that would be needed for the war in the Pacific.
>
> At that point we felt much better about our chances of living through the war, to get through it, to be able to go home. The troops in Europe considered the atomic bombing

of Japan to be a good thing because it increased our chances of living.

It favorably affected us individually, as an army unit, as a company, and as an army. It affected us in so many ways, in that we could see that the war was going to be shortened. To the troops in Europe waiting to be sent to fight in the Pacific, and ultimately to fight in the invasion of the home islands of Japan, the dropping of the bombs on Hiroshima and Nagasaki were wonderful events. It was a terrible thing for the Japanese but a great thing for the American GI.

It saved a lot of lives in the long run, allied soldiers and probably even Japanese, and maybe mine. There would probably have been more persons killed during the extension of the Pacific war than were killed by the bombs that caused the Japanese to surrender. We've never known for sure about Japanese casualties, but we positively know that the bombs saved more American and allied lives.

Back home the wives and lovers felt the same as their men overseas. Shirley remembers.

Back then, at that time, it was encouraging to us at home to know about it, about how devastating the atomic bomb was. That our side was the one that had the bomb, not the other side. We knew it could end the war and that our men would be coming home. No more of them would have to die. That Brice would be coming home. I had been afraid for him. That he'd have to go to the Pacific. It was a big boost to the morale on the home front. All of us with men overseas became optimistic for the first time in a long while. Came out of our years-long depressions.

# CHAPTER NINETEEN

## *"JAPAN QUITS"*

A mid-August, 1945, letter to Shirley from Brice contains a copy of the original Tuesday, August 14th, 1945, issue of the Stars and Stripes, Southern France Edition, containing the famous headline quoted above. Parts of the accompanying articles read,

> "Japan has accepted the Allied terms of surrender, a Tokyo radio report picked up by OWI announced early today. No further details were immediately available. . . . [It] touched off unprecedented victory celebrations in Allied capitals and the towns and villages whence come the bulk of the fighting men. The surrender of Japan was foreshadowed by two sensational events in the Pacific war within the last few days. The incredibly destructive atom bomb, which was dropped on two Japanese cities, and the Russian declaration of war."

On an inside page are two almost forgotten articles.

> "Ike Denies Reds Asked Elbe Halt - Gen. Eisenhower said today that he had ordered U.S. troops smashing across Germany last spring to stop at the Elbe River because he wanted to break up Hitler's national redoubt in the south - and not because the Red Army or Stalin had requested it."

The other article is about the Russian invasions of Manchuria and Korea.

Brice immediately responds to the article and rumors in a letter of the same date.

Sweetheart,

Although not yet official, we are fully convinced that the war with Japan is finally over. This morning before noon there were strong rumors that the official word had come through, but I guess that was just a rumor. The Stars and Stripes put out an extra about 4PM this afternoon with 4" headlines stating that "Japan Quits." It hasn't as yet come thru official channels, but the news was given out by Tokyo radio. The town went wild (being more than 50% GI s on the streets when the extra came out.) The soldiers would buy a paper, read the headlines, throw it in the air, and give a big yell. It was so wonderful to see everyone so happy again. It means more to the soldiers here than in most parts since the larger percentage of them are sweating out a boat directly to the Pacific. A friend of mine boarded a ship here this morning. Now I don't know where he will be going. Maybe the fellows that are on the boats [going to the Pacific] will be the lucky ones - they will be sure to change their course from the Pacific to the States. Celebrations are still going on. Be a lot of headaches tomorrow.

I really won't feel like a celebration until I am at last home - then we will make up for all the celebrations that we have missed. . . . . They had to collect all the guns and ammunition from the fellows in the staging areas - think they shot up everything. . . . . Sparing the ships that haul all the ammunition and equipment plus all the ships that were carrying all the troops directly to the Pacific, plus the thousands of planes that can now be used, the speed of the troops moving to the States should be doubled and redoubled. . . .

I took off a couple hours this afternoon and went for a little shopping (window shopping) but I didn't buy a thing. . . . . [Women's]Bathing suits sell for around $50 and believe me that is robbery as there is very little to a French bathing suit.

# CHAPTER TWENTY

*Going home?*

In the months after the war was officially over the concerns of the GI s, including Brice, were primarily related to going home. In several letters the Army's policies are questioned as Brice yearns for home, and for Shirley. There are also discussions as to what will happen when he returns to Hoopers Island. With editing of the more personal material, the letters contain the following passages.

> I think we all agree that the awards given to make high points aren't at all fair. Some of the fellows that never left England have enough battle stars for 30 points - that surely isn't right. Four [more] battle stars were requested for us, but didn't come thru. We missed a battle star in Germany by moving in just a couple of days late.
>
> . . .
>
> The time passes so slow and I miss you more every day. How I wish they would speed up this discharge system. Everything seems so indefinite. If they continue to use the point system it is damn unfair. . . . The 66th [Brice's Unit] had more time on the front than a lot of units that have more stars. Just because our campaign was a long one, shouldn't be a reason why we should have less credit than units that

moved from place to place, usually in rear assignments . . . Why should someone who has never left England get 6 battle stars? Battle stars are supposedly awarded for actual contact with the enemy.[23]

. . .

I gain 8 points on the new computation giving me 43. . . which doesn't sound too good. I would be much happier if only I had two more. Seems as if all the divisions are going home with the exception of the 66th. Not even a good rumor. I guess we will continue to operate the staging area here for some time as 1/3rd of the troops that are now being returned are coming thru the Port of Marseille, approximately 100,000 per month [these figures, relating only to American soldiers in only one theater give context to the scope of World War II in comparison with the current conflicts - our fathers were truly "The Greatest Generation"].

. . .

Yes, Marseille is [apparently an indecipherable section of this letter was answering a worry expressed by Shirley about the character of Marseille and its reputation for being a wide open, immoral city] the worse in the world, but wherever a person may be, they can live by their own standards, at least morally if not physically. The old saying "when in Rome, do as the Romans do' is applicable only to those who accept it

[23] Apparently, battle stars were more frequently awarded to units for different engagements, rather than the more serious long engagements. If a unit was associated with one battle it got one battle star regardless of how long the battle. Thus, a unit that was in three different engagements over a period of six months would get three battle stars while a unit in continuous combat for the same period of time would get only one battle star. The system of awarding battle stars was thought to be unfair for at least two reasons. The unit in continuous combat in a single battle, often was at as much, if not more, risk as the unit that was pulled out of an engagement and sent to another battle. Additionally, rear echelon members of a unit whose jobs required them to stay in non-combat areas such as England, were also awarded battle stars although they never saw combat. This was important at the conclusion of the war in Europe, because a soldier's status in respect to returning to the United States depended on a point system and, among the things that were considered in computing points, were battle stars.

as a means to justify actions committed due to the lack of, or possibly to the flexibility of their ethics. Considering, the GIS here are very well behaved.

Brice is reassigned to Germany. Writing from "Frankfurt on Main" beginning on the 24th of September, 1945, he says,

> This is my first day at work here - spent most of the morning getting records straightened out. . . .
>
> The town has been pretty well battered - block after block completely destroyed.
>
> I miss you more everyday - its even worse that I have to stay behind now while so many fellows are going home - everyday I expect to hear that they have revised the point system, but no one seems to know what the score is.
>
> If you would rather not work this winter, I could make a larger allotment - let me know! There really isn't much to spend money for here in Germany - course the small amount that I earn here wouldn't go far at home. Don't try to save the allotment checks [Shirley had been investing the checks in bonds, saving for a house]. Be sure to buy some new clothes for the winter and other things you are sure to need. How about that long overdue vacation? You could spend some time with Harry & Bernice and Dot. . . . . . .
>
> There is practically nothing new on the discharge policy - in fact they seem to have just about forgotten it - what happened to this 2 year discharge plan. The senators and congressmen are proposing all kinds of asinine things - there must be someone other than an army officer that understands and could propose a fair plan.

# CHAPTER TWENTY-ONE

*Homeward bound*

Frankfurt, Germany
15 October 45
Sweetheart,

This is the letter you have been waiting to receive and this is the letter that I have been waiting to write for a long time, and now I don't know what to say - can hardly believe it - yes, I'll pinch myself again, it's time, the best news possible.

Tomorrow, I am flying to a staging area in France for redeployment to the States. I had promised myself that I wouldn't tell, but this is one bit of news that I can't keep - maybe I shouldn't mail this. I had always planned it to be a surprise, but I know you are anxious to know - so here's spoiling my surprise. Yes, I am surprised, too. Our "lucky break" came thru.

Now please don't think I will walk in the door tomorrow, or next week, or even in a couple of weeks. . . . I am flying to France, but returning to the States by water. . . . I will have to wait for shipment and usually that is two weeks and more, often a month or so. The redeployment schedule is now all 'screwed up' since the British have [requisitioned] their ships which were a very large part of our transportation, and I am

> sure our return will be delayed sometime by that, but with all the difficulties it's still wonderful news, wonderful news.

In an interview for this book, Brice notes the unusual circumstances of his trip home, and wonders whether he was ever actually discharged.

> When I came back to this country we came into Boston aboard a ship. I had an interesting way of getting to Camp Meade. In Boston we were assembled in a big room. They called the names on the list and assigned the various returnees to different barracks on the basis of where they were to be sent next in order to be discharged close to their homes. My name was not on any list. It was as if I wasn't there. And I'd been fighting for months to be there.
>
> I went around to the various barracks late that night and I found out where each group of men were to be transported the next day. I finally found the barracks of the men that were going to be transported to Fort Meade. Early the next morning I was hanging around that barracks when they called the roll and lined the men up for transport to a train station. After they had called the roll and lined up, I just slipped into the rear of the line. I kept slipping into the rear of the lines until I ended up at Fort Meade.
>
> Everything was a little confused at that time. They didn't know what was going on really, so I just got on the train for home with the rest of the guys. I guess I took advantage of a situation.
>
> When we got to Fort Meade, they didn't know what to do with me either. I wasn't on the list, so they gave me a furlough to go home to Hoopers Island for a month so they could figure out what to do with me. I reported back when I was supposed to. Eventually, someone told me to go home. I don't know whether he had authority to do it, but, I presumed he did, so I went home. Never went back. I still don't know whether I was ever discharged, I presume I was, but I have no recollection of it. It was a lot harder to get out of the army, then it was to get

in. That's if I am out. Maybe I was never discharged, maybe I'm still on furlough; if I am they owe me a lot of back pay.

When I got home on the first furlough, I met Shirley and my mother and father in Cambridge when I got off the bus. That was a beautiful picture, Shirley, and my mother and father meeting the bus. It had been almost two years.

[Question by interviewer.] What was the first thing you did when you got back to Hoopers Island?

I'm not going to tell you.

# CHAPTER TWENTY-TWO

*Hoopers Island, the next decade*

Brice went to work in the packing plant immediately upon his return from the war. Captain 'Ellie' wasn't well. He had heart trouble and needed Brice to take over the operation. Brice would be the hands-on manager of the business. In the beginning he would meet with Captain Ellie in the evenings, tell him what had happened each day and seek his advice for the next day. But he soon realized that change was needed. He had recognized a different vision for the seafood industry while he'd been overseas.

He had written of his thoughts and plans to Shirley. In one letter, Brice, worried about Shirley's finances, wrote of the post-war situation.

> How are you making out financially? You never mention it. I worry that you don't have the money to buy lots of things that you should have. Don't try to save a lot of money. I appreciate it, but we can start when you and I are together again. I have no definite post-war plans, but once this sentence has served and once again I have my freedom, we'll make the most of life - and make every moment count.
>
> Do you have any definite post war plans -any suggestions - where would you like to live? I received a very nice letter from mom yesterday. Everything seems to be going fine at

> home. She mentioned that Dad would probably want to turn the factory over to me when I come home. It would be a lot of responsibility and take me a long time to learn, but it is a wonderful opportunity. Small business should present a better opportunity than any other field after the war. The seafood business is very young, concentrated and under-developed. What do you think? Let me know any plans or suggestions you may have for after the war, which can't be too far away. If it helps to hope, wish and keep your fingers crossed.

During our interviews, Brice discussed the vision he had for the seafood industry upon his return from the war.

> When I first got home from the war, I realized that things were going to need to change. Prior to that time, seafood had been packed in bulk, in wholesale sizes. In other words, crabmeat was also packed in gallon cans, or larger cans, just like oysters. I realized that there was a market for packing the product in smaller retail sized containers, like we do now.
>
> I also wanted to get into more prepared foods. Like the restaurants do now. I wanted to be involved in preparing seafood in different ways. Additionally, it had been apparent even before the war, that the supply was dwindling or the demand was drastically increasing, or both.

Shirley remembers,

> Brice saw the way seafood had been handled was changing drastically. People had developed a taste for hot steamed crabs, were beginning to buy them instead of buying crab meat in large cans the way they had always been doing. A market was developing for steamed hard crabs and the people, the restaurants, wanted the bigger crabs for steaming. This for the most part happened after the war. It wasn't the culture in the pre-war years. It came to be a trend, the fashion. It became really, really popular after the war.

As Shirley and Brice both note, before the end of WWII, the commerce in crabs was almost exclusively in processed, canned crab meat. Restaurants specializing in steamed whole crabs were just beginning to be popular. This phase of the industry was embryonic, but poised for rapid growth. The public was fast developing a taste for steamed crabs in the shell. The Phillips' packing plant, as well as others, became involved in developing that industry, initially from the supply side.

One of the problems in getting live crab to restaurants was getting them there alive. Dead crabs would be rejected, and couldn't be brought back to the plant and used for picking. Dead crabs were disposed of at the packers' expense. This was compounded by the fact that as the live crab industry grew, the packers began to pay the watermen premium prices for the large male 'jimmie' crabs that were the first (and in the early days only) choice of the steaming restaurants. The premium price paid to the watermen for the 'culled' larger crabs was sometimes as much as 75% higher than the price paid for smaller sized crabs. Initially, in order to transport live crabs in the high heat of mid-summer, a small stove pipe was placed vertically in the middle of an open barrel. It was filled with ice, then the live crabs were packed around it, filling up the barrel, and off they went to market. As the live crab market continued to expand, other methods, including refrigerated or ice cooled truck bodies were used.

After the war, Gorden's on Orleans Street in Baltimore was one of the first restaurants to buy live crab from the Phillips' packing plant. Gorden's had combined several small garages into a crab house and a carry out. Over the next ten years, crab houses and carry-outs began to spring up in many places and Brice and Shirley continued to expand the Phillips' operation.

And they began to expand their buy boat operation beyond the local waters where it had operated. They would sail the *Gertie V* to fishing ports as far away as the western shore, to the James River, Solomons, Reedsville, Annapolis and other areas across the bay, and motor right in among the tongers and the crabbers, depending on the season, to buy product.

From the beginning Shirley was involved in all aspects of the operation, going on the buy boats, helping out in the packing house, driving a ten-wheel truck to other packing houses ("I felt so good, so powerful, sitting up there behind the wheel in that big old truck.") buying and selling oysters and crabs, helping with the books, doing the quarterly reports and the payroll. She was always good at getting things done. Always reaching for the result.

The business was a joint operation from the beginning. They would take their visions, and with the impetus supplied by the restaurant's treatment of the packers in the early 50s, they would begin another part of the amazing Phillips' journey to success by starting their own crab house in Ocean City in 1956.

But first, they were lovers, he was a husband home from the wars. There had to be time for holding hands, making a home and a family.

# CHAPTER TWENTY-THREE

*Settling in at Fishing Creek*

Shirley has strong memories of the war years, the worrying about Brice, its impact on her, and the picking up of their lives.

> When Brice went overseas it was a tremendous loss for me. I missed him terribly, but I couldn't let him know how miserable I was without him. I knew he had problems of his own being in a war, problems I couldn't solve. I would write him and tell him I loved him and tell [him] things were fine at home, even when they weren't.
>
> I knew that as hard as it was, it was still easier for me because I had my family, his family, our friends and my job to keep me busy. I worked in Cambridge and lived with another girl named Shirley Dunn whose husband was also overseas in the service. I was able to go home to Hoopers Island most weekends or somebody from our families would come up.
>
> When I would get his letters I always wondered even more about him, whether he was safe. He never talked much in the letters about the danger. I didn't even know that he had spent the winter of 45 at the front until he told me after VE-Day. He had kept it from me. I had wondered if he was keeping knowledge of the risks from me. I often asked myself if I would ever see him again. It was hard times and you just

> hoped and prayed. I prayed a lot that God would take care of him and bring him back to me. Home safely. It was a long time apart for a young woman who had just been married and not knowing what was going to happen.
>
> I remember where I was when Brice came home. I was working in Cambridge and he got off the bus. His mother and father were there. I really wanted him to myself, but I understood that they needed to see him as much as I did. Well, not as much, but they needed to see him. His coming home from the war is just like yesterday to me. I've remembered it vividly for over fifty-five years. That's how afraid I was for him, that's how thrilled I was to get him back.

While we don't have any of Shirley's letters to Brice about her desire for children, it is obvious that children had been the subject of much of the content of her letters to him when he was overseas. To one such letter, Brice responded,

> I'm still sleeping on the subject - your letter of 5th. Should we try the first nite? Bet we could have lots of fun, too . . . . Just wait. (Better not get started on this subject.)
>
> What do you mean when the war is over I will be 27 - don't tell me that I'm going to be in the army for 3 more years. When do you think we should start a family -you asked the question - give me your opinion. I will most likely agree with you. It's that I have done very little post-war planning - but we will get along - just you and I - we will be together, that is the most important factor to me.

He had previously written her that after the war the two of them *and a "Joe or two"* would take up housekeeping, would travel, make a life. He had responded to her thoughts about building a house after the war.

> About the house - an excellent idea. I appreciate your attempt to plan for the future even though everything is so discouraging, indefinite, with the odds stacked against us

in numerous ways. I agree with you 100% that a place of our own is a must when I return, but, at this moment it is impossible to plan; if it can wait for a few more weeks, I feel sure that the future will be predictable to the extent that we can begin to make some plans. Anyway, I have high hopes for that long shot or lucky break.

Shirley remembers that

As soon as Brice got home he wanted, we wanted, to have a child right away. . . . We had rented a house on Hoopers Island when Brice first came home, then his father obtained a house for us across from the packing house so that Brice and his family would be near the plant. It was a present for Brice's return, Captain 'Ellie's way of saying thanks for his service during the war. It was a real nice home and is still there today."

Brice was home from the War. It was time for children. Steve was born in 1947, in the hospital in Cambridge. When Jeffrey was born in 1952, frugal Shirley was experienced at giving birth and at saving money. The island doctor just managed to get to the house and he and Brice delivered Jeffrey. When it was over, practical Shirley's first comment to Brice was, "Isn't this wonderful, we don't have to pay all that money to the hospital." She's still not sure Brice, who had delivered his first and last baby, agreed it was worth the money they saved.

Shirley remembers,

They [Steve and Jeffrey] were very involved in the business at a young age. In Hoopers Island they'd go over to packing plant when we'd steam the crabs in the evening and crack claws, just like I did when I was a little girl. Once they learned to crack claws and pick crabs, Brice and I would take them out on the buy boat, the Gertie V, a 50 foot long drake-tail boat. We'd take them with us when we were going all over the bay buying oysters. In the winter it was oysters - in the summer crabs.

Then on the weekends we'd have the boat available to take trips on the bay. We'd go on weekend trips. Brice or I would run the boat, but we'd be teaching the boys as well even when they were young. Almost every summer weekend before we started the businesses in Ocean City, we'd pack up food, chicken, sandwiches, of course crab meat, and I'd bake a cake. We'd take off for the western shore, over to the James River, Solomons, Annapolis or some other place. Steve was about five or six years old and Jeff was a toddler.

Brice or I would con the boat through the Hoopersville bridge, then say, 'Come here Steve," and we'd sit Steve up on a stool and tell him, "Take us to Solomons. Or wherever it was we were going."

We'd get there [Solomons] dock the boat and go to the little resort area where the boys could swim and we'd spend the day on the beach. When we'd get ready to leave, Brice would put Steve back on the stool and tell him, "Take us home." Since that time, when he was only six, Steve has had a love for the water and for boats. Now he's into sailing, he's a world champion-class sailor.

The boys have been a part of all of our ventures - from the beginning. Now much of it is turned over to them and to their children to manage, but Brice and I still are there to help them when it's wanted - and sometimes when it's not. But it all works well in the family, it always has.

# CHAPTER TWENTY-FOUR

*The wreck of the Gertie V*

In the middle of one season the Gertie V, with a hired captain aboard, was sent on a buying expedition across the Bay to the western shore in the area of the Potomac River. After a full morning's and early afternoon's buying, she turned, left the mouth of the Potomac, and headed northeast up the bay for home, for Hoopers Island. A storm came up out of the north and soon the Gertie V was burying her bow into very steep seas and into a rising wind. As the seas would come on, the bow would rise with each one, then abruptly fall off the back of the seas because the troughs were so deep.

On the course she was heading, unknown to the captain, was the site of an old abandoned pound fishing operation. Fishing pounds are fish traps where nets are arranged attached to long pilings extending from the bottom in order to funnel fish into a net trap at the end, or the center, of the pound. Boats would come to the pound at regular intervals and remove the trapped fish. When the pound is active, being fished, the pilings extend well above the surface of the water, normally readily seen. When fishing pounds are abandoned, the pilings are removed and taken ashore, or moved to other locations for use in other fish pounds.

When this particular fishing pound had been abandoned, the fishermen had failed to observe that one of the pilings snapped, leaving the top of what remained just under the surface of the water. It had unknowingly been left imbedded in the bottom, its top just below the surface.

In the middle of the storm the Gertie V fell off the back of a wave and landed on the top of the submerged piling. Her bottom was holed, water rushed in and she swiftly sank. Brice described the recovery operation.

> The captain was able to secure a line to the boat before she went completely under, and was able to tie the other end of the line to a life preserver. The captain was able to swim until another boat, a competitor's buy boat was passing, saw him, and rescued him. He was brought to Hoopers Island where he told of the sinking.
>
> In those days the Coast Guard was permitted to assist in recovery operations on the bay, or if they weren't permitted, did it anyway. They really were a part of the sailing family . . . . The Coast Guard was called, and the next day I had another boat take me, and Mr. Jim Simmons, a master motor mechanic, to the site of the sinking. There I met a large Coast Guard boat equipped with a heavy winch.
>
> We first attempted to winch the Gertie V from the bottom with the line the captain had attached as she was sinking. It would only winch her part way off the bottom because of the weight of the wreck, the strength of the line and the power of the winch. She hung below the Coast Guard vessel, partially on the bottom and partially off it, with only the point of her bow near the surface. The line had so much strain on it, that it had been stretched so far that it had lost half of its diameter and couldn't bear the strain of any other weight.
>
> A conference was held on the Coast Guard vessel and it was determined that she'd have to be 'planed' to the surface. In other words the Coast Guard vessel would run in circles around the wreck with lifting tension on the line and cause the rest of the Gertie V to rise off the bottom and, with the effect of a circular movement through the water, plane to the surface where jury-rigged repairs could be made to the hole in

> the bottom. She could be pumped out, and eventually towed to a boat yard for permanent repairs.
>
> However, the strain on the one line then in place was so great that there was a fear that it would break if the action were taken while it was the only line on the boat. If the line were to break, given the strain it was under, it could whip back toward the Coast Guard ship, and seriously injure anybody it would strike. Because of the danger, the captain of the Coast Guard vessel would not let any of his crew members assist in attempting to get another line attached to the Gertie V. It was my boat. So it was my job.
>
> The line from the Gertie V was warped to the bow of the Coast Guard vessel, and I attached another line to the Coast Guard vessel and lowered it to where the bow of the Gertie V was near the surface. I lowered myself into the water, made my way to the stanchion on the Gertie V, and was able to make the extra line fast.

After getting the extra line fastened, the Coast Guard vessel began pulling on the Gertie V, by running in circles around her. Soon the vessel had spiraled completely to the surface, and Brice jumped aboard her with several other lines. Before long they had her fastened to the side of the Coast Guard boat. A pump was put aboard her and they began to pump her out. Soon they had enough water out of her that they could put a temporary patch on the hole in the hull.

She was towed to the boat yard in Reedsville, Virginia where she was hauled out. Overnight they replaced the temporary patch with a permanent patch. Mr. Jim Simmons worked on her engine all night and got it working. The buy boat was back in business less than 48 hours after it sank.

The Gertie V continued in service for years as both a buy boat and a recreational vessel for the Phillips' family.

# BOOK TWO

---

*Ocean City and beyond*

# CHAPTER TWENTY-FIVE

*Ocean City beckons*

The demand by crab houses in the late 40's and early 50's for live crabs to steam for serving whole was rapidly changing a large part of the crabbing industry. The immediate effect changed the operations of the packing plants on Hoopers Island, and in other crabbing villages as well. Prior to the war, while there was special pricing for peelers, all other hard crabs were generally priced the same when the packers were purchasing them from the watermen - by the pound of the total catch. There was little culling of the hard crabs according to size. The males were thrown in with the females, and all the crabs, regardless of size were put on the pickers' tables for picking. Once the live steamed crab market was established, the pricing system changed drastically. The larger crabs, almost all of them males, were culled from the catch and sold separately to the packers [or even retailed by the watermen themselves] at much higher prices.

Additionally, the packers had to develop a different delivery system, their own trucks. The live crabs had to be transported to the crab house restaurants as speedily as possible. In time, however, the opening of the steamed whole 'crab house' restaurant business began to create serious problems for the packers, including the Phillips' operations. Brice and Shirley explain.

When the restaurants began to want to have live crabs to steam and serve whole, they only wanted the largest crabs. This meant that the watermen would separate the crabs by size and the largest crabs would cost the packers much more money, sometimes 70% more than the picking crabs. However, the significantly higher costs the packer incurred in obtaining the larger crabs contained the seeds of economic problems for the packer. After a restaurant had opened up several different sources of supply, we would arrive at a restaurant in Baltimore or elsewhere with the quantity of crabs they had asked for, only to find that they had obtained others, and that they wouldn't honor their understanding with us and buy ours. This meant that the only thing we could do with those large crabs was to take them back to the plant and steam those that survived the two-way trip and pick them for crab meat. When this happened, and it began to happen more and more frequently, we lost considerable sums of money because we had, in essence, overpaid by 70% for picking crabs. On top of that there was the crab mortality problem and transportation overhead, our time on the road as well. Because we couldn't depend on the restaurants to buy the crabs as promised, the live whole crab business too often was a losing proposition for the packing houses.

We discussed it, and decided that the only way we could protect ourselves, was to go into competition with the crab house restaurants. We would open our own steamed crab retail carry-out or restaurant that would use all our large crabs. We were sort of forced into the restaurant business. We began to look around in Baltimore and Washington at first. But then we thought of the boys. They'd have to spend the summers in the cities if we opened a restaurant there. Our thoughts turned to Ocean City next. It fit right in with the seasons at Hoopers Island. The crab season at Hoopers Island was short and the season in Ocean City was short back in those days. And the seasons were the same. We'd have the market for crabs at our own restaurant in Ocean City when the crabbing season was at its peak, then just about when the crabbing would start to drastically slow down, Ocean City would drastically slow down. There would be a short break when we could close up a summer operation, and then the oyster season would start back at Hoopers Island. Time-wise, in those days before Ocean City became a year round resort, it was a perfect fit.

On top of being a perfect fit, we thought we'd have plenty of time to spend with the boys on the beach. Time for swimming, fishing, doing other things with them. They'd be out of school in the summer, we'd open the restaurant in the summer. It just looked like it would work.

We went over to Ocean City in the wintertime when everything was closed looking for a place to convert into a small carry-out. We were referred to a Mrs. Swindler, who had an old small hardware store, not much larger then one of our plant's shacks over at Hoopers Island.

With some money from the packing house operation we rented the place on what is now 21st Street and Philadelphia Avenue. In those days it was considered way 'up the beach'. Later on we bought it. My mother lent us $2000 to equip the place so we could open it in the summer of 1956. We had noticed, but really hadn't paid much attention to the larger building next door. As we began to put our place in shape to open, the business next door opened. We had opened right next door to Ocean City's only crab house. "Buck Griffin's."

It was generally thought among the Ocean City old-timers, that they were crazy. They were laughed at. They had built their restaurant way 'up north'. "Wasn't anything up there but Buck Griffin's, and the dang fools from over on the bay have gone and opened a crab business right next to the only crab house already here." But, as Shirley says, "A problem is an opportunity disguised in work-clothes."

The first year was the perfect example of a shoe string operation. Things were borrowed from all over. Brice had stored an old used meat case in the packing plant on Hoopers Island. It was liberated and was used to ice down cold carry out items for display. Brice found and old counter, took it to the east. For the most important item, a boiler, Brice and Shirley discovered an old discarded one on the packing plant property. Now they were in business. All of the old equipment ended up in the Ocean City carry- out business.

They remember the early days,

> My [Shirley's] cousin, Tom Flowers and his wife, Francis, were our first choice to help us get started. As Tom was a supervisor in the school system, most of his summer time was free and he'd be able to help us. They would handle most of the weekdays and we'd do the weekends. Fran and I would look to the customers, thinking up recipes and things, Tom and Brice would do the steaming. . . . . [After the first year] because people wanted cooked food, crab cakes and crab imperial, we began to experiment with recipes, brought an old cooking stove over from Hoopers Island, and began selling cooked food. Our shop grew, unexpectedly, into a restaurant. Actually, it didn't remotely deserve the name "restaurant;" crab-shack comes closer to describing it.
>
> Tom and Fran Flowers loved to cook. He experimented with our now famous crab soup until he perfected it. We haven't changed it from those first two years. It is still the same.
>
> We were open from Memorial Day to Labor Day. After Labor Day Ocean City emptied. You could shoot a cannon down Philadelphia Avenue and not hit anyone. The moment the season was over, we closed and went home to Hoopers Island and the boys started school. During the winter Brice shucked and packed oysters.
>
> In 1958 the Crab House was still unpretentious, decorated with fish nets and a few oyster and clam shells. We couldn't have been more limited for funds. Still, it was a great time. All of us having been born in a small community, we were thrilled to be in Ocean City. It had a summertime population of around 50,000 people in those days.

And initially, that is all that was planned - a carry-out to dispose of large crabs, one that would be only minimally demanding on everybody's time. It was to be a small business that would give the family time to go on the beach, to spend the summers having fun, summers as they had discussed in their letters while Brice was away during the war. They anticipated that it would be a small business, just to complement the packing house on Hoopers Island. It didn't work out that way.

Right away, before they were able to steam the first crab, there was a serious problem. The most essential item in a steamed crab business is the boiler. The one they had was an old coal fired boiler but Brice had it converted for use with an oil fired burner. He'd bought an old oil burner for $40.00. The conversion required that new fire bricks be laid in the boiler. Brice hadn't thought of that. Brice couldn't fit through the hatch in the boiler. None of the men could fit. They needed someone small, skinny-hipped, with a small waistline. Soon Shirley was lifted up and inserted head first through the hatch into the sooty, dirty old boiler. When she had finished laying the bricks, they pulled her back out. She'd been clean when she went in.

That first year they opened the business solely as a carry-out - selling only steamed crabs and Phillips' packaged crabmeat. The boys would sit out on the curb, folding the cardboard boxes that were used in the carry out operation, and yell in whenever a customer appeared - "Customer coming, customer coming." Shirley remembers, "In those days crabs were consistently larger and were $4 a bushel as compared with today's prices of over $70 a bushel sometimes - or more even for the premium crabs. In those days all of our crabs would be what are considered premium crabs today."

By the end of the first year, ( a year in which the profit from the carry out was $1,000) they realized they didn't know how the Ocean City tourist industry operated. The carry out had not done as well as they had thought it would because of the nature of the vacation business. In the 50's it was primarily based upon hotel rooms. The rooms generally were not furnished with stoves to cook raw seafood (including steaming crabs) and were not furnished with refrigerators in which to keep food until it was cooked, or if cooked, until it was eaten. The hotel rooms did not have plates, silverware, or cleaning facilities. Today, of course, with the extraordinary growth since the 50s of the condominium and apartment industry, that is not so. Today, the Phillips' carry out business flourishes to such an extent that it requires separate kitchens and separate staffing (a set-up first championed by Jeffrey.)

To address the problem learned that first summer, they realized that they needed some dining-in capacity. The second year they purchased picnic tables for dining on the premises. When they decided that they were going to operate a sit down restaurant, albeit still a rudimentary one, they realized that they would need servers and additional help. Brice remembers,

> We initially brought four girls over from Hoopers Island. They were our first 'Phillips Girls'. They were Judy Flowers, Joyce Flowers, Judy Taylor, and Charlotte Parker, now Charlotte Sours. The two Flowers girls were Shirley's cousins. And Charlotte was Bernice's daughter, Shirley's niece. Judy Taylor was probably related in some way as well. We also brought another couple over from the island to help us. We were all a Hoopers Island family.
>
> We had built a small room in the back of the building. We divided it down the middle with plywood and put two bunk beds, each with an upper and a lower on one side, and the same on the other side. The girls stayed on one side, we stayed on the other. There was one bathroom used by all of us.

It was the second year of operation, the first year when they had table service, that they decided to offer a crab cake on the menu. Both of their mothers were renowned cooks and Shirley had learned from both of them. She took what she had learned from the mothers, all she had learned from the other great cooks of the island, and began to experiment back in the kitchen to develop a distinctive Phillips' crab cake. The recipe was created, and it is the same recipe that is still used in all the Phillips' restaurants. Now, tens of thousands are sold through various outlets every day. At the end of the second year they had made $5,000, but more importantly they had found the formula for success.

They asked for an appointment with Reese Cropper, Sr., the decision maker at the Calvin B. Taylor Bank in Berlin. They asked to borrow twenty thousand dollars to build another dining room. He suggested that they borrow forty thousand dollars and build two. For seven of the next eight years they went to him to borrow money from the bank to add new dining rooms. They had bought out Buck in the third or fourth year and were rapidly expanding into that space. At the end of the eight years they had a restaurant that seated 1400 people. At that time it was the largest restaurant in the State. They built it on hard work, vision, guts, and by developing great employees through loyalty to those employees - but most of all they built it from the delectable crab.

# CHAPTER TWENTY-SIX

*The Crab House*

The 21[st] Street Crab House for all of the Phillips, but especially for Brice and Shirley, is the primary memory maker. It is their third child. They virtually raised the boys in its shadow. As Steve and Jeffrey grew to be young men, the restaurant was growing apace. Many of the most important events of all their lives relate to it. If something important happened, someone at the Crab House had to be notified. If the location of someone that was needed, wasn't known, the first place called was the Crab House. It is the foundation stone. It is a place of memories for almost anyone who has come into contact with it over the years, especially from 1960 on. There are literally thousands of 'Phillips Girls' and 'Phillips Boys' who came of age under its roof and under the eyes of its mistress, haunted by the ever present 'Semore' Dofflemyer. Thousands of young men can recall Shirley hovering over her girls, protecting them, chasing away the neer-do-well young men that were attracted to the dorms like bees to flowers.

It was after the third year of operation, a year when another dining room was added, that both Captain Ellie and Captain Ivy died. That spring both of their widows, Miss Lillie and Miss Leone, became involved in the operation of the restaurant. The legendary Miss Lillie, (nicknamed Lillie Bird by the kids that worked at the Crab House) the great Hoopers Island musician, would continue working with the Phillips' enterprises until she was in her nineties, entertaining guests at the piano bar at the Phillips by the Sea Beach Plaza Hotel, the first Phillips' hotel.

The first year that she and Miss Leone, Brice's mother, came to Ocean City, they brought with them many of the great recipes of the islands to the west. The crab cakes were formed by using one hand to round them into the exact shape. Miss Lillie's left palm was the perfect size for the crab cake they wanted to serve. The Phillips' crab cake is still the same size.

In the fourth year, the business began to boom. Brice and Shirley had found the formula, hard work, loyal employees, taking risks and giving customers what they want. Always giving the customer what he or she wanted. There was only one exception and in time that, too, would be addressed. They did not sell any alcoholic beverages, including beer, in the early days. Customers were welcome to bring their own beer (but not liquor) to eat with their steamed crabs but the Phillips declined to sell it. Eventually, however, that would change as Brice and Shirley realized that it was what the customer wanted.

The Crab House began to take on the Phillips' 'look', a warm and colorful look that would almost embrace the customer with warmth, an atmosphere that complimented the great service and great seafood. Brice could look several expansions ahead to see what the layout of the Crab House would ultimately be, and how the outside would look. Today Steve has the same ability to visualize what the business will be like years into the future

Shirley, on the other hand, has a flair for decorating. A Vice-President of Phillips Restaurants, Paul Wall, who has been with the organization since 1967, says - "Shirley can look at a vacant room, and in just minutes she knows just how it should be decorated to give it that Phillips' look ."

Joyce Flowers remembers that

> In the off-season Shirley would come home to Hoopers Island and we'd go hunting for driftwood. Shirley could look at a piece of driftwood and see in it things I couldn't see. She could see how it could be used to decorate. She could just see special things in the wood. We'd go up to Punch Island [the island where the Indian Chief and his group went after

> leaving Barren Island], you can't go there anymore. We'd go all around the shore. A lot of the drift wood pieces in the restaurants were picked up by Shirley on the shore of Punch or Hoopers Islands.

They were a perfect couple, Brice was handy with tools; he'd had to be. On Hoopers Island in those days, when something broke at the plant or at home, you fixed it yourself. It didn't change when they started the Ocean City operation. They were short of money so they did almost everything themselves. Shirley explains:

> Brice gets all of the credit for building the Crab House in those early days. He knew building skills because on Hoopers Island we didn't have plumbers and electricians. The nearest plumbers and electricians were in Cambridge twenty-five or thirty miles away. If you needed anything repaired you learned to do it yourself. When we came to Ocean City we were well acquainted with the do-it-yourself process. I sanded and painted, while Brice hammered and sawed.

As the business expanded with the additional dining rooms, they wanted to create a certain ambiance. Shirley wanted a warm cozy feeling, imbued with subdued and muted color, but, there was little money for decorating and none for professional assistance. She needed to decorate 'on the cheap'.

Shirley was (and is) an inveterate habitue' of second hand stores, old stuff retailers, and what passed for yard or garage sales in those days. She had seen several colorful Tiffany lamp shades. She could visualize that a lamp within such a shade would strike just the right tone as she sought to create the environment she wanted. When she looked in the classified sections of the Baltimore newspapers, she saw that Tiffany or Tiffany style lamp shades were included in many estate furniture sales. To her surprise they had apparently gone out of style and weren't bringing very high prices. They were within her self-imposed decorating budget.

She began to frequent the sales in the off season, went to antique shops, second hand stores, even junk stores looking for the shades. She limited herself to $3.00 per shade and most were bought for a dollar. She bought hundreds of them. She turned down hundreds and hundreds of Tiffany shades because the sellers wanted more than $3 for them. Now unsigned Tiffany shades bring as much as $1,500, and signed ones as much as $50,000 or even more. She notes that if she had bought all she had turned down because they were over her $3 limit, they'd probably be worth more by now than the Crab House.

With the continually expanding restaurant there was a constant need for more tables, but they couldn't yet afford to buy commercial restaurant tables. Shirley saw several old Singer pedal action sewing machine tables for sale, without the attached sewing machines. She realized that with the advent of electric sewing machines the old pedal machines had become obsolete. What intrigued her was that they had a flat metal top, not large enough in and of themselves to be table tops, but large enough on which to affix a larger table top, and she had a handy-man husband. Because the pedal machines were obsolete, but not yet antiques, they were inexpensive and she began to buy everyone she could find. Initially, Brice would take plywood sheets, cut out the right table top size, cover the plywood with oil cloth and affix the tops to the pedal machines, and they had their tables. Then Shirley would sit down at her electric sewing machine and make the table cloths they also couldn't afford to buy. The result was signature furnishing.

In time, a local surfer and surfboard maker, the late Jon Phillips (no known relation to Brice and Shirley) developed a process whereby he could apply surfboard making techniques to the making of furniture. When Brice and Shirley saw what he was doing they made arrangements for him to make their table tops. They were made by covering a harder core, usually wood, with a fiberglass and epoxy mixture, sanding and reapplying the mixture until the right look was achieved. They added more of a nautical look to the dining rooms and they replaced the old oil cloth covered table tops as fast as Jon Phillips could make them. Eventually, the process was copied by other makers.

# CHAPTER TWENTY-SEVEN

*'Oysterin', seaside style*

There came a time when Brice couldn't stand not having a 'fishing' venture closer to Ocean City than Hoopers Island. He decided to get involved in 'oysterin' in the back bays. He explains it,

> There was little leasing of oyster bottoms over in the Maryland portion of the Chesapeake Bay. It was frowned upon. Sometime after we started the Ocean City business, I realized that it was thought of differently on the sea-side, as opposed to the bay. I decided to investigate the feasability of a bottom leasing operation in the back bays. The water was saltier there. The oysters would be tasty.
>
> We leased some bay bottom in the back bay behind Ocean City and Assateague. We planted around ten thousand bushels of seed oysters just south of where the Route 90 bridge is. We didn't have much luck with them.
>
> However, I was also partnered with a couple of men down south near Girdletree. Brimer and Jones. Howard Brimer and Chester Jones. They were two honorable people. We worked together. I furnished the seed oysters to plant on the leased bottoms and they took care of them, and brought them in. They were shipped in barrels to Baltimore.

> We worked together and split the profit. It worked fine. We all made money, too. There was also a Mr Duke down there that did some oystering around Greenbackville, Virginia with a Mr. Nelson Collins. They were all good people. In those days we had about 30 oyster shuckers at the plant in Hoopers Island. The oysters would be shucked at the plant, then I'd bring the oyster shells over to the back bays in Worcester County. The oyster shells from the Honga River always had lots of spat, small oysters about the size of your thumb nail attached to them. We'd save all of these, take them over to the sea-side and plant them out.

It must of been a thriving business for a while. Brice was driving back and forth between Hoopers Island and Worcester County so much that it almost wore him out. Jane, recalls, "Brice got so tired when he was running the Hoopers Island plant, the Ocean City restaurant and also 'salting' oysters down at George's Island Landing [in Worcester County], that he would stop at our house in Cambridge en route between the two places, just to sleep. Then get up and go again."

Ultimately, the demands of the restaurant would take precedence over planting oyster spat, and Brice would leave the seaside aquiculture business.

# CHAPTER TWENTY-EIGHT

*The irrepressible William 'Semore' Dofflemyer*

Up until the second or third expansion, all of the back of the house (kitchen and bookkeeping) was family. Brice took care of it (except for creating recipes,) doing much of it himself. In the third year he was still operating the steamer. Shirley took care of the front of the house, (wait staff, bus boys and cashiers.) It was decided, by approximately the third expansion, that the business had grown so large that it needed a professional chef and kitchen staff. A chef was hired, a grand opening planned.

In the meantime, out west [To an Eastern Shoreman, anything west of the Chesapeake Bay is 'out west'.] a young man was getting ready to come east. He explains it best.

> I lived in Hagerstown. While I was going to school, and in the summers, I had been working for my uncle who owned a restaurant, so I had a little experience. I had sent an application to the Phillips for a job, along with my picture. I had already packed, when I received a call from Shirley Phillips. I had never met her, but we had talked. She told me in the call that "I know I told you that I thought there would be a job, but I can't put you on right now." I told her, "Mrs. Phillips, I'm coming with or without a job."

I took a bus to Ocean City, made my housing arrangements with Mrs. Mabel Pierce at Pierce Hall (renting a bed on a plywood section over the rafters in the attic, with shower facilities out back - but the rent was right and Mrs. Pierce was great.) When I got settled, I decided to go up on the boardwalk to scout out opportunities for jobs. Soon I was at what was then the north end of the boardwalk. A couple of blocks north of me, a little bit over to the west, I could see this little red building. It was the Phillips' Crab Shack. Out of curiosity, I walked the two blocks, opened the door and walked in.

Mrs Phillips was in front, looked up, noticed me, and recognized me from the picture I had sent with my application. Suddenly, she said, "Oh my! Do I need you." She handed me an apron, and took me back in the kitchen. Well forty-seven years later, here I am still in the kitchen. It's been a 47 year long 'endless summer.'

He was 17 years old that summer. Shirley remembers the day he showed up.

In 1959, we opened our new 125 seat restaurant. It was a totally traumatic day. Opening night was scheduled for the Friday right after Memorial day. We had hired a chef and several other people, non-family for the first time, to help us with the crowds we hoped would be filling our brand new dining room. The restaurant was due to open at 6 p.m., but as the time grew nearer, we began to realize that we had a big problem. The tables were set and the food was in the kitchen, ready for the magic touch. But the chef's magic touch was exactly the problem. He couldn't provide it because he didn't show up. And the other hired help didn't show up either. We looked at our watches, looked at each other, and in walked Semore. We all went back to the kitchen and went to work. Fortunately, we had our mothers and the Hoopers Island girls to help us in the front of the restaurant. The dining room filled immediately and there were lines of people waiting outside.

> We had been successful as a carry-out operation and the word had spread about our food.
>
> The opening night the menu was limited. We served Maryland crab soup [Tom Flowers' recipe,] entrees were seafood platter, soft-shell crabs, crab cakes, jumbo shrimp and fried flounder, along with a choice of four vegetables and a salad. Nothing was broiled. We didn't have a broiler. Everything was either baked or fried.
>
> By the next day Mr. Dofflemyer was a chef. He's been with us ever since and is now our executive chef in charge of five kitchens.

And that's how Semore started. He says "it's been a way of life, more than a job. It's not really a job, but a way of life when you work for the Phillips." He went through all of the expansions over the years, eventually moving in with the family, and built and painted, cleaned the antiques Shirley was always buying in the off-season, running kitchens in season. He remembers,

> "Every year we added something. Brice just couldn't stay still, had to add something, build something, do something. . . . Started with furnishings no one else wanted, and we'd fix them up and that's how we kept going. Just kept building and building. We just never stopped. Used to do everything ourselves, but after a while it grew so big we had to get outside help.
>
> . . .
>
> Shirley kept her finger on everything. She and Brice were in the kitchen day and night. Nobody can ever say they didn't work. And they still work. Even now, when it gets busy, you can still catch her in a dining room busing a table or seating a guest.
>
> . . .
>
> Brice and Shirley still come to the restaurant every day and work, do anything that's needed. Even now, when they're in their eighties, they still work up in the office lots of nights. I'll be heading 'up the beach' around ten or eleven in the evening,

I'll glance up at their offices and the lights will be on. They're still up there working and they've been there all day.

They're not the type of people that will ever retire and sit on a porch.

Semore quickly became one of the family. Before long he became a combination confidant/ baby sitter/and later friend, with the two boys, Steve and Jeffrey. In his first week the boys were still living on Hoopers Island during the middle of the week. They were scheduled to come over on the weekend. He remembers, "They came over with their grandmother. I looked out of a window and here came this car wheeling around the corner with the boys leaning way out of the windows, yelling at the top of their voices, 'Here we are! The Gila Monsters are here. The Gila Monsters are here." I remember saying, "Oh my god, who are those kids?" Shirley answered. "They're mine." He describes his relationship with them, and how they grew and matured.

We have had a good relationship over all these years. Part of it was that I wasn't that much older than them, I was only 17 or 18. After the second year, I was living with the Phillips and did do some baby sitting. When they'd take a vacation, sometimes I'd be taken along. All of it was just a lot of fun, the work, the kids, Brice and Shirley. It was never like work. We did things together, it was like a family.

They had a dog they brought over with them, a black cocker spaniel. Everywhere those boys went, the dog followed. When a boy would run through a dining room, right behind him was a dog. I don't suppose you can let that happen now. But, that's the way it was. Informal. Still is for the most part.

Later as the boys were ten or eleven years old, or even younger and started in the business, there was rivalry and competition, and like all boys, they had their teenage years and what goes along with it. But they were good boys, smart boys.

In school it was like if Steve was the best pole vaulter in his class, Jeffrey'd have to be the best in his, if Steve made a great sandwich, Jeffrey would try to make a better one. They really competed growing up, but, at the same time, they were completely different personalities.

Back in the old days before piped in music, when we had our first upstairs dining room, there was a big coin operated juke box up there. Each evening after the restaurant closed, it was our job, the boys and me, to sit up there and fold up the boxes for the next day's carry-out business. The boys would turn the volume all the way up on the juke box while we were folding boxes. Then they would leave it up.

The next day when the first customer went up to play the juke box, it would blare out at top volume, and here would come Shirley, running at break-neck speed to the juke box. Before long it was automatic for her, anytime she first entered the room to go to the juke box to check the volume setting.

He remembers the very early days when the yellow Buick convertible was Brice's fancy car, before the limos. "It had a problem. The top wouldn't go up." But every evening nearing closing time, Brice would come get him so they could check parking lots. If it started raining they'd get wet, sometimes there would be an inch of water on the floorboards. They'd ride by all the other restaurants, and see how many cars were parked in their lots, as compared to the lot at the Crab House. That was the way they checked on their competition. Brice would always end up saying, 'Hey, we're not doing too bad.'"

As they continued to grow, Brice would do all the carry-out and the business end, the books, payroll, taxes and the like. "Shirley stayed in the kitchen with us. It was her recipes. We're still preparing things today from Shirley's old recipes, or her mother's or mother-in-law's. They were all great cooks."

Brice and Shirley were there every step. They never left us there alone. They helped us to do everything and they worked just like everybody else, just as hard or even harder. For them the job was never over.

. . .

Shirley tells it like it is. She knows what she wants and when it comes to the restaurant she'll tell you, "This is the way

> I want it done." We do it that way. She knows what works, what doesn't, because she has been there from the bottom up. When she says, "This is not right," we change it.
>
> . . .
>
> Every now and then we might not agree on something, but it was always minor stuff. She likes to pick on my fried chicken. I'd get in a scrap with her over it in the early days. She'd say "It's too fried." or "It's not fried enough." She's still keeping me straight on my fried chicken. Even now, after 47 years, she comes in every evening, walks back in the kitchen and, making sure I see her, goes and gets a chicken leg and leaves with it - just to check on me.

Restaurant people from other areas often ask to tour the Crab House, to see how it works. They are asked to come on a busy night to the back of the house. Almost without exception, they have difficulty in understanding how it works, and some of them are famous in the field. They stand in the kitchen area for a while, then say to Semore, "We've been in the restaurant business for twenty, thirty years, and we've never seen anything like this. How in the hell does this place work." Semore explains it, "It's chaos, but its organized chaos. We knew in the beginning that it was chaotic, but that if we could organize the chaos, it would be a winner. Underneath the surface of what looks like chaos to you, is order to me." Interestingly, another of the early employees made an independent statement of how it all worked when he was a cook, "Out of chaos comes order is how it all worked."

One of the reasons it probably works so well, is the 'family', the 'team' personality of the operation. Semore notes, correctly, [the writer spent a 9 year stint working in restaurants] that;

> In most restaurants they're always bickering, the cooks are fighting with the waitresses, but here it's not like that. Here there's a harmony that somehow works. The back of the room helps the front, and vice-versa. The cooks help the dishwashers, they help the cooks. In the beginning that was the way it started because it had to start that way. Everybody was on the bottom, there wasn't any up. In the beginning everybody did

everything because they had to, everybody helped everybody because they wanted to, and we've just kept doing it that way. It's still the way we do it. If the prep people are asked to help with dishes, they just do it. It's a team effort. It's a family business, still. We're all part of the Phillips family.

We have people working in food prep that have worked for us for over twenty years, people in the crab room that have been there for fifteen or twenty years, a lot of other long-time employees. And it wasn't and isn't the money. It's a loyalty to Brice and Shirley, a loyalty to each other, it's wanting to see each other from season to season. And Steve is creating the same ethic across the bay [Mr. Bill Sexton, the head chef in charge of Phillips Foods research and development kitchen in Baltimore began his career in the food business as a cook at the Crab House when he was 17 years old. Mr. Dean Flowers, the Comptroller of Phillips Foods is the son of Tom Flowers who was one of the first managers of the old Carry Out in 1956-57, and created the Phillips' Maryland crab soup recipe still in use today.]

When one of us dies, we're devastated. We had a man that had been a cook in the service, we called him Virgil Joins, who came in one day looking for a job. Said he'd do anything and he always did, although he was a great cook and mostly did that. He died while he was still working for us - 30 years later. Another cook, Jack O'Hara from Pennsylvania came for a summer, stayed until the summer he died, years later. He'd been like a father to a lot of the kids. It really hit us, the deaths, especially hurts Brice and Shirley and the kids. You don't see that kind of caring in most restaurants.

If an employee is injured on or off the job, or gets ill, they're right there. Just yesterday an employee got injured, thankfully, as it turns out, not too seriously, but initially it was thought it might be serious. When Brice and Shirley found out, they got their daughter-in-law, Janet, to be their driver and started following his movement up the shore, eventually winding up at the burn unit at Johns Hopkins. They left here at eleven in the morning and they stayed at the hospital with him until after ten in the evening, when they found out that his injuries were not life threatening and that he would be released in a day or two. They didn't get home until after one the next morning. They're both in their eighties. And that's not the only time.

Four months ago I had a health situation that put me in the hospital for a couple of days. I looked up, there were Shirley and Brice. They were with the two Pauls [Paul Wall and Paul McKinley] when they needed it, with Jay [Jay Newcomb, manager of the Hoopers Island plant]. It's just what they are, and what we are. Family. We're treated like family as long as we act like family. It's our choice.

As the businesses began to take off, when there was finally a little money to do extra things, they started going as a group to restaurant and hotel conventions in order to get ideas. Often they would go to New York, and the Phillips family and Semore, and often Brice and Shirley's mothers, who were still working in the businesses, would go along. When they went to a restaurant or club with live music, Miss Lillie, Shirley's mother, would always go up on the bandstand and sing with the band. She was in her 80s.

When we would come back from these conventions, we'd all sit down and discuss what we had seen in the displays, the new items, the different methods of doing things. After a while, Brice or Shirley would say, "Hey, compared to what everybody else is doing, we're not doing bad, we're already doing as good, usually better than the other restaurant operations are doing."

. . .

Another reason for the success is devotion to customers. In hurricanes, after everybody else closed, Brice and Shirley would stay open, knowing it wouldn't be a profitable day, but they'd say, "Some of our customers are out there, there are city workers, police and emergency people. If we close there won't be anywhere to eat. We'll stay open." And they would, and lose money doing it, but they felt their customers had been loyal to them, and they owed loyalty in return.

One winter when I was living with them in the living quarters on the second floor there came a loud banging on the door downstairs. We'd been closed for months. Shirley and Brice went down and found a group of Phillips' customers that had come from somewhere in the middle of the night. They told her that they had come all the way to the Crab House only to find it closed. They asked her what she would suggest they do. What she did, was she invited them into what at the time of the year was her home, went to the family refrigerator where she'd saved some pasturized crab meat, used the family cook stove, and cooked and served a crab cake dinner to all of them. And didn't charge for it. I guarantee you, that somewhere those people are still eating Phillips' crab cakes.

Paul Wall remembers how William Dofflemyer got his nickname.

Semore Dofflemyer is probably a legend. He got the nickname as he was handed more and more responsibility from the early years on to supervise, or oversee the various operations. Shirley and Brice discovered that he had the uncanny ability to see things, and in a short period of time it became one of his functions to check on everything. He was immensely loyal and he would see immediately anything that was amiss. Over a period of time, when Semore would venture out of the kitchens, the 'Phillips Girls' would begin to pass the word, 'Semore's out,' or 'Watch out, here comes Semore.' [ Another version of his acquiring a nickname comes from Joyce Flowers. According to her, in the early years there was a Cuban cook that had trouble with the name Dofflemyer, so he would say, Mr. Senior, but with a heavy Cuban accent. The waitresses had a hard time understanding the Cuban cook, and thought he was saying Semore. So they started calling him by that name. In either event, the nickname stuck.]

Semore was really the first non-related employee of Brice and Shirley in Ocean City. He was a cook that became a buyer.

> For a while he did all the buying, hired most of the kitchen staff. Over the years he has performed many of the functions in the Crab House - knows all the operation. Currently he is in charge of the food preparation room at the Crab House. When the Baltimore operation was started, he went to Harbor Place, helped set up the restaurant. He is one of the operations' best trouble shooters, because he still sees everything. When he first started he even baby-sat the boys, when necessary. Semore is an integral part of the Crab House. Brice and Shirley have always treated Semore, and me as well, as members of their family, and we have always been grateful.

William 'Semore' Dofflemyer remembers an especially meaningful event, that perhaps distills what being a part of the Phillips' Family means.

> The 45th Anniversary celebration of the business was held here at the Crab House a couple of years ago. At first, I wasn't going. I'm getting older now and don't go to as many things. But, I went. And I'm glad I did. People kept coming up to me telling me how grateful they were and how much they had learned with me, working at Phillips. To me, it almost seemed like it was my night, because after all the years and all the kids, a lot of them were coming back to see me.
>
> I hadn't realized that I had been that important to the kids that worked here. They had gone on, grew up, got jobs as doctors, lawyers, judges, and they were saying to me, 'Semore, I just want to thank you for helping me, because things you taught me, I'm still doing.' There was a famous guy in our business, from Chicago, who owns a big, top of the line, restaurant out there, who had started in the restaurant business as one of our kids here at the Crab House. He came over to me, put his arm around me and said, 'Semore, I would like to thank you for the things you did for me when I was working here.' I asked, 'What'd I do?' He answered, 'First of all you kicked my butt out of bed many a day to get me here to work. You know I still have some of the same bad habits. I

don't schedule any appointments until after eleven a.m. I still can't get out of bed.'

Everybody wanted to see me. They were all telling me that I didn't know how many people I had affected over the years.

A lot of the people at the reunion had gone on to open their own restaurants. Were now in the business on their own. A lot of them, of the couples at the reunion, had met here, then had married each other and had started families together.

Dr. Geoffrey Robbins, a former cook at the Crab House remembers the reunion:

I saw kids I hadn't seen in 30 years. Everybody still looked kind of young. People came from all over the east coast, even one former employee from California. It was interesting finding out how many of the kids had made their goals, or had made changed goals. Most of them had made them. Made their goals.

Semore agrees,

We have kids working for Phillips now, who were referred to us by their parents who themselves worked for us years ago, and the kids tell us that their parents tell them, to go work for Phillips for the experience of it. It's become a tradition.

Semore best sums up his thoughts by noting,

I've held virtually every job in the Crab House at one time or another. Now, I'm like Walt Disney. I don't know what I do, but I do a little bit of everything. When I was younger I did all the ordering and buying, did most of the back of the house hiring. I'd fire a few, but not too many. As I got older, I mellowed a little. Besides, you can be pretty understanding of a cook getting to work late, when you realize if you fire him you're going to have to do his job as well as your own. Usually, I 'd stop and think, 'Now, Semore, if you fire him, you're going to have to do it,' and by that time I preferred not to wash dishes.

In the early days, especially, it was a real family working together, still is to a large degree. And everybody can become a part of the family. But hard work, loyalty, caring and consistency is what built it. We worked, but the work was fun.

It didn't seem like such a difficult job because we grew up with it. If we had to start out cold today, we probably couldn't do it. But, as the job grew, we were growing with it, growing at the same time and it never seemed particularly hard. We'd add a little job here, another one next year, piece by piece. Now that I look back on it, I don't know how we did it. We worked so hard and so long - but it was great fun.

I never heard either Shirley or Brice complain about the rough times, even in the rough times they always knew they were going to make it, and make it big. They are the two most optimistic people I've ever known.

The Crab House is my home. It's not the money, although my time with the Phillips has made me wealthy through the profit-sharing plan. It's just been a remarkable life for me.

# CHAPTER TWENTY- NINE

*Home at the Crab House*

By the time of the fourth expansion, the original one room out back, divided by a plywood sheet, with one bathroom, shared by the family, the managers from Hoopers Island, and the Phillips Girls was outgrown. Brice and Shirley realized that their dreams of an idyll at the beach in Ocean City, weekends with the boys fishing and crabbing in the back bays, was being ruined by success. The Crab House had taken over, displacing old dreams with new dreams.

As the business grew, and its staffing grew, and the boys grew, it became apparent that more and more of everyone's time would be spent in the crab house and that they'd have to move to Ocean City in order to manage their growing business. There would also have to be a change in the living arrangements.

They rented an apartment from Betty Frame behind Newt and Amanda Cropper's 8th Street Shopping Center, near Jack Sanford's house, while they modified the Crab House. For two years after they moved to the Crab House apartment, they still kept the 8th Street house for Miss Leone and Miss Lillie. They built living arrangements for themselves, an apartment within the Crab House. The living room and kitchen were over-top the carry-out, Brice's and Shirley's bedroom, a dormitory for Steve and Jeffrey and a bathroom were constructed above the Tiffany Dining Room.

They built their living arrangements to be convertible. At the start of the season they would move all the living furniture out of the living room, and have the boys double up with them in their bedroom. They would move restaurant furniture into their living room and into the dormitory. The apartment kitchen became a warming kitchen for the two new upstairs dining rooms.

In the fall, when the season was over, they would move their furniture back. As Paul Wall puts it, "There were thousands of people that ate in Shirley's living room and never knew it. When I came over to be interviewed [in 1967] I couldn't believe it. They moved the furniture out and moved in restaurant tables, in the spring, and vice-versa in the fall."

As the restaurant business grew, the upstairs living arrangements continued until they were able to build their house on Mallard Island. The apartment would be moved around as the various expansions occurred and be extensively enlarged. The larger the wintertime living quarters, the more people could be seated in the Crab House in the season when the apartment was converted to 'front of the house'. Of course, after the season, the apartment was a great venue for parties, these parties would expand as well, as Brice and Shirley became full-fledged members of the Ocean City community. There was always plenty of room, plenty of seating space for social gatherings - in the winter.

During the expansion periods, Steve and Jeffrey matured. They were no longer little boys, sitting out front folding carry-out boxes, and running in and yelling "Customer coming, customer coming!" Privileged to graduate from such lowly duties, they first became workers in the crab room (the toughest job in the Crab House where the rite of passage, an initiation, so to speak, required the beginning employee to bite the face off of a live hard crab.) Then they were promoted to garbage handlers and then dishwashers. Wherever the bottoms were, that's where they would start, each in his time. Brice and Shirley had done the same; it was expected.

No idyllic days at the beach, no crabbing and fishing in the back bays for the boys. They were Hoopers Islanders. That meant they went to work. It's what Hoopers Islanders do, even when they are young, go to work with your parents. They lived in their work, literally. As with their parents, the Crab House became part of them. They never left it, it never left them. It still has not.

It wasn't absent rewards, though. By the time they went to college they would have literally worked at every job in the restaurant, including working in the crab room and being bus boys. And bus boys worked with the 'Phillips Girls,' the pettiest, smartest, most vivacious group of young ladies anywhere, hundreds of them. A boy's dream, a young man's heaven on earth.

When Jeffrey was asked about growing up with 'Phillips Girls', he responded,

> Oh Shoot. Why do you have to talk about that [his mother was present, his wife was not]. The 'Phillips Girls" were a great, a good, a wonderful blessing. The Crab House identifies with them. It was a wonderful thing and one of the best starts of my life. My life began with the wonderful things that can happen with so many beautiful, beautiful girls on the staff. [Of course] there were bad times, too. There can always be bad times and good times. The bad times from those days are forgotten, but the bad times are what make the good times look good.

In order to better prepare them for college, when each entered the tenth grade, he was enrolled at McDonogh, a boarding school in Baltimore. But in the summers each would return to live and work in the Crab House, working seven days a week. Shirley remembers: "Thankfully, our sons were enthusiastic about the restaurant and the hotel we bought in 1967. They worked side by side with us over the years. We were a team in which they each played increasingly important roles as the years went by."

# CHAPTER THIRTY

*Menus and recipes*

Brice, perhaps because of his gastronomic experience on the front during World War II, ("Most of the food we have [at the front] is canned and not very well seasoned.",) was determined from the onset of their retail venture into the restaurant business, that their steamed crabs would not suffer from blandness. In the spring before their Memorial Day opening in their first year in Ocean City, he experimented. By opening day, he had it down pat. He had developed a unique blend of seasonings for steamed crabs that has endured the test of time. It is still used in the Phillips' restaurants.

It was quickly recognized locally as well. Their steamed crabs quickly became the favorites of Ocean City steamed crab gourmets. Many efforts were made by others over the years to come up with a formula that was comparable, most failed. The taste for Phillips' steamed crabs became so prevalent that some subsequent crab house competitors gave up and literally joined the Phillips' operation. Instead of steaming their own crabs, they would buy bushels of Phillips' steamed crabs, add on a profit factor, and then sell them as their own crabs. This information was not furnished to me by anyone in the Phillips' organizations. I come by it firsthand. In the era 1959 to 1965, I worked in various eating establishments during the summer, usually two or more at a time. During one period I worked at a boardwalk crab house, advertising and selling "[name deleted to protect the guilty] Crabs".

In the evening a phone call would be made to the Phillips and I would be sent to the rear door of the Crab House. There I would wait with others on similar missions. Shortly, a door would open, a body would emerge and announce the name of a particular crab house. The person representing that particular crab house would speak up and its steamed crabs would be put in a truck, then another name would be called. In the entire summer I worked at the boardwalk crab house, not a single crab was steamed there. They all came from Phillips. At that time, most of the steamed crabs eaten in any of the crab houses, or any of the items made with crab meat, probably originated in the Phillips' operation.

Other than the seasoning for the steamed crabs and the Maryland crab soup recipe, Shirley was primarily responsible for formulating the recipes for all the other items. She readily acknowledges that she had the advice of some of the best seafood cooks in the business, her mother, Miss Lillie, Brice's mother, Miss Leone, and Francis, cousin Tom Flower's wife. They all brought with them to the operation the great Hoopers Island tradition of delicious seafood. They ate so much of it growing up, the recipes had to be good. They would try this, try that, taste this, taste that, and then Shirley would decide on the final recipe. Shirley's crab cake recipe that resulted from the experimental process is still the recipe for crab cakes used by all of the Phillips' entities.

New seafood items were only added to the menu after an exhaustive experimental period in which the members of the family and, in time other employees, acted as tasters. When the particular process produced an item that she could not improve any further, it would be put on the menu. Other than the steamed crabs, crab soup, and the crab cakes, almost all of the other menu items resulted from requests from regular customers that a particular item be added. Shirley explains,

> As time went on the menu grew as customers made suggestions. In fact, one of the unusual aspects about our restaurants, is that just about everything on the menu came about because somewhere, sometime, a customer asked for it, and we didn't have it. I remember one of the first additions which came from a customer's request was crab au gratin.

When the request came from a customer I had a problem. Not only didn't we have it on the menu, I didn't even know what it was. I went out into the dining room, went to the customer, asked him how it was made. I experimented for a week. Thanks to that customer, the next time he came in crab au gratin was on the menu. The first time the restaurant served sauteed crab lumps with Smithfield ham, it was because a customer had asked for it. Again, within a week we were boiling our own Smithfield ham, slicing and shredding it, and adding it to the crab meat. These menu items, and many others, came about because of the first policy we put into place when we opened. Please the customer. If they wanted it, we'd prepare it, and on the menu it would go.

One day a woman asked for a bowl of cream of crab soup. It wasn't on the menu. I went out and talked to her finding out all she knew about the dish, then I went back in the kitchen experimented for a couple of weeks. From talking with her, I believed that the soup should include half and half cream, butter, seafood seasonings, and of course ample shell-free crab meat. I experimented for a week and Phillips Cream of Crab soup was born. We use the same version all over the world today - because one of our customers wanted it fifty years ago. Many of our other items were developed because of requests from customers. . . . If you enjoy your work and accept it as a challenge, the challenge becomes a game; a game of knowing you have done your very best in always remembering that the customer comes first. It is customers that lead you to success. We knew that early on, and because of it we have one of the finest menus of any sea food restaurant.

Eventually, mostly at the customer's suggestions, the menu grew with the addition of fin-fish, clams, oysters, lobster dishes and many other items, including soft-shell clams - manteos. The addition of soft-shell clams, commonly called 'piss clams' on the Eastern Shore, gave rise to one of the favorite stories of the early days. Tom Flowers remembered the day when a city woman came in and ordered a seafood platter because she wanted to taste all of the seafood items that were available. He related what happened.

> We served her a crab cake, crab imperial, all the usual items. Then we served her a bucket of steamed manteos. When the lid was lifted off, she looked at the manteos with their snouts sticking out [the water siphon of a manteo is elongated and sticks out from the shells,] and said 'I can't eat these things with their peters hanging out.' Another woman eating in the restaurant, yelled over, 'What's the matter lady, don't you know an old piss clam when you see one?' No matter whether you battered them, fried them, or steamed them, you always soaked them so that they would spit the sand and grit out. Some people chopped them and some ate them whole.

Paul Wall remembers that,

> Shirley came up with all these recipes to make the crab cakes, the crab imperial and all the menu items, with the help of the first two waitresses - Miss Lillie and Miss Leone. Brice did all the steaming in the early days and Shirley stayed back in the kitchen doing the other cooking, making up recipes and the like. Eventually, she did the recipes, menus, and ran the front of the house - where the customers were accommodated. Brice ran the back of the house, the kitchens and the book work. He had been the only employee in the kitchen when they began, and in 1967 he was the only employee in the office. Eventually, that would change. But first a living trademark was created.

# CHAPTER THIRTY - ONE

*The 'Phillips Girls' (and boys)*

There are times when it is not possible to determine why a thing, a concept, an image has been created. That is not the problem when one considers the creation of the 'Phillips Girls' concept. Even though it may have been completely unintended, the reasons are easily understood. Shirley was, and is, as Paul Wall says, a mother hen. All of the girls were her biddies (baby chickens,) for whom she had to set the example. They were her girls.

The first 'Phillips Girls' were four young ladies from Hoopers Island, most related to Brice and Shirley. In those days, Ocean City was considered to be 'faster' than Hoopers Island. One can surmise that their parents were depending on Brice and Shirley to make sure their daughters were safe. As we have indicated, in the first years the girls and the Phillips virtually lived together. Shirley was the mother in place, Brice the father.

It may have been this combination that inadvertently created the 'Phillips Girls'. Shirley started out mothering and kept right on mothering in all the years she was responsible for the 'front of the house' at the Crab House. Shirley remembers the earliest days, the first year with seated dining, the first year with the girls. Writing in a draft introduction to a proposed cook book, she says:

For years, Ocean City had been known to have one of the most beautiful beaches in the world. Families flocked to it yearly, making it a family-oriented vacation spot. Many young people of high school and college age spent their summers working in Ocean City. We followed this tradition and hired four high school girls from Hoopers Island. We dressed them in white Bermuda shorts, white blouses and red aprons that I designed to resemble crabs. The body of the crab was the part that was worn at the waist, the straps resembled the claws of crabs. We also decked them out in red tennis shoes and they tied their hair back in pretty red bandannas. Because they were Hoopers Island girls and understood how to pick crabs, they had plenty of fun teaching customers to remove the meat from our steamed crabs. The customers seemed to like the girls as much as the crabs.

Working at the crab shack for the girls from Hoopers Island was fun for them, for us, and for the customers. We all lived dormitory style in one room. The small room we lived in was probably 9 feet by 16 feet, with a wooden partition down the center. The girls slept in bunk beds on one side and on the other side were four bunk beds. Brice and I slept on the bottom bunk, while Steve and Jeff occupied the top. Our manager and his wife, slept on the other bottom bunk with their two children on the bunk above them. We all shared one toilet and one shower. That means that there were eight people on one side of the partition of this tiny room. The amazing thing is that we never had a cross word, even the girls got along well.

During an interview for this book, when discussing the 'Phillips Girls', she noted:

Loyalty to those that support us, to those that worked for us, and to family is what has always been one of the most important things to us.

It was the second year when we also built a small dormitory on the back of the restaurant for housing for four waitresses.

> That was the beginning of the 'Phillips Girls'. We've had thousands of 'Phillips Girls' over the years. Later, we bought a place across the street, the Skyliner, and turned it into a dormitory for a number of the girls. Right from the beginning there was a curfew as to the dormitory. One in the morning, I think it was. That was part of the reason we got so many good young women working in the restaurant. Their parents knew we'd control the things that went on in that dormitory, and that their daughters would not be allowed to wander all over town at night. In time, a job as a 'Phillips Girl' was much sought after. We'd get calls from all over the state. We always hired the best young ladies we could get. . . . They helped grow our business.
>
> . . . It was people like Miss Myrtle [Myrtle Phillips the depression era store keeper on Hoopers Island] and our parents that make us so grateful for our employees. Giving credit to the people that work for you always pays off because they grow your business.

The writer interviewed Joyce Flowers at her daughter's home near the bridge on Hoopers Island. From the rear of the house was an expanse of lawn leading down to the Honga River. From the front of the house I could see Tar Bay. Mrs. Flowers, still as peppy and peppery as I suppose she was fifty years ago, remembers,

> I went down at the end of the first year, and went down for all of the next summer. The second year was the first year they had table service. I was 17. We all got put together in a room in the back, eight or nine of us. We had a community bathroom and a shower. We had close quarters, but we got along well.
>
> We worked from opening until closing. Long hours and hard work, but we were used to it. That's how you worked on Hoopers Island. You worked until the work was done. When we went to Ocean City we didn't know that people didn't work twelve hours. Shirley and Brice didn't know either. They'd worked back on Hoopers Island just like the rest of us

- until the work was done. They worked so hard you wanted to work hard too. None of us thought there was any reason to change the work habits we were used to.

Shirley was real busy that first year. Well, she is always busy, even now.

She would even wait on tables in addition to everything else she was doing, but she'd always complain that "They never tip me right because they know I'm an owner." That's when she started instilling in us her feeling that the customer was always right. She emphasized all the time that we should be friendly with the customers. And we were. I think the friendliness of everybody made a big difference at Phillips when we were still competing with Griffins.

And we had a good time. Laughed a lot. Once Brice was in cleaning up, and when he came out, all of us burst out laughing. He couldn't figure out why we were laughing at him, until we told him that he'd shaved off half his mustache. Then he laughed with us. And it was neat to eat steamed crabs with Brice because he never fooled with the claws, so I got to eat his claws. When he and Shirley were eating, Shirley would take care of the official tip. But Brice would be slipping the waitress a little on the side where Shirley couldn't see him. But she probably knew it, anyway.

One time I was working in the carry-out when I noticed a customer eating shrimp he'd just bought. He was eating them shell and all. When he finished, I couldn't help myself, I went up to him and asked if he had enjoyed the shrimp. He answered, "They're very tasty, but they're a little tough." I figured that it must have been the first time he'd eaten shrimp.

And after she'd gotten a little experience in the restaurant business, Shirley started 'salting' the cooking sherry. She'd noticed that it was disappearing at too rapid a rate, so when they would get a case in, the first thing she'd do is 'salt' the cooking sherry so the drinkers wouldn't want it.

Over the years the Phillips became friendly with many of the families of the girls from other areas as well. Their relationships with these families was creating a wide-spread group of friends, friends that came to influence their subsequent expansions into other areas.

As the Crab House grew, so did the number of 'Phillips Girls' until, as Shirley notes, their alumni grew into the thousands. As the numbers grew, the Phillips family continued their personal interest in the well-being of the young ladies. Organized activities were created for their off duty hours, things designed to make them realize that the Crab House was their business and that they were part of a family. Paul Wall remembers some of the activities that went on after the Crab House had fully expanded.

> Shirley was like a mother hen with the girls in those days. She laid it on the line. When you work, you work. You don't come down here and not work.
>
> We had three employee meals a day during that period, the 60s and the 70s. Shirley wanted to make sure the girls were well fed. Breakfast, before the rush meal - around 3 in the afternoon, and a late meal. That way she knew that the staff had access to three meals. There was no charge for the meals. That was part of the experience of working at Phillips. Shirley usually worked in the front of the house, in the dining rooms with the girls. There she could watch over them, guide them, discipline them, and when needed, protect them.
>
> If the girls did not abide by the rules, or misbehaved, and Shirley found out about it, she would call the girl's parents and tell them whatever the problem was, and then ship the girl home. You probably couldn't do it today, somebody would sue you, but back in those days Shirley did it whenever it was needed.

Dr. Geoff Robbins, probably the only licensed dentist to ever work as a fry cook while he was a successful dentist, remembers the meal policy during the time he was at the Crab House

> Three meals a day were provided, good meals at no cost to the kids. They had a special cook, Jack O'Hare, whose only job was to feed the employees. For breakfast you could order anything you wanted, eggs, omelets, pancakes, whatever. Lunch was the big meal of the day because the timing worked better for more of the kids. It was always the hot meal of the day, roast chicken, roast beef, with the side dishes and everything. Then right after the Crab House closed the doors in the evening, there was a light meal available, sandwiches and such. All the employees, whether front of the house or back of the house, were permitted to partake of all the meals whether they were on that particular shift or not. At that time there were probably a couple hundred employees, maybe more.

But it wasn't all work. There was plenty of time for fun, and Phillips helped organize activities. Phillips sponsored a uni-sex softball team that played in an Ocean City league. Steve was usually in charge of the after-game refreshments. As Steve grew into his teenage years, and then college years, he assumed the role of 'thinking up fun things' for the employees to do when they weren't working.

One of the major events was the annual Phillips' Christmas Party. In August! The kids would draw names for giving gifts to each other. The restaurant was decorated for Christmas, with a tree and everything. The services of Mr. Pete Richardson, a local Santa Claus, were obtained and he'd come around in costume and distribute gifts to the various employees. The gifts from the Phillips would generally be money or an extra pay-check presented in envelopes by Santa.

Then there was the famous end of season party. It was held after work on the last night the Crab House was open. Tables were cleared, a band was brought in and there was dancing and singing. The walk-in coolers were opened and all the remaining food was cooked and brought out. It was hoped the kids would eat it all. Everyone gorged on the food. The next day the kids would pack up and go home. Dr. Robbins remembers other activities:

There was also mid-night flag football for the kids, sponsored by the major restaurants in Ocean City, including the Crab House. Each restaurant would have a team. The games were played at mid-night or later, after the restaurants closed. They were played up on what was then called "Holland's Island" because it was owned by Charlie and Elvine Holland who let the kids use it. [The area is now called "Sunset Island,' and is being developed as a townhouse/condominium project.]

Sometimes there would be several hundred spectators, the wait staff and back of the house crews. Phillips had a team [It was called 'Shirley's Studs'] and Steve and Jeff both played.

Jeff also started, and Phillips supported, a Phillips' competitive surfing team.

Then there was always a 'party house'. The regular staff at the Crab House, almost all of them young people, would work every night until late. There wasn't much time for partying during normal hours. Every year a group of guys, young male employees ('Hondo', 'Willie T.' and others) would rent a house up the beach, where, when the restaurant closed, the party would start.

One year it was at 61sth Street. Then Vice-President Agnew rented the house next door. One evening they were rousted by the Secret Service detail. They had to give their names, addresses and their backgrounds were checked. But, by the end of the summer, the interaction between the two groups had mellowed and the agents became Phillips' regulars.

As the writer was leaving the Crab House on July 6th, of 2005, after interviewing the amazing Mr. Dofflemyer, a homemade poster caught his eye. It said,

SERVERS - BUSBOYS

7TH Annual Servers - Busboys

Basketball Game

July 8th

## Northside Park

> Note: [name omitted to protect the culprit] will be sober for this game so servers beware.
>
> Bathing attire permitted.

It still goes on. Working at Phillips is not just a job, its an experience.

Periodically, in each of the summers after the home on Mallard Island was finished, Brice and Shirley would invite groups of selected Crab House employees, as many as forty at time, from both the 'front' and the 'back' of the house, to their home for lunch or dinner. Shirley would cook for them, and there would be age appropriate drinks, other fun things. The kids would bring their bathing suits and swim in the pool. Roam the garden. It was a chance for the kids whose days and nights were involved with supplying dinners to hundreds of tourists, to have a regular home cooked meal without having to cook or serve it themselves. It was a sharing by Shirley and Brice of their home with kids, whose homes were far away. It was giving them a 'normal' day away from the restaurant.

Additionally, most weeks they would take a group of 20 to 25 kids to the Beach Plaza for dinner, and then on to a night out on the town. When I asked them why they did these things Shirley replied, simply "We did it because they were good to us. We became attached to them." Brice said "We were all family. We felt like they were our children."

In the winter there were the Thursday night parties where the year-around employees would meet at Paul Wall's house. They would each bring a dish, there would be music, Miss Lillie would sing and entertain and games were played. It was a group united by work, as well as blood (in some cases.) It wasn't employer/employee. It was family.

The activities all created a unique comradery among the Phillips' group, unusual in the restaurant business, a bonding of a place, a business, and the people that made it possible.

Mr. Wall remembers:

> After Steve began to be involved we usually had plenty of appropriate beverages at our parties for those entitled to partake.

But, even then steps were taken to make sure that only those of the appropriate age drank, and then not to excess.

The kids were also involved in beach activities galore. Kids were kept busy. Because most of the kids that then worked for the Phillips and still work for the Phillips, were of very high caliber, the problems were few. We'd make mistakes every now and then, but we tried to see the good qualities we were looking for when we hired employees, especially the 'Phillips Girls'. A lot of parents felt, and still feel, that they wanted their child to get a job at Phillips because they felt their children would be looked after and taken care of. They would be safe and have a nice place to work.

A lot of our girls and boys were the children of our customers and, as time went on, were the children of those who had worked for us. That made us, and makes us, look after them all the more. We felt and feel that they are family. A lot of people fell in love here and ultimately got married after leaving for their permanent careers. Met at Phillips, started a relationship, got married, had kids. At one time Shirley even kept a marriage roster.

In the earlier days Shirley interviewed every girl that was hired to be a 'Phillips Girl', a front of the house girl. Even in the early days there were thousands of applications. In time as the Crab House expanded, the season extended, a north restaurant was built, the Beach Plaza bought, the applications became greater in number. As the business grew, Shirley needed assistance and a head hostess was hired, Ms. Doris Moore from Cambridge, who herself became a Phillips' fixture over the years. She began to help Shirley with the interviewing process and in the supervising of the girls at work, and after work. She stayed with the operation for years. Mr. Bruce Pendleton was assigned the duties of interviewing for bus boys, using the same standards. He was with the operation for at least twenty years.

Shirley remembers one special interviewing session,

Each winter, one of my main tasks was painting the restaurant. One year when I was on a ladder painting one of the dining rooms, I was simultaneously interviewing several college freshmen for the following season. [As Shirley had described the depression years, they didn't have much but time, but they knew what to do with time. Obviously, she still knew how to do two things at once.] I was on a ladder painting this particular room a salmon color. I got engrossed with the interviews and got careless with the painting. Unfortunately, I stepped into the paint bucket on the ladder, spewing a gallon of salmon-colored paint all over the floor. To make matters worse, I then slipped on the wet paint on the ladder and fell backwards, right into the little lake of vivid-colored paint. The fall didn't do much for my dignity, and the three girls I was interviewing couldn't hold it in, and all three of them sat down and laughed their heads off. Eventually, I joined in. The scene was funny; however, the cost of all that paint going down the drain was not. We were always doing two or more things at once. Time was at such premium, we had no choice.

She thinks she hired the girls.
Semore remembers all the years of the 'Phillips Girls."

The kids were hard workers; they needed to make the money. Mostly, the kids today are still the same. We get a sour apple now and then, but we always did. The numbers may be different, but, at the same time, it's still the same.

We still have housing for a lot of the kids, sheer economics dictate that we have to charge, but we charge at reasonable, well below market rates, and we monitor the facilities.

Now the former 'Phillips Girls', or boys, who are now parents, will have a son or a daughter working here, and they still remember the way the Phillips looked after them, imposed limits. These former employees feel free to just stop by, or call, and they'll ask, "How's so-in-so doing." Usually, we're able to say that the daughter or son is doing fine. Often the parent will tell us, "If he or she gives you any trouble, just kick their butt." We don't do it, of course. At least as best I can remember.

What is unusual is to try and think of any other large sit-down restaurant, where parents are calling up the employers to find out how their children are doing at their jobs, how they're behaving.

It's almost a tradition here for parents to check up on their children. It's probably why we get to choose the cream of the crop of young people. The Phillips genuinely care for their kids. And all of these people are customers, too. It really is, again, a matter of loyalty.

Joyce Flowers notes

> There are no words you can use to describe my time as a 'Phillips Girl'. Brice and Shirley were probably the best thing that ever happened to us girls. I learned so much just by watching Brice and Shirley. Every time Brice sees me now, and I'm 67, he always says, 'I've never had another one like you.' Sometimes he would call me into his office and he'd make me call off all the orders that I had served that night. I could always remember all of them. . . . They never knew the good they were doing. They were the type of people that just did things. They had great business sense, were creative. Shirley was a great hostess, even before they went to Ocean City.

Charlotte Sours, who was a 'Phillips Girl' for over eight years in the 1950s and 1960s, remembers

> But the best part of all are the wonderful memories of all the people who worked there, the times shared and all those special customers who brought a special blessing to my life. Some have passed on, other I haven't seen again, but all the special times and people have enriched my life. Shirley and Brice ran an establishment where people and friendships mattered, where work, learning and fun were all part of working at Phillips.

Shirley has never forgotten those early years and the young women and men she hired. She still acknowledges that

> A special bonus for us over the years has been the young men and women who have worked for us during their summer break, to help defray their college expenses. Some of them went on to become doctors, lawyers, ministers, successful businessmen and women. Almost all of our kids were college kids, or went on to college, even the cooks in the back of the house. . . .
>
> In order to have our employees remain loyal, we hired dependable people and attempted to make them feel as though they were part of our family. . . .
>
> We tried, and still try, to offer management positions to those employees that come to understand our business from the bottom up. It's preferable to hiring someone off the street. Most of our management staff consists of young men and women who worked here during the summers while attending college. They had served as dishwashers, bus boys, waitresses, waiters, cooks and in the office. They were bright and anxious to learn the business, worked very hard, with great dedication to our company.

Shirley summarizes her feelings for the young people who helped made the Crab House, and all the subsequent businesses, successful:

> When I look back at those years, I am teary-eyed with gratitude.
>
> We are so grateful that the college kids we hired back at the beginning now have children of their own who are working for Phillips. How could we be so lucky that we would now be rewarded with a second generation of wonderful young folks. What draws these students back? Is it the lure of the beach, or associations with their peers, the need for college tuition, or all those parties? It was probably a combination of all those things. . . . But it's more than that. These are the kids that are willing to take on responsibility and are looking for a chance to prove themselves.
>
> At Phillips they learn our work ethic and learn to take pride in what they do, no matter what they go on to do, they remain 'Phillips Girls and Boys' to us. . . .
>
> Most of the young people that come to our restaurants to work, even today, seem to have their heads on straight. I am proud of the young people of today. They live in a different world than the one I grew up in, there's a lot more temptation out there for them, but they can still get my admiration.

Mrs. Leone Simmons Phillips and Captain Augustus Elsworth Phillips (Capt. Ellie) - Wedding day 1919. From the collection of Mrs. Jane Phillips Groff.

The H. I. Phillips packing plant 1914. A. E. Phillips and Son acquired this plant after the 1933 hurricane destroyed their first plant. Verified by Mr. Charles Shockley Fishing Creek. Picture from the "Groff" Collection

Brice Phillips and his sister Jane. 1924-1925. From the "Groff" collection.

Mrs. Lillie Flowers, Shirley Phillips' mother and Mrs. Bernice Murphy, Shirley's half-sister. Bernice survived the hurricane of 1933 on the roof of the original A. E. Phillips and Son plant when it was destroyed, by clinging to the roof section of the plant as it was blown out into the Honga River - and then back to shore when the wind changed.

"Mrs. Bernice Murphy (center front) with members of her family and the author. Standing to Mrs. Murphy's right is Mrs. Charlotte Sours. Mrs. Sours is one of the original four 'Phillips Girls' of the 1950s. Mrs. Murphy, now over 91, is the last known living survivor of the girls that rode out the great hurricane of 1933 on the roof of the demolished Phillips' packing plant as it floated out into the Honga River. Photo taken at Boca Raton - 2006."

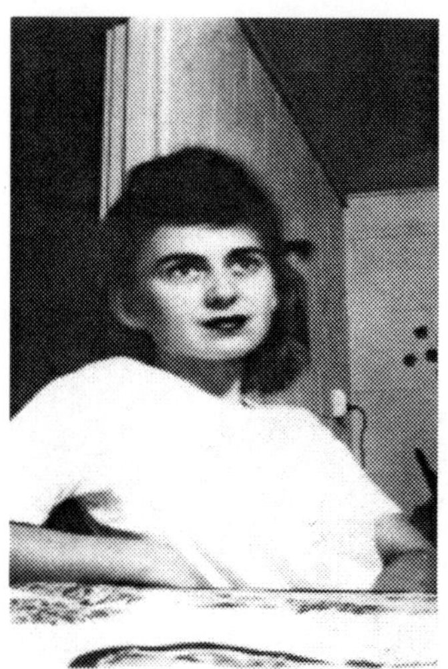

Shirley Phillips, wartime bride. 1944-1945.

Brice Phillips. V-E Day Chateaubriant, France.

Brice Phillips - Matapeake Ferry. 1940-1943.

Captain Ivy Flowers wading for soft crabs.Approx. 1930-1940.

Yacht at Gibson Island which Captain Ivy Flowers, Shirley's father, captained when he first returned from World War I. 1920-1922. From the collection of Mrs. Bernice Murphy.

Captain Ivy Flowers in a dingy at Gibson Island. 1920-1922. From the "Murphy" collection.

EXTRA | THE STARS AND STRIPES | EXTRA

# JAPAN QUITS

**TOKYO REPORT:** Japan has accepted the Allied terms of surrender, a Tokyo radio report picked up by OWI announced early today.
No further details were immediately available.

## PACIFIC COST 321,052 YANKS

### *Ike Denies Reds Asked Elbe Halt*

MOSCOW, Aug. 13 (AP)—Gen. Eisenhower said today that he had ordered U.S. troops smashing across Germany last spring to stop at the Elbe River because he wanted to break up Hitler's national redoubt in the south—and not because the Red Army or Stalin had requested it.

The former supreme Allied commander declared there had been complete coordination with the Russians. He said he told his commanders weeks ahead of time to pull up at the Elbe at certain places and to turn southward at others with all possible speed. It had never been his plan to stop at any military or political zone, he added.

As long ago as January, Eisenhower revealed, U.S. Ambassador to Russia W. Averell Harriman and Maj. Gen. J. Russell Deane, chief of the U.S. military mission to the USSR, worked out a plan of cooperation with the Red Army.

Eisenhower's current visit to Moscow was made at the suggestion of the Soviet government.

## ATOMIC BOMB, RUSSIAN ENTRY HASTENED END

Two events hastened Japan's capitulation to the Allies, while her main armies were still undefeated.

They were the unleashing of the atomic bomb and Russia's entry into the Pacific war.

At 9:15 AM on Aug. 6 the first atomic bomb was dropped on the city of Hiroshima, an army and QM base of 318,000 people. It caused explosions described by the pilot of the Superfortress which carried it, who already was ten miles away, as "tremendous and awe-inspiring."

This weapon, the best kept secret of the war, was estimated, after examination of American reconnaissance photos, to have leveled 4.1 square miles or 60 percent of the city. Tokyo Radio said Hiroshima was "completely destroyed."

"The destructive power of the bomb is indescribable," the Jap broadcast stated. "Every living thing outside simply vanished into the air because of the heat."

And then two days later Russia entered the war, and Soviet troops began moving immediately across the borders of Manchukuo, in a two pronged pincer attack, and the following day invaded Korea.

Headlines and articles, August 14th Southern France Edition of The Stars And Stripes. For a current perspective, compare the total number of American casualties just in the Pacific during that war, with the current number of American casualties in Iraq and Afghanistan.

Headline and part of front page of an "Extra" published by the France Edition of Stars and Stripes on August 14th, 1945. For a current perspective, compare the total number of American casualties just in the war in the Pacific with the current number of casualties suffered in the actions in Iraq and Afghanistan

Steve and Jeffrey Phillips - Hoopers Island days. 1950 - 1953

Phillips plant on Hoopers Island around 1945-1950.

The mother ship, Phillips Crab House, - 1960s.

Brice and Shirley with "Aunt Shirley's Studs", the Phillips flag football team. Year unknown. Believed to be in the 1980s -1990s.

The family - Shirley, Steve, Jeffrey, and Brice. Before the accident.

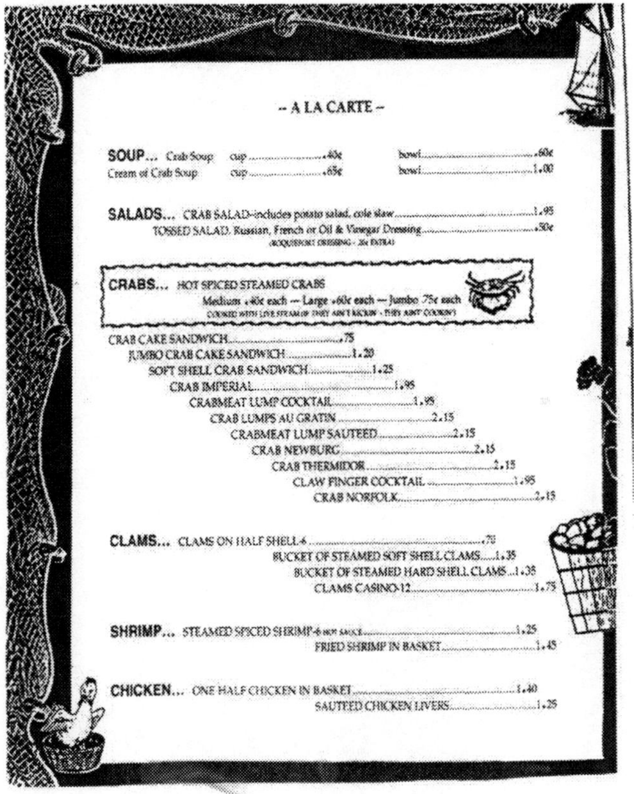

-- A LA CARTE --

**SOUP...** Crab Soup cup .......... .40¢ bowl .......... .60¢
Cream of Crab Soup cup .......... .65¢ bowl .......... 1.00

**SALADS...** CRAB SALAD-includes potato salad, cole slaw .......... 1.95
TOSSED SALAD. Russian, French or Oil & Vinegar Dressing .......... .50¢
[illegible]

**CRABS...** HOT SPICED STEAMED CRABS
Medium .40¢ each -- Large .60¢ each -- Jumbo 75¢ each
[illegible]

CRAB CAKE SANDWICH .......... .75
JUMBO CRAB CAKE SANDWICH .......... 1.20
SOFT SHELL CRAB SANDWICH .......... 1.25
CRAB IMPERIAL .......... 1.95
CRABMEAT LUMP COCKTAIL .......... 1.95
CRAB LUMPS AU GRATIN .......... 2.15
CRABMEAT LUMP SAUTEED .......... 2.15
CRAB NEWBURG .......... 2.15
CRAB THERMIDOR .......... 2.15
CLAW FINGER COCKTAIL .......... 1.95
CRAB NORFOLK .......... 2.15

**CLAMS...** CLAMS ON HALF SHELL-6 .......... .70
BUCKET OF STEAMED SOFT SHELL CLAMS .......... 1.35
BUCKET OF STEAMED HARD SHELL CLAMS .......... 1.35
CLAMS CASINO-12 .......... 1.75

**SHRIMP...** STEAMED SPICED SHRIMP-6 .......... 1.25
FRIED SHRIMP IN BASKET .......... 1.45

**CHICKEN...** ONE HALF CHICKEN IN BASKET .......... 1.40
SAUTEED CHICKEN LIVERS .......... 1.25

Early menu at the Crab House. Note that a cup of crab soup was 45 cents, a crab cake sandwich was 75 cents and clams on the half-shell were 70 cents.

Representative 'front of the house' staff of "Phillips' Girls" and "Phillips' Boys" at the Crab House. Year unknown

Representative 'front of the house' staff at the Phillips Beach Plaza Hotel. Year unknown.

Typical Phillips sponsored employees' sports team- post-game naturally. Year unknown.

One of the famous August Christmas parties with the "Phillips Girls" all dressed up and having fun. Year unknown.

The Phillips boys also having fun. Post-1971 after the accident.

Grand opening party at Phillips Harborplace. Shirley left front. Then Mayor Schaefer (since Maryland Governor and Comptroller) on the left side. Semore behind him and Brice behind Semore. 'Front of the house' and 'back of the house' staff scattered throughout.

Party aboard ship- East China Sea. From left: John Dale Showell, III, Earl Brittingham, Billie Brittingham, Ann Showell Dr. Frank Townsend, Lil Townsend, Shirley Phillips, Brice Phillips

Economic development trip to Europe. Maryland Governor (now Comptroller) William Donald Schaefer on the left, Brice Phillips on the right.

# CHAPTER THIRTY-TWO

## *Paul Wall*

By the time the season of 1967 rolled around, the Crab House was at its maximum seating capacity of 1400 seats. Over the years office work had also increased. Brice had been in charge of all the pay-roll, book keeping, paying invoices and such, but the amount of paper work had grown to the extent that it was beyond the capabilities of one person to do. As Paul Wall puts it, Brice "found himself staying up half the night doing paperwork and then spending all day in the kitchen." Brice went looking for help.

In the school year of 1965/1966 a young man graduated from East Carolina University with a degree in Business Education. A vacancy existed for such a teacher at Snow Hill High School in Worcester County and he was hired.

That winter, the winter of 1967, Brice finally realized that if the business was going to continue to grow, it was essential that he find a business educated person to assist him with the paper work and the bookkeeping load. He passed the word around the community and in time was referred to the young East Carolina graduate.

Paul was interviewed for the job before the season opened, in the Phillip's living room (while it was still a living room.) He recalls,

> My timing was great. I was hired. I worked seven days a week just like everybody else in Ocean City - Memorial Day

to Labor Day. I continued to live in Snow Hill and commuted. They also hired my wife, Billie, to help in the office taking care of the paperwork for the servers, the 'Phillips Girls'. She would designate and distribute the order books to the girls and after the shifts were over, would check for any errors in the computations.

We both commuted from Snow Hill. I really liked the job. But in the fall, Billie got really homesick for our hometown of Winston-Salem, North Carolina. I was able to secure a teaching job down there and Billie and I moved back home, permanently - we thought. We intended to spend the rest of our lives there.

We hadn't counted on Brice. Didn't know him well enough yet. When he wants something, he never gives up. He had made up his mind that he liked me and wanted me to be in the operation - and that was just the way it was. At first, although I was flattered, I declined his offers. But, Brice just doesn't give up. He called me just about every week while I was down in North Carolina. He'd ask me, 'How's everything going down there?' 'Things all right with you?' 'Thought I'd just call and check on you.'

Things began to get a little more aggressive around Christmas time. He then started asking, 'When are you coming back to Ocean City?' 'Are you going to come back this year?' This was in January or February of 1967. I told Brice that I intended to stay in Winston-Salem because my family was happy there.

He kept calling, anyway. To this day my wife won't let me forget that I was alone sitting in the kitchen at our home in Winston-Salem when I finally gave in. He called that particular day and was very persistent. He kept making offers. Finally, he said 'Paul, I really need you up here.', and made me an offer I would have been a fool to refuse. Finally, after the months of entreaties, I responded, 'Okay Brice, we'll be up there.' I said it right as my wife and her mother were walking in the door. Billie started crying, said 'We haven't even discussed this.' But I knew that I had a better future with Brice and Shirley than

> I had in North Carolina, because Brice had these dreams of expansion and had shared them with me. He dreamed of other restaurants, perhaps a chain of carry-outs someday in different areas of the country. I realized that I wanted to be a part of it. I came up that next summer and never went back and never looked back. And I made the right decision.

A figuratively shanghaied (maybe the practice is in a Hoopers Islander's genes) Mr. Wall began a lifetime relationship with Brice and Shirley, not only as a valued employee, but as a family member and friend. Much of the material contained in this book comes from information furnished directly or indirectly by Paul Wall. He was in at the creation of almost everything that followed.

In addition to the normal Phillips practice of turning employees into members of the family, Paul believes that Brice and Shirley saved his life - that but for them he would be dead.

> When I got seriously ill, the local medical community was having difficulty in diagnosing what was wrong with me. I'd had a grand mal seizure and it was so bad it had broken my shoulder. I had been rushed to the Salisbury hospital. While I was there Brice and Shirley spent every day at the hospital with my wife. When they realized that I was not getting better, Brice told Billie, 'We've got to get him to [Johns] Hopkins. That's the best hospital in the State.' Brice arranged for me to be flown to Hopkins by helicopter, but it couldn't fly because a hurricane had arrived and flying conditions were too dangerous. I was taken to Hopkins in an ambulance in the middle of the storm.
>
> When we arrived at Hopkins, Brice and Shirley made sure I had the best doctors at that hospital. I ended up with a Doctor Mary Newman who was able to diagnose me with a condition 'Consistent with, but not diagnostic of encephalitis.' She began to treat me as if I had encephalitis. Still she called the family together, including Brice and Shirley, and told them that she didn't think 'I would survive.' Later they again told

my family and Brice and Shirley to prepare for the worse. At best I would be in a nursing home for the rest of my life. . . .

Later when I was well enough for therapy, my primary problem was that I had completely lost my memory. I didn't even know my wife or my children. At intervals over an extensive period of time, Brice and Shirley would walk me up and down the hallways of the facility I was in, talking to me, explaining the nature of things I couldn't understand, things I couldn't remember. They constantly talked to me about all the memories that I once had, they constantly repeated my past to me. They would show me photo albums to bring back memories.

With the help of Billie, and the efforts of Brice and Shirley, my memory started coming back. Brice kept saying 'We're going to get you back in the office. These memories are going to come back.'

In six months I was back in the office, most of my memory restored. If it wasn't for them I wouldn't be here today.

I had a spell four or five years later that was probably related to my prior illness. I became very depressed and didn't think things were clicking right in my thinking. I remember very clearly walking up to Brice's office and saying to Brice, 'I can't make it. I think I'm going to have to quit. I just can't do it, anymore.' Well Brice never gives up on anything, neither does Shirley. Brice looked me in the eye, said 'You can't quit. You are going to make it, now get downstairs to that office of yours and get back to work! We'll give you a period of time, the rest of the season, and then if you still want to stop, come back and talk to me again. Right now you're going to make it, and you're going back to work!' I turned around, did what he told me. I went back to work and I haven't stopped since. And I am not the only one they have done these types of things for. There have been other people they have helped in the same way they helped me, that it's not for me to identify.

I won't say they're stubborn, but when Shirley gets something in her head she'll let you know directly. She was, and is, much more aggressive in business than most women of her generation. I've had Shirley, after listening and considering my viewpoint, look me in the eyes and say, "This is what I think." And that is what she thinks! She may agree or disagree with you. Either way she is going to directly let you know what she thinks. Brice is less abrupt, gets his point across in a less direct manner. Had it not been for the both of them I wouldn't be where I am now. And I wouldn't have learned so much about business and how to live a life worth living.

# CHAPTER THIRTY-THREE

## *The boys*

Brice and Shirley have raised two extraordinary boys - now men. One has created an international seafood empire, arguably has progressed further than any person ever born on Hoopers Island and raised in Ocean City. The other son, in a different way, has accomplished as much, perhaps more.

During my initial interview with Steve Phillips, an interview that I scheduled and planned in order to understand the operations and successes of Phillips Foods, the discussion somehow came to the relationship he had with his brother. I noticed that Steve's eyes filled with tears, and soon a tear was moving down his cheek. He said then, totally unsolicited,

> Jeff is my hero. To have had happen what happened to him, and to still be able to make a constructive life for himself and his family, raise kids, still participate in the management of the businesses is something I don't think I could have done. He's a great man. And he's my friend.

Still, with all the achievements of Steve and Jeffrey, Shirley has never forgotten that they are boys, her boys. She still is the mother hen. When Shirley was asked how she wanted to be remembered, her answer was a simple, "I want to be remembered by my two sons for being a good mother."

The story of both boys begins of course on Hoopers Island. Jeffrey being the cheap kid, because he was born at home saving the money not spent on hospital bills. One supposes that they grew up as did all the boys on the island, doing the things that island boys did. In time, as has been indicated, there were the weekend trips on the Gertie V throughout the areas of the bay.

But then came the summer moves to Ocean City where the boys sat outside the crab shack, folding carry out containers and acting in a way, as shills, or at least as door-boys for the carry-out, announcing - 'Customers coming, customers coming!' There was the living in bunk beds in the rudimentary dormitory out back of the store. There were the days of being invited by Mrs. Weaver to come hop in the pool at the Islander motel across the street, maybe a time or two when one of the first 'Phillips Girls' might have taken them up on the beach for a swim, or 'down the boardwalk to the rides'. Later there was Jeffrey waking Joyce Flowers up early in the morning to go watch him surf. The summer moves to Ocean City continued until Jeffrey was in the fifth grade. Then they moved to Ocean City on a year-round basis, and after a short hiatus on 8th Street, they moved to a larger and more comfortable space in the Crab House, at least in the off-season.

There was the usual brotherly love thing, older brother protecting younger brother.[24] There were disagreements as well, competitions, teasing, but the almost four years difference in their ages minimized these. At an early age they were indoctrinated into the business. Starting at the bottom, learning all of the tasks, pleasant and unpleasant, in hands-on fashion. Steve, the oldest, passing through the system first - was groomed first. But there are those, in and out of the organization, that considered Steve in his younger years to have been more the playboy of the two, Jeffrey the more serious. Among them is Steve, himself. Jeffrey was considered more the scholar, an honor student at Cornell. As one long time knowledgeable person puts it:

[24] Prominent local business man, Bobby Jester, is believed to have some knowledge of this trait of the brothers.

Both boys went to McDonogh School in the tenth grade. Steve was a big athlete on campus, on the football team, other sports teams. Jeffrey followed him, not expected to be an athlete, yet he broke the school's pole vault record that Steve had set before him. Steve graduated from the University of Miami, reinforcing his playboy image, Jeffrey graduated from Cornell, consistent with his alleged more serious nature.

Dr. Robbins recalls the playboy's McDonogh and college days:

McDonogh was a very good military prep school. I went there a year before Steve did. We'd been in school together since the 4th grade. Steve came up the year after I got there. He was a little more rambunctious than most kids. Brice and Shirley started looking for some structure for him. He had become a little bit of a free spirit. So Brice and Shirley enrolled him in the tenth grade year.

He did really well. He was a great athlete. Played on the football team, broke the high school record in the pole vault. He was a great wrestler on the wrestling team.

He was one of those kinds of people that didn't have to put a lot of effort in academics, but always seemed to do well. He was always, even back then, quick on his feet and had a lot of street sense. He just didn't have to study very hard like the rest of us.

Upon graduation from McDonogh, Dr. Robbins and Steve both enrolled at 'Cardboard College', also called 'Sun Tan U.', also called 'Party School', the University of Miami. There a somewhat storied college career began. As Dr. Robbins says, "I was on the four year plan, Steve was on the five year plan.' At one point it was said that with Steve college was, "Five years or five million dollars, whichever comes first."

Early in his University of Miami career he managed to acquire a sports car with the help of his father. He promptly loaned it to a fraternity brother who then "totaled" it. Later he acquired a motorcycle and one evening rode it through the front door of the girls high-rise dormitory, onto the elevator, took the elevator to the seventh floor, exited and rode the cycle around the $7^{th}$ floor halls, then reversed the process, down the elevator, through the lobby and out the front door and on down the highway. He once asked Geoffrey to go for a ride on the motorcycle, put him on the back and made Tampa in less than an hour and a half. Apparently, the speeding gene of his father that had so worried Miss Lillie when Brice started dating Shirley, had been passed on to him.

As Dr. Robbins remembers, even in those days Steve was lucky. When he was pledging a fraternity, the initiation rites included the pledges being taken at midnight way out on Alligator Alley, the road to Tampa, in undershorts. There they'd be left out in different places. After the upper brothers let Steve off, he noticed that they had put him out near a power sub-station and that a utility man was working there. Steve went over, introduced himself and found out that the utility man lived right next to the University of Miami. Steve promptly arranged for a ride and was back in the fraternity house before the upper classmen returned. Shortly, he had earned the nickname 'Hoot', probably in a comparison with the old saying, "He's a hoot." As Dr. Robbins recalls, "Now a lot of the stuff he did might seem tame, back then he was considered a bit of a hellion."

Eventually, Steve and a young man named Virgil Price became friends. Price would go on to fame as a world class big game fisherman. The huge marlin hanging at the front of the Crab House is a Black Marlin caught by him in Cairns, Australia. Price and Steve moved in to a house on Key Biscayne that had a pool. Even then Steve had a flair for organization. Geoff describes Steve's studying practices:

> Steve would position cold cans of beer at strategic points on the apron around the pool. Then he would throw a big inner-tube into the pool. He would get whatever books or papers he was studying, climb into the inner-tube with his study material, and push off. No matter where the breeze took him, sooner or later he'd bump into the side of the pool. There would be a cold beer to refresh him. That was his idea of studying.

Dr. Robbins recalls thinking at the time, "I knew how I was studying, looked at how he was studying, and thought, 'He must know something I don't.'"

Semore remembers the before and after. He laments, "We used to do bigger parties when Steve was here and in charge of fun. Sometimes we miss the old Steve."

Both boys, as their college years approached and during the summers after college began, were gradually placed in supervisory positions, were groomed for management. They were very different. As one confidant put it,

> Steve and Jeffrey were different when they were younger. Jeffrey was the more serious one. He taught himself to play the piano and clarinet. While still in his teens, he did a lot in helping reorganize the kitchen at the Crab House so that the carry-out and in-house operations were serviced separately in the kitchen, which increased the efficiency of both operations. Jeffrey was much more the studious one, always serious, a Cornell type. While there, he consistently made the Dean's list, was considered a top scholar, and, in spite of his serious accident would go on to graduate in the allotted time.
>
> Prior to Jeffrey's accident, Steve, as is very evident, appears to have been a happy- go-lucky character. The type of guy you think of when you think of the University of Miami. Full of fun. He worked hard, but he played hard, too.
>
> After Jeffrey's accident, I think Steve stepped back and said to himself, 'That could have been me instead of my brother.' At that time I saw Steve take an about face, especially in the business. He began to really take hold of the reins and shortly became a much more important part of the operation, helping his parents in the management of the restaurants, and later becoming the more dominant force in the future of the companies, although Brice and Shirley were always there, always involved.

Semore remembers the time of the accident.

When Brice and Shirley went up to New York to stay with Jeffrey, everyone buckled down and worked all the harder because we didn't want to let them down. Steve led us while they were away. He did almost all of the management decision making, took over doing the books, doing the payroll. Because he, and all of us, were trying so hard, the restaurant was probably run the best it had ever been. We didn't want to disappoint them. It brought everybody together, closer, because we were all family, shared in the heart-break.

From that point on, Steve began to take more and more responsibility. He knew he had to do everything while they were gone, so he just took the bull by the horns and did what needed to be done. Made the tough decisions, and he's never looked back since. For him, everything is always ahead.

There was a time when you went to Brice for every little thing, then when Brice came home after the accident we'd go to both of them, and then we would just go to Steve for most things, because he was real good at working things out. He had become a decision maker. From the time of Jeffrey's accident on, decisions never fazed him.

Dr. Robbins remembers the time:

Only Steve, Paul and Semore were there running things. Brice and Shirley were with Jeffrey. For big decisions there seemed to be no one but Steve. He simply picked up the reins; he had to, because even though Semore knew how to run the back of the house and Doris Moore was familiar with the front of the house, and Paul the books, no one knew it all. Someone had to run the overall business of the Crab House. For Steve it was swim or sink, on the job training, so to speak, but he took over and the rest is history.

Before the accident, Steve and I used to do a lot of partying on the weekends, but after the accident his entire demeanor changed - he became much more serious. When he had to step into Brice's shoes that spring, Steve's involvement in the fun activities of the 'Phillips Kids' ceased. He was too busy, too serious. And he stopped partying. He was a different Steve. Jeff's accident was a life altering experience for both boys.

I don't think I would have continued working at Phillips, but for the accident. When I became a dentist, Brice had taken me out of the kitchen and put me in charge of the Cash Control operation in the office. I think he wanted to get my hands out of danger. But after the accident, and after I became a dentist, I stayed with Brice, Shirley and Steve for six more years. A dentist in the daytime. At the Crab House in the evening. I stayed because of them. Because of the Phillips.

Brice and Shirley remember Geoff with special fondness. In one interview session, they said

> Geoff Robbins is one of our family members. Even after he got his dental business going to where he was overloaded with patients in the daytime, he still kept working for us in the nighttime. For six or seven years. He did it because he wanted to and he knew we needed him. All the money would come to him when he got there in the evening, all of it, he was the cash flow coordinator. He'd come winging in at around six in the afternoon and straighten it all out. Shirley describes the relationship "I just love that boy to death. He is a wonderful boy and he's been really good to us."

Dr. Robbins describes how the community felt at the time of Jeffrey's accident:

> The community just opened their hearts to the Phillips family. Out of every tragedy, so much good can come out of it. The Phillips' attitudes, especially Jeff's, have been a great example to many people, that no matter how bad your morning might be, there are people with worse problems who still maintain a positive attitude. When Jeff is riding down the boardwalk, he's not having a bad day. He's having a great day no matter what physical problem he's coping with at the moment.

As Steve put it recently, "When we were younger, before the accident, I always thought that Jeffrey would be doing something like this. Not me."

Jeff's accident changed everyone's life.

# CHAPTER THIRTY-FOUR

## *The accident*

Shirley says that Jeffrey wanted to go to Cornell:

> Because it had a College of Hotel Administration. And we had bought a hotel in Ocean City, the Beach Plaza, and he felt like he might want to manage that hotel, and others we might buy in the future. Once he got out of college he'd be in a position to have a large role in our future hotel expansion plans, he could manage our hotel operations, and still be in the restaurant business. He could get a top education in both hotel and restaurant management because Cornell had strong programs in both fields.

Steve was home in the apartment at the Crab House. His parent's new house on Mallard Island was still under construction. Brice and Shirley had gone to Baltimore for a business meeting scheduled for ten the next morning and were spending the evening in a hotel in Baltimore, but Steve didn't know what hotel. Shortly after midnight, the morning of December the 7$^{th}$, 1971, Steve took a call for his parents.

Jeffrey's car had been run over by a tractor-trailer and he was critically injured. He was in a hospital in Elmira, New York. It was doubtful whether he could survive.

Steve took several minutes to attempt to find his parents at the hotels in Baltimore, but was unsuccessful. He phoned Bernice Murphy, his aunt who lived in the Baltimore area, told her of the situation, and asked her to go to the office where the meeting was scheduled the next morning. He asked her to tell Brice and Shirley what had happened and to tell them to get to the hospital in Elmira. He and Olivia[25] would go up to Jeffrey, would wait for his parents at the Elmira Hospital.

Steve and Olivia sped through the darkness, six or seven hours to Elmira. They went to the hospital and stayed with Jeffrey through the long hours of the night.

Shirley tells of the events of that day.

> The day before . . . Brice and I were in Baltimore on business . . . and had a business appointment at ten o'clock the next morning, December the 7th. When Brice and I were arriving at our meeting the next morning, I looked up and saw Harry and Bernice [her sister] coming towards us. I initially was glad to see her, and started to greet her, when I noticed a utterly desolate look on her face. I knew immediately that something had happened to one of my boys. Bernice told us, 'I am the bearer of bad news. Jeffrey has been hit by a tractor-trailer and he's not expected to live.'

Brice first called the Elmira Hospital and talked to Steve. Steve told them that the doctors at the hospital were only giving Jeff a 50/50 chance to make it through the day. He told them to hurry. Brice and Shirley remember:

> We tried to charter a plane to go to Elmira, but it was too foggy and the planes couldn't fly. We had to rent a car and we sped there driving as fast as 90 miles per hour in the fog, wondering with every mile whether we had lost Jeffrey. Several hours later we pulled into the parking lot. Steve was waiting in

[25] Olivia Harrison Phillips, Steve's former wife and now a prominent Ocean City attorney. For a number of years she was active in the operations of the Crab House and contributed to the success of the restaurant operations.

> the parking lot and gave us a thumbs up signal and we knew that we had made it while Jeffrey was still alive.
>
> . . .
>
> When we went in the hospital room, Jeff was just lying there and I didn't know whether he was going to live or not. We were told that it was touch and go that he would even live. It was a horrible, horrible feeling.
>
> The doctors told us that Jeffrey had a terrible brain injury, and although they hadn't completed all of their examination, they believed the injury was deep in the cerebellum. They told us that they couldn't guarantee that he would even live. He was then in a coma, and if he survived the brain damage would be massive.

They were told by the experts that if Jeffrey did live, he would only last a year at most. In the first several days they had him examined by five experts, including a brain surgeon. They came up with a similar consensus - "He might be able to live for six months, but he won't live for a year." They were told that he would never leave the hospital alive. Even though they thought he was going to die anyway, the doctors still made herculean efforts to save him, and he stayed alive, and stayed alive. They gave Jeffrey every chance that modern medicine offers. Deep inside somewhere he was responding. Responding in ways that no one could see, and still can't understand. Perhaps, it was the never give up gene that is prominent in the Phillips. Perhaps it was the praying. Perhaps it was a mother's and a father's and a brother's love. Whatever it was, he lived. Shirley remembers:

> Jeffrey was in a coma for several months. We asked Steve to take care of the business until we could get Jeffrey home, if we could get Jeffrey home. Steve was a god-send. He'd gone to Jeffrey, for himself and for us, when he couldn't contact us. Now, he took the load of the businesses off our shoulders so that we could tend to his brother.
>
> Brice and I stayed in Elmira for the whole time Jeff was in the hospital there, several months, during most of which he

> was in a coma. I prayed every day, several times a day, went to the hospital chapel and asked God to make him well.
>
> John and Sue Hess from Salisbury knew people in Elmira who owned a department store, Larry Schuler and his wife, who was a weather person and newscaster on the local television station. They came to the hospital every day we were there to be with us, to lend us their support. Additionally, through them the people of Elmira learned of our problem and immediately opened their hearts to us.
>
> On New Years Eve as we were sitting with Jeffrey in his room, the Schulers brought a bottle of champagne to share with us. Mrs. Schuler took a little champagne and wet Jeffrey's lips with it so that he could toast the New Year, even though he was in a coma and being fed through tubes [Later the Schuler's son would become a 'Phillips Boy' at the Crab House.]

The hospital made room for them during the first days in a lounge, then gave them a place to sleep in the nurse's quarters where they stayed for the rest of their time in Elmira. Apparently, Jeffrey's plight, and his family's reaction to it, had struck a responsive chord among the hospital staff. Brice and Shirley remember that, without exception, everyone at the hospital was great. The nurses and all of the people of Elmira were "extremely kind." Brice remembers, "Everywhere we went people knew us, would stop and ask about how Jeff was doing, how we were doing. People we hadn't known before. Wishing us well. It was like we were adopted by the people of Elmira."

There was nothing else in their lives during the stay in Elmira, but to watch Jeff, react to the doctor's reports, and to appreciate the kindnesses of the Elmirans. During the first months when Jeff was unresponsive, there was a lot of time spent sitting, looking at a son lying in a hospital bed. Shirley remembers one instance where an advertisement on television seemed to incongruously relate to their situation.

> It's funny sometimes how your mind works when you're in a time of tragedy and stress. We didn't have a chance to watch, or at least pay much attention to television while we were up there, but both of us remember one program. We saw for

> the first time Frank Perdue's 'It takes a tough man to make a tender chicken', advertisement. Other than the fact that Jeffrey was still alive and that the people of Elmira were treating us so great, that's the only thing that cheered us up. It was like someone we knew was talking to us. Right then we needed a little bit of toughness and tenderness.

The days went by day by day, week by week, and then month by month. Everyday Brice and Shirley would try and get Jeffrey to respond to them. Nothing happened. After a while his eyes were open, but there was no sign that he was seeing anything, let alone recognizing them. His eyes just looked up at the ceiling. They would try to get him to respond by signs, asking him to squeeze their hands.

Day after day. Nothing. Then, as Shirley describes it,

> From the beginning we would often hold his hands and speak to him, telling him that if he recognized us or our voices to squeeze our hands. This went on for three months with no response. Then one day, in response to my question, he squeezed my hand for the first time. This was when he was still in Elmira. Until he squeezed my hand that first time we didn't know whether he'd ever snap out of it. I can vividly remember the day when it happened. After hundreds of times asking him to squeeze our hands, he was finally doing it. And squeezing intelligently, responding specifically to specific questions. It was a big thrill, one I can't even describe. I knew then that his mind was reacting. That he was understanding what we were saying. We knew that in a mental sense, at least, there was a good chance that he would become completely viable.

The day of his "squeeze reaction" was the first time they knew that Jeffrey was out of the coma. Jeffrey had known it earlier but had not been able to physically respond. Jeffrey continued to progress while at Elmira. During the long time he was in a coma he had been fed through a tube; he had taken no food by mouth in three months. He was now able to eat and the staff, and his parents, began feeding him hospital food. During their time in Elmira, Brice and Shirley had became regular customers at a nearby restaurant as they would take turns going out for meals. The proprietor, knowing of their situation through a daughter that worked at the hospital, had gone out of his way to support them, had encouraged them, had become a friend. One afternoon shortly after Jeffrey had 'awakened', the restaurant owner sent over a complete steak dinner for Jeffrey. He was able to eat it - 'even the crumbs.'

After another period of time, they were able to move Jeff to the Dean Rusk Institute in New York City to begin his rehabilitation, to attempt to regain as much of his motor skills as possible. Among their initial inquiries at that facility was whether his mental faculties were intact. They were assured that they were.

Jeffrey stayed at the Institute for several months, gradually improving as his physical rehabilitation progressed. They were able to bring him home for the weekends, returning to New York for weekdays of rehabilitation.

Later he moved home, but would go to a Baltimore facility for physical rehabilitation. After a month that hospital announced that he had advanced as far physically as was possible. Nonetheless Jeff continued with out-patient treatment, first at a facility in Key Biscayne, Florida and later at Johns Hopkins Hospital in Baltimore. That was the end of his physical rehabilitation. Now, as Shirley puts it;

> He has a wonderful wife, Janet, four great children. Janet understands his physical problems, is very patient and a great mother. They live in a home next to ours on Mallard Island. Jeff is very active in the management of our Ocean City hotel, the Beach Plaza, goes there every day. One of his sons is also a part of the hotel's management team and his youngest son works there. Jeff's aware that God gave him back his life.
>
> He never gripes over his physical problem. He's gone all the way from being in a comatose state for a three month period or longer, being severely physically handicapped, to living a regular life. He's made himself an internet expert, he still loves piano music. He's done this, turned tragedy into triumph, with the help of his family, especially his wife, but primarily with his own will.

Dr. Robbins comments on Jeff's accomplishment: "It shows a difference in the two boys. Jeff looked at the problem as a challenge and took the challenge. Steve might have looked at it as a mortal defeat. To Jeff it's just another job to get done because it's important."

Shirley summarizes,

> Today, Jeff . . . is walking. He is a happy, wonderful, delightful person, who never complains. Although he cannot work in the ways he once did, he visits the restaurants and hotel daily. He has a far more important task to perform for us, talking to our employees, making each of them feel that they are a part of our Phillips family.
>
> He's a very special person.

# CHAPTER THIRTY-FIVE

*Jeffrey - "It's just that the gear is different."*

*Janet: I really want to say what I've learned from being with Brice and Shirley and Jeff. The biggest lesson I learned from Brice and Shirley was about what you can do. I remember when our children were small, and they would want to do things and I would gently explain why it couldn't be done, either for reasons of danger, or tactical reasons, or for whatever reasons. They would go right next door to 'mom-mom's' and say, 'Mom-mom, we want to do this.' Shirley would never say no. She would always say, 'Let's see how we can make this work.'*

*I've now learned through the years that, even if eventually you get to no, the process of working through it, trying to figure out how you can make it work, often ended up with yeses.*

*I think that's the way we should all live our lives. What are the possibilities instead of what are the limitations.*

*From Jeff my greatest lesson has been patience. I've always been an impatient person, and to be around somebody who knows how to go slow, and enjoys going slow, has been a trial, yet a gift. Because when you slow down, you notice the little beautiful things in life.*

*What I learned when Jeff and I had children was that I was not their teacher, they were mine. They were a reflection of my behavior and attitudes, and if I didn't like what I saw in them, I needed to change what was going on with me.*

*I think Jeff has achieved something so much greater just in terms of existence. I've been around him for twenty years and have seen people coming up to him, just wanting to touch him, just wanting to come up and say hello because he always has kind words for everyone and he's just full of love. People want to feel that. People need him. They need that boost from him.*

*I remember going down the boardwalk last fall [2004] with Jeff on his three- wheeler. People were rushing out of their stores and shops as we'd go by, just to say hi to Jeff. It was touching, but a little funny, also. It took us probably two hours to get up and down the boardwalk because everybody wanted to come and say hello to him. It was a beautiful experience and I realized then, that he's doing just exactly what he needs to be doing in this world.*

*I think he's spreading love, giving hope. I've had a lot of people say to me, 'Gosh, you know I was really feeling bad, feeling down on myself. Then I saw Jeff. He's happy. You know what I said? I said to myself, 'You have no excuse for not being happy.'*

*I think he changes people's perspective on what you need to be happy. Like Jeff said, it is simple, 'just be happy.' His lesson is that happiness is a choice you make. Sure, things happen to us, but that's part of an experience of life. But we choose how we feel and how we think. That's the gift Jeff reminds us of, that's a gift we all need to know we have.*

Brice and Shirley were our success story, the town's success story, as well as their own. Jeffrey and Steve became to be among the most loved of the resort's sons. And when Jeffrey's accident occurred it was a tragedy for the town, as well as the family. His progress was followed, his return home celebrated, albeit silently (although there was that great birthday party in October of 1972.) Upon his return he became an active member of the community.

Throughout the years, I've had the occasion to be seated at a table with Jeffrey, to be standing beside him, to simply be in contact. It had always been extremely difficult for me to understand him amidst the din of social gatherings and with my own hearing problems. For this reason I scheduled an interview with Jeff after I had interviewed the other members of the family (except for Janet whose reaction to Jeff's interview I wanted.) I was concerned that I would not be able to understand him sufficiently to have a valuable interview, so I wanted to have as much background as I could to help me understand what he would say.

At the appointed time, I met with Jeff in the atrium at the family compound. Shirley and Brice were there. The first thing I realized was that without the din of background noise that exists at parties, that in the relative quiet of the atrium, with concentration, I could understand most of what he said.

The story of Jeffrey Phillips was and is extremely difficult to write. The impact he has had on the writer, colors, as it should, the interview and comments that follow. In some small way my contacts with him during the writing of this book became a mini-story of us. The reaction between us. His acceptance of his life, his understanding of my difficulty in understanding his speech, his helping me to understand him, when in truth he easily understood me, his obvious mental completeness, all of it combined to make Jeff, as Shirley puts it, "a special person" to me. At the conclusion of our interviews I knew I had been blessed by being permitted to see into a serenity that God, or nature, gives to few people. He is not only "special", he is exceptional. He is, as Janet says, a gift for all of us. Here is that gift.

> Jeff: The first thing I remember when I awakened was that I was trying to figure things out. I was trying to understand, because I didn't know what had happened. There wasn't any real physical damage. I had all my limbs and I had no big cuts on me. So I was okay. I thought I was okay. I couldn't understand what I was doing sitting there in a bed in front of people. I was talking [he thought he was talking but at first he wasn't] and they couldn't understand me. I thought something must be wrong with them. They weren't responding. They didn't know what I was doing. It was as if I was living on a distant planet, and I didn't know what had happened. But, all these people who were so close to me, that loved me, were

there whether they could understand me or not. [After a while] I figured they knew what I was trying to talk about.

. . . .It was so odd that I had this crash up in a place where I knew no one and no one knew me and it was as if [I was one of their own]. That's why I'm so grateful to Doctor Schaffer and all those people from up there who were so instrumental in my recovery. I'm so thankful. I'll never forget what I was trying to say [to them].You talk in the same language you've used all your life, but people can't understand you. It was frustrating because you are saying what's on your mind. I understood myself clearly and was communicating with them. [Jeff could not understand why they weren't hearing him].

I was, I am talking, Judge, just as if you hear it the way I hear it when I talk. I hear myself without any impediment. What I say to you is very clear and simple. I know you don't hear it with the same clearness. But, I do.

[Question by me.] In other words you hear yourself talking exactly as I hear myself talk?

Yes sir. Judge, I know it doesn't turn out exactly that way, because it took me a year of talking at this level for even my folks to understand me, but I understood myself clearly all the time. And I was trying to communicate with them.

[Question by me.] You wondered what was wrong with their ears? Their hearing?

Exactly. It's what I was trying to figure out lying in the hospital bed when I woke up, because I knew there was nothing wrong with me. My mind was normal. I felt good.

[Statement by me.] You must of been saying to your parents, 'Look, it's not me. It's you.'?

You're right.

I then began to discuss his rehabilitation efforts at the Institute in New York. He responded,

> To me, I remember thinking at the time that it was very bad. I was going through a hospital and that was understandable. That was good. But I wondered why I was in that hospital that I thought was for people with different problems, people that needed it. For instance, I was in a room with four people in it, and it was a zoo. One boy had his arms cut off, one guy had been run over by a train and he had no legs. I had all my arms and legs. I didn't know why I was in that part of the hospital.
>
> It really frustrated me because as a boy growing up I was the type of guy who always tried to do things for myself, making my own decisions and making things work on my own.

[Question by me.] It was frustrating because you are the type of person who wants to do things your own way, but you were being handicapped . . . . because other people had to make your decisions for you?

> You have an innate understanding of my feeling during that period of my life. That was a character trait [making one's own decisions] that I got mainly from these two people [gesturing to Brice and Shirley]. But they had to be the ones to make the decisions back then, because there were no others [during my coma and rehabilitation]; my brother couldn't be with me very much because he was running the family businesses while the rest of us were in New York.

[Statement and question by me.] In one of your father's last letters from Europe to your mother in World War II, he foresaw that the seafood industry was going to have to change, so he and your mother changed it. I get the impression that you think similarly about things. You have your share of ambition, certainly your share of brains?

*I have everything that I used to have, it's just that the gear is different. The gear is different now from what it was in 1971.*

[Question by me.] You arrived at the point where you began to finish your rehabilitation on your own?

Yes. People should always rehabilitate themselves if they know how, if they know what to do.

[Question by me.] What do you think was most important in your rehabilitation process? What was your strongest personal characteristic? Was it that you were stubborn?

Please don't use the word stubborn. Persistence is it. Exactly. That's what I was. I will be persistent until my last breath. There's no other word that fits, that I can give you to explain it. Honestly. I know what it's like when you are on your last breath. I am so thankful for the experience I've had. Thank God it's all over and I came out on top. I enjoy living and look forward to each and every day.

[Question by me.] What would be your goals for everyone's children, not just yours?

My first goal for everybody in living, in growing up, is to be happy. To want your children to be happy. Whether it's in your play, your work, your life - be happy. That's the number one consideration in life.

[Question by me.] When you can't reach that goal because of a tragedy, what do you do?

*You have made the mistake of saying that you cannot have the same goals because of a tragedy. That's a mistake!* I always believed, even after the accident, that I could attain my goals quite easily if I was smart enough and wise enough - and lucky.

It doesn't have to be a bad thing at all. It's easy - just be happy. In life, it's the most important thing for anybody.

[Question by me.] I think your perceive yourself as a happy man?

Thank you for saying that. I sure try to be.

[Question by me.] What does the future hold for you, for Janet, the children, your parents, this family?

That could go on for volumes. [Interestingly] shortly after the crash while I was still in a hospital, I remember having a dream about Phillips opening a restaurant in a space station, orbiting the earth. I was in the space station and looked around and there was a sign. It said "Phillips Crab House."

[Question by me.] Anything else you want to say?

Before my accident, my main hobby was surfing. But my earliest real involvement was in the family business, and all the different jobs I did there. But the one I managed to claim for my own was the carry-out business at the Crab House and that was very special to me. We had a carry-out from the inception of the business.

I love the Beach Plaza. We bought it in 1966 and started operating it in 1967. From the very start, I was happy with having it as well as the restaurants. I was so lucky because I had a choice. I could have remained with the Crab House, the most important business at the time. But from the day we bought the hotel I was very happy that it was ours. I love the Beach Plaza.

Then my brother has the tremendous seafood business he has built from scratch. A great accomplishment.

I have four children. Three boys, Jeff Phillips [who is the soup chef at the Crab House], Hugh Phillips, who you met at the hotel. He managed it for two years - he and Joseph

> are surfers, like I used to be. Joseph Phillips works at the Beach Plaza, and then there is my little angel, Carmen, who is away in college in Maine [Carmen, like her father was, is an accomplished pianist, and as can be seen from the beginning of the book, a poet. In addition to the poem she wrote when she was only twelve or so, at the age of ten she wrote, illustrated, and published the children's book, *Cleocatra,* about a cat.] They are so special. All of them. I don't want to be egotistical and I hope you know I'm not that way, but I am so proud of my family. So naturally, I named my first son Jeffrey Phillips, II, because I want him to have at least as good a life as I've had. And Jeffrey the III will be on the way soon [Jeffery II was engaged to be married at the time of the interview.] Hugh and Joseph are my surfing dudes, just the best guys ever.

[Question by me.] Hugh and Joseph follow in your footsteps in more ways than one, then?

I am blessed that you would credit me with the ability to surf. I was really a beginning surfer [before the accident but a wonderful] beginning surfer.

Then God has given me my wife, my Janet. She is the perfect person.

[Question by me.] What makes you angry?

Sir, there's nothing that makes me mad down inside, because it doesn't do any good.

Jeffery Phillips is indeed, 'all in there', a complete and happy man. Each day he teaches us all a lesson. Persistence, determination, happiness, a guy living life to its fullest. His story is an inspiration, a celebration, an affirmance of the power of will.

# CHAPTER THIRTY-SIX

*Loyalty returned*

By the late 60s and early 70s the Phillips had realized that their concept of what makes a business special, includes, in large part, creating employee loyalty, a sense of family. They had done everything they could to emphasize the importance of loyalty. It had always been stressed as a two-way street, and, once success was assured, they were looking for ways to repay the amazing dedication many of their employees had exhibited to make the Crab House the success that it had become. They began to put together for their year-round, permanent employees programs that would address the welfare of their workers. The first steps had been their commitment to promote from within whenever possible, and in the process they created a cadre of experienced young people thirsting for a career in the restaurant business. Employees wanting to make the ride up the ladder that Brice, Shirley, and the boys, were just beginning to climb. Now, the time had come for the Phillips to do more.

They began something that had not yet been done, especially in the hospitality industry, and especially in Ocean City. They developed a profit-sharing plan, as Shirley says, "To reward the employees; to return loyalty." As explained by a member of management,

> When they [Shirley and Brice] first started they had meager resources. They just didn't have much. They were

> very humble people, and still are in spite of their success. They give a lot of credit for their success to the hundreds of thousands, if not millions, of satisfied customers, and to the loyalty of their employees; the two groups of people they have always considered family. Summer employees tended to return year after year, other employees stayed with the business for periods unheard of at that time, or even now, in the restaurant business. Customers came back year after year.
>
> We now have scores of twenty year plus employees, which is very unusual in the restaurant business. Back in the late seventies or early eighties, Brice and Shirley were looking around, trying to find a way to reward the long-time employees by looking to their future. They came up with a profit sharing plan, originally fully funded completely by the Phillips (as costs rose it later became funded on a 50/50 basis with the employee's contributions returnable if he left the company before vesting.) It was designed to be a retirement plan for the employees and it was well ahead of its time.

It was available to any returning employee that had worked at least a 1000 hours in the preceding calender year. As originally conceived, an employee became fully vested after ten years of employment, later it was changed to seven years for vesting. The contributions by the Phillips to each employee's plan was based upon the salary of the employee. There are employees that have become wealthy because of the profit-sharing plan. Even some millionaires.

Semore Dofflemyer notes,

> They have been exceptionally generous with employees. We have a great profit-sharing plan. I'm wealthy because of it, and so are others. And I started out as a cook. It's been great for employees. Some don't fully understand it, but, for the ones that do, it's been fantastic. Whenever I leave here, if I ever do, I don't have to worry. I will be able to take care of myself. It's been a big benefit and a relief.

> I've been able to buy a place in Florida because I have worked in this operation. I spend time there every winter after the Crab House closes. I can take vacations; I do take them.
>
> There's probably no restaurant in the United States that has treated its employees any better. Not many restaurants, if any, do anything like what is done here. With all the programs. With what Brice and Shirley do.
>
> If someone in the community really needs something, they are the first ones there. But they don't want to talk about it. They do it all the time, but won't tell any one that they're doing it. A church burns down, a civic organization needs a new carpet, storm damage, all of it they help with, sometimes do it all. Charity parties are going on all the time in the restaurants. Then there's the church thing every year.[26] Much more. They simply want to be nice to the people that work for them, give to their community.

Brice and Shirley advise that the profit-sharing plan fund is now managed by professional managers, and that, "Its been one of the secrets to the loyalty we get from most of our employees. Loyalty is a two-way street. The plan is part of how we respond to our great employees." "We want to repay the people that helped us."

In addition to the profit-sharing plan, at about the same time they created a term life insurance plan for long-time employees, with the same 1000 hour eligibility requirement. Phillips pays one hundred percent of the premiums. There is maximum coverage of $50,000 based upon the salary levels of the particular employee. It lasts as long as the particular employee remains with Phillips, but can be carried away by the employee if he leaves employment, albeit he becomes responsible for his premiums in that event.

Brice and Shirley had seen incidents involving employees who had died and their families become almost destitute overnight. The term insurance was a way to help, to repay the deceased employee by having a fund available to help the family over the most difficult time.

[26] The "church thing" is a fund-raiser. It is further explained in Chapter 56 *Giving*.

Even now, if Brice and Shirley learn in time of an employee's or former long-term employee's death, a Phillips' vehicle often pulls up at the church hall, or the home of the deceased, with a load of Phillips' food for the reception. Paul Wall remembers a particular employee who died.

> If there has been an employee who has died, the Phillips family always tries to send food to the family during the viewing and the funeral reception. A case comes to mind. The employee had come to Phillips right after he got out of the army and worked for the company until he died years later. He was a chef; became a great chef. He had been a godsend when he 'd been hired. He had taken a lot of the responsibility off of Semore over the years. He died, and the Phillips took care of the food for that period. They do it all the time, and not only for employees. Sometimes for people not a part of the Phillips family of employees.

Dr. Robbins remembers the death of the long time employee and much beloved cook, Jack O'Hara.

> When Jack O'Hara died, it was like Brice and Shirley and the boys had lost a member of their family. It was that way for the employees, too. Steve was visibly shaken by his death. He went into the kitchen and gathered up all of Jack O'Hara's cutlery, had all of it sharpened, and before they closed the lid of the casket, placed it inside the casket with his body."

They also obtained a contributing health insurance plan for employees and their families, in which Phillips contributes part of the premium and the employee the other part. As costs of health insurance rise it is a struggle to keep the insurance, but they've managed to do it.

Later, wanting to make sure their giving will extend after their death, they created a charitable foundation.

Then there is present recognition. Paul McKinley describes the concept of the "President's Cup,"

> Steve had begun the practice for the restaurants on the western shore, and the Phillips brought the concept to the Ocean City operations. Once each year awards banquets are held in the respective venues to honor employees who are paid by the hour. It does not include supervisors and the like. Each department nominates its best hourly employees, and from them as many as 30 or 35 employees are selected for awards. A special dinner is prepared for them and their families, there are speeches from, as one of the higher ups himself puts it, "the high level muckedy-mucks", awards are presented and mementos handed out.

They have many other ways of showing their appreciation, not the least the expressions of their direct concern about the health of their employee. Their reaction to Paul Walls' illness is just one example. Semore was ill, in the hospital for several days not long ago. When he looked up there were Brice and Shirley at his bed side. Paul McKinley's step-daughter became ill with a form of cancer. Off she went to John's Hopkins, with Brice and Shirley giving the full use of their Baltimore home to Paul for the weeks-long duration of his daughter's illness.

Jay Newcomb, the manager of their packing plant operations on Hoopers Island (more about him later,) and a restauranteur on the side, came down with cancer while managing the packing plant. He explains:

> In around 1992 or 1993 I started noticing I was having some problems with lymph nodes. I had previously had them checked but been given a clean bill of health. That previous time I had been hit on the head with a thrown bottle and when I was in the hospital getting sewed up the doctor had noticed a lump in my throat. Not wanting to leave scars, the doctors took a bunch of lymph nodes the size of a mound of grapes out from under my arm. They were checked and everything came back fine.
>
> But then another growth came under my arm and I felt bad and was running a high fever. The surgeons took it out and

it tested positive for Hodgkin's disease. That was about 1993 or 1994. After seeing a doctor in Cambridge and not being satisfied with the way he perceived the urgency of my situation, I called Brice and Shirley to tell them of my illness.

Mrs. Phillips was on the Board of the University of Maryland Hospital at the time and knew all the top doctors in Baltimore. She told me right away, 'Jay, you need to go to Baltimore. I'll see what I can do for you up there.' She called up one of the top people up there, Dr. Rappaport, and within a half-hour he was on the phone with me, he told me right then, 'I want you up here tonight!' I didn't make it that evening, but was up there the next day. He put me through a bunch of tests, every test they had I think.

They found some enlarged glands and found out that my spleen had to be removed, and they did it, took it out. Then they scheduled me for radiation treatments, once a day for 42 days. Except for two days, I was able to drive myself. Eventually the doctors told me that while 'We can never give you a guarantee, we can say there's a ninety-three percent probability that we've put it in remission.'

It was a great hospital and Dr. Will, who ended up as my cancer doctor was great. She even came down to the island for lunch one day, just to visit me.

Through it all Brice and Shirley were opened armed with me. Always wanting to make sure I had everything I needed. They set up everything in Baltimore for me. Told me to take off work, but through it all I only had to take off two or three days once I got out of the hospital after the operation. They were always calling to check that I had transportation to the hospital, asking me if I needed any extra money. That I'd have my salary no matter what. They just kept wanting to know what they could do for me.

Later in the same interview Mr. Newcomb again shared with me his feelings about the Phillips.

Brice and Shirley are two remarkable people. I'm proud of them. They treat me like a son. Anything I ever needed they take care of it. I don't care how busy either of them are, they come to the phone when I call. They are constantly calling to see how I am, if I need anything. I don't know how they have kept up with so much over the years. They are both just down-home Hoopers Island people. They will never change. Wherever they are they're still talking about Hoopers Island. They'll always be coming home.

Dr. Robbins remembers an incident in the 70s.

When someone got hurt, the first thing that was done was to get them to the nearest health care facility. Brice and Shirley never worried about the costs, about insurance, about paperwork, it was just get them where they could be helped as fast as possible. We'll worry about the rest of the stuff later. One day Tommy Collins [now a prominent Ocean City businessman] lit one of the gas stoves. Everyone was always told, you light the match first, then turn on the gas. Tommy reversed it. In short order he was absent his eyebrows and his hair was on fire. Right away it was off to Dr. Townsend's office. No paper work, no questions. Just go. They really took care of the employees.

It's how you treat people. That's why they're so successful. Customers, employees, and even purveyors. They are as loyal as it gets. Brice and Shirley couldn't change if they wanted to. It's ingrained in them. You don't learn it. You can't go to a Tony Robbins' seminar somewhere and learn it. You have to have it - it has to come from within. It probably has a lot to do with their upbringing on Hoopers Island and the values they were taught. I don't even remember anyone ever getting fired. When people went to work for Shirley and Brice they stayed there.

On July 5$^{th}$ of 2005, as explained by Semore, an employee was injured in a similar flashback while lighting a pilot light on one of the gas stoves, but suffered more serious injuries. There are hundreds of management people that could have seen to the boy, but he was one of their family. It was their responsibility. So they went to make sure he was taken care of. It has never changed. Finally, there is their policy of creating restaurant management careers for their valued employees. It all adds up. Loyalty is a two-way street. Brice and Shirley's inherent belief is that if they look after employees as they want the employees to look after them, their businesses will be successful. Brice still remembers that his father, Captain Ellie, always stressed the golden rule. As Brice restates it, "Always treat people the way you want them to treat you."

# CHAPTER THIRTY-SEVEN

## *The first expansions*

In 1967, Brice and Shirley bought their first hotel, the Beach Plaza hotel at 13th Street on the boardwalk in Ocean City. It was somewhat of a legendary hotel, having been built by one of the great ladies of Ocean City's history, Mrs. Ethel Kelley, the mother of the late Harry Kelley, a Mayor of Ocean City from the late 1960s into the 1980s.

Back then, Ocean City was a unique resort in at least one important way. It was a matriarchal town. Many of the great hotels in the town's early history were built and managed by the women, the wives of fishermen, who, around the turn of the 20th century, had started renting out rooms in their homes to summer tourists while their husbands worked in the offshore pound fishing industry that had evolved on the island. Gradually, they would add more rooms, then build cottages for the tourists, and then over time the matriarchs began to build hotels. As the town grew its northerly boundaries, the matriarchs had begun moving north with the growth of the town.

By the late 50s and early 60s the Beach Plaza was THE hotel on the boardwalk (along with the Commander and one or two others.) Mrs. Kelley had intense pride in her kitchen and her dining room.

Even into the early 1960s the guests dressed for dinner, there would be assigned seatings (usually a first seating around 5:30-6:00 p.m., and a second around 8:00 p.m.) When the hotel guests arrived for a week's vacation, they would be assigned a seating time and a table. They would have the same waiter or waitress for the period of their stay and, generally, would leave a gratuity at the end of the week. Mrs. Kelley continued the gracious dining standards of a prior era, bringing them into the last half of the 1900s.

When Mrs. Kelley died, the business was continued for a number of years by her son, Harry Kelley, who would go on to be one of the more famous mayors of Ocean City. Through all its years, it had been one of the establishments to which the better college students gravitated for summer jobs. They were required to wear uniforms and conform to certain standards. There was a special hostess in the front of the dining room (Mrs. Blanche McCabe,) who was concerned with the well being of the wait staff, the girls particularly. In the early 60's Harry Kelley was in charge of the 'back of the house'. There were rooms available for some of the staff underneath the hotel. (At one point the writer worked at the hotel, painting, and stayed in one of the rooms.) Many of the young people that worked in the dining room or the kitchen came back year after year, until they graduated from college and went on to other careers.

Eventually, Harry Kelley sold the hotel to a lady who continued to operate it, but not with the same style as before. Brice and Shirley came to covet the hotel. Its history and its operation intrigued them. In its recent past, it had been operated somewhat similarly to the way they had begun, and its employees in its heyday had exhibited the type of loyalty to a business that many of the "Phillips Girls and Boys" displayed in respect to the Crab House.

In 1967 or 1968 its then current owner, Mrs Fleming, contacted them through either Ann Showell or Dr. Frank Townsend, or both, and negotiations began. As Brice recalls, there were four or five separate negotiating sessions, with Mrs. Fleming pretending she didn't really want to sell and the Phillips pretending they really didn't want to buy. Eventually, the two positions closed at a figure and the famed Beach Plaza became the "Phillips by the Sea Beach Plaza Hotel and Dining Restaurant."

They relaxed the seating in the restaurant/dining room, going to a regular reservation system rather than a 'seatings' system. At first guests retained the old time 'dressing for dinner' style of dining. Today the dining room is more casual.

Over the next few years the hotel would take on the distinctive traditional decor of Phillips. Collectibles, antiques, Tiffany Lamp Shades, and sewing machine tables were added to the public rooms. The dining room was decorated with red walls and the tints and hues of the decor created a specially colorful, yet gracious, up scale ambience. They would impart to it all the appropriate ideas they had from the Crab House, yet would maintain its special historical style.

Miss Lillie[27] (Shirley's mother) lived and worked at the Beach Plaza. She was an entertainer, playing the piano at the piano bar in the lounge and regaling the upscale customers with stories and song. She continued doing it into her nineties.

Brice and Shirley had bought property 'up north' for a future restaurant site. And Steve wanted to expand. They built a new restaurant in an area where many Phillips' customers had purchased homes, and condominiums. They built it in response to their customer's wishes for a north end Phillips. Diners wouldn't have to drive 'down the beach' for Shirley's crab cakes. It has traditional dining in the front, buffet style dining in the rear.

Shirley describes the next move - the biggest. Shirley and Brice believed it would be the riskiest. Again, it was a move that Steve pushed.

> Our business prospered and our family seemed to have unbounded energy. We began to think about opening restaurants in other areas. Many of our young men and women who had worked summers while they were going to college, would call after they graduated, and ask "Mr. Phillips, do you have any openings in management for me?" We realized that we could open in other areas and have potential managers who knew and understood the Phillips' system

By 1968 the 21st street Crab House had reached its limits. It sat 1400 people in a pinch, 1200 any time, and there was nowhere else

[27] The spelling of Miss Lillie's name is uncertain. Many of the acquaintances of Miss Lillie believe that her name should be spelled 'Lily' or 'Lilly'. I use the spelling, Lillie, because that is the spelling that Captain Ivy used when he wrote his 1945 letter to Shirley. If she was 'Lillie' to her husband, then she is 'Lillie' to the writer.

on the site to expand. In the years since the move to Ocean City in 1956, the Phillips had built a steady and repeat clientele from all over the northeast, especially in the Baltimore area. That area had became one of the largest non-Ocean City customer bases at the Crab House. In addition, many of the 'Phillips Girls' and 'Phillips Boys' who had worked in Ocean City had come from city area families and were now raising their own families. At about the same time Shirley and Brice "began to get people, large numbers of customers, asking us to open a restaurant in Baltimore."

There was one special regular customer at the Crab House, a man who lived in a trailer park when he was in Ocean City. A man who would go on to become a great friend, William Donald Schaefer, then Mayor of Baltimore (later to be Governor and then Comptroller of Maryland.) He was one of the customers asking them to open a restaurant in the city, but he asked them in a very special way.

> Governor Schaefer became friends with us. He was the Mayor of Baltimore back then. He kept pushing for us to open a restaurant up there, a seafood restaurant. Eventually, he put us in touch with Jim Rouse the developer of Harborplace, the new to-be, center piece of the inner harbor redevelopment.

An employee remembers the management discussions about the feasibility of opening a restaurant in the inner harbor.

> The opportunity was presented to the Phillips by Mayor Schaefer and Jim Rouse.
>
> They told the Phillips that in order to make this Harborplace go, 'we need a Phillips. So many of your customers are from Baltimore. They'll come downtown to a Phillips. We need a Phillips as an anchor.' Brice and Shirley were advised against going. Were told by some of their friends, 'The harbor is filthy. Nothing but old dilapidated buildings and warehouses. You'd be out of your minds to build a restaurant up there - to expand to Baltimore. You wouldn't take your children down there on a Sunday afternoon.'

But Mayor Schaefer told them, 'There's going to be more. We're going to build a convention center, an aquarium, all sorts of things. New roads. But we need a Phillips here as an anchor to get people started coming back downtown again. A lot of the existing buildings will be replaced with better buildings.'

Mayor Schaefer and Mr. Rouse kept working. Creating incentives to get the restaurant open as an anchor for the project.

Shirley remembers the mixed emotions of the time.

Many of our friends discouraged us, others favored the idea. But, our love for Baltimore goes way back. When we were courting, Brice lived in Baltimore. When we got married, we first lived in Baltimore. The boys had gone to McDonogh, just north of Baltimore. Steve was for it. No amount of discouragement could hamper our decision. We simply came to want to do it.

For Steve it was a dream come true. He would have his own restaurant to manage. Jeffrey was also very excited about our new location. Semore helped to set up the kitchens, but Steve was the main man. He worked everybody hard to make our opening date, a lot of the work outside in freezing temperatures and winter weather. We scoured Maryland for antiques for the restaurant. It was great fun looking at all the roadside antique shops for fretwork, old barn-side wood, Tiffany lamp shades, and beautiful old Victorian sideboards.

One of the proudest days of my life was opening day. The Park Service provided the final brick, and Jeffrey laid it despite good natured cat-calls from the union workers about him having no union card. And we were open. Steve's baby was under way.

One of the many, many nice things that happened to us during that opening week came from friends in Ocean City, John Dale and Ann Showell. They had purchased the State yacht, the Maryland Lady, and motored to the Inner Harbor and docked it there at the quay directly in front of our new restaurant for us to use. During that final hectic week it was our living quarters and our conference place. That we were able to take periodic breaks during that opening period was a blessing to the family. We set up an office on the yacht, were able to greet many of our old Ocean City customers who were flocking to the new restaurant, were able to hold promotional dinners and entertain.

One evening, Mayor Schaefer, Ms. Snopes, Mr. and Mrs. Rouse, and Mr. And Mrs. de Vito were all aboard the boat. As we were standing on the top deck looking out over all the thousands of people on the promenade, Mayor Schaefer, said, with tears in his eyes, 'Just look at all the Marylanders out there. They're all types, all races, and every one of them is having a good time. This is a dream come true for Baltimore.'

For the opening day many of the key members of the Crab House went to Baltimore to help make it a smooth transition. Paul Wall was one of them and remembers vividly that opening day.

When the restaurant opened lines formed that were almost out of sight. We wondered how in the world we were going to handle the crowds. But we did. The restaurant stayed open way later than had been planned, until the a.m. hours of the next morning to make sure everyone was served. We had a carry-out as well as a restaurant and it was all we could do to take care of everything, but we did. It exceeded everyone's expectations, except perhaps Steve's.

We only had one kitchen at the time and one small office. There was so much money coming in by midnight that I was back in the office stuffing it in paper bags.

It was almost unbelievable how much support the people and officials of Baltimore gave us.

Shirley and Steve had trained the wait staff. Made sure they were dressed the same as they dressed in Ocean City. They did the same with decorations. The interiors were very similar, sewing machine tables, Tiffany style lamp shades, and all. The Phillips brought the food and the ambiance to Baltimore. And it worked.

It was like a marriage - Ocean City and Baltimore. The Baltimoreans came to Phillips. They came downtown as Schaefer said they would. Schaefer kept his promises. He rejuvenated downtown Baltimore.

All doing that opening day Schaefer was everywhere, mingling. He'd come in and talk to the customers. He would be outside mingling. He was the Host of Baltimore, as well as its mayor. You knew it when he was around. Rouse was a great gentleman, as well. He was there. In manner he was a lot like Brice. He was a visionary, too. Schaefer, Brice, Rouse, and now Steve, they're all visionaries.

Schaefer knew in his mind what he wanted for Baltimore. And he got it.

Semore remembers that time.

The first day that Harborplace opened, I don't think I ever saw so many people in my life. They just kept coming, and coming, and coming. We had so many customers, and they were all spending so much money, that we'd have to go around to the various cashier stations in the Phillips' venues with a duffle bag to put the money in. Then we'd take it back to the office and dump it on Paul Wall's desk, and pretty soon he was stuffing it in paper bags.

The people never stopped. We stayed open from one morning to early in the next morning to get all the customers taken care of.  Governor Schaefer, I know he was the Mayor then, but everybody at Phillips still calls him Governor. Anyway, he came over and was getting a soft-drink, when he said to me, 'I've never seen this many people in one place downtown in my life.' It was really exciting. It was our first venture away from Ocean City and it obviously was going to be a great success story, and it is.

Shirley had put her touches in, Brice had put his in, but Steve was the one who really got it all going. He was great. He had taken on most of the responsibility for day to day decisions. He was great. He really led us. If something happened, something broke down, he knew right where to go to fix it, because he'd probably helped install it; and he could fix almost anything.

After those of us from the Crab House who had gone up to help get the restaurant opened had returned to the Crab House, the success of the Harborplace Restaurant just kept on. They were so busy that first year that they couldn't keep up with making crab cakes, which was part of their signature dishes. We were called on to help out, and our prep room in addition to preparing the crab dishes for the Crab House, started making and sending 6 or 7 thousand crab cakes a day to Harborplace on refrigerated trucks.

It was really fun.

The Phillips sum it up.

We have never regretted a single day of our expansion to the Baltimore market. It was great.

The family's thirst for expansion, for growth to be managed by the hundreds of former 'Phillips Girls' and 'Phillips Boys" had yet to be assuaged. A restaurant, the Flagship, was waiting in Washington, D.C. for someone like the Phillips to revitalize it. It had been a family run business on the waterfront for years.

It had been operated by two sisters and their husbands. The husbands had died and it was becoming too much for the sisters to manage. After a series of negotiating sessions, it was purchased. At the same time the management of the western shore restaurants was turned over to Steve to operate.

Steve had told Brice that the new Washington restaurant needed interior modifications. Brice and Shirley turned the remodeling project over to him; it was his restaurant to manage.

When Brice next visited the site there was nothing of the old restaurant standing, except the exterior walls. The old interior had clearly been modified. It was gone, completely gutted. Steve told Brice, "I told you there were going to be some interior modifications." When I asked Brice if it happened that way, he answered "That's exactly right." Shirley said "He sure did." Steve has a way of getting things done. He just does them. Just like his father - like his mother.

In any event, the Washington restaurant opened. There were a few opening period glitches, but Brice and Steve put their heads together and decided to "just be Phillips - lets not try to be anything else." It worked. It was an overnight success. Steve later turned it into an all buffet restaurant, and it's continued to boom ever since. The buffet style of dining would be imported back to the Crab House where it was equally successful.

Paul Wall remembers the period of the opening of the Baltimore and Washington operations.

> By that time Steve was taking a much more active role in the decision-making process. He was becoming a dominating force, in a constructive way, in the management decisions of all the operations. The great business sense of his father and mother was showing up in him, with a lot of additional vision and willingness to take risks. From this point on, Steve took over most of the operations, all of them across the bay. I help when he needs me.

Then there came the Norfolk and the Annapolis restaurants, and more recently the Myrtle Beach restaurant. Another is being developed in Atlantic City, and Steve has started a new group of smaller restaurants, and there are Phillips' operations being started in several major airports. All of them were built on the back of the mighty crab.

Today, the restaurants combined (the Norfolk restaurant no longer operates) seat almost 7 thousand people at one time. On a busy three day weekend they will serve over 30,000 customers. In a year Harborplace will serve over 410,000 customers, the Crab House over 285,000 people, North Ocean City over 165,000 people and the Phillips Flagship over 400,000. Over a million, two hundred thousand customers served in a year, not counting the Annapolis, Myrtle Beach, Rockville, the soon to be opened Atlantic City restaurants and the

Phillips' facilities in airports. During exceptionally busy periods the restaurants will gross almost $360,000.00 - per day. That is a lot of crab.

# CHAPTER THIRTY-EIGHT

## *A. E. Phillips & Son, Hoopers Island - 1987-2005*
## *Jay Newcomb, manager*

In early 1987, Tony Shockley, manager of the Phillips' packing plant on Hoopers Island, told Brice of his plans to retire (Tony's father, Charles Shockley had been the manager before him.) Tony's wife Debbie also was working at the plant. Jay Newcomb was a local man buying crabs for another businessman (Jay Newcomb attaches a caveat to the local characterization. He says that to true Hoopers Islanders he's still an outsider because he lives in Golden Hill on the wrong side of the Hoopers Island bridge.) Tony Shockley approached Jay, apparently having told Brice and Shirley of him, and asked Jay to go with him to Ocean City to meet the Phillips. Brice remembers that both Tony Shockley and Dave Flowers recommended Jay as a new manager.

When Jay met Brice and Shirley, they offered him the management job, he accepted, and as he puts it, "I've been here ever since - 18 years." He notes about that interview with Brice and Shirley:

> It was the first time I ever met the man. He's the same today. Just a down to earth man, smart, intelligent, a business man. He is remarkable. He's very successful and it hasn't gone to his head. He just sits down and carries on conversations just like everybody else. In some respects he's a man of the world

now, but when you sit down to talk to him he's a Hoopers Island man.

I have liked him every day since. At the interview we talked about the business, talked about crabs in general. I told him I'd been driving a truck for Mr. Parks and buying crabs for him. I told him I didn't know much about managing a crab picking plant. He hired me anyway.

The Shockleys helped break Jay in and, except for when Steve shanghais him to go looking for the ultimate crab, he's been managing A. E. Phillips and Son ever since. He has a great understanding of the relatively recent problems in the industry, seen from a waterman's, a packer's. and a restauranteur's perspectives. He has thought a lot about the crabbing industry, and has, in some ways been a pioneer himself.

When I started here we had plenty of crab. Some days we had so many crabs we just couldn't buy them because we couldn't pick them. Back then we had one crabber come in one day with 201 bushels of crab. We had two pickers. In those days we had buses running into Cambridge for pickers. Even then we had so many crabs we couldn't get enough pickers to pick the crabs. Sometimes we'd run two shifts.

When we still had plenty of crab, it began to be harder and harder to get pickers. This is a pretty remote island to begin with, then a lot of the people started retiring. The restaurants were yelling and hollering that they wanted crab meat and I had crab but couldn't get them picked. Ten years or more ago the watermen worked on the water and their wives picked crab while their husbands were on the water. But a lot of the older guys retired or died off.

Then a lot of the local residents began moving out as they were bought out by people looking for vacation homes on the water. And vacationers aren't interested in picking crab. The island has changed to second homes and they don't generate people looking to be crab pickers in a packing house.

At that time we could have hired 24 pickers but we couldn't get them. We had job fairs, we ran ads in newspapers. We went to Baltimore and Washington, offering jobs, trying to get pickers. When we'd hire someone up there, for whatever reason, they would never show up on Hooper's Island. That's when I went to the foreign worker program. It's fair to say I had no choice. It was find pickers or close.

I talked to some people in the Carolinas who were using workers from Mexico in agriculture. I found out the name of a recruiter that was used by the Carolinians. I got up with her and told her that it just made sense, if she was recruiting men to come up to work in agriculture, she should be able to find women who wanted to work, and that I could train them and use them.

It started with just a few at first. The first year was a little rough. That first year she had recruited from areas near the border and they weren't the right people. Then she started recruiting from further south in Mexico.

The foreign workers were also a big change for Hoopers Islanders, as well. Until then we'd always used local pickers. We'd been a very local community. The Hoopers Island people thought what I was doing was going to change the island. That there would be problems. It was hard for everybody to get used to it.

Steve remembers the time,

If we hadn't used the Mexican program we couldn't have picked the crab. And we were really criticized down on Hoopers Island when we started using the Mexican workers' program. We were threatened. Jay's life was threatened. We got threats that the plant would be burned down. Sometimes I think that we're so close to the crab we get like him. Have a crab mentality. If one crab is trying to crawl out of a basket to get away, the other crabs grab him and pull him back.

We told the people opposed to it, 'Look, who's going to buy your crab meat if you can't get the crab picked.'

Jay continues:

"A lot of people here were right upset. A couple of the other plants said they'd close their doors before they used foreign workers. They said it until they were at the point of closing their doors, then they started using foreign workers. All of the plants that objected when A. E. Phillips and Son started using the workers, are all using the same workers today. Or they're out of business. Nobody else will pick anymore. Now, with the foreign workers it's not the problem it was.

Steve comments: "You can't complain we're taking American jobs. Americans won't take the jobs anyway. Now the only people that will pick American crab are the workers from Mexico." Jay explains the beginning of the practice,

> When the foreign workers first came up here they had never seen a crab before. It took them a while to get it down. Now they've got it and are good pickers.
>
> I was the first one to use them. It was two years before the rest started coming aboard because they couldn't find local pickers.
>
> There was such a high demand for crab meat that we had to get the foreign workers. The Phillips Crab House was using several hundred pounds of crab meat a day.
>
> Foreign workers started out with just single workers from different families. But now its gone to where we have different workers coming from the same families. We have one lady that's been coming for ten or eleven years. She comes back every year. Lots of the women have been here for five or seven years. One worker who has been here a long time, has had two of her sisters here, two of her brothers working in the steaming room. Another family that started with us with the mother, has seen her daughter, her daughter-in-law, and her other daughter come to work here, and today her two sons are working in the steam room. Over time it has become families.

Now I don't use recruiters anymore. I learned enough that I do it myself. Recruiters don't cost us money, but they charge the foreign workers. By not using recruiters I save the workers money. I just do all the paper work myself, contact the Consulate in Monterey that handles the program and send the information down. There is no law saying you have to use recruiters, so I don't use them and the workers save money. I know most of them from the years before, I don't need anybody to help me find them. A lot of the people in the state get me to help them with the paperwork. I've done so much of it I have it down.

When we first started, the first several months, we housed workers in a motel in Cambridge. We had some quarters atop the crab house, so when we did the renovations we said 'Lets change the upstairs.' We got a permit, and made worker's housing on the second floor. Worker's dormitories. We still didn't have enough room and we'd rent what houses we could, but pretty soon everything was getting sold to summer people. That's when we also started using Brice and Shirley's apartment for housing.

Now we're building the Phillips a small apartment overtop the cooler right alongside the Honga. Mr. Phillips wants a place to be able to come home to - to come home to Hoopers Island and spend the night. Hopefully it will be ready by late fall.

We've had very few problems. After the picking is over for the day you'll see the pickers walking, seeing what Hoopers Island is like, they fish some. But mostly they work and generally rest a lot. They all go to Catholic mass once a week. Save their money for the winter. They've been a godsend.

After the crab picking problems were solved with the use of foreign workers, the supply of crabs then became the problem. Over time there was a drastic reduction in their numbers. Jay surmises;

It's a lot of reasons probably. About the only thing it's not is the rockfish. We used to have loads of rockfish at the same time we had loads of crabs. It was that way for years. Fish and crabs, no problems. So when some says it's the abundance of rock, I don't buy it.[28]

The peeler potting (Jimmy potting) has changed everything. They put a male in the smaller pot to attract female crabs and loads of them go in. Most have never mated, never been sponged, never laid eggs. Never produced any crabs

[28] Whether there is a correlation between the populations of rock (striped bass) and crab populations is still an open question for watermen and scientists. I have examined the commercial catch records of both species from the years 1963 to 1997 (the last year for which landings are included in the study *A Historical Background for Striped Bass Landings in Maryland 1928-1998.)* I have selected from those years the five highest landings years and the five lowest landing years for striped bass in Maryland. Then from the Maryland Department of Natural Resources, *Annual Commercial Hard Blue Crab Landings - Chesapeake Bay Region,* reports, I have extracted the hard crab landings for the years following the highest and lowest landing years for striped bass. Over the period the average yearly landing of striped bass was 2,189,840 pounds, the average yearly landing of hard crabs was 32,829,246 pounds. The comparisons follow:

| Highest striped bass catches | Next year's crab catch |
|---|---|
| #1. 1969 - 5,088,200 lbs | 1970 - 24,935,400 lbs |
| #2. 1973 - 4,975,900 | 1974 - 24,660,300 |
| #3. 1968 - 4,453,200 | 1969 - 23,013,900 |
| #4. 1967 - 4,150,200 | 1968 - 9,345,000 |
| #5. 1970 - 3,997,500 | 1971 - 26,075,000 |

All of the next year's crab catches were considerably below the average catch when the previous year's striped bass catch was at its highest.

| Lowest striped bass catches | Next year's crab catch |
|---|---|
| #1. 1990 - 42,486 lbs | 1991 - 45,750,632 lbs |
| #2. 1991 - 151,389 | 1992 - 29,654,788 |
| #3. 1983 - 445,589 | 1984 - 46,801,878 |
| #4. 1982 - 518,215 | 1983 - 47,583,968 |
| #5. 1992 - 609,257 | 1993 - 54,997,934 |

All but one of the next year's crab catches were considerably above the average catch when the previous year's striped bass catch was at its lowest.

Throughout the book, when discussing the landings of crab in pounds, I am referring to the poundage of live crabs, not pounds of crab meat.

of their own. They are going in the pots for the most part for the first mating with a male crab. Then they're caught. You're only catching that one crab, and you can only catch her once. If they catch all the peelers before they get a chance to mate, then you get only the one crab - you don't get her offspring.

Years ago when the Japanese got into the soft crab business, there was so much demand, a crabber could get 75 or 80 cents for a little old peeler to be shed-out for the Japanese market. You could only get maybe fifty dollars a bushel for regular crabs, so most of the crabbers went to peeler potting. Did it for the money. It's hard to blame them.

When they catch tens of thousands of these small crabs, they don't have a chance to grow up and reproduce. That's also why we don't have many big males around any more, not as many as we used to have. They're catching them when they're small. Jumbos used to be 6 inch crabs, now they're 5 inches and up.

A male crab has to be at least 5 inches, a soft-crab 3 ½ inches, but a peeler only has to be three inches. The size for immature females also has to be 5 inches, if it's not you're supposed to throw it back until it's a mature female. There is no minimum size on a mature female, because once they are mature they stop growing bigger. A mature female, we also call them 'Bitch Crabs' or V8 crabs, have a full apron, one that is in a V shape. Immature females' aprons aren't full. They're narrower.

Another serious problem is the winter dredging of the crabs down in Virginia where many of them go to winter. The crabs burrow down into the mud before the water gets too cold in order not to freeze. Then the Virginia crabbers pull dredges along the bottom in the winter and dig them up. Virginia says they don't get enough to really hurt the population. But its not what they land that's the problem. They only land a small portion of what is scraped up. When the bottom is torn up the crabs go everywhere, blown or pushed aside everywhere and only a small portion of them end up on the crabbers' boats. But every crab forced out of the bottom freezes and dies because he is too lethargic from the cold to dig himself back into the mud. They kill a lot more crabs than they catch.

Another thing is some people keep sponge crabs (crabs with eggs.) We won't buy sponge crabs [she-crab soup is made from sponge crabs.] We're allowed to, but we don't do it. We also work real hard to keep undersized crabs out of the plant.

Up north they tell me there's lots more private pots, than there is down here. That could be a problem with just too many pots. Usually, the crabs are bigger the further north you go in the bay.

Then there's hydraulic pullers. In the old days pots were pulled by hand which meant they were fished in shallower water for the most part because it was a job to get them up from deeper water. With hydraulic pullers you can pot in deeper water and fish a lot more pots because they get to the boat faster. Sometimes if they are in deep water, some crabbers will use strings of pots. You couldn't do that when they had to be hauled by hand. If a crabber has two helpers, he can legally set as many as 900 pots from one boat. But, at the same time it takes a lot more pots nowadays for a crabber to catch enough crabs to meet his expenses. Again, you can't blame the crabber, he has to do it, or get in some other line of work. He can't make a living otherwise.

Another change is the conversion of crabbing from trot-lines to pots. Trot-lining can't be done right in as deep a water as crab-pots can be 'fished' and was generally done in the shallower waters of the rivers and the shallower parts of the little bays. Trot-lining is better in areas where there are grasses, mostly in the rivers and smaller bays. It might have been done some in the shallows of the big bay in the old days, but not in the deeper water. The bottom is different in the big bay, where it's deep, and there's lots of debris for the lines to snag on. Trot-lining is still done, but only in the rivers. By law, pots are not supposed to be set in rivers. Trot-lining is way off down here from what it used to be. Aren't as many of the old guys in the smaller boats that used to do it .

> With the advent of potting, there were more pots set out in the deeper water of the bay, opening up what might have been areas free from crabbing before. Potting opened up pressures on crabs in areas where there didn't use to be any pressure.

Other changes in the industry having to do with customer preferences also affected the way the packing plants had to process product in order to stay in business. At the same time pasteurization also changed the way the product could be handled once it was picked. Now the packer could hold product over the winter months, have it available for the restaurants in the spring before the next year's crabbing season began. Now the packer and the restaurants can get through the winters.

Jay explains why a good picker picks 40 or 45 pounds a day now, when a good picker could pick up to a hundred pounds in the old days when Shirley and her sister, Bernice, were picking:

> In the old days when the great pickers could get a hundred pounds, there were larger numbers of big crabs in the picking crabs because there was no live-crab market. Everything, all the crabs were used in the picking - used for crab meat. You can get a lot more meat, easier and faster, out of a big crab than you can out of little crabs. Everything, all kinds of crabs, used to be mixed together.
>
> Back then they didn't take out the bigger, fat crabs or the number ones. Everything they caught went into the picking crabs. Now all we pick is the 'trash' crabs [only small crabs not big enough to sell live], the poor [not fat] sooks [female] crabs. Now all the number ones are sold live, all the number twos are sold live, and then the Japanese buy up the larger sooks.
>
> In the old days we used to throw the sooks back because there wasn't any market for them. No one wanted them for picking and no one wanted to buy them live. Now crabbers are 'fishing' as much for the females as the males. So now we're picking what we call the 'trash', it's the poor [not fat] she crabs. Now it's even getting worse with the large number of 'All you can eat,' places. They use the 'trash' crabs because they're cheaper and people can't eat as many of them because

they take longer to pick and the people get tired of picking. All that doesn't leave much for the packing houses.

Now there's fewer crabs, fewer crabbers, and more of a demand for 'basket crabs' [the larger crabs sold alive to restaurants or alongside the road]. It's hard for a Maryland packing plant to make it. Three more plants have closed down this year.

Steve generally agrees with what Jay says about the shortages of crab products:

We still buy, pick and process as much or more crab meat from Maryland crab as we did before we decided to look for other places with crab. We simply had to find more product to supply our business, or close it down, begin to shut it down instead of growing it. The problem has been a growing demand and a diminishing supply of crab and shell fish over the last thirty years. A perfect example is the oyster shortage. There used to be 450 shucking houses. Now there are two.

The crab shortages have been well documented. We move somewhere between one and 2 million pounds of crabmeat a month through our Baltimore facilities, more than another million a year through our value added plant in Asia. That's much more than eleven times the entire Maryland production of meat in a year [Fifty percent more than the entire annual production of crab meat in the United States.][29]

There are a lot of reasons for the shortages. My parents and Jay have told you most of them. And everybody that works on the bay differs a little on the reasons. . . .

But, another thing that is happening is that crabs are getting smaller. We rarely see the large Wye River crabs we used to see. Some of us wonder if the way we're catching crab

[29] In 2002, the International Trade Commission reported that the entire United States production of processed crab meat had declined from 19 million pounds in 1990 to 10 million pounds in 1998. Since then the production has certainly continued to decrease further - probably drastically. With the ravages of Hurricane Katrina in the center of the Gulf Coast's prime crabbing area, the supply of crabs from the area will, in all probably, decrease even further in the near term.

now results in breeding down-sized crabs. In the way the regular crab pots are required to be built, there are now sleeves for the smaller crabs to leave the pots and the larger crabs can't get out. If the larger and smaller crab are of the same line and year class, and only the smaller crab can get out, over time the smaller crabs' genes might be having a disproportionate effect on the breeding stock. Genetically smaller crabs may be breeding with other genetically smaller crabs and over time a population of smaller crabs takes over, dominates the population. There are scientists looking into it now.

Recreational crabbing has changed and is probably adversely affecting crab populations. Back around the time of the Second World War, recreational crabbers were 'chicken neckers'. They would handline baits from bridges and docks, and dip crabs when they pulled them to the surface. One recreational crabber might have five or six hand-lines affixed up and down a dock, baited with chicken necks when they could get them, hence the name 'chicken neckers'. When they went home they'd take the lines with them, but even if they didn't the lines couldn't kill crabs when no one was there dipping them. If they were left in the water the crabs would just finish off the baits laying on the bottom and move on to do what crabs do.

For both the recreational and the commercial crabber the advent of crab-potting after the war changed everything. But, the commercial crabber would still 'fish' his pots every day, throwing back the smaller crabs, separating the peelers and culling the larger crabs to sell on the live market or the smaller crabs to the picking houses. The commercial waterman's pots were 'fished' each day until the season ended.

The recreational crabber, the former 'chicken necker' was mostly a weekend crabber, meaning he would only 'fish' the pots on the weekends. And it wasn't unusual for the recreational potter to leave the pots overboard from one weekend to the next. The first crabs in would die and then attract more crabs, only for them to die. By the time the pots were 'fished' the next weekend, or a month later, most of the crabs in the pots would be dead. The wastage of crabs was high in the recreational sector once crab pots became available after the war. The wastage was much higher in the recreational side than when they were 'chicken neckers'.

Another problem is that over time the water has been getting cloudier, which reduces the amount of grasses in the bays and rivers; and that's where the young crabs and shedding crabs hide from predators. The cloudiness is probably due to many factors, none really attributable directly to the commercial watermen. Septic system problems as the bay's coastline has been built up, water run off, farming operations, storm drain runoff and -  not the least of the problems - the effluent from the two major river systems that end up in the bay. Another cause is the lack of oysters. There aren't nearly enough to have any impact on straining the water.

Steve talks about possible solutions to the shortage

Science is just beginning to catch up. In the process some old thoughts are going to be changing. One of the laboratories [that Phillips indirectly financially supports by contributing $400,000 to $500,000, or more, to date] has had a female crab that has produced five different egg clusters. It was thought for years that female crabs only had one brood in their lifetime and thus after they had one clutch of eggs, it was ok to take them. That's not necessarily so.

It was also thought that crabs only bred and laid eggs in the wild. That is not so because we have been successful in breeding crabs in the laboratory and bringing the crabs and the eggs to hatching stage. It's been thought that it couldn't be done, but now it has. We've actually been able to bring the young larva crabs to the stage where they are of a size to release into the wild.

Most important is the success rate we've achieved with survival levels. Each time female crabs breed, they produce anywhere between a million, and a million, two hundred thousand eggs, or even more. In the wild, only one or two survive to become mature crabs, and most of the crabs that don't make it are eaten or killed at the very youngest larva stages. We've been able to achieve a survival rate of 70 percent in the laboratory and that means we can release 700,000 or more crabs into the wild from one egg sponge of a female crab and that could drastically increase the numbers of crabs in the bay.

Once they're in the bay they belong to all the creatures in it or on it, including the watermen. We're excited at these scientific successes. They could constitute a major step in re-establishing crab populations throughout the bay's ecosystems.

Jay sums up the attitude that every waterman and packer must have, just to keep doing what they do:

Our crabbing season normally starts on April 1st and lasts until the end of November. The Governor can change the dates. We can usually catch them all through that time, but normally it starts off slow with not many crabs, but in the fall it's usually better. The crabs are bigger and fatter then. By the end of November it's mostly over.

Every year, everybody worries about how good or bad the crabbing season is going to be. Everybody but Mr.[Brice] Phillips. He's the most positive man I've ever met. If the crabbing is poor in the Spring, it's 'Well they're going to get better; we'll have a good Fall.' If it isn't good in the Fall it's, 'Remember how good it was in the Spring.' I don't care what happens, he always talks positive. This year when everybody was talking about the poor spring, he'd call me just to tell me not to worry, that we're 'going to have a good season.' Just yesterday he told me, 'I think we'll have a good Fall.'

The oyster shucking business in the bay area is almost all over. Nobody is commercially shucking. There's no oysters; if there were oysters, there'd be no shuckers. About the only oystering going on is boxed oysters [Live, un-shucked oysters sold in boxes]. The boxed oysters are used privately, and to some extent in raw bars.

The southern states have taken over the shucking business and the market. They have a bigger oyster and a longer season. In respect to live oysters they only charge around fifteen dollars for a hundred pound burlap sack full. Up here we have to charge around at least fifty dollars a bushel. At these prices, we can't compete. Lots of the guys tried buying oysters down there, bringing them up here and shucking them out, but they couldn't make any money at it. Just didn't work economically.

Jay sums up his feelings about the Phillips:

They've never lost the Hoopers Island in them. Brice and Shirley are both proud to be from Hoopers Island, and they'll tell anybody that. They say that A. E. Phillips & Son will always be here [In an interview with Steve, he said, "Hoopers Island will stay open forever."]

# CHAPTER THIRTY-NINE

*Isabel the Jezebel - 2003*

*Jezebel - A shameless, impudent, scheming woman.*

*She wasn't supposed to be bad, not real bad. Just a little wind. Just a little high water. The weather people still advised evacuation, but anymore they talk evacuation with any blow - hoping to make themselves important in the process. They cry wolf so often that after a while no one takes them seriously. No one listens.*

Some of the people on Hoopers Island did evacuate - most of the non-natives were gone by the time the storm arrived at Hoopers Island. But the locals, for them blows and storms are part of life on the islands. Storms came and storms went. Some like the great blow of 1933 were bad, most were not.

The women in the dormitories had made a decision that they wanted to stay and didn't want to evacuate. Jay would stay with them at the plant. They were his to look after. The crab plant was his to look after. Besides, it wasn't supposed to be bad - not bad according to Hoopers Island standards. Jay explains;

> Some people evacuated. But the women and myself, we stayed here. They didn't want to leave. They were upstairs on the second floor over the picking room. We figured that the

water wasn't going to get that high, and it didn't. But, it got higher than I thought it would. We knew we'd have some seas and wind, but nothing like what we got.

I had filled the ice bins with ice while we were waiting for the storm to get here, so we'd have ice for the women's food if the electricity went out. We had brought most of the floats ashore, filled them with water so the wind and seas wouldn't take them. Had put some of them in the building near the big walk-in cooler where the crab meat was kept. Went around and battened down the hatches, so to speak. Tied things down, secured things. Did what we always do in storms. Then waited for it to go on by.

After a bit the wind began to come up out of the southeast, and it kept on coming up. After a bit it was blowing hard. The wind gage across the street registered wind blowing a hundred and twelve miles an hour. The water was coming up and up. I called the storm center, asked them about the storm. They said it would be a while before she'd get to Hoopers Island. I told them, 'You're not in the same place I am, because the storm has already gotten here.'

I knew then we were going to have a long night, but I didn't tell the women because I didn't want them to be scared and we couldn't get off the island anyway. Boats were already floating over the streets. Worrying wouldn't stop anything.

I kept moving around outside in the rising water trying to save things. Made the women stay up on the second floor. The seas started breaking on the water side of some of the buildings and sheds. I could hear things breaking up, walked around the rear of the buildings, on the river side, and as I rounded the corner of the building the seas were hitting me chest high. I braced myself there in the chest high seas and had to watch the sea and the wind take apart the big cooler. I couldn't get to it. It was the one we had all our pasteurized crab meat in. It just busted apart. They found the stainless steel door a quarter mile away up the creek after the storm was over. The crab meat was found as far away as Taylors Island. All of it was lost.

> We lost two or three of our other coolers, all of our shedding floats, lost compressors, and the knock-down coolers we had out back.
>
> The storm ripped up the guardrails on the bridge up the island and almost washed it through there. There was lots of damage to many of the homes on the island, mostly flood damage from rising water. The wind had come up out of the southeast and tore up the east side of the island, then it switched over to blowing out of the southwest and tore up the west side of the island. It got it all.
>
> Most of the watermen's bigger boats had been hauled out before the high winds and seas got here, so there was very little damage to them. And no one was injured on the island. We were very fortunate.[30]

There was, however, extensive damage to A. E. Phillips & Son. And a winter's supply of crab meat was spread about the bay. All together the damage to the plant and product amounted to between $350,000 and $500,000. But like his father before him, like their parents in the old days of the 1933 hurricane, Brice and Shirley began immediately to repair the damage, to make arrangements for product until the next season would mute the ravages of Isabel the Jezebel.

[30] During the hurricane, Jay was able to use his cell phone to contact Doris Lewis, the Dorchester County Register of Wills. She received the last call from Jay Newcomb as Isabel intensified. His last words to her were "I'll call you in the morning if we make it."

# CHAPTER FORTY

## *Demand and supply economics*

The Phillips' restaurants, three in Ocean City, one each in Baltimore, Washington, Annapolis, Rockville, Falls Grove, Silver Spring and one in Myrtle Beach, with combined maximum seating of between 6 thousand and 7 thousand, were now serving as many as thirty thousand customers, or more, on a busy summertime weekend day. Most customers wanted a serving containing crabs, or crab meat in one form or the other. Crab dishes made up 60 per cent of the menu.

With the drastic increases in business, the operations had to deal with severe shortages of crabs and crab meat, even though they were acquiring all of the product from their plant on Hoopers Island, and were buying all the crab products they could obtain from other Chesapeake area producers.

In order to help address that problem, Brice and Shirley had acquired a majority interest from members of the Abbott family in another packing house on Deal Island. Initially, it provided a source of large crabs, but, over time the large crabs diminished to such an extent that crab meat picking became less feasible. However, it was an excellent soft-crab producing facility and still today provides many of the soft-crabs used in the Phillips' restaurants.

But, even with the addition of another packing plant, there simply wasn't enough product to supply the restaurants. Shirley recalls;

Right before we went to Baltimore, and in the first year there, we were still using all of our own product from the plant on Hoopers Island. Then we had to acquire an interest in another packing plant on Deal Island. It still wasn't enough. The demand from the restaurants was for more crabs and crab meat and we were already producing and buying every available pound of Maryland crab meat.

At the same time, the crabs were becoming less plentiful in the Chesapeake. Fewer and fewer crabs. Right when demand was rapidly increasing, the supply was rapidly decreasing. And we were buying all we could buy, but it was a constant battle to find enough crabs and crab meat. We bought them from anywhere in Maryland we could get them. From Virginia. Then we began buying them from the Carolinas, from Texas and Louisiana, and all over. We could never get enough for our customers.

Crabs were getting scarcer for many reasons: less grass caused by pollution; more and more waterfront development eliminating the marshes; the proliferation of private crab pots, killing crabs 24 hours a day.

We started buying product out of state because we were forced to. By February, in our Baltimore and Washington restaurants we were running out of crab product. . . . It became a crisis.

Brice recalls,

Even when Steve was still in Ocean City, Chesapeake crabs and crabmeat had gotten so scarce that, even though we used all of the output of our own plants and bought all the Maryland product we could get from other vendors, it still wasn't enough. We had gone as far as Florida, North Carolina and Texas, looking for product for our Ocean City restaurants. When we opened the Baltimore and Washington operations, we were running out of product around the first of the year. As the businesses grew, so did the crisis in supply. It was at the point where we would have to curtail operations, let alone continue to expand, unless we could find product somewhere else. And we employed over 1800 Marylanders, mostly Marylanders, in our restaurant operations alone. It wasn't just our livelihood, it was theirs as well.

Semore comments that;

We had to get crab meat from somewhere. We couldn't buy enough from Maryland at any price. Brice and Steve were on the phone all the time trying to find crabs and crab meat, to find product. It got really tight, especially when the winter came around.

We' be selling spaghetti now if Steve hadn't found the overseas sources, developed Phillips Foods. We'd be like a steak house without steaks. You'd have to sell something else.

Paul Wall comments on the always increasing shortages of crabs and crab meat.

We supply ourselves with all the product we can produce.[31] We bought from other Maryland vendors. Steve went all over looking for sources, looking for areas where there were sufficient resources to justify constructing plants to economically process the product. He went to North Carolina, Florida, Texas, Louisiana, all over. There simply wasn't enough product available to sustain our then present operations, and certainly insufficient to sustain growth.

Brice and Shirley discuss the product supply problem after the successful opening of the Baltimore and Washington operations.

[31] The A. E. Phillips & Son packing plant produces approximately 100,000 pounds of crab meat a year. About 90% of its production is used in Phillips' restaurants, leaving them around one million, six hundred thousand pounds short of meeting their demand from their own packing plant. (Various sources within the Phillips' operations.)

Each year fewer and fewer crabs were available to us - at any price. . . . Every new waterfront homeowner had to drop a couple of pots off the dock, and they just left them out there 24 hours a day, day after day, killing crabs, most of which never got to the steam pot. Often a weekender would leave his pots in the water during the week, and they'd kill crabs all week long and this was going on all up and down the bay from May through October. Female crabs were being dredged and killed in the winter down in their wintering areas in Virginia. It was everything, really. The pressures on the crabs and the environmental effects gradually diminished the crab populations to the point where it was impossible for Maryland watermen to come anywhere close to meeting the demand of the ever-growing in-state Maryland retail and restaurant markets.

We started buying product out of state because we had to. It was that or stop our growth, and, if we couldn't get product we'd have to eventually retrench our businesses.

Then there a came a year, don't remember which specific year, when we realized we were out of crab meat. And couldn't buy anymore in Maryland. It was only February. It was a scramble the rest of the winter and spring to get product here and there on a hit and miss basis. We didn't know what we were going to do. It was a crisis.

Then, Steve said, 'Dad, we've got to do something. We've got to start looking for another source of crab meat.' In the spring of that year, Steve began to visit all the blue-crab producing states looking for sites where packing plants could economically operate. He went to the sounds behind the Outer Banks, South Carolina, Georgia, Florida, the Gulf Coast, Texas, all over for locations to put new packing plants. He couldn't come up with a good location.

He came back, said 'Dad, with all the shrimp we're buying from the Philippines and Asia, there's got to be crabs over there. We need to look over there. I'm going to check it out, have it checked out.'

We hated to see it happen. We wanted to buy in Maryland. We were reluctant and really non-supportive of Steve at first. We were afraid for him. Afraid that he might get hurt where he was talking about going, afraid he might fail. We didn't want him involved in a project so far away from us. But he went, anyway.

Steve was right and he proved it. It was time to try to find crabs overseas, as a last resort.

We still obtain all the Maryland crab meat we can buy. We're Marylanders, Hoopers Islanders, and if we could get all the product we need here we wouldn't be going anywhere else. Maryland's crab meat is the best in the world. But, there is very little difference in what Steve has found overseas. We can hardly tell the difference and we've been crab meat eaters every day of our lives.

If we bought all the Maryland crab meat produced it still wouldn't be nearly enough. It wouldn't even be close. We had to get crab meat from somewhere else or stop growing. If it weren't for the overseas operations we couldn't operate our businesses like we're doing today. And we're giving people work, giving a lot of Marylanders jobs that we wouldn't be able to do if Steve hadn't discovered the overseas sources and started that operation. We've added hundreds and hundreds of Maryland jobs as a result, maybe thousands of additional Maryland jobs.

Every crabber knows you have to go where the crab is to be successful in this business. We're still just crabbers, and proud of it, but our water is now worldwide. We go, Steve goes, where the crab is.

In addition to all the restaurants, five in Maryland alone, Steve has started the worldwide wholesale and retail business of Phillips Foods; our headquarters operations are in Baltimore. They employ hundreds of Baltimoreans, new employees that resulted from what Steve has accomplished in finding crab.

Now Phillips' products are on retail shelves all over the country, being used in other restaurants all over the country. He's expanding into markets outside the United States.

> Steve saw very early on the advantages that pasteurization held, that it provided the opportunity to do things differently than they had been done for the previous hundred years, or more. It allowed people with vision to see things other people couldn't see yet, to see things that hadn't been done before. Pasteurization, combined with a hundred years of crab knowledge, vision and not a small amount of courage on Steve's part, produced Phillips present world-wide operation.

According to the Maryland Department of Natural Resources, the average Maryland catch of hard crabs, (*including* 'basket crabs'[32] and 'all you can eat crabs'[33] and peelers and soft crabs that generally are not used in packing plants that process crab meat,) averaged in the four years of 2000 through 2003(the last year for which figures are finalized as this part of the book is being written in May 2005,) just under 21,600,000 pounds per year before processing.[34] Deducting the 'basket crabs' and 'all you can eat crabs'(small female sooks that would be described as 'trash' crabs that if not for 'all you can eat' crab houses, would be available for picking,) peelers and soft crabs and allowing for mortality (crabs that die before they can be steamed for picking,) the poundage of crabs available for picking is estimated to be at least 20% less than the total catch.[35] Accordingly, the approximate poundage of

[32] The large, premium crabs sold live to retail outlets for steaming and normally sold in crab houses by a set price per dozen or half-dozen crabs. In 2005, the writer observed that in some establishments a dozen of the large premium steamed crabs sold for $70.00 or more.

[33] The smaller, cheaper, 'trash' crabs sold live to eating establishments that offer "all you can eat" crabs for a fixed, relatively inexpensive price. Smaller crabs are preferred in "all you can eat" establishments because it takes much more effort to extract the meat from the smaller crabs and while many people might have the capacity to eat large amounts of picked crab meat, they don't have the patience, or the time, to pick the meat from large numbers of smaller crabs. In 2005, the writer observe prices in the $20.00 to $30.00 range per person for "all you can eat" crabs.

[34] *Blue Crab Regional Query - Annual Commercial Hard Crab Landings - Chesapeake Bay Region,* See http://mddnr.chesapeakebay.net/mdcomfish/crab/careadefquery.cfm.

[35] The 20% figure is as estimate by Jay Newcomb. Some estimates go as high as 30%. Interview with Steve Phillips.

crabs available for picking for the restaurant and retail trade is about 17,600,000 pounds of hard crabs per average year.

Jay Newcomb says that it takes between 10 pounds and 18 pounds of live hard crabs (depending on the size of the crabs) for a picker to produce one pound of crabmeat. The small crabs that he generally calls 'trash crabs', which make up the vast majority of all crabs picked in packing houses today because the larger crabs are culled from the catch by the watermen to be sold as basket crabs, take the most pounds of hard crabs to produce a pound of crab meat. Using not 18 pounds, which is probably what it actually takes, but 16 pounds of hard 'trash crabs' to produce a pound of crab meat, the total available commercially processed crab meat that could possibly be produced in Maryland from the total annual catch of hard crabs in the Chesapeake and its tributaries, is, on average, somewhat less than one million, one hundred thousand pounds of commercially processed crab meat a year. And this presumes that every picking hard crab landed in Maryland's Chesapeake basin is sold to packing plants, or to others who commercially pick, which it is not. Steve Phillips estimates that the amount of commercially processed crab meat produced in Maryland averages around seven to eight hundred thousand pounds.[36]

The Phillips' restaurants in the year beginning July 1, 2004 and ending June 30, 2005, used approximately 1.7 million pounds of crab meat (this does not include the poundage of crab claws that are used in crab claw cocktails in the various restaurants; it also does not include soft crabs.) Steve's Phillips Foods in the same twelve month period used 9,806,866 lbs, or more, of crab meat to produce its products. Phillips Foods estimates that it will use 14 million pounds of crab meat through its Baltimore facility in 2005/2006 and use an additional million pounds in its Asian value added facility, for a total of around 15 million pounds a year. Combined, the Phillips' operations use around

[36] As this book is being edited there are newspaper articles stating that there will be an above average landing of hard crabs in this year - 2005. If so, and usually estimates are high, there may be a slightly larger supply of crab meat in 2005, but still way below the demand. Even if the landings were consistently at the Maryland average, there would still be serious shortages as the demand far exceeds the average supply and exceeds even the largest recorded catches of hard crabs in Maryland. Demand, as much as, if not more than, supply, is responsible for the shortages of crab meat.

15 times as much crab meat in a year than is produced annually in Maryland.

The International Trade Commission report of 2002 indicated that the entire United States production of crab meat had declined from 19 million pounds in 1990 to 10 million pounds in 1998. In other words, all of the Phillips' entities in the current year will use in excess of 50 per cent more than the total annual production of crab meat in the United States. If Phillips used every pound of meat processed in this country, they would still be 4 or 5 million pounds short of their needs, and with Hurricane Katrina in 2005 the short term shortage could be even greater.

There really wasn't any answer in Maryland - or even in the United States. The problem of supply dictated the action that had to be taken. While going beyond Maryland and the United States might not have been desired by anybody, the choice was clear. And today approximately 3000 restaurant, and Phillips Foods, and packing house employees still have jobs in Maryland, and millions of crab meat loving Marylanders, and other millions all over the world, can still enjoy one of Shirley's crab cakes - a crab cake that is the result of the cooking of generations of great Hoopers Island cooks.

Steve went looking for product for the restaurants; he created a whole new level of the Phillips' family of businesses. Captain Ellie did this when he bought a schooner at age 18 and went in the cargo business. He eclipsed his father, the first Captain Augustus Phillips. Brice and Shirley went beyond what Captain Ellie had done on Hooper's Island by starting the Ocean City and the other restaurants. Steve went far beyond what Brice and Shirley did with the restaurants when he created Phillips Foods.

# BOOK THREE

---

*Asia and Steve*

## *Asia*

*It had been a 30 hour trip from home. Through several airports. Thirty hours from the marshes of Maryland. We had taken off into an easterly wind, circling out over the Eastern Shore and the Chesapeake Bay. I was on the port side of the plane when she leveled, and could see down the bay. I imagined I could see Hoopers Island way down to the south. Maybe I could as we climbed. That's where it had all started. In one of the Empires of the Crab. In the great bay, and Tar Bay, the Honga River and all the rest. Where the schooner McCready had home-ported, in whose aft-cabin Miss Leone, my grandmother, and the second Captain Augustus Phillips had created my father.*

*It was just down there as we climbed, just under the wing, in sight really, where Brice had sat me on the stool at the wheel of the old Gertie V and, leaving Annapolis, had told me, "Take her home, Steve." I'd been six or seven then. Conning the Gertie V on the bay I loved. Heading for the Honga. A long time ago.*

*And then we'd left our home on Fishing Creek, went to another island, to Ocean City. We loved it there and we had prospered, my parents, my great brother Jeff of the unbending spirit, and me. But we had a restlessness. An irresistible desire to see what's on the other side of the hill.*

*And they'd come, the emissaries from the west, from the great city at the head of the Chesapeake. 'Come', they'd said. 'Come'. 'We have a place on the harbor.' And we had gone. It was great. But, it wasn't enough.*

*And now I had flown half way around the world looking for another place where they reigned. It had been near as we began our descent over Manila Bay into the international airport. Been near when, after a short trip to Thailand, I'd caught an inter-island Philippine plane the 400 or so miles to Cebu Island, situate between the Tanoft Strait and the Camotes Sea. Now I'm sitting on the deck of an outrigger 'pump' boat, moving over the Visayan Sea, twenty miles or so to a special island, to Bantayan.*

*It's a beautiful twilight as we approach the white beaches framed by the green of the mangroves. I look over the side into the crystal clear waters of this remote island. They are down there. I know they are down there, relatively untouched over eons of time. In their other Empire.*

*I can feel them, smell them. Crab. I've come for crab.*

*Steve*

*Maxine: It is this part of Steve [putting something together that nobody expected him to be able to do] that inspires those around him to do more, to be more. Steve is a man who knows and lives the honor and the dignity of hard, physical labor. . . . I have come to recognize that it is the work ethic of his youth that has earned him a position of leadership in our community. . . . After a long day's work at corporate headquarters, he comes home only to get right back on the phone with business associates in time zones that are just starting their work day. Many times in the middle of the night he is sitting at his computer, writing a memo or at his drawing board designing a new restaurant. . . . He does this, of course, along with some other Phillips' folks (that's the name I give the amazing part of his company that is comprised of mostly long, long time and loyal employee/partners that despite their last name not being Phillips, work side by side with Steve growing this company because of their shared belief in its mission.) For me, there is another part of him that I love and value. For someone who is driven by achievement and success like he is, I know of very few people that at the same time, exude humility, generosity and compassion the way Steve does. It is this apparent dichotomy that he lives and is, that I find most appealing and amazing.*

*And, as I have come to know, admire and love Steve's parents, Brice and Shirley, I see so much of their amazing work ethic, drive and ambition that they have passed on to Steve. I know they have to feel great satisfaction knowing that part of them is living on in their son; but there is something more for them to know. He has added his unique footprint in a profound manner that has changed the nature of what they began in ways they could never have imagined. The sort of courage and achievement Steve displays is every parent's dream for their child and I know that such a legacy is a source of their boundless pride.*

*I see Steve as a man who is as comfortable walking through his grandfather's oyster and crab processing plant on Hoopers Island, as he is discussing trade issues with a Washington politician, negotiating a lease with a Mexican land owner or presenting a donated boat to an Indonesian fisherman who lost his family and livelihood in the tsunami.*

*He is a man whose fairness, environmental respect, ethical business practices, sensitivity to differing cultures, and honesty, builds friendships with both fishermen and businessmen throughout the world. . . .*

*So, when that same man is duct taping his sandals together because he thinks he can get another year's use from them, I have to smile.*

# CHAPTER FORTY - ONE

*Bantayan Island - Philippines*

> I was determined to go. To go to the Philippines. To Asia. And I did. But, truthfully, I was scared to death, not in respect to my own personal safety; I was afraid that after I had committed to the project, I'd fail. No one in the family had wanted me to do this. To go to Asia to look for crab. For whatever reasons they were afraid. They opposed me. And that made the pressure to succeed heavier and the fear of failure greater. I simply wasn't going to fail.

When Steve decided to go to Asia, his family, as Brice and Shirley acknowledge, was strongly opposed. Certainly a part of that opposition was the fear that loved ones have for the safety of those who go to far away places. The families of the old time 'Whalers' out of Nantucket had it. The parent on land, while a storm rages on the sea as her waterman son is attempting to cross the bar, knows the same fear. But there is often more to it than a concern for the physical safety of the son. Part of it may be that parents don't want the children to suffer the torment of failure. Whatever the reason, it is not forgotten by sons. Although, it is understood.

Skepticism from one's own family can be a heavy burden. Steve would bear it over the first years. It's the same cross that Brice and Shirley bore when they made the momentous decision to make the move to Ocean City. It is the same burden borne by the 18 year old Captain Augustus Elsworth Phillips, Jr. when he bought the schooner *McCready.* It may be what the next generation will experience. It is the natural way of things, especially for the Phillips.

On that first trip to Asia, Steve was accompanied by another relatively young and successful businessman from Ocean City, Hale Harrison. Steve and Hale belonged to an international organization called the Young President's Organization (YPO,) and there was a conference being conducted in Manila sponsored by YPO called "Opportunities in the Philippines."

They didn't fly directly to the Philippines, but first went to Thailand. The restaurants had been purchasing large quantities of shrimp from a company operated by another member of YPO in Thailand named Yong Areechareonlert. He had three prawn (shrimp) processing factories in Thailand where he processed squid and octopus as well as shrimp. Additionally, he raised shrimp in ponds that he later processed and shipped throughout the world.

They were in Thailand for about four days on this first trip. They met Yong and were shown around the various seafood processing facilities. While they were in Thailand, Steve, Hale and Yong took a day and went down to one of Yong's factories in the middle part of the coast.

On the way there Steve first saw the Asian crab (*Portunus pelagicus.*)[37] As they were passing through the various coastal fishermen's villages on the way to the factory, he noticed that vendors were selling crabs, large crabs. While Yong really didn't know much about the crabs, Steve learned from him that the only market for the crab in Thailand, other than roadside vendors, was what was called the 'Wet Market' in Bangkok. In other words there was no processing of crab meat, only a small market for whole crabs. But that first glimpse of the Asian crab brought out the Hoopers Island in him. There was crab here.

Before Steve had left the United States for the conference he had heard rumors of the presence of crab in the Visayan Sea area of the Philippines. Earlier he had met a businessman in Louisiana who was

[37] The scientific name of the Atlantic Blue Crab of the Chesapeake Bay is *Callinectes sapidus.* It is found in Atlantic waters and in the Gulf of Mexico as far south as Venezuela. A sub-species of *Callinectes sapidus* has been found to be present in commercial quantities by Steve and the other Hoopers Islanders along the Pacific coast of Mexico and in the Sea of Cortez.

selling feed in Asia. When he learned that Steve was going to the Philippines he gave Steve the name of a person in the Philippines, Barry Deeney, an Englishman who had married into a Filipino family.

Steve and Hale went on to attend the conference in Manila. Afterwards, Steve contacted Mr. Deeney. He was very familiar with the Central Visayan area because his wife was from that area. He agreed to take Steve and Hale there and to act as an interpreter for them.

They flew into Cebu Island, a large island between the Tanoft Strait and the Camotes Sea. From there they took a small ferry boat to Negros Island and went to a little fishing village called Balcolod. At the village they hired a fisherman and his boat, a small boat with outriggers for stability. They started going around to the various islands in that vicinity. There are over 8,000 islands in the Philippines so there was no shortage of islands.

They were island hopping around the Visayan Sea, stopping at this island in the morning, spending a couple of hours talking to the fisherman there, asking about crab, then going on to the next island and the next village. Steve notes: "We were just going around, trying to figure out what was going on, trying to learn. I was basically doing a feasability study."

They'd ask the fishermen, "How much crab is out there?" "What to you do with crab?" "Do you have a market?" "What are the prices?" They found out that there wasn't any commercial market for the crab of the Philippines. But all of the fishermen constantly said that there was plenty of crab. Steve notes that, "My curiosity was about to kill me."

Ultimately they made their way to Bantayan Island. On that very first trip Steve sensed a kinship between the fishermen of Bantayan and his Hoopers Island roots. It wasn't necessary to go on any further. He knew the crab was there. The answer to the problem of crab shortages in the Chesapeake, in the United States, the problems of lack of supply for the restaurants was to be found in the waters of the Visayan Sea, in the islands of the Philippines, perhaps in all the waters of Asia.

The taste of the Asian crab was very close to the taste of the Maryland crab, the size was bigger, the lump meat was bigger. The only question left open was whether the crab could be commercially fished in sufficient numbers to make it economical to create facilities to process them for meat. He was confident that if the crab could be fished in sufficient numbers, he could create the way to get the crab on the world market. And he had the feeling that they were here, multitudes of them.

Steve still has vivid remembrances.

> On that first trip to Bantayan Island, as we approached, the sun was just going down, twilight. A beautiful, beautiful night. Bantayan is part of the Visayan Islands in the Visayan Sea. It is just a beautiful part of the world. That part of the Philippines is so beautiful, it's just breathtaking. When we came up on Bantayan, I just had a sense of energy. It was the same feeling I had as a young boy growing up on Hoopers Island. I instinctively knew that it was a peaceful place, but full of energy like Hoopers Island. I knew, then, that things were going to work out. I had this strong feeling that the boat was passing over crab. Just waiting for me. I knew crab was there. I could smell crab.
>
> . . .
>
> . . . I was coming to another island like the ones I'd known all my life. I was coming to island people, people that make their living from the water. I felt as if I was coming home to Hoopers Island. Islands exude energy and optimism. Watermen, fishermen, the world over are sure the next set, the next line, pulling the next pot, is going to result in a great catch. And I felt that Bantayan was the next set. We're like treasure hunters, watermen and fishermen. Islanders are born with it.

Bantayan Island and its associated islands were the last islands that they visited on that first trip to Asia. They retraced their steps to Manila and caught a flight for home.

# CHAPTER FORTY-TWO

*Bantayan Island - Philippines - Second Trip*

The relevant governmental entities in Thailand and the Philippines had no data as to the population levels of crab because at that time they were not considered a product. No one had ever attempted to catch crab for the production of pasturized crab meat[38] in commercially viable quantities. They were primarily caught when other types of seafood weren't available, and then they were caught mostly in nets. As soon as Steve returned to the United States, he acquired crab pots and shipped one to Yong Areechareonlert in Thailand and one to Barry Deeney in the Philippines. He asked each of them to have about 50 pots fabricated in the respective countries so that they would be available.

He was missing one necessary item before he could return and complete a feasibility study - Hoopers Island watermen. Down the Hoopers Island chain he went. He acquired the services of Jay Newcomb and Lawrence Rhea.[39] He notes: "I wanted them with me so I could get everything right. What I didn't know about crab, Hoopers Islanders like Jay and Lawrence did." He wanted to see if the crab could be potted.

[38] There may have been at some time in the past an attempt by someone to market sterilized crab meat from Asia, but the sterilization of the crab meat left an unpleasant taste, and the effort was unsuccessful. The writer has been unable to verify this information.

[39] Mr. Lawrence Rhea is now deceased.

How many could be caught? Was netting the best way to catch the Asian crab?

He describes some of what then happened:

> When I was growing up I remember Lawrence Rhea as a baby almost; he was four or five years younger than me. I got a big kick out of him on this trip. I don't think he'd ever been far from Hoopers Island before. I know he'd never been on a plane. So the first plane he would ever ride on was going to be a Boeing 747.
>
> When I told him where we were going he really had no idea of the extent of the trip we'd be undertaking. When he went to Washington to expedite the passport process, he returned, told me, 'Steve, I've never seen anything like it before. My God, they've got ho'ses piled on top of each other. Ho'ses on top of each other.'
>
> When we were about to board the plane I've never seen anyone so excited. He shot about twelve rolls of film just on the plane. He took pictures of the stewardess, of the seats, the windows, out of the windows, everything.

On the second trip they landed first in Thailand. Initially they stayed in a small hotel in Serrittanni. They continued on to the southern part of Thailand and obtained a boat and began to set Hoopers Island style crab pots at different depths and on different bottoms. Then the pots would be pulled so they could check population densities. How many could they catch? Where could they catch crab? Were they in shallow water? Were they in deeper water? On sandy or muddy bottom? They did it all over the area of southern Thailand wherever the three Hoopers Islanders thought conditions were right.

They found that crab population levels at that time in Thailand were "iffy." In some areas it was fair, in other areas not so good. So they moved on to the Philippines. Steve describes the explorations of three Hoopers Islanders in the Visayan Sea of the Philippines.

> It was great having both of them on this trip. Hoopers Islanders have a great sense of humor, and the three of us did.

It was a lot of fun being a Hoopers Islander in a sea halfway around the world from Tar Bay.

We got on another one of these little outrigger boats and started island hopping again, going from island to island. Going out to the little fishing villages. Lawrence was like a rose that was blooming. The people just loved him. And he loved them. He loved being there with them. He didn't understand the language but he understood the people. He had a natural way about him that as soon as the people saw him, they instinctively liked him. He fell in love with the people of the islands.

I felt pretty much at home, too, everywhere on the various fishing islands in Asia, the Philippines, Indonesia, all of them. Fishermen are very much the same the world over. Hoopers Island, Bantayan, anywhere. . . . We're all the same. It's got to be born in us. It's everywhere you go. It's true on Hoopers Island, in Ocean City, in the Philippines, Mexico, all over.

Jay Newcomb remembers that first exploratory trip of the Hoopers Islanders to the Philippines.

Steve wanted to take some Hoopers Island watermen with him when he went to Asia looking for crabs. He wanted our expertise; wanted to make sure that the test crabbing was done right. He asked me to go, and another Hoopers Islander, Lawrence Rhea.

We prepared trot-lines and our other gear before we went and Steve shipped them over so they'd be there when we arrived. I think the first place we went was to Thailand. I remember that the food was so spicy I could hardly eat it. I remember how great it was when we moved on to test crabbing in the Philippines. The food in Manila wasn't near as hot. One time though, all of us were eating real tasty hamburgers at a hamburger place in Manila. Even though I liked it, after I had eaten almost all of my burger, I noticed that the meat was mushier than normal and pinker then our hamburgers. I was afraid it was some kind of dog meat and I didn't want to eat any dog. I called the waitress over and asked her what kind of meat they used in their burgers. She said "earthworms."

Jay survived the 'wormburger' and describes the actual application of Hoopers Island crabbing practices in the waters of the Asian crab.

When we first got over there we had a lot of difficulty getting the local fisherman to sell us oily fish. They couldn't understand why anyone would take a fish that they caught for food, and put it in a contraption and put it overboard for crab to eat.

We set the pots in likely places, but just caught a few, not enough to be commercially feasible. Then we set the trot-lines just like we always had back home. That didn't work very well either, the water was so clear that the crabs wouldn't hold on long enough where we could dip them. The only thing we could get to the surface, and the only things we caught on the trot-lines were octopuses. They'd hold on. We kept trying different things with the pots and the trot-lines but nothing seemed to work. Plenty of crabs, but we couldn't get them with the pots and trot-lines. We kept at it for three weeks that first time.

During that time we noticed that the local fishermen were catching crabs in their fishing nets. So we adapted, tested out the netting, and that's how we ended up doing it, and that's how crabbing is mostly done today over there. Netting. Set the nets in current in areas where the crabs are and let them swim into the nets. Pull the nets in, untangle the crabs, and set her out again. They don't catch as many crabs per crabber as we do at Hoopers Island, but there are lots of fishermen doing it, so many that it produces crab in commercial quantities. And there appears to be lots of crabs.

They're a little different in looks than our crab back here. They're not quite so blue and green, and they have some spots on their shells. They have longer bodies and longer claws, and generally, are bigger than our crabs here are today. The shell isn't quite as hard as the Chesapeake blue crab.

> We went all over. To Cebu Island, to Bantayan Island, lots of little islands all over. Steve, myself and Lawrence were going back and forth between these little islands in canoes with outriggers to keep them stable. The water around most of the islands was shallow and you'd have to get out of the canoes and wade ashore to these beautiful white beaches. It was so beautiful. Everywhere there were beautiful beaches and beautiful water. We went to one island that hadn't had any visitors at all for two years, and hadn't seen an American in four years.
>
> The island people were great, in fact the people everywhere were great to us. When we'd approach some of the islands, the people would come out and greet us on the beach. We were welcomed with open arms everywhere we went in the Philippines.
>
> We were going everywhere in just a short period of time, about three weeks - looking for where the crabs were most numerous. We slept in huts. Open sides. Slept with nets draped over the beds to keep scorpions and bugs off of us. We were so close to the equator it was always very hot. On the different islands there were different dialects spoken, so we had different interpreters for the different islands.

The results were much better in the Philippines than they had been in Thailand. They were very encouraged at the population level of crab. It was at that point that Steve determined that he could build a viable new industry in Asian waters on the back of the Asian crab. It would be a Phillips' operation beginning in the Philippines. He remembers,

> Before we got there crabs were mostly a by-product of other kinds of fishing. We'd ask them if they were net fishing for crab and they'd say 'No we're fishing for something else, there aren't many crabs.' What they really meant was that at that point in time something else was moving through that particular piece of water and that they had stopped catching crab, to catch tuna, shrimp or whatever. I asked the fishermen, 'Is there a season for crab?' They'd say, 'Yes, there's a season.

> There's no crab caught during [a particular period of the year].' I asked about fifteen different fishermen and got the same answer. Come to find out what was happening was that during that period of time the shrimp came through, or the tuna came through, or something else came through, they stopped fishing for crab. There was no good market for crab, so when anything else moved through they stopped going for crab. It was really the economics of it and markets. There wasn't a market for crab. So when anything else was around it didn't make any sense to go for crab. . . . That was true in a lot of the fishing areas in Asia before we built up a market structure for crab.
>
> The crab were there year round and while their numbers might go up or down, it was related to rainfall and drought. If it rained excessively the fresh water debouching out into the ocean would make the water brackish further out and the crabs might move to deeper water. But, they were always there.
>
> The Philippines, all of Asia, had crab. We had the need and we had the market. All we had to do was build the structure, the business structure to serve the market. I knew building structure wouldn't be easy, but I also knew it could be done. We knew how to do it. We'd been doing it for a hundred years on Hoopers Island. I was convinced that what had worked for a hundred years could be adapted to work anywhere there was crab.

Bantayan Island was to be the first attempt to build that structure. It would be successful, and, to a large extent guide the development of the industry throughout Asia. Steve first met with the appropriate officials and was pleased to hear that they were supportive. Throughout some parts of Asia, including the Philippines, there has been a large influx of people to the urban areas, an influx so large in some cases that it is impossible for the local economy to absorb the immigrants from outlying areas. Accordingly, in the Philippines the government was discouraging the opening of businesses in the urban areas for fear it would attract more immigration into the cities, but was encouraging development, including foreign development, in the rural and outlying areas.

That is exactly where Steve wanted to build, where he needed to build. From the very beginning the government was extremely cooperative. The one concern it did have related to issues that might upset already existing industry or economic matters. Therefore, the government set the minimum wages, but strongly suggested to Steve that in respect to wages above the minimum wage, he should try to keep within the average wages of the already existing salaries in any particular area of the Philippines. As they expanded throughout Asia, Steve would be told by the various governments that "We've had trouble several times with American companies who come in and don't understand the situation and pay large amounts above the existing scales thinking they are doing a good thing. But what they really do is upset all of the other elements of our economy." They would always request that the impact on pre-existing entities be considered. With only that one concern, Steve was encouraged to proceed. Steve explains the process of creating an industry in Asia.

> Here's how it worked. Because of the fragile nature of the Asian crab, it dies very quickly when removed from the water compared to the Chesapeake crab,[40] it was going to prove to be difficult to transport live crabs long distances from fishing areas to an all- inclusive processing plant. In most instances, by the time I would get the crab to the factory, it would be dead, or so far gone as to affect the quality. If that happened, I certainly wouldn't get the quality I needed for the markets I wanted to serve, and we would lose a lot of money due to crab mortality.
>
> The first factory in Asia was on Bantayan Island. Because we were getting all of our crab from the fishermen of the one island, the time from water to cooking was not a long time

[40] Steve said in one interview, "The Asian crab will sometimes die in a matter of hours. You can take a Maryland crab, throw him on a parking lot and he'll crawl off, find some shade and be alive the next morning. He's a tough guy." This toughness may be a special characteristic of crabs found in the Chesapeake. According to fishing guides in the Florida Keys, the blue crab in that area dies very quickly when taken out of the water.

> and the crabs would arrive at the factory alive. We could steam them right at our first factory, pick them, process them at the one site. The quality of the meat was top grade. But the demand for our crab meat continued to increase, and I was forced to go to many of the other islands in the Philippines to secure live crab. Many of the islands were long distances from the large factory on Bantayan Island, and all of the transportation back to Bantayan was by boat. Many times, especially during bad weather the trips were so long that many of the crabs would die and could not be used in producing our quality of crab meat. It couldn't meet our standards. To solve this problem, we created what we first called 'cooking stations' at the other islands. We would steam the crabs in these cooking stations, ice them down and then transport the crabs to the large factory for processing. This first mini-operation was steaming only.

At first this new concept was a large plant that would do every step in the production of the crab meat except the catching and steaming of the crab. That would evolve over time into a much more complex, yet, in practice, a simple mini-plant concept.

Steve had spent a large part of his youth on Hoopers Island where it was not unusual to see several ladies sitting at their kitchen tables picking crabs for dinner, and of course he had grown up seeing scores of women picking crab at A. E. Phillips & Son. Halfway around the world, on another island, he sees women doing what he had always seen back on Hoopers Island. Picking crab.

# CHAPTER FORTY-THREE

## *The concept*

Steve: The final mini-plant concept came to me one night when I was at the house of a fisherman in an area called Gebang along the north coast of Java. I was talking with this fisherman at the door of his house, and inside I could see his wife in a small kitchen sitting with two of her friends. They were sitting around a kitchen table picking the meat from crabs that I had rejected that day because they were of poor quality. The thought came to me, 'hey, why can't I also do the picking in each fishing village?' This would help the livelihood of the fishermen because it would provide jobs for their family members. The very next day I had a site for our first full fledged mini-plant picked out, and in two more days construction started. We opened the first mini-plant about 6 weeks later and it was so successful that in the next week we had 10 sites under construction. This made our entire logistical chain much easier and we were able to build these types of mini-plants longer distances away from the large factory they served. We found that we could develop entire areas at one time - build a large factory and several mini-plants almost simultaneously. We'd be building 4 or 5 mini-plants at a time.

. . .

It worked so well that in about four months we had transformed the entire Philippines operation to the mini-plant system. The quality immediately improved since the crab was steamed as soon as the fishermen returned from the sea. After we had the system going we were transporting cooked picked meat in ice to the large factories. It consistently gives us the top quality product that our customers demand and deserve.

The nature of the species, the animal itself, the Asian crab, in essence told me that I had to build factories right in the fishing villages near where the crab was caught so that I could maintain the quality levels I wanted for our products. The mini-factories or plants, turned out to be terrific for everybody because, in almost all of these little fishing villages, there was little or no industry. No jobs. Many of the wives of the fishermen had never had a job because there simply weren't any. With the advent of the mini-factories there were now jobs. It was a great help to the community and it worked very well for us.

It was amazing, the money it pumped into these little communities. Our concept was tailor made for the goals of the governments as well. We were creating thousands of jobs in rural areas right where they wanted them. The product was underutilized and a hundred percent exportable.

Steve and the Phillips' people train the villagers. They are indoctrinated into what has always been the creed at A. E. Phillips & Son back in Hoopers Island. Sanitation first, quality second, and all else follows. The mini-factories and the large factories they support are built to the highest sanitation and quality standards, an essential in the seafood business where one mis-step can be ruinous.

In each plant, including the hundreds of mini-factories to come, there would be locker rooms for the pickers with fresh clean and sanitized uniforms each day, rubber boots for each worker, face masks, and each picker would have to walk through sanitizing liquids in foot baths and through bacteria killing ultra-violet rays on the way into the picking rooms. As Steve notes: "It would be stupid to do it any other way. I'm using the product in our own restaurants, selling it to other restaurants and stores all over the world. I'd be a fool not to do it. I have to make sure it's done right."

The fishermen land their boats on the open beaches, or in some cases on the banks of little rivers and creeks, wherever the village is located. The fishermen bring the live crabs to the mini-factory in baskets. Dead crabs are never bought so the fishermen have a huge incentive to keep crabs alive. The crabs are weighed and the fishermen are paid per pound of crab. The live crabs are then washed to remove any debris, sand, mud, weed and the like and are then taken to the cooking room where they are steamed. After steaming they are taken to a cooling room or area where they are permitted to be cooled until they reach picking temperature.

They are then moved into the 'de-backing' station where the backs are removed from the steamed crabs and the crab is dressed - the innards, gills ('dead man's fingers' to Eastern Shoremen,) and the like are removed. The claws and fingers are also removed at this station, put aside. They move through the processing area in separate containers. Now the crab is basically ready for picking. The bodies are moved into another room, the cool picking room where the crab meat is removed. The meat is put in large sanitized coded containers, special in one type, back-fin in another, lump in still another. The fingers and claws are also packaged at this stage. Lids are then affixed to the various containers, and they are sent to the packing room where they are packed in ice and wait for transportation from the large factories to pick up each day's production. This goes on seven days a week.

There is a constant exchange of supplies and product between the large factories and the mini-factories, by truck or boat. The next day's supplies, ice, containers and the like, are delivered to the mini-factories. The crab meat is taken back to the large factories. Generally, when the crab meat is picked up from the mini-factories it has not yet been pasteurized or had its final quality check.

The crab meat from the mini-factories is delivered to a receiving department in the large factories where each container is opened and the crab meat weighed to insure that the same quantity that leaves the mini-factories arrives at the large factories - that none disappears en route. It then goes into what is called 'grading.' The meat is dumped on sanitized surfaces and is re-graded. Then it goes into 'cleaning', a room where there are large numbers of women utilized. Cleaning the shell from crab meat is very labor intensive. There, they attempt to remove every little bit of shell from the meat. Steve notes,

> That is really one of the great advantages we have over what our competitors were doing domestically. We spend a lot of time getting shell out of the meat because we realize, having been in the restaurant business for forty or fifty years, that there are only three types of people that can get the shell out. One is us at the factory level. Another is the worker at a restaurant, and the last is a customer picking it out of his or her mouth. So we take an extra effort to get the shell out. We're in the restaurant business and we don't want the customers doing it.

After the cleaning process the meat goes into a blending area. Phillips Foods will tailor-blend crab meat for customers that buy in sufficient quantity. A particular large scale purchaser may want a blend of 20% special with 80% lump. It's blended to the customers' specifications. The blending area is also where the special, the back-fin, the lump, and the colossal blends are created. Once blended the meat is placed in specially designated metal containers, or plastic containers if a customer requests.

It then goes through the pasteurization process. This is a hot bath where there are carefully controlled temperatures during the various phases. The temperature is closely monitored. That process normally takes five hours or more. Once completely through the hot bath process it is removed and immediately chilled. The cans or containers are then packed in cardboard master cartons, put in cold storage. Each customer's specially blended meat is kept in separate marked cartons and containers. When there is enough product to fill a forty foot refrigerated container, it is shipped out on container ships. At any given time there may be three or four containers en route to Baltimore, or one of the other destinations. Containers have been shipped directly to the west coast, to Florida, to Australia, to cities in Asia, even to England and other countries in Europe. Each container holds approximately 36,000 pounds of crab meat.

# CHAPTER FORTY-FOUR

*Padre Pio Beach -Bantayan Island - Philippines*

As indicated, the first Phillips' crab meat processing facility in Asia was on Bantayan Island. The best potential plant site was located on a part of the island near Padre Pio Beach. The Padre Pio Beach parcel had two nipa huts that Steve would need for sleeping quarters while he put the plant together. The nipa huts were made out of bamboo with thatched roofs, open on the water side, with mosquito netting covering the sleeping area. There was no electricity or plumbing. None-the-less, the Padre Pio Beach nipa huts, however rudimentary, were the closest sleeping accommodations to the plant site.

The nipa hut parcel was owned by a lady who was then living on Cebu Island. After contacts had been made through emissaries, the lady agreed to come to Bantayan Island to enter into negotiations with Steve over the sale or lease of the proposed site. She came over on a small inter-island ferry. Steve met the ferry. The lady got off the ferry and was followed by her maid. The maid was about four feet eight inches tall and was very slim, weighing much less than a hundred pounds. The maid's function was to follow the property owner everywhere she went, carrying in her arms a five feet tall wooden statute of Christ. Steve notes, "The lady had her maid bring the statute of Jesus with her to bless her position in the transactions and to bless her discussions with me. Brought it along to help her. Kept it near her. Here's this little old lady bringing a life size statute of Jesus to the negotiating table. It certainly gave me something to think about during the discussions."

In the process of preparing to build the first plant, Steve also had to obtain the approval of the village leader, the equivalent of a mayor in United States terms. It was brought to Steve's attention that the village needed a chapel. Phillips built the chapel. Then it was brought to Steve's attention that the school needed an addition. Phillips built the addition to the school. All of this occurred before the commencement of the factory construction.

Steve instinctively knew how to do business in Asia:

> One of the first things you have to do when you go into another country assessing the potential for doing business there is to learn what their culture is, because that's the culture you're going to be doing business in, and you have to quickly determine whether you can accommodate your business needs to their culture - not the other way around.
>
> And you want to learn their culture anyway. To me it's exciting to learn about the culture of other countries. If you're willing to really listen you can learn a lot from them, from their culture. My grandfather, Captain Ellie, back on Hoopers Island used to say, 'That's why the good Lord gave us two eyes and two ears, but only one mouth.' So I try to spend a lot more time listening than I do talking when we go into a new country.
>
> Americans, everybody really, going into new countries to do business there, or even to visit, need to look and listen, and not talk so much. You'd be surprised what you can learn in the process. The people in these countries have a lot to offer us. They have a lot to say and sometimes they're just looking for someone to listen. I try to be that listener as often as I can. Anyway, it's a good thing we don't have two mouths like we have two ears. One mouth gets us into enough trouble.
>
> . . .
>
> For an American doing business in Asia, a sincere willingness to listen and to consider local ways is an important

> part of creating a successful operation. Americans know a lot, but so do the Asians and Mexicans and people of all cultures. Our operations in Asia, and elsewhere, are learning experiences to us. We all learn from each other. An open mind is a valuable asset in Asia and in Mexico. Anywhere actually. Especially in Americans because it's not always expected from us.

While the first plant was being built, Steve sent back to Hoopers Island for more islanders to come to the Philippines to continue the training of fishermen and to train the Philippine pickers as soon as the plant was ready to process crab. Lawrence Rhea returned, Jimmy King went over, and Debbie Schockley went over to train the pickers. Steve explains what happened then, the positive results from listening .

> I brought Debbie over there with me to train them. Of course the Philippine pickers were the wives and family members of the fishermen, just like it had been back on Hoopers Island when I was growing up. Even though there had been no commercial market for crab before we began our operations, these ladies had been eating crab all their lives. One day a group of ladies came to me and said 'Mr. Phillips we will do anything you say, we will pick crab anyway you want until the day we die, but we do it differently here and we'd just like to show you how we do it.' So I sat down and watched these ladies pick the Asian crab and they were rolling that jumbo lump out of there like I'd never seen before. Beautiful. They picked an entirely different way that actually got more of the jumbo lump out and improved the yield on the crab by 3% - just by the way they picked it. Debbie looked at it, said 'Steve, I don't have anything to offer these ladies. They can teach me the Asian way.' Debbie and I than sat down with the ladies, said, 'Ladies you are right. You get more lump out and increase the yield by doing it your way. We are not going to teach you our way, we're going to do it your way.' They applauded us, and then they thanked us - just for listening to them.

Earlier, while the necessary property and the local approvals were being obtained, Steve drew up plans for the plant and for its equipment, drawing for the most part on his experience with the layout and equipment used in the packing plants on Hoopers Island. When all the negotiations were consummated satisfactorily, Steve went to Manila and using the plans, had the necessary equipment fabricated, or otherwise obtained.

Now came the problem of transporting the materials to Bantayan Island from Cebu Island. Years earlier when he had been a boy, he had conned an A. E. Phillips & Son work boat called the *Shirley* to Norfolk. There they had purchased an old Navy landing craft of World War II vintage for the purpose of dispersing oyster shells in the Chesapeake. He recalled that trip, knew that a similar craft would be just what was needed in the Philippines. In a short time he had made arrangements for transport on an old troop landing barge. "We obtained this old World War II barge with a ramp that lowered horizontally and used it to take materials from island to island as we built the various factories in the Philippines [it was probably an old 'Higgins Boat'.][41] Most of the materials were obtainable on Cebu Island, just twenty miles or so from Bantayan.

The construction of the first plant was begun, initially using only hand tools because there was no electricity. Steve learned an important lesson at the very beginning. In many of the outlying areas in Asia, Phillips was going to have to produce its own power. He immediately purchased generators and power tools in order to expedite construction. Thereafter, the Phillips' plants would have backup generators when they were situated in areas served by electricity. In areas not served with electricity, Phillips would include generators to produce the needed

[41] A 'Higgins Boat' was a type of troop landing craft of simple design. It was designed by a man named Higgins. Thousands were manufactured, mostly in Louisiana, during the course of World War II. They were the major troop landing craft used in the first wave during an attack on a coastal objective. The bow of the boat was a vertical ramp that could be lowered into the shallows, or on the beach if the water depth was sufficient close to the beach. When the ramp was lowered the troops would scramble onto the beach, or on another objective. Then the craft would be backed off the beach if able, and return offshore to the troop ships for another load of troops to transport to the beach. They were used extensively during World War II in all theaters of the war, but primarily during the island campaign in the Pacific.

power and additional generators to back up the primary generators. He also learned the necessity of having back up tools and equipment. He notes: "In some areas if you need a screwdriver or a screw, the nearest store that sells them might be on the next island down the line, or the one beyond it. A screw might be two days away." So, from the earliest days, with the construction of the first plant on Bantayan, redundancies on top of redundancies were the order of the day. It was especially important given the type of product to be produced in the plants.

> When we build something like our boilers, we have to have extra transformers, extra blowers, extra belts, things like that. We had to stock parts because if something were to break it might take days to get replacements, even for simple parts. We had to assess that type of situation on a plant by plant, island by island, village by village basis. On some of the islands there was no electricity so we'd have to have generators to supply electricity for our plants, and then back-up generators to support our generators. On Pina Island, we actually electrified the whole island, it was a small island, but we ran an electric line from the plant down the street and the people were able to electrify their homes from our generators.

The approximate cost of building the first plant in Asia, on Bantayan Island, was $360,000.

# CHAPTER FORTY-FIVE

*Igbon Island, Hilaturon Island, Back to Bantayan Island*

On the trip when Jay Newcomb, Lawrence Rhea and Barry Neeney accompanied Steve, they were island hopping in an outrigger boat and came to Igbon Island that had about 600 fishermen and their families. It was only about a mile long and a mile wide with a village on either end. They landed directly on the beach and were met by six or seven hundred people. The village mayors (called Barranbia Captains) had let the schools out when they heard the Hoopers Islanders were on the way. Everywhere they went the children followed them. They were taken to various houses on the island. Steve explains:

> One thing I love about the Philippines and some of these other areas that reminds me of Hoopers Island, is that we would land on these islands and immediately they would take us to the Barranbia Captain's house and we would meet his entire family. Then they would always sit us down at the kitchen table just like they used to do, and still do, on Hoopers Island, and they would put all their food on the table and expect you to eat as much of it as you could. Pretty much like my mother still does.
>
> It made it difficult sometimes, particularly in the Philippines when we were going from island to island by canoe, first one island, than another, all day long and into the

> twilight. You couldn't be impolite, you had to eat. And eat a lot. At every island. We'd have a full meal about every two hours. I gained ten or fifteen pounds. It was just like Hoopers Island.

While their reception was always great at every island, Igbon Island's seemed special. They found out why there was so much attention being paid to their presence. One of the elders in one of the villages told them that they were being honored because they were the first Americans to come to the island since the island had been liberated from the Japanese by American marines in 1945. During that war the Japanese troops stationed on the island had killed 40% of the islanders, including the parents of both Barranbia Captains. They were told that they were being especially honored as a way for the islanders to say "Thanks," to America. They had never had the opportunity to thank the United States until that very moment.

Phillips put a mini-factory on Igbon Island.

### *Hilaturon Island*

Hilaturon Island is a small island just a short distance from Bantayan Island. There are only about thirty fishermen and their families on the island. As do most of the islands in the Philippines, Hilaturon has a yearly festival. On one of Steve's trips to the Philippines he and Barry Neeney were asked to be guests of honor at the Hilaturon Island festival. Again they traveled to the village in a small outrigger boat, a 'punt' boat. Barry, who was familiar with the local customs, had suggested to Steve that they go over early. They arrived fairly early in the morning, went ashore and entered the village along with the village elder. Steve relates what happened the rest of the day.

> As we entered the center of the village, I noticed this dog tied to a tree that looked half-dead. Looked strange. Then I saw children bring bowls of water and rice to the dog, and the dog eating the rice and inhaling the water as if it had been half-starved. Then two children wrapped a wire around the dog's muzzle. I said to the elder I was with, 'Look what those

kids are doing to that dog.' He said, 'That's ok, that's ok.' At that point we went to the other side of the island, actually went out on one of their boats to look at a certain shell fish that they thought might be an oyster, but wasn't. It was a couple of hours before we got back to the center of the village.

When we got back these same two kids are beating this dog with bamboo sticks. I started to run over to stop them, when the elder put his hand on my arm, said, 'Leave them alone.' So I backed off. The kids almost beat the dog to death. Then they put him in a burlap bag, carried him out on a small pier and threw the bag in the water. They drowned the dog. I just kept my mouth shut, but it was hard. I'm from Hoopers Island and we love our dogs.

We took another walk around the island looking at one thing or another and then went back to the center as the feast was starting. I was seated at the place where guests of honor are seated. As I looked over the preparations, I saw the dog again. It had been skinned and was being rotated on a spit over a fire; being roasted. I knew then what was going to happen. You don't insult your hosts when you're the guest of honor in Asia, and the guest of honor is served first.

### *Back to Bantayan Island*

When the first factory on Bantayan Island was finished, and production was to begin the next day, the villagers came to Steve and told him that the factory would have to be blessed before it could be opened. The ceremony took most of the day. The priest insisted that all the machinery be turned on and he then spread holy water on the equipment, buildings, the fishermen's boats and the people, blessing one man twice because he had twenty-two children and needed extra blessing. But the priest forgot to bless the water tower.

Later that evening as Steve was sleeping in his nipa hut a procession of islanders came down the road, got him from his hut and they all returned to the factory site. They had come to the factory to make animal sacrifices. They were mostly the same people that had been there during the day-long Catholic ceremony. This time they were led by a shaman to honor their ancestral spirit gods. They slaughtered the animals, saved some of the blood, then cooked and ate the animals. They mixed the blood with crushed ancestral bones, and went to each corner of the plant and to the doors, and smeared the mixture on them, and then chanted.

Later Steve asked one of the participants who he knew had participated in both ceremonies, why they were doing the two different blessings. The reply was simple and in baseball terms. "We like to cover all the bases." Steve understood the concept. It's what is done in the seafood business.

Some time later they made another trip to Bantayan Island. In a short time all of the Hoopers Islanders were sick except for Steve. There were twelve table leaders (ladies that were in charge of each of the picking tables in the plant.) They went to Steve, said "Mr. Phillips, you have to get the priest." He responded, "For what?" They answered, "When the priest was here before he forgot to bless the water tower. You have to get him to come back and bless it so your people can get well." Steve said, "Ladies, they just have a little bug, they'll be fine tomorrow." But they weren't, or the day after. They appeared to be getting worse. The women went to him again and begged him to call the priest, told him that if the priest blessed the water tower his people would be better in four or five hours. Finally Steve gave in and called the priest who blessed the water tower. The Hoopers Islanders were all well in five hours. Steve comments, "You figure. Whether the blessing made them well is not for me to say. But, I do know that people in Asia appreciate it when an American doing business in Asia defers to local tradition and belief. And who's to say a blessing by a priest is inappropriate. Not me."

# CHAPTER FORTY-SIX

*Indonesia*

Once the Philippines plants were operating and looking successful, Steve was looking for another area to prospect for crab. The success of the Philippine's operation had spread the word throughout Asia that Steve and Phillips Foods knew what they were doing. Steve went to Indonesia several times, not getting the right feeling that all the pieces were in place, the 'people factor' just wasn't there. He was trying to find the right company or the right person to work with. He had agreements with several human resources firms looking for the right setup, the right person for Phillips Foods. On his various trips he had conducted fifteen or so interviews looking for the right situation.

One day back in Ocean City he received a resume by fax from a gentlemen who identified himself as Muchlison Zaini whose nickname was 'Sonny.'

> Sonny's uncle owned a small accounting firm in Jakarta and had told Sonny what I was looking for. On my next trip to Indonesia I interviewed him and really liked what I saw and found out. I told Sonny, 'I have to leave and I'm not going to offer you a permanent job with Phillips Foods now, but I'm going to hire you as a consultant to conduct a feasibility study for us all around the island of Java.'

Sonny was put on a salary. Phillips provided a car and the gas.

Java is a very large island. Indonesia itself has approximately 90 million people and is over 600 miles long. Sonny was to have three months to complete the feasibility study, with periodic reports back to Phillips Foods in the United States. Steve notes "I told him I wanted to know everything he could find out about crab." Arrangements were made for Steve and Sonny to meet in Indonesia at the end of the three month period. During that three month period Steve received regular reports from Sonny. Sonny would spend a month in the field then return to his home, prepare reports, fax them to Steve and then go out in the field again.

When Steve returned to Indonesia, Sonny took him to the various fishing villages that Sonny had concluded were worth Steve seeing. Steve notes,

> I was really impressed with him because he related so well to the fishermen. The fishermen loved him. In our business that's always the first step. And he seemed to have a genuine fondness for the fishermen and their way of life. So I hired him on in a permanent position. He ended up as President of Phillips Indonesia. He helped me build the six large factories we have in Indonesia, with all their supporting mini-factories and cooking stations. In addition to the six large factories, we probably have a hundred and twenty-five mini-factories supplying the large plants in Indonesia.

As always when setting up the factory operations, sanitation and quality control were the paramount considerations in the Indonesian operations. And that, for the most part, meant getting the people and training them properly. Steve explains.

> It's always a challenge to find the right people. No one in Indonesia had ever done any crab meat processing or pasteurization of crab meat. We started from scratch, literally. Initially my major function in setting up the plant complexes in Indonesia was getting our kind of people. Then when you have the right people you have to work hand in hand with them, teaching the Phillips' way of producing a

> superior product. Teaching 12 to 14 hours a day about our sanitation requirements and why it is so important, teaching the importance of ice, teaching about temperature abuse - the importance of always keeping the right temperature during the various stages of processing the crab. We conducted seminars for large numbers of our people, using translators when it was necessary. Many times the people didn't understand the special importance of sanitation when you're entering the commercial market with a perishable product. We had to explain why it was so important and why we insisted that processing had to be done our way - that the standards had to be at the level we required. That all else depended on the proper sanitation in the factories.
>
> We didn't just want them to understand that we wanted it done, but why it was necessary to do it. We had to go through a whole educational process for our people. Really people are the most important challenge, not only in Indonesia, but also in the United States, anywhere in the world where we operate. We've been fortunate that in Indonesia, and throughout Asia the people are extremely capable.

When he took the initial tour of the fishing villages with Sonny, they would go from dawn to dusk and then half the night on the road. They'd have daily meetings along the way. Explaining to villagers and fisherman on all the coasts, the Phillips' model of the crab processing industry that Phillips wanted to establish in Indonesia. They told the Indonesians what they wanted to do, and inquired as to whether Phillips would be welcomed in this village, that village, and so on. They were seeking the blessing of the local populace in the various areas, for as Steve puts it, "We did not want to go anywhere we weren't wanted. Our type of business only works if it is wanted and welcomed. It doesn't work otherwise."

He explains the significance of a country's major religion.

> The Muslim religion, as it's practiced by almost all of the Muslims in Indonesia is a beautiful thing to see when you go

> over there from back here. I've been exposed to most of the world's religions over the years and they're almost the same. They all have the same God that wants the same things. It's just a different face when you move from country to country and religion to religion. It's a shame that such a small percentage of a particular religion can give the religion a bad name at a particular time in history. The people in Indonesia that I've come to know are wonderful people - some of the best I've ever met. They're like all of us everywhere, they want a good life, want their children to have a good life, want them to do better than their parents. It's a universal, everywhere.

In Indonesia they didn't encounter any governmental problems, other then the normal start up problems that always occur every time they built a factory. As in the Philippines they received a hundred percent support from the Indonesian government, for a lot of the same reasons. Phillips was creating industry where the government preferred new industry and new jobs to be - in the outlying areas of the country, not in the major urban areas. The cooperation was so great, that Steve remarked at an interview, "Wouldn't it be nice, be wonderful if it happened the same way in this country. If when you went to create a business that is going to create jobs, governmental people were actually concerned with helping you get it built, helping you create jobs, helping to control costs, instead of always being concerned with stopping you." He continued,

> Some of the people back home, back here, ask me, 'Wasn't it hard, difficult to go to Indonesia and build a factory, build an industry?' I always answer, 'No, actually it's a heck of a lot easier than building something in the United States, because you have so much cooperation from the officials of the governments in that part of the world.' They needed the industry; we were bringing it to them. They want you to build, they want you to succeed over there. Some of the countries have 40% unemployment rates. When you're bringing and creating jobs you are doing the same thing they're trying to

> do. They want the industry and the job creation. We needed them; they needed us.
>
> I had thought when I was first flying to Asia, that I was going to have all kinds of problems, but the opposite occurred. I got all kinds of cooperation. Every businessman ought to branch out with operations in that area. Do it right. Do it in accordance with their customs, but do it.

In acknowledging the customs of Indonesia, when Steve built a large factory in Pemaland, Indonesia, he built a Mosque within the factory, with a minaret so that the employees have a place for prayers. Muslims pray at set schedules five times a day. Not only was the Mosque a response to the religious customs of a country that is over 90% Muslim, but it was smart. The workers could honor their religion with less disruption to their work day than otherwise would have occurred. Similarly, it was relatively easy to configure the plant in conformance with religious practices. In other words, prayer rooms were available, religious garb accepted so long as it didn't interfere with sanitation requirements, doors were placed to face in certain directions. Steve found that being accepting of the practices and customs of the host country wasn't only the right thing to do, but the best thing to do.

With one exception that was quickly corrected, Steve found that the businessmen he dwelt with all over Asia, including Indonesia, were ethical and honest. Negotiations more often than not were conducted without lawyers present. Sometimes the opposing party would bend over backwards to make sure Steve was treated fairly.

On one occasion in Indonesia, Sonny had taken Steve to a separate island called Suliwese. They had flown there by plane, picked up a car and went exploring up and down the coast looking for fishing villages and possible factory sites. At one village they were told that there was a shrimp processing factory that had opened three years before but had closed after a year of operation and that it might be available for sale. It was in a place called Para Para.

Steve and Sonny made the four hour ride to Para Para and found the closed factory in a location that appeared suitable for their operations. Although it was closed it had a guard and he told Steve and Sonny who the owner was and they called the owner. He lived in the same area they had left just four hours before. They set up an appointment for the next day and drove the four hours back.

The next day they sat down with the owner, with no lawyers present for either side, and negotiated a price in the half-million dollar range for the factory. When the deal was done, all parties went to what is called a Notary in Indonesia, a person that can draw up legal documents. They met with her for a while and she then retired to prepare the documents while Steve, Sonny, and the factory owner waited. It was to be Steve's responsibility to pay the Notary's bill. After a while the Notary returned with the documents and they were executed. The deal was done.

Before the Notary could present the bill to Steve, the now former owner of the factory demanded to see it. It was shown to him. Steve explains what happened next.

> He became enraged and that is a very unusual thing to see in people from that part of the world. Anger is considered a weakness. But he was mad, anyway, and was vigorously arguing with the Notary. I couldn't understand the language so I asked Sonny what was going on. He told me the man was angry because he thought she was charging me too much for the work she'd done. Sonny also thought the charges were unreasonable. Soon Sonny and the former owner of the factory were both arguing with her. Eventually she went over and redid the bill.
>
> This was a half-million dollar deal, and the factory was probably worth a lot more. When the Notary's final bill was presented it was for seventeen dollars. The first bill had been for twenty-seven dollars.
>
> That's one of the things that's fun to me about doing business on that side of the world. There's a whole different mentality and it's so easy. Sometimes I compare what we pay for professional services over there and what we pay here, usually pay for a lot of hassle. For those of us in business in Asia, the differences explain why the United States has one sixth of the world's population but eighty-seven percent of the world's lawyers.

> What they do in Asia is a lot of arbitration. And it really works. It gives the parties a better chance to work things out.

In Indonesia Steve initially believed the configuration of most of the fishing villages on the shores of the large island of Java, which had a road network, would permit him to truck the live crab to the large factories he would build. It didn't work. It took the trucks several hours too long to transport the crab. There were roads linking the areas between the large factories and it appeared to be feasible. It didn't turn out the way. The condition of the roads caused the truck trips to be too long and the crab mortality too high to sustain a viable operation totally dependent on road transportation of live crab. The circumstances dictated that he had to adapt. It was at then that he found himself talking to a fisherman at the door of the fisherman's house and saw the three ladies picking crab at their kitchen table. And he realized that he could create a special system utilizing the ability of the wives of the fishermen,

He put into place in Indonesia for the first time a complete mini-factory/large factory complex: one large factory located on the coast with five mini-plants east of it and five west of it.

It was also in Indonesia, during the creation of the mini-camps where the only exception to the innate honesty of the Asian businessmen occurred. The exception furthered the evolution of the mini-factory/large factory concept to what it is today.

During the initial creation and early operation of the mini-factory/large factory system, Phillips hired managers to run each mini-camp, and put mini-factory workers directly on the Phillips' payroll just as the workers were in the large factories. As Steve explains:

> Before long, human nature set in. A couple of the managers started hiring their relatives, putting people on the payroll that didn't show up for work, began to make side deals with the fisherman, overpaying them and pocketing part of the proceeds, buying ice from relatives with only half the quantity purchased making it to the factory and other games. Sometimes I'd walk into a plant and there would be 40 people working and when I'd check the payroll figures we

were paying for 60. Our costs were going up, and our yields and quality were going down. I told Sonny we had to change the nature of the Indonesian structure.

I have an old saying that sometimes the best way to achieve control over a situation is to give up control. I met with the mini-plant managers and fired half of them. I took the other half, along with some potential managers that I now had time to be more selective about, and now I had people I thought I could work with. We set them all up in their own businesses.

Through contractual means we leased the operations to the managers, keeping control of the land and ownership of the facility itself. Each mini-factory became a separate business, the pickers worked for the managers. The receivers, the pasteurizers, the weighers all worked for the managers. The managers, now owners of their own business, bought ice for their own business, bought crabs from the fishermen at negotiated prices between the managers and the fishermen.

With contractual arrangements, Phillips agreed to buy all their product so long as it was produced in accordance with Phillips' sanitation standards and the quality was Phillips' quality, and they agreed to sell all their product to us according to negotiated prices set in advance.

We set them up in business, helped them get up to our standards on the sanitation requirements, the paperwork requirements, remained available to advise whenever they needed it. In doing what we had been forced to do, we created a new class of entrepreneurs. And they were happy with it.

In the first full week of the new operation, Phillips' product costs went down 30%, our labor costs went down 39% and yields went up tremendously. And quality stayed at Phillips standards. It was a win-win situation. We gave up a lot of control and were the better for it.

Now when Phillips moves into a new area, it normally uses the system of entrepreneur/managers. Steve sends people into a new area ahead of time where they think a mini-plant, large plant complex is feasible. And Phillips will identify people in the area that they think have entrepreneur/manager potential for the mini-plants. When they are identified, Phillips goes in and buys or leases the appropriate piece of property; then, because the entrepreneurs don't have sufficient finances to build and equip the factory, Phillips does it. They put in the cooking stations, the stainless steel tables, the sanitation facilities, furnish all the equipment, supply the uniforms; and, most important, impose the quality controls necessary to produce the high grade Phillips' product. Everything that is needed to start a business is provided up front. Then everyone is trained. The entrepreneur's employees are trained by Phillips' staff when necessary. Everything is covered by Phillips, including all the start up costs - costs necessary to get the factory running at profitable levels.

The entrepreneurs then enter into exclusive contracts with Phillips to produce product for the large factories according to Phillips' sanitation and quality control standards. Phillips agrees to buy the product. The start up costs are amortized over appropriate periods of time through the pricing of the product. Steve comments,

> If I had to personally manage all those thousands and thousands of crabbers and tens of thousands of mini-plant workers and managers, and the hundreds and hundreds of mini-plants we have now, as well as the large factories, I simply couldn't do it. I could do it in the beginning, but it has outgrown the early times. Now we have all these former managers who are business owners worrying about their own bottom lines instead of ignoring our bottom line. In taking care of themselves they take care of us. It's almost a symbiotic positive relationship. Everybody is making money.
>
> I was asked one time, 'Why would you do that, why would you give up the profit you could make from operating the mini-plants?' I answered, ' Because we are much more profitable with the new system. It's a win-win situation for everybody.
>
> When I was asked about the former managers, I merely answered what we in the Phillips family have always known, dishonesty is not a good long-range business policy. If there

are any dishonest officials in the areas we operate in, they don't come to us. Everyone knows we'll walk away first. We just don't play those games. Some of the other American firms have people lined up at the doors because they don't chose to avoid politics and they don't keep a low profile. For them, it never stops. With us it never starts.

Everything had begun to click, going good everywhere we expanded into Indonesia. The secret to the whole thing is the people. You have to have the right people. It's been all about people since the Crab House opened in Ocean City in 1956 to Asia in 2005. We operated like a family at the Crab House and I tried to keep the same philosophy going everywhere we went in Asia.

At the present time about 95% of the Phillips' mini-plants in Asia are operated by entrepreneur-owner/managers under contracts with Phillips. All of the large plants are operated directly by Phillips. As of the summer of 2004, there were 19 large Phillips' factories in Asia and around 250 to 300 mini-plants. There are large plants in the Philippines, in Indonesia, India, Borneo, Vietnam, China, East Malaysia. There is a large plant and mini-plant complex on the Sea of Cortez in Mexico that came on line in the summer of 2005, and three more complexes planned there on Baja California and near Mazatlan. Feasibility studies are under way along both coasts of Africa.

The mini-plants are set up for between 50 and 250 workers per mini-plant, depending on the area. Phillips, and its associates throughout the world, employ over twenty thousand people. Fifty years ago Phillips started the restaurant operation with 4 paid employees!

# CHAPTER FORTY-SEVEN

*India*

Before long the demand for Phillips' crab meat, their value added crab products, and other products as well, was outpacing Phillips' production in the Philippines and Indonesia. Steve had never been to India at this point, but had heard that the Asian crab also lived in the coastal waters of the subcontinent. No one was producing pasteurized crab meat in the entire country.

Steve was back in the United States attempting to create a marketing division in Florida where increasing numbers of Phillips' customers were located. He had gone down to find someone to head up the project and found an excellent person for the Florida position.

During the process, Steve had interviewed a gentlemen from India. The conversation had strayed to the feasibility of a Phillips' production facility there. The Indian man had excellent references and he was hired to conduct a three month feasibility study in India. During the three month period excellent feasibility reports were faxed back to Steve. Eventually, the Indian notified Steve that he had found a factory that was for sale. An existing seafood company (one that did not process crab) had opened up a seafood factory between two of its other factories on the South East coast of India opposite Sri Lanka. After it had opened they determined that the three plants were too close and were economically unfeasible. The Indian company, Baby Marine Inc., one of the most respected and successful firms in that part of India, had decided to sell the middle factory. The company was owned by the Thomas family, one of the most respected families in India.

Steve flew over; and, along with the man working for Phillips, negotiated a deal for the plant over a period of five days. There were several things still to be done. There had to be meetings with governmental officials, but they were to be handled by the employee. When the appropriate approvals were obtained, the deal would be consummated, and Phillips would have a production presence on the subcontinent.

He returned to his office in Baltimore and faxed his representative in India pages and pages of things that needed to be done to get the factory operating in the Phillips' mode, making arrangements with watermen, obtaining pickers, training instructions and the like. Two weeks went by and he didn't hear anything from his representative. Another two weeks went by and he still hadn't received any word. He called the Thomas family, the people from whom he thought he was buying the factory. They told him they were also trying to find Steve's employee and that they had experienced some problems. They wouldn't tell him anymore about the situation.

Steve flew to India and when he arrived he couldn't find his man. He discovered that his representative was an alcoholic and had been drunk for two months. While he was drunk he seriously embarrassed the Thomas family by showing up at meetings with various officials completely inebriated. Now the Thomas family declined to deal with Steve. The negotiations were rescinded and the deal for the plant was off. It was one of Steve's few mistakes in judging character during the start up periods in all of Asia.

Steve went to the other side of India, to the northwest coast, found a factory, bought it, modified it, and after making arrangements for the mini-plant system, brought it on line. Ten to fifteen thousand pounds of production a week of Indian crab meat entered the Phillips' world wide system (by now products were being sold in Europe, Australia, Central America and in many other areas.)

Steve was still enamored of the missed factory deal with the Thomas family and remained personally embarrassed by the actions of his alcoholic former employee.

The Thomas family was extremely prominent in South East India. The elder Mr. Thomas had started life as a fisherman, working on someone else's boat, saving his money. When he had enough money saved he bought his own boat, then another and another, until he owned and operated a fleet of 150 fishing boats. Then he built his own processing factory, then another one, another one, and so on. And he always gave back to his community. The Thomas family built schools, other civic facilities. The large local hospital was called, "Baby Marine Hospital" after the Thomas family who had been instrumental in its creation.

Steve flew back to India to attempt to meet with the family to express his apologies and to attempt to reopen negotiations to purchase the factory from them. The father in the family wasn't as conversant in the English language as was his son, Alex Thomas; so Steve called the son and asked him if he would go with Steve to speak to his father and help Steve express his personal apology and the apology of Phillips Foods. Steve describes the process,

> Alex Thomas is one of the nicest men I've ever met, who you would ever want to meet and he is super smart, very intelligent. He's about my son's age. Thirty or so.
>
> I first apologized to Alex, then with his help I made a formal apology to the entire Thomas family. But I still wanted the factory. I asked Alex to tell his father for me, that I felt I was in a very difficult situation. I said to Alex, 'I respect your father, your family, very much and I know he is a highly respected leader in the community, and I know it's proper for me, if I want you to come to work for Phillips in India, to go to your father and ask his permission.' Alex told me that I was correct. Then I stated the obvious, that I didn't speak his father's language, and his father didn't speak my language well enough for us to understand each other. I asked Alex if he thought it would be proper for him to act as my interpreter during my discussions with his father about Alex working for me. He agreed to be the intermediary between me and his father over whether his father would approve me hiring him.
>
> In that culture the salary, incentives, and benefits for the son you are hiring have to be negotiated with the father.

So there I was negotiating over Alex's package and position through Alex with his father.

Things are done differently in other parts of the world, not better or worse, just different, and you have to adapt.

Alex was brought into the Phillips' business family as the head of the Phillips' India operation and they have had a great relationship ever since. Steve went on to become close friends with the Thomas family, sometimes being a guest in their home on his travels to India. He regards the entire Thomas family as a special family. He pays them the ultimate compliment, "Their family is a lot like my family."

The Indian crab is the same Asian crab found in most of the rest of Asia, *Portuntus pelagicus.* The methods used to catch the Indian crab are much the same as elsewhere in Asia. Today Phillips Foods has two large factories and approximately 25 to 27 of the entrepreneur mini-plants in India.

# CHAPTER FORTY-EIGHT

*Vietnam*

Phillips Foods had no real problems beginning business in Vietnam. Steve saw little of what he used to imagine as communism. Today Steve perceives it as a beautiful country; and the people there that he does business with he describes as "wonderful people" that love their country. And moreover they like their form of government. He considers the pickers and workers in the plants as especially hard workers. "An industrious people." He notes that in the times he's been there, he's not "seen anything . . . that was really restrictive in terms of freedoms, and it's a great place to do business." He describes the Vietnam operation.

> We have a large factory in Nha Trang. Once again I did the same thing. Sent a guy over to do a feasibility study looking for crab up and down the coast for three months. From that study we determined that the heaviest concentration of crab was near Ho Chi Minh City, but we decided not to go there with our first setup but to go up the coast further north because that seemed to be where there was more fishing actually going on. And the area was less congested and less competitive.
>
> Nha Trang is a beautiful area along the coast of the South China Sea. We got lucky there. We found a man who had just built a brand new factory to process fish. It was built very well and the layout was suitable to our purposes. He had never

been in the fish business before and after six months was losing a tremendous amount of money. He wanted out. We wanted in. We negotiated with him privately and there was absolutely no interference by any governmental officials. We didn't even have attorneys during the negotiations. I'm just sitting there doing the deal. Working it out with the guy. After the deal was worked out we got attorneys to formalize what we had negotiated.

I didn't have any problems in Vietnam. I really didn't. Actually, the governmental people I met were very supportive. They appeared happy to have Americans coming to their country. They felt that, in current times, Americans have the wrong concept of their country and that they were still being viewed from the perspective of thirty-five or forty years ago. Their country has moved totally away from that, totally beyond the war, and they feel that the United States hasn't; and, frankly, they want us to. I think they really like us; I know it's a great place to do business.

# CHAPTER FORTY-NINE

## *China*

Steve went to China for the first time in 1997 and it didn't work out.

> A Hong Kong Chinese came to me, telling me that he had contacts in the fish processing business in mainland China. He wanted me to come and take a look at the plants and, hopefully, be able to set up a Phillips' operation in China to produce meat from the China crab, the same Asian crab we were working with elsewhere in Asian waters. I went over to China and took a look at the situation. No one was processing pasteurized crab meat in China at the time.

One of the factories wanted to work with Phillips, but their factory wasn't up to Phillips' standards. Changes would be necessary. Phillips, at its expense, set up all the equipment necessary to process crab in the China factory with an agreement that Phillips would recoup its cost over a period of years through the adjustment of prices for crab meat. After the factory was in a position to produce crab meat according to the Phillips' sanitation and quality requirements, Steve sent a team of experienced Phillips' personnel to the factory in mainland China to train the workers in the sanitation and quality procedures necessary to produce quality product. The training team spent a month training the

Chinese workers, and then reported to Steve that the training process had gone well.

The first container of 36,000 pounds of crab meat received by Phillips Foods in Baltimore was pretty good. The second was the same. The third container of 36,000 pounds of crab meat was bad and was destroyed. There had never before been any spoilage or other serious quality problems with any of the Asian product. The crab meat is shipped in specially refrigerated containers that are constantly monitored by devices within the container that keep a record of the temperatures within the container throughout the voyage from Asia to Baltimore. The records are always reviewed upon the arrival of each container. The devices indicated that there had been no refrigeration problems during the voyage from China. So immediately Steve knew that the problem had not occurred in transit, but that the problem had begun in the factory.

At the time of the arrival of the first bad container from the Chinese factory, there were two more containers from the Chinese factory at sea en route to Baltimore. When the next container arrived with its contents in the same condition, Steve was soon on a flight to China. Upon his arrival at the factory he immediately realized the Chinese managers had changed what the Phillips' people had set up. They weren't monitoring temperature; they were buying bad crab, changing the way things had to be done from a sanitation and quality point of view. They had become so cost conscious that they had changed everything to reduce the cost of production. They were more concerned with efficiency and volume, than with quality. Steve made a preliminary decision to close the plant.

But before he left China, the Chinese managers met with him and ultimately convinced him to give the factory another chance. After Steve received assurances that the process would be conducted in the Phillips' way, he agreed to restart the operation.

Phillips went through the set up period all over again, sent two training people over from the Philippines to retrain the Chinese workers in the sanitation and quality measures that are absolutely required in the Phillips' operations. The plant was restarted and the product in the first container arriving in Baltimore was fine, the product in the second bad, with two more containers in route. As Steve puts it, "I closed the China operation. I just didn't have the right people. I left China. But, it wasn't China's fault, it was my fault. I didn't have the right people."

Back in Maryland several months later, Steve received an e-mail message from a man named Yi Lifu. He told Steve that he wanted to process crab meat for Phillips in China and wanted to meet with Steve. He would come to Baltimore at his own expense if Steve was willing to talk with him. Steve knew there was crab in Chinese waters, the man wanted to talk crab, so Steve e-mailed him back saying he would meet. Yi Lifu showed up at the appointed time with a translator. He explained to Steve that he was catching crab in Chinese waters on big boats, 180 feet long or bigger, dragging nets along the bottom in deeper water than the inshore fishermen. The crab Mr. Yi Lifu was catching in his net was th Asian crab, a *portuntus pelagicus* crab, but a slightly difference species of it. It was called the 'Hanna crab'.

He explained to Steve how he was able to maintain quality and sanitation controls on the ships and impressed Steve with his general commitment to quality and his understanding of the need for strict sanitation procedures. He was already processing his crab in a factory he leased in China, and was willing to modify it to bring it up to the Phillips' standards for producing pasteurized crab meat products.

Phillips gave it another try in China with Yi Lifu and has been satisfied with the process. As always, there are issues, but they're always worked out. Mr. Yi Lifu has done such a good job that it has caused Steve to want to expand the China operation further, with Mr. Yi Lifu as part of the Phillips' team. As Steve says,

> . . . this guy is street smart. He was a fisherman, his father was a fisherman and he appears to be real sharp. He knows seafood, not only crab, but other products. I said to myself, well here's a guy that can help me reach one of my other goals. One of my remaining goals is to develop other products and this guy has the knowledge and the ability.
>
> So four months ago [this interview is taking place in August of 2005] I said to Yi Lifu, 'We've been buying product from you, now I want to expand the business. The factory you're in now would cost too much to fix up to handle the expansion of the business into other products. We're going to

have to get another factory. What we're going to do is pay you. If you agree, I'm going to buy your equipment.' It was worth about a half a million. 'We'll put that equipment on the floor in the new factory. You will be an employee of Phillips Foods at a [certain] salary with [certain] benefits and incentives.' He agreed, was happy with the proposal. He wanted to work for us, wanted to be involved in developing new products. He told me that he could grow faster with us than by himself.

Now we're in a good situation in China. I'm pretty happy with it. It has a lot of potential.

# CHAPTER FIFTY

*Mexico*

There was still an insufficient supply of crab to satisfy the ever growing market for quality Phillips' pasteurized crab meat and value added crab meat products. The market just kept out-running the supply. Phillips Foods had people conducting feasibility studies all over the world including Africa and South America.

Preliminary indications were that Mexico might have crab in sufficient quantities to support commercial production of Phillips' style crab meat. After an initial look at the east coast of Mexico, Steve took a group of Hoopers Island watermen, including Jay Newcomb, to Mexico. There they discovered crab on the west coast that, although it was a Pacific crab, was of the same general species as the Maryland blue crab, albeit somewhat different, and its meat tasted closer to the taste of the Maryland blue crab than any they had discovered elsewhere. And after the Hoopers Island watermen had tested the waters, they believed crab was there in sufficient quantities to be commercially viable. Steve explains the early trips to Mexico.

> Three or four months ago [this particular interview was conducted on the fifth of August in 2005] when I went to Mexico, we must have traveled three thousand miles. All up and down the east coast, then all up and down the west coast including the Sea of Cortez area and the coasts of Baja

> California. It took two weeks to do it because I wanted to see every crab and seafood area in the country. I decided to put the first factory in the estuary area around Los Mochis, which is on the east coast of the Sea of Cortez opposite Baja California.

Phillips Foods built the first large factory in Mexico at Los Mochis and it will be served by six mini-factories, not all of which were completed at the date of the interview above. It is anticipated that all of the mini-factories that serve this new large factory will be completed by the first of September. The first week of August Phillips Foods received at its Baltimore plant the first 9,000 pounds of Mexican crab meat. It is anticipated that the crab population in the waters around Los Mochis will allow this first large factory and its supporting mini-factories to produce 30,000 pounds of product a week when they are at full capacity. As Steve notes, "Just out of this one factory in Mexico we will be producing 1.5 million pounds of crab meat a year, and that's a lot more than the entire average annual production of pasteurized crab meat in Maryland, and it might double the Maryland production. Just from that one factory complex."

The mini-factories serving this first large Mexican factory run from just opposite Cabo San Lucas on up the east shore of the Sea of Cortez almost to the top of it. Phillips Food's Mexican goal is to have, within three to five years, four large factories, each supported by its complex of mini-factories. One of the other complexes will be in Baja California on the west shore of the Sea of Cortez. There will be another complex south of the existing complex, and one more further south on the west coast of Mexico. It is anticipated that one of these complexes will have a value added capability.

The mini-plant complexes in Mexico have started out as 100% Phillips' operations, and will remain Phillips until they grow to the profit level necessary to maintain an entrepreneur type operation similar to those in most of Asia. For the three or four month start up period, Steve notes: "We're basically subsidizing their losses."

Steve further explains the Mexican venture.

> One of the advantages we see in Mexico is that, although we are the largest producer and seller of Asian pasteurized crab meat in the United States, there are some customers that prefer the meat from domestic or Mexican crab. For that reason we're already processing all the domestic crab we can get our hands on. But we're missing out on part of the market because we can't get enough domestic meat, and pasteurized meat hasn't been produced in any large quantity in Mexico. So now we're in Mexico to serve the needs of our wholesale and retail customers. We can process the Mexican crab, produce pasteurized meat and better satisfy a part of our market.
>
> In Mexico we are on the doorstep of the United States and I want to look at trying to promote fresh seafood of all kinds imported from Mexico. I think we can do that and the factories we're building can be used as the structure. There are lots of tuna and other marketable fish in Mexican waters, and lots of shrimp.
>
> I'll be able to put something in Tucson. They have an international airport there. Put a buying station in Mexico with cold storage and ship everything to the United states fresh and cold. Our regional managers all over the United States could call in their orders every day. Our Mexican buyers could then buy the fish fresh, ice it and ship it. Sometimes all in the same day. Often within hours.
>
> From one part of our factory complex on the Sea of Cortez we're less than four hours from the border. We're really close. We're four, maybe five hours by air from any point in the continental United States. We're within easy reach of the rail networks. There's plenty of shipping structure, we have the buying, processing, packing and marketing structure already in place. When the product is available and you have the right people, from that point its about logistical structure.

Steve has sent a willing son down to Mexico to be trained towards ultimately becoming a part of management. But Aaron is starting at the bottom. At the time of the 5 August interview with his father, Aaron was living with the family of a Mexican fisherman and working on the

Mexican's boat in the Sea of Cortez under the control of the fishermen, fishing for crab. The very first step in the vertically integrated Phillips Foods' crab meat operation. Steve's other son, Brice, is now playing a prominent role in the Washington operation, but he too started at the bottom. As to family involvement in the businesses, Steve says

> We don't want to force any of the kids to work in the businesses and the ones that stay with us are doing so because that's what they want. It's an opportunity, but I know there are plenty of other opportunities out there for them. Heck, I took out on my own looking for other opportunities when I created Phillips Foods. Went to Asia, scared of failing but went anyway. You can't live for your children. You have to set them free to be what they want to be. Everybody has to use their own wings to fly.
>
> Sometimes I think there's a lot to say for your kids not coming to work for you, lot to say for them striking out in different directions. Anyway, its pretty hard for parents to keep kids with Phillips' and Flowers' genes under their thumbs. Captain Ellie struck out in a new direction when he bought the schooner McCready; Brice and Shirley did when they moved to Ocean City; we all did when we moved to Baltimore; and I have with the creation of the Asian crab industry. All of us probably ended up amazing our respective parents. I guess that's how it works.
>
> I started the buffets at the Crab House while Brice and Shirley were in Florida. When they left Ocean City there was no buffet, when they returned there was. I was just using my own wings. Then I was totally immersed in the Harborplace operation for a year- the hardest, and maybe the most satisfying, work year of my life. It was a big move for Brice and Shirley growing up on Hoopers Island to start the Ocean City restaurant business. It was another big move when they sank virtually everything they had into buying and restoring the Beach Plaza to its former glory. It's the way I was raised. I was raised by two of the best entrepreneurs and visionaries of their time, business people taking huge chances, risking

> everything for what they believed would pay off. How could I have been different? How could I be different from that? How can my children, Jeff's children, be different? They'll be using their own wings, I might not always want them to, but I know they will. It's in them.
>
> That said, all of us, mom, dad, my brother and myself, sure love seeing our children working in the family businesses. All of the children that want to work there.

Aaron has apparently committed to a future with Phillips Foods. As Steve has indicated he's working at the entry level - he's catching crab working under the supervision of a fisherman. After a period of time fishing for crab, he will be put in the cooking room of a mini-plant working alongside Mexican workers, under the supervision of whatever Mexican employee is in charge of the cooking room. When he has that process mastered, he'll even be sent to the picking room so that he can learn first hand how it feels to be sitting at a stainless steel table surrounded by women, picking crab. Then he'll be in the packing room, spend a lot of time working in the pasteurization processes at the large factory. Then he'll be in shipping, in the administration end of the Mexican projects. He'll come back to Baltimore for a brief period between Thanksgiving and Christmas and then be sent to Asia to work with the Asian crab and to be trained by Sonny, Alex Thomas, Yi and the extended members of the Phillips Foods' family.

# CHAPTER FIFTY-ONE

*Tsunami*

The tsunami raged in many of the areas where Phillips' facilities were operating and some of the villages of Phillips' employees or fishermen in various countries were seriously damaged. In two areas Phillips mini-plants were destroyed; but, over all, the remaining physical facilities quickly picked up the slack. More importantly, no Phillips' employee was killed. Some though, sadly, had family members either killed by the waves or who were missing after the tsunami retreated.

Steve explains some of the efforts of Phillips to assuage the immediate effects, and some of the long term assistance generated by Phillips.

> After the tsunami, the manager of our Indian operations began to arrange for immediate relief for the affected areas. Alex Thomas, on our behalf, and the entire Thomas family, began to address the needs in the affected areas of India. All of the available trucks from our respective businesses were pressed into service and were loaded with all the rice and other foods, water, blankets, other supplies, everything we could get together, and were sent out every day to the affected areas. It was a constant stream, an immediate stream. It didn't take us weeks to get there. We were already there throughout Asia. Everybody else that could do so was participating throughout the affected areas in Asia. It was a great effort.

We were participating in one way or the other wherever we had facilities in an affected area.

Some aid that came from outside the respective countries was just deposited on beaches. Food just sitting there in cartons on beaches after the people had fled elsewhere. Food not going anywhere. We'd try and take it to where the people were. It helped immediately to have trucks on the ground transporting aid and people within hours after the tsunami hit. We did that right away and in the right way.

Too many people think that you have a tsunami and half of the people of a village are killed and the other half stay there, so they deliver aid on the beaches where the wave struck. The problem is that the survivors have gone into the hills, into the mountains to get away from the sea. They're scared and they stay scared for a long time. Sometimes they migrate to the cities, inland villages and the like. What they're not doing is hanging around all that misery. Why would they? A lot of the foreign relief agencies simply didn't understand. So a large amount of aid was being unloaded along the beaches where no one was.

There were all these people raising money for relief, and they didn't have the slightest idea what to do with it. They'd just send stuff over. The infrastructure wasn't where they sent the aid. It made the donors feel better but a lot of it wasn't able to be used. In some cases the aid just sat there because there weren't any people to use it. That's one of the things we put our trucks to work doing when it was possible. Moving the aid to the people.

Some of the people out of our Bangkok office went to the affected areas immediately to attempt to save lives. We had an English guy, A. J. Simpson, and two Americans, Michael Halogher and Chris Kegan (who used to be an Alaskan crabber,) who worked for us in Thailand and lived down near Phuket. For a week they helped with the gruesome, but necessary job of finding, removing, and disposing of bodies and aiding in any way they could down there.

Adrian Simpson e-mailed the home office from Thailand,

> All the disaster relief efforts that were visible were directed towards the main tourist areas. My concerns were for all the small villages up and down the coast that have fishing communities that are out of the spotlight and do not receive the brunt of the effort under the spotlight now shining. These are also the people that we - 'Phillips' - deal with daily. I heard that forays by Anthony's staff found deserted villages, whether the people have been lost to the sea or are still hiding in the hills scared of the tsunami is not clear. . . . The thoughts . . . . go out to all the people who live normally in the cash existence economy day by day. Getting them back their means to scratch a survival income is the highest priority now. Fishermen are in desperate need of boats and nets. . . ."

In Indonesia, India and Thailand, everywhere they had resources, Phillips, and its people, helped in any way they could, especially prior to the beginnings of substantial aid from abroad. After a while there were so many people coming in from abroad that they were getting in each other's way. Persons affiliated with special political groups came in and started problems attempting to investigate their own pre-conceived thoughts on alleged human rights abuses in the various countries, trying to obtain information about rebel groups and the like. At least one of the major foreign countries involved in the tsunami disaster actually refused foreign aid workers for that, and other, reasons. Phillips and Steve decided that their efforts would focus on long term assistance.

In one country, Phillips, at its own expense, developed long range proposals for rebuilding fishermen's villages in safer and more environmentally friendly ways. A complete plan for rebuilding villages of eight hundred fishermen's houses, along with government buildings, mini-plants and the like was prepared at Phillips' expense, and furnished to the government free of cost. Phillips offered to get the projects started.

In some areas where Phillips operated, all of the fishermen's boats were destroyed. The sea, as Mr. Simpson had e-mailed, was the only way that the fishermen could support their families. Phillips created the "Buy-a- Boat" program to respond to the fishermen's needs. President Mark Sneed put the idea together, and it has been immensely successful. By the time this book is in print it will have resulted in providing more than a hundred boats for over four hundred fishermen's families who had their means of livelihood washed away in the tsunami(often one fishing boat will be operated by several families.)

Phillips Foods created the Phillips Foods Tsunami Fund, Inc. on January 19, 2005. Its announcement of the fund's creation, included the statement:

> Many of our plants and their employees were affected by the devastation that hit the islands of Asia. We feel we are in a unique position to organize a localized effort in rebuilding these communities. We understand the culture and have first-hand knowledge of the true needs of these coastal villages. In an effort to restore the means of income to the fishermen within the coastal villages, we have launched a community-based boat building program: Operation Buy-a-Boat. This program will build boats for affected fishermen, giving them back their means to feed their families and generate income.

The motto of the program was, "Give a man a fish and you feed him for a day. Build a man a boat, you feed his family for a lifetime." The money collected, well over a hundred and sixty thousand dollars in the early months, has produced more than a hundred boats so far, and the effort is continuing.

# CHAPTER FIFTY-TWO

*In General*

Phillips was the first entity to go to Asia and set up a system to process and market the Asian crab. In Asia Phillips was also the first business to pasteurize crab meat on a large scale, giving it the shelf life necessary for a product on the international market.

Initially it had been a desperation move. A source of crab meat was needed for the restaurants, to sustain that part of the family's businesses. Steve was the first one to have the idea, the willingness to take risks, the drive and the perseverance to get it done. Steve comments that

> We were the first. But as with any successful venture, you soon have people who come in and copy your structure; but I knew that in the beginning so it wasn't a shock when it happened. I knew that if it worked the way I thought it would, we'd be creating a whole new industry in Asia and the industry couldn't be limited to us. I knew that going in.
>
> When you're out creating something its important to have an accurate idea of the size of it, the potential impact. Then you take it one step at a time. I've always had the talent to visualize where I want to go, where I want a business to go, to be a year from now, five years, ten years ahead. I can close my eyes and see it. That this is where it needs to be down the road. Here is how much business it needs to be doing.

Then I say to myself, 'What kind of structure do I have to create to support where I see this company going?' When I have that figured out, and it doesn't take long for me, I start looking for the quality people I need that I can plug into this structure to make the whole thing work. To make the vision a reality.

I think you have to be able accurately to define what you're going to look like in the future in order to end up there, to get to that point. First it's accuracy in the visualization of the future; second it's creating the right structure to carry you there; and finally, and probably most importantly, it's people. That's really the way it's always been in our family. Brice and Shirley may not have realized it, but it was that way with them. Vision, structure, people. You have to have the right people.

After we got started in the Philippines and every thing was going good we made our move into other areas in Asia. The secret to the whole thing is really people. You have to have the right people. It's all about 'people' from the Crab House in 1956 to Asia in 2005. We've always operated like family in the Crab House, and I tried to keep right on doing it in Asia, and for the most part it works just as well there. Take care of your people, give them a better life, and they'll take care of you.

These fishermen, these watermen in Asia and Mexico have the same pride as the watermen of Hoopers Island. They want to be independent. They don't want to work for a company; they want to work for themselves. But, many of their wives and family members work in the factories that are supporting the crab fishery. It's almost like it was in the old days on Hoopers Island and what I learned back then - works in Asia now.

When Phillips goes into a new area, they make sure that they learn early in the process what the people in the fishing villages really need, things that Phillips can address. If Phillips goes in, as Steve says, we're "extending the Phillips' family and that means we're going to be giving to our new family members just like we always have back home." Steve considers that it was a successful formula for Brice and Shirley and it's worked everywhere Steve has taken the company in Asia, and now in

Mexico. As he notes, "We don't just plop one of these factories down on one of these little villages." Phillips tries to become a part of the village. Because Phillips has the strengths to do it, the company feels an obligation to share in resolving problems.

If it sees something that needs doing, and Phillips can do it, it is usually done. If they see teeth that need fixing, cleft lips that need repairing, boats that need building, they arrange for whatever can be done, to be done. Generally, Phillips has made a decision for its companies to deal directly with the people needing the help, rather than with officials of government. Its motto is to avoid all politics and to keep a low profile whenever possible in any country they are in.

Sometimes they have to deal with officials in order to get a project done because they're a foreign company, but even then the aid is directed to the people for whom it is intended. Steve recalls that,

> Sometimes officials will come to us and say 'Can you give us this or that so that we can give the people this or that?' We say no - but. In other words if we feel the need is legitimate and we can meet the need directly without going through intermediaries, we'll often go ahead and do it. Electrify the island, build the basketball court, the soccer pitch, the volleyball court, the cisterns, a dentist, a doctor. And we'll stand aside and let the officials, the political figures take the credit. Our concern is that our people have the benefits. At that point there's plenty of credit to go around.

Steve has found out that in Asia, as in other areas, foreign businesses are generally treated the way they deserve to be treated. As he sees it, that's the way it was on Hoopers Island and that's the way it is on the islands of Asia. Steve says,

> Early in our Asian ventures, we'd sometimes be asked by political figures, just like business people in the United States get asked, 'Will you support me in the election?' We just say no. We tell them that we won't get involved in another country's politics. I tell them we have a rule, 'no politics and a low profile.' We believe that American companies should not

get involved in the politics of foreign countries. It's just not right. We'll help directly with community projects instead. Most of the governmental officials I meet understand our non-interference policy and I think they appreciate it.

I learned this very early in Asia when I was just starting our search for crab. On one outrigger boat trip to a little island with Dean, Jay and Lawrence, a local governmental official brought to my attention that a local church on a particular island needed extensive roof repairs. Dean told me not to give him money for the repairs but I did it anyway. That's the kind of things the Phillips family, Brice and Shirley and my brother and I have been doing for years. It seemed right up our alley.

Several months later I went back to the island and went to the church and the roof still wasn't repaired. I complained to the priest and his response was, 'What money?' It dawned on me then what had happened. I told the priest I'd get it straightened out and headed for the village official's house, when the priest told me, 'He doesn't live that way anymore.' I asked him where the official had moved and the priest pointed to the top of a nearby hill. There was a sparkling new home. I just sighed, gave the priest the money to fix the roof. Every time I see the roof I think of the fact that Phillips paid for it twice. But that taught me a lesson that was worth the money. That's when we adopted our policy on giving and it has worked well ever since. The first time you give money inappropriately, there are fifty people lined up at your door the next day. It's not smart to start, so we don't. We'll take a walk, well, a boat ride anyway, to the next island, the next country.

But Steve is quick to remark that he has never been approached in Asia or Mexico by any high level governmental officials and asked to do inappropriate things. The national governments were glad he was creating the industry, creating the jobs, and were supportive, not hindering.

He acknowledges now that it was scary going to the other side of the world from his Hoopers Island roots, against the wishes of his family, to attempt to create something that no one else had ever done, at least as far as he knew. "To create a completely new world wide industry, to create the product and the market."

> What I felt in my mind on the way over there to start the first factory, based on my experiences growing up and being a Hoopers Island boy, was that crab was there, the pieces of an industry were there; I knew that based on our feasibility studies - on the work that three Hoopers Island boys, me, Jay and Lawrence had done island hopping through Asia. There was crab, there were boats, there were fisherman, there were fishermen's families. They had everything we had on Hoopers Island but the structure. And I knew I had the experience to put it all together because of growing up on Hoopers Island, being in the crab packing business, being in the restaurant business and knowing what the consumer wants. I'd been dealing with crabbers in one way or the other since the day I was born; I'd been dealing with restaurant customers since I used to sit on the curb at 21st street in Ocean City with Jeff when we were young boys, both of us yelling in to Shirley, 'Customer coming, customer coming!' Everything was in my genes. All I had to do was set up the factory system and the shipping system, and then create the market. Of course I knew it wouldn't be simple, but I did know it was doable, and one of the traits I'd gotten from Brice and Shirley was confidence."

The way the structure is set up now, each piece of it helps the rest. Asian fishermen sell their crabs to mini-plants owned by or under contract to Phillips. Phillips then further processes the crab meat, blends it to the customers' specifications, ships it, passes some of it on to large customers unchanged (and some to its own restaurants unchanged.) The rest, in either its Baltimore factory or the new value added factory in Asia (and the planned value-added factory in Mexico,) is turned into value added products that are then sold to restaurants, used in Phillips' restaurants or sold to wholesalers or bulk users that sell it in retail outlets. It is vertical integration in the crab industry. All the way from the waters of the Honga and the waters of Asia, to the mouth of the ultimate consumer, Phillips is present.

Now Steve thinks about the new generation of Hoopers Island Phillips - bearers of the genes.

> For our kids, they're going to want to move on; just like all of us have done before them. Now we're Phillips Foods, not just Phillips Seafood. We already have the structure, the people, and new goals, areas we can branch out into as we grow.
>
> That's one of the reasons we're excited about opening Phillips' outlets in airports. It gets our name out there. We just opened in Baltimore-Washington International Airport at the Southwest terminal. We're also in Savannah, in Charleston. Basically, we're working with Host Marriott. We're hoping to be in four more airports in the near future.
>
> We've got our products in Europe. We're expanding into the entire European market. I was there about two months ago [two months before August 5th, 2005] and flew into Dublin and went to a Tesco Supermarket, walked in and there was a huge display of Phillips' crab meat right there in Ireland. I flew to Paris, went to the huge seafood market they have and there was Phillips' crab meat. We're starting to sell fish and some of our other products there as well.
>
> There hasn't been much consumption of crab meat in Europe in the past and Europe has a larger population than the United States and a much higher per-capita consumption of seafood in general. If you look at the two figures, Europe is a market five times bigger than the United States. And we want to be a major player in that market. We believe that if we do our job right, we will eventually have more sales in Europe than in the United States. The major growth portion of our business in the next five years is going to be the development of markets.
>
> Larry Sims [President of the Maryland Watermen's Association at the time the book was being written] said that what Phillips has done by finding enough crab product, is to promote crab meat throughout the country and in the process opening markets to Maryland watermen as well. Larry has the

vision to see the importance of future markets, and that you can't have future markets, or even keep the ones you have, without crab.

Jay Newcomb also recognizes the importance of markets.

"There's a bunch of overseas operations now by a lot of producers. But Steve was the first, the pioneer, and he's the best. What Steve did and the Phillips did just opened the market for crab meat. There were millions and millions of people who had never even tasted it because it wasn't sold in their markets. Especially out west in this country and internationally. Prior to Steve going to Asia, the states that had crab meat processing facilities couldn't even satisfy the market for crab meat in their own states. Picked crab meat, as well as crabs generally, were an east coast and southern thing. There wasn't even enough product to meet the demand of the east and the south. Crab meat just wasn't available outside those areas. Now, because he went over there, crab meat is eaten all over the world. London, everywhere. Everybody has a chance to taste that very special flavor.

And it's been great for the restaurants, not only the Phillips, but all of them, to have a steady supply. And people at home love the already prepared crab dishes that they can buy in the market. Just slap them in the oven, sit down to dinner without the mess of preparation. Getting the same crab cakes they ate fifty years ago at the Ocean City restaurant.

Steve is confident that the structure that he's put together that works so well in producing crab meat and creating markets, will work just as well for other products. While the emphasis may always be on seafood, Phillips Foods has a structure that can be used on an international scale, to produce and market other seafood and other food products as well. Phillips has just begun to market a line of products called Asian Rhythms - a line of Asian influenced seafood. He looks at the children coming up. "For the Phillips kids the business will have to move on. We're Phillips Foods not just Phillips Seafood. We already have the structure, we have great people, and our new goals are to branch out into other lines, non-seafood lines. We're already working in that direction."

Steve gives a large part of the credit for the success of Phillips Foods to his early life and his family.

> Although Brice's family was okay economically in Hoopers Island terms, Shirley's family would probably have been thought of as money poor under any terms. But, because of where they were, and who their families were, their economic status wasn't very important.
>
> I've always thought of myself, even when I was a little boy before all the restaurants started, as being rich. Not in money. It wasn't even important. I was rich because of where I was, who my family was, how I grew up on Hoopers Island and Ocean City. Rich in being able to learn about nature, being on the water, running boats when I was seven or eight years old. Growing up on Hoopers Island was great. Ocean City was great.
>
> That's why when I make all these trips to Asia and see what others call poverty in the way the fishermen and their families live, I don't see it that way. When I see the kids fishing near the shore or in the creeks, they're doing what I did back on Hoopers Island fifty years ago, what my mother did, my father did. According to the standards of the islands of Asia, there isn't poverty as we understand it. The fishermen and their families eat well, have the shelter they need. You are more likely to see malnourished children on the street corners in some areas of our major cities, or in many rural areas, than you are likely to see in the fishermen's villages in Asia.
>
> Are they rich. Not in money. Not in the terms of most Americans. But they are rich in a way of life and they are happy. They're the happiest people I've ever seen. They don't see themselves as victims. We never saw ourselves as victims back on Hoopers Island just because other areas may have had stronger economies. The Asian fisherman lives off the sea and

> the land just like we did back at Fishing Creek. We ate better back then than you ever could today. My grandmother grew her own vegetables. She had a chicken house in the back, fruit trees. She canned. We ate rockfish, crab, oysters whenever we wanted. How could you ever live a life better than that?

It seems especially fitting that Hoopers Island men and women opened up the rest of the world to the pleasures of eating crab. They left their 'remote' island in the Chesapeake, journeyed half-way around the world to other remote islands to make sure crabbing was done right. They, these Hoopers Islanders, were the pioneers. Not only Steve, Jeffrey, Brice and Shirley, but Jay, Lawrence, Debbie and the rest who helped. Hoopers Islanders are still bringing crabs to the tables of the world. It's what they have always done. Every crab now caught in Asia, every crab cake eaten in London, has a Hoopers Island connection.

# CHAPTER FIFTY-THREE

## *The future*

When interviewed Steve isn't afraid to say what he thinks and he put no limits on my quoting him. He is an inveterate thinker, even during an interview. He simply never stops thinking. When he's not thinking, he's pacing, looking for information in files on the computer, going to get a quick cup of coffee, introducing you to the corporate counsel, others on the headquarter's staff, listening with one ear to a report from the research kitchens, another report from the far ends of the sea, hiring, everything, without missing a beat in the interview. I should have filmed it.

He has some innovative ideas about the future. He shared many with me. With only a little editing, I share them.

> Sometimes the seafood industry doesn't put enough back. It just takes. So what we have throughout the world is a decline in seafood resources. Some of our fisheries are no longer sustainable at current harvest rates. I think there's going to more of an outcry from people all over the world, saying, 'You can't keep taking, taking, taking. You have to make sure the resource is sustainable.'
>
> I think you're going to end up in the future with demands from governments in regards to conservation and maintenance of resources. Governments in the future may end up creating

quotas, or some other method, that limits the importation or exportation of certain types of seafood products between areas and various countries throughout the world.

All that's going to happen in the future. Should it happen? Yeah, probably it should come, because what's good for industry is to make sure you have something to process. Sustainability! This whole equation, industry, fishermen, all that, what's the most important thing? For us the most important thing is crab, fish, oysters, whatever, because that's what everybody depends on. From the bottom to the top of the industry. These big fishermen's families in the Philippines live off the resource in one way or the other, and there is no other resource that can sustain them. How will they eat in the future if the resource is gone? Who is going to feed them? We, as a concerned company, have to understand that. And we do.

When I was a young boy in my grandfather's boat on the Chesapeake in fifteen feet of water you could see the bottom. There was plenty of crab, rock, other seafood. You could see it. We thought it would last forever. Well, we all know now that if you don't take care of it, it doesn't last forever. Our oysters in the Chesapeake are basically gone, our shad are gone. Rock were almost lost forever. Crabs are left, but they're fewer every year. That's just in my lifetime and that's a relatively short period of time. We can screw things up pretty quick.

How do you rebuild all that? You probably never will. There may not be enough money in the world. Population pressures, development pressures throughout the Chesapeake region argue against it. And you can't stop those pressures, more and more people come into existence every day. But, there are things you can do to give Mother Nature a helping hand.

They saved the rockfish with the moratorium and that caused me to ask myself, why can't we do something for the crab? We helped the rockfish, we need to help the crab. I went to State officials some time ago and asked about crab nurseries for the bay, breeding crabs, things of that nature. They said it couldn't be done. I asked them if we could try it, would they try it? They declined to try.

I went back over to Asia and worked with the Departments of Fisheries over there. In some parts of Asia they are light years ahead of us in things like aquiculture and hatcheries, marine science and fisheries management. If you look around over there you see thousands of thousands of hectares devoted to aquiculture, prawn farms and like. What they've done with shrimp, breeding and hatching shrimp eggs and stuff like that.

So I went over there and we started working with crab. They had never worked with crab before because there had never been any market until Phillips Foods began its overseas operations. I arranged for a couple of their scientists to work with crab. We found that the secret to hatching crab, is water quality. We also grew algae and other microscopic creatures that early stages of crab feed on. We were able successfully to do what had been said couldn't be done. We took a female crab's million or so eggs and ended up after they went through the various larvae stages with seven hundred thousand little crabs. To me that was significant.

I came back to Maryland all excited about what we had been able to do with the Asian crab. I went to the University of Maryland Bio-Tech Center and asked them if they would work on it. They said they lacked funds. With Larry Simm's help funds were funneled to them, almost a half million dollars over a period of time.

I'm not saying that aquiculture will ever take the place of regulation or anything like that, but, along with regulation and enforcement, in the future the industry as a viable concern in the Chesapeake may be significantly helped if we can establish a string of hatcheries along the shores of the bay. Raise crab and turn the baby crabs loose in the bay to serve the industries. We have hatcheries for fresh water trout, a purely recreational resource - why not for crab, a much more significant resource; at least for people that love crab and for the economy.

We could get watermen involved in working alongside scientists in the hatcheries. We found in Asia that you have to grow the algae and other foods for the different stages of the process in small enough sizes for the little crabs to eat them. It doesn't work if the food is three times the size of the organism that's trying to feed on it. When they're really small they shed every day so the size of the food has to change. It is difficult, but it can be done. We did it in Asia. Feed it until it looks like a crab.

Also keep the water at the required level of salinity for each stage of the process. We found that to be essential in Asia. It is probably not a coincidence that our crab move around the Chesapeake Bay during the hatching and growing stages. Over long periods of time the crab may have adapted to particular salinity levels for the various stages of the hatching process. We have to try and duplicate it in the hatcheries.

Then, instead of taking them from the hatcheries and putting them into ponds like they do with shrimp in Asia, just release them into the bay, tens of millions and even more of them. Instead of just a couple of eggs from a female making it to the adult crab stage, there will be hundreds and hundreds of thousands from each female, if successful. And I'm confident that what was done in Asia can be done here.[42]

Steve summarizes,

Of course anytime you broach new ideas not everyone is receptive. The current Maryland model is regulation and enforcement - and I'm in favor of it. It is always going to be necessary. I just want to add to the equation. Put crabs in the bay and still regulate how they're harvested. I think the combination could restore crabs to historically high levels, or higher. At least there will be something to harvest.

[42] The *Virginian Pilot*, in an article about crab aquiculture, reported in 2001 that Japan had developed a hatchery process for the Asian crab. The Japanese were releasing 50 to 60 million crabs a year into the wild. It certainly appears that it can be done, if the will to do it is there and entrenched interests are accommodated.

Steve Phillips with an Asian crab in the 'Wet Crab' market in Bangkok, Thailand.

Hoopers Island crab pots on the way to the testing waters in Thailand. First feasibility trip of the Hoopers Islanders - Jay Newcomb, Lawrence Rhea and Steve Phillips

Hoopers Islanders, Lawrence Rhea and Steve Phillips, 'on the beach', along the coast of Thailand.

Jay Newcomb meets King Cobra. Thailand.

Wading ashore somewhere on the coast of Thailand.

Fishing (crabbing) boats on the mangrove coast in Thailand.

Island in the Visayan Sea, Philippines. Land's end is to the left of the picture. A Phillips' mini-factory is behind the palms along the beach.

Miss Chesapeake, inter-island outrigger boat in the Visayan Sea. In addition to Miss Chesapeake, there is now an A. E. Phillips and Son sailing the waters of the Philippines

Nipa hut, Philippines where the Hoopers Islanders stayed during their hunt for crab.

Hoopers Island crab pots on the rear of outrigger boat heading to the testing grounds in the Visayan Sea. Steve Phillips among the pots.

Hoopers Island's Ambassador of Good Will, Lawrence Rhea, with a friend in the Philippines.

Phillips' early mini-factory on an island in the Visayan Sea. Philippines.

Outrigger fishing boats at a fishing village in the Philippines.

Outrigger fishing boat with fishermen removing Asian crab from nets. Visayan Sea, Philippines.

Brice and Shirley in the Philippines.

Shirley Phillips with the ladies picking crab at a Phillips' mini-plant in the Philippines.

Large Phillips SEAFOODS INDONESIA state-of-the-art factory at Pemalang, Indonesia

Dignitaries and Phillips' officials at the opening of the Pemalang factory.

Steve Phillips addressing the crowd at the opening.

Typical Indonesian fishing (crabbing) harbor.

Large picking room in the Phillips' plant in Indonesia.

Closer view of ladies in the picking room in the Indonesian plant.

Typical sanitizing foot bath at the entrance to a Phillip's plant in Asia.

Crates of large live Asian crabs heading for the steaming room at a plant in Asia.

Typical boiler at Asian plant.

Callinectes sapidus, the Maryland and Atlantic blue crab. The Maryland blue crab is considered to be the tougher crab in that it can survive out of water much longer than the Asian crab. (For a color and size comparison see pictures of both types of crabs contained on the back flap of the dust-jacket.)

Portunus pelagicus, the Asian 'blue swimming crab'. On average the Asian crab is larger than the Maryland blue crab. See the photographs of the different crabs on the back flap of the dust jacket.

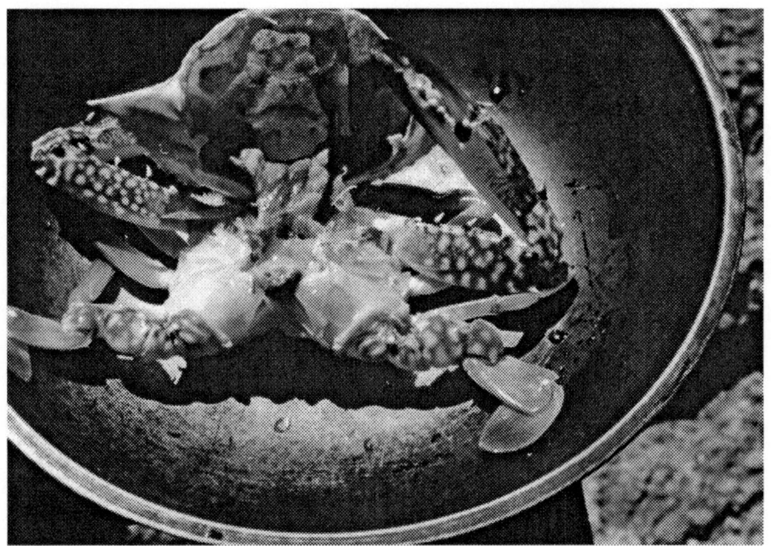

A 'debacked' Portunus pelagicus, the Asian crab, showing the large back fin crab meat lumps. As can be seen in the photographs on the back flap, there are different configurations of the two types of crab. The Asian crab is larger and has more of a variation in color. Some of the Asian crabs have spots that are absent in the Maryland blue crab (there is an Atlantic crab, the 'calico' crab, that has spots, but it is not utilized commercially.) The Asian crab's claws are also longer and proportionately thinner in respect to its body than are the claws of the blue crab..

A 'debacked' Callinectes sapidus, the Maryland blue crab, showing its back fin area. Blue crabs are remarkably consistent in coloration. Their claws are fatter in proportion to their bodies than are the Asian crab's. It is a more compact crab.

A Phillips with his bride on a sailing vessel - again

Steve Phillips - Chief Executive Officer - Phillips Foods.

Jeffrey Phillips - Captain Happiness - 2005.

# BOOK FOUR

---

*Living and Giving*

# CHAPTER FIFTY-FOUR

## *Living - Steve*

All of the Phillips at one time or the other enjoyed a good party. Some still do, although to hear him tell of it, Steve is mostly retired from the party scene. Steve likes to read, but generally has little time except when he is on a plane.

Fishing was a passion in early years, and, one suspects that passion could be rekindled if the bill-fish returned in large numbers to the waters off Ocean City. In the past, as is natural with Hoopers Islanders, and like his parents before him, he loved to fish. In college he roomed with Virgil Price who had a sport fishing boat. Steve explains;

> At the University of Miami Virgil Price and I were roommates. We arranged our classes where we could fish almost every Friday, Saturday, Sunday and Monday. For the five years I was in college, if you wanted to find us on the weekends we'd be out at the 20 to 40 fathom line, trying to catch sailfish. One day we caught around thirty-five - of course they were Palm Beach releases where we used extraordinarily long leaders, backed up to a group of sailfish 'balling bait', hooked up, snubbed the swivel to the rod tip, count it as a release [The author described the Palm Beach release in his first book *From Lands Over*.] For a Hoopers Island boy that wasn't really fishing, but it was fun and we won tournaments.

> We fished all the tournaments when I was in college. We won the Ft. Lauderdale Blue Marlin Tournament one year with two blue marlin. We fished the Masters, the Gold Cup up off Palm Beach.
>
> Later, after college, when I was back in Ocean City I went to Florida and bought a twenty-five foot Chris Craft with a tuna tower on it and ran it up to Ocean City. The first day we fished it off Ocean City we caught a white and a blue marlin. I love fishing.

But his greatest passion is competitive sailing, a passion he shares with Maxine (He calls her Max,) his wife. He readily acknowledges it.

> Sailing is absolutely the passion of my life. I love it. It's almost like I'm one with it. It just re-energizes me. And I really like the competitive part of it. The racing. My grand father loved it. Anybody who is on a boat that has a sail on it and meets another boat with a sail on it, is going to start racing.
>
> I feel like growing up on Hoopers Island I have saltwater in my veins. I could never live and not be on the water. When I get home the first thing I do is go out on the porch and look at the river. Study it, see how the wind is acting, how it comes off the shore, eddies here and there. I'm setting up a race just sitting there on the porch. Checking how the wind shifts. In my mind I'm figuring out where my header is, where to tack. In fact, I did that for three years before we had a race on the Severn River and I won the race because I knew how the wind acted on the river better than anybody else.
>
> Max and I have two racing sailboats. One is a J105, a one design boat[43] 33 feet long. There are about 50 boats in the Annapolis area that regularly race in this class. We've won the national championship in this class twice. Once in Annapolis and the last time in Chicago in a field of 51 qualifying boats.

[43] In one design class racing boats, all the boats in a particular class are built and equipped exactly the same to maximize that importance of the crew's skill.

> Our other boat is a Farr 40, which is probably considered to be the most competitive one design class in the world. We won the world championship in that class in 2002 at Nassau in the Bahamas.[44] I call it *Le Renard* for Marvin Foxwell who really taught me to sail.

A yachting association's publication[45] described that world championship: "In the end it was all about the man and his boat rather than the place. . . . Steve Phillips had stayed true to a promise among crewmembers to 'keep it clean'. Having bought *Le Renard* only last summer, he was truly the dark horse. He sailed to a 22 point lead over a fleet that not only represented eight nations but also brimmed with Rolex Yachtsmen of the Year, Olympic Medalists and veterans of the America's Cup and Volvo Ocean races."

For Steve nothing comes close to sailing, nothing compares with it. Even to me, someone who is not a competitive sailor, Steve's passion is especially understandable. Sailing gave him Maxine.

She remembers her first experience with the Hoopers Island man.

> Ten years ago I was sailing in the annual Annapolis to Oxford Race and after three long tacks, the boat appeared to be well ahead of the other boats in our class. As I commented on our good fortune to my team's tactician, he at first nodded in the affirmative, but then squinted his eyes far down the bay, close to where the Choptank empties into the Chesapeake. He pointed to a boat so far in front of us that I wouldn't have seen it except for its breeze filled spinnaker literally sailing us out of sight. He said then, 'Yes, we're ahead of everyone except my old Eastern Shore buddy, Steve Phillips. He grew up on Hoopers Island and he knows just where to sail to take advantage of the current and the breeze. . . .'
>
> Were it not for my defeat on the race course that day, I wouldn't have had to congratulate the victor, and would never have met the man who ultimately became my permanent sailing partner and life mate.

[44] They also won the East Coast Championships in that year.

[45] The Farr40 Association.

. . .

Most people approach sailing as the ultimate way to spend quiet days in relaxation. For us, that will never be the case. Once in the early years, . . .we chartered a sailboat in the Caribbean for a 'quiet and serene' vacation. We left St. Thomas in a balmy 12-knot breeze, supposedly heading for a relaxing sail to St. Martin. About ten minutes out of St. Thomas, however, we spotted another sailboat on approximately the same course and heading as ours. Within minutes Steve was running all about the boat, trimming a sheet, adjusting the leech line on our jib, and hardening up our main halyard. He was obviously tweaking every knot of speed out of the cruising boat that could be tweaked. We were in a race. The other boat had no idea that a frantic competition was taking place, but nonetheless it was a race for Steve. Never mind that we were sailing a 40 foot, tubby keelboat and the other vessel was a state of the art . . . catamaran. Of course we sailed into the harbor at St. Martin just ahead of our unsuspecting 'competitors.' At that moment, I knew that my life with Steve wasn't destined to have much quietness or serenity.

Steve's zest for life, his uncompromising drive to compete, influences every part of his day. Just as he inspires those in his family business to share in his vision and direction for the company, he does the same on the water.

. . .

Several years ago I urged him to get into the prestigious Farr 40 class. . . . . Many people, including his trusted sailing mentor admonished him not to enter such a demanding class. Another friend counseled Steve to give himself a couple of years to work his way up to a middle ranking in the class. He went on to warn Steve that because of his not getting into sailing until relatively late in life, he would never be able to dominate in the class since he would be competing against others who had Olympic sailing pedigrees.

That same year, just a few months after that conversation, we won the World Championship. Right after winning, Steve got that twinkle in his eyes that he gets when he knows he has just pulled something off that nobody expected him to do. I'm sure being told that it couldn't be done, factored strongly in our ultimate victory.

# CHAPTER FIFTY-FIVE

*Living - Brice & Shirley*

*They had lost the most precious time in the lives of young lovers, time taken by a war to save mankind. But, even in that war they had been lovers still, across the thousands of miles of sea and land. In love letters. Not a day went by when he did not tell her he loved her.*

*He had told her in the beginning, told her that he would make up for the years they'd lost during the war. They would have a time, he said, for living. There would be time for parties, for traveling. Time for her to see Europe, to see the world. Time for a Hoopers Island girl to become a woman of the world.*

*Not a day went by in the years of the war that she didn't tell him that she loved him. In love letters. Not a day went by during those years that she didn't worry over him. Cry over him. Miss him. And then he'd come home from the war, stepping off the bus in Cambridge. If anything, handsomer then when he'd left.*

*He had told her on the night they'd wed that he'd always loved her, would always love her and he had loved her every day of their lives. But he'd also told her on that night so long ago that she'd have a yacht and a captain to go with it. She had told him on the night that they had wed that she had always loved him, would always love him. And she had loved him every day of their lives. But, she'd also told him on that night so long ago, that, in time, she would make him a millionaire.*

*And the time had come.*

Once World War II was over and Brice had returned home to start managing the packing house, the two of them always managed to find a way to have fun, usually with other friends. Steve and Brice remembered a trip they all made in an A. E. Phillips' work boat, the old *Shirley,* from Hoopers Island down the bay to Norfolk, to pick up an old World War II landing craft to tow it back to Hoopers Island.

Shirley as a girl back on Hoopers Island had been known as a great dancer. As his letters before they were married indicated, Brice recognized - and worried on occasion about it when he was in Baltimore in the late 1930s. In a letter dated 10/14/38 to Shirley back on Hoopers Island, he said in a serious context, "Don't dance too much."

On the trip to Norfolk. Steve was at the wheel, running the boat. Brice recalls him being a young teenager. Tom Flowers and Fran, his wife, were along for the trip. Shirley and her cousin Tom were great dance partners. Along the way Brice got some music playing and Shirley and Tom started dancing in the open cockpit of the boat, jitterbugging down the Chesapeake to Norfolk. It is easy to imagine what some gnarled old sea captain heading down the bay in a freighter or tanker must have thought as they overtook the old *Shirley*, a work boat, with a kid at the wheel and a couple jitterbugging in the cockpit at the stern.

One interesting social story of a special Halloween has survived. It shows the length that Brice and Shirley will go to liven up a gathering. It happened at an annual party at a fire house on Hoopers Island. In Asia it would have been known as the 'Year of the Horse'.

There was a costume contest and Shirley was determined to win. The person who told of the party, and who wishes to remain anonymous, says that Shirley had obtained a real stuffed horse's head and had managed to find an especially fine horse costume that matched the head of the horse.

They made their grand entrance into the Fire Hall, Shirley, dressed in a cow girl costume, leading the horse, and shooting a cap pistol in the air. Brice had stuffed his head inside the horse's head, and

Charles Shockley[46] was concealed to the rear. Atop the horse was Charles Shockley's wife, a tiny women, also dressed in a cow girl's outfit shooting off a cap pistol. Shirley's genius then became apparent. Behind the horse came her brother, Billy, in a sanitation worker's uniform with a bucket and a shovel.

Shirley had somehow rigged the costume with a way to dispose of horse droppings from within the costume out the appropriate place on a horse. Underneath the costume, Charles Shockley was kept busy. He had a large bucket of real droppings inside the costume with him and periodically would cause some to be expelled from the rear of the horse. Billy would promptly shovel it up and put it in his bucket. At one point when passing near an older gentleman, Charlie Parker, whose eyesight was failing, Mr. Shockley made the horse perform that peculiar function. Charlie Parker saw what was expelled better than he saw the horse. Even after everyone else understood what was going on, Mr. Parker was still arguing, "I've seen a lot of horses in my lifetime and I've seen what they do. I tell you - that was a horse."

The Phillips and the Shockleys won the first prize.

Later, after they had expanded the Crab House with several second floor dining rooms that they converted into living quarters in the wintertime, they would hold great parties at the Crab House for many of their local friends. Ann Showell remembers one dinner:

> What a time. Shirley and Brice would invite large numbers of families to the second floor of the Crab House for New Years. Great camaraderie. Imogene and Earl Pierce were always there. One year, not realizing that Imogene had a pet pig that she really loved, Shirley got everyone sitting down at the tables, and then on a huge platter had a whole roasted pig brought in, head and all, probably had an apple in its mouth,

[46] I interviewed this Charles Shockley by telephone.( As earlier noted he was the source of the information that the Henry I. Phillips plant was the plant that Brice and his father bought after the 1933 hurricane.) There were several Charles Shockleys in the phone book. I picked a number at random, called it, and when I received an answer, started out by asking, "Are you the same Charles Shockey who was in the hind end of a horse at a Halloween party on Hoopers Island 50 or 60 years ago?" The answerer began to laugh as soon as I asked the question and I knew I had the right Charles Shockley.

and sat it at the center of the table right in front of Imogene. Imogene broke down and started crying, cried most of the night. What Imogene loved, she loved greatly; and she loved her pig.

Ours was delicious, anyway.

Ann and her late husband, John Dale Showell, had met Brice and Shirley soon after they opened their initial Ocean City carry-out and a year or so later, the restaurant. At the time, John Dale was working at a bank as a teller at a relatively low salary. John Dale met Shirley because she would take deposits to the bank. Ann remembers,

> Johnny started going up there for lunch at the Crab House every day and Shirley got so worried about how much money he was spending, that she started charging him half price for everything. She felt that bank tellers worked for low wages and she felt sorry for him. After that we became best friends in the world. Later when we were all able, we traveled a lot together.
>
> One time Shirley even gave me Brice. We were in Singapore at the Mandarin Hotel and sitting around partaking of some libations and Shirley said, 'You know Ann, I really love you and want you to have Brice. If anything happens to me you are going to have Brice.' She sort of ignored the fact that Johnny was still living and quite healthy.
>
> So, I've always felt that I have to look after Brice. I really wanted to stay healthy so that Brice would be taken care of if anything were to happen to Shirley.
>
> We were always like teammates. One year the two couples and our children took a trip to England on the first Queen Elizabeth on its last voyage. It was my first cruise and Shirley's second. All of us were on the top deck when we passed the Statute of Liberty. Brice and Johnny started to tip the various crew members heavily and they gave our husbands some of the flags flown on the last voyage of the Queen Elizabeth.

Ann and Shirley decided to go to their cabins and unpack for the voyage. They agreed to meet the husbands for lunch in the dining room. When lunchtime came, no husbands. They weren't there. The ladies went back to their staterooms, still no husbands. They went up on the top deck, they weren't there. They looked around the ship. They couldn't find their husbands. Ann describes what happened thereafter,

> Shirley said, 'Ann, somebody has robbed them and thrown them overboard.' She became very concerned. We kept on looking and looking - still couldn't find them. Finally we went to the purser. Shirley said, 'We're having a terrible time. We've lost our husbands.' He responded, 'Don't worry lady. I have yet to see a cruise where that doesn't happen. Don't worry. They'll show up - they always do.' That didn't help Shirley stop worrying, and she said then, 'Suppose someone has robbed them?' The purser replied, 'No madam, that didn't happen. You've just lost them temporarily. They'll show up.'
>
> Well they showed up about three sheets to the wind and Brice went to his bunk and fell asleep. Johnny joined us in the dining room. Where they had been was a mystery for awhile.
>
> The next day when we were all walking on deck, two of the girl members of the crew passed us, looked at our husbands, and one said 'Hi big John.' Another one said 'Hello Brice.' They had to confess then. When they had first got on the ship they had found their way into the bowels of the ship where many of the crew members were having a last voyage party, and John and Brice had joined it.

Finally the ship arrived at La Havre, France. It hadn't been scheduled for a passenger stop there, but had stopped to let off crew members and to take aboard provisions. It was early in the morning and most of the passengers were asleep, but the four of them had managed to stay awake so they could see France. As they walked around the decks, they got hungry and went looking for a place on the boat that was open where they could get something to eat. Nothing was open. Ann explains how they resolved their dilemma

As we were walking around the decks we found an open porthole into a galley. It was high and small. Shirley was the only one who had a chance of fitting through it. So we hoisted her up, and slid her through the porthole and into the galley. All she could find to eat was a half a pineapple and a gravy boat half full of gravy. As we pulled her back through the porthole she spilled the gravy all down the front of her clothes. It made her so mad that when she finally got out she took the pineapple and the rest of gravy and crushed it on top of Johnny's head. I still have the gravy boat.

They were all in their sixties.

On another cruise Brice got Ann to made a heavy investment.

We were taking a voyage out of Singapore around the Indonesian Islands and we took a side trip on a volcanic island. We had to ride in the back of a pickup to reach the top of the mountain. People would try to sell us stuff every time the truck stopped. Brice saw someone trying to sell little stone statutes and thought they were very old and possibly very valuable. He bought a lot of them and talked me into buying a lot. We were making an investment. After we bought the statues we continued on up the mountain.

There was a tribe that lived on top of the mountain and there was a crypt or coffin like object that had carvings of human sacrifice on its side. Shirley got a little frightened and I had to calm her down. Then the chief of the tribe came over and grabbed Shirley and she was too frightened to refuse. They began to dance together. Red tinted saliva from chewing betel nuts was coming out of his mouth as he and Shirley gyrated. He went into a trance while he was dancing with her. Shirley's eyes were big as saucers.

Five days later the little stone statues that were going to make Brice and me rich, crumbled in our hands. They were

> made of sand temporarily bound together by some substance. We'd been duped. Taken.

Brice and Shirley love to travel, and as they became financially able, they traveled further and further. At first it was the day trips to Solomons Island, Maryland, later the weekend trips to various ports on the Chesapeake Bay in the old Gertie V. Later, in between seasons, they'd travel in the United States, taking the boys when they could. Ultimately, they traveled throughout the world, sometimes taking their entire family, including grandchildren, with them.

Often they would travel with friends like Ann and John Dale Showell, Dr. Frank Townsend and Lil, Earl and Billie Brittingham, the Frank Perdues. Sometimes they'd travel alone. Often they'd take business related trips to other countries with Maryland economic officials, always at their own expense. Over the years they've been to Russia several times, to Egypt, trips through the Panama Canal, to China, Canada, Indonesia, the Baltic countries, Germany, and England. They still travel, going up the Mississippi in 2003, more recently taking a cruise on the new Queen Mary.

Brice also has a passion for cars. Still has a De Lorean in his garage. Ann Showell remembers a trip with Shirley in the De Lorean.

> Once we were going to Salisbury for an important lunch meeting. Shirley wanted to drive the De Lorean, but she wasn't very familiar with it. First of all Shirley is not the best driver. We got in the car and at first Shirley couldn't reach the pedals. Then she drove into the drive-through lane at a local bank to get some money and didn't know how to get the windows down. So she opened the door, it would only go a foot or so because the doors opened upwards. Then when she finally got the bank situation straightened out, we headed on over to Salisbury. About half way over it started to rain, heavily. Shirley didn't know how to turn the windshield wipers on and we rode all the way at a very slow rate of speed in the rain without wipers. All I said to her was, 'We're going to be late.'

Dr. Frank[47] Townsend and Lil, his wife, the Showells, the Phillips, and others became close friends. There were the parties at the Crab House, at each others' houses, but there was a special place 'down the beach,' a hunting club called 'High Winds'. High Winds was built by Glenn L. Riddle, the owner of the race horses Man of War and War Admiral(the horse that was prominent as the match race opponent of Seabiscuit in the recent movie of the same name.) Mr. Riddle owned a large horse farm several miles west on the mainland that is now the site of a high end housing development.

Eventually 'High Winds' was bought by Dr. Townsend, Walter Clauge,[48]Harry Aydolette Jarvis, and Daniel 'Spriggy' Trimper.

Ann Showell remembers that 'High Winds' was made from two or three shanty boats hooked together at the middle with another big room. The shanty boats were bedroom wings. The big room in the middle was a 'communal room.' Lil Townsend remembers it more specifically, 'It had a nice kitchen, pantry, big dining area, a stove for heat in the cold months, rocking chairs, three couches, four bedrooms and two baths. According to Mrs. Townsend:

> We all cut up. We used to give theme parties. Come as someone you wished you were. Once Frank came as Eric Sevareid and Ann came as _______tight. One time we all got a little tipsy [drinking stingers] and formed a congo line and went around 'High Winds' singing 'Hi Ho, Hi Ho, it's off to sea we go,' as we went out on the dock to take a ride on the *Love Boat* [Dr. Townsend's boat]. [Ann Showell managed to fall into the boat attempting to board it, and never spilled her stinger - an event she remains proud of today.]

New guests were regularly exposed to that old game - the snipe hunt. But there appears to be no recollection that Brice and Shirley ever bit on the old gambit. It would be hard to trick Hoopers Islanders to go on a snipe hunt. But there was hunting, too. It was a gunning

[47] Dr. Frank Townsend was Ocean City's preeminent doctor for fifty years, or more, as had his father been before him. A son follows in their footsteps.

[48] Walter Clauge, together with his family would later drown trying to get across the back bay when his boat capsized in a bad storm. His dog was also thought to have drowned but was later found stranded on an island in the bay.

club. But, the only remark the writer has been able to glean from those that were there about hunting, is Brice's cryptic repeat of what he said about Hoopers Island hunting, "Were there limits?" From personal experience the writer is aware that the particular area was not one known for rigid adherence to hunting laws.

Lil Townsend comments that "They [Brice and Shirley] were strangers when they came to Ocean City, but within a year or two they were full fledged members of our social group. To us, it didn't make much difference what anybody did, just that they did it well."

Later, after Steve bought his Chris Craft sport fisherman, Brice bought a sports fisherman, naming it after his wife. He even had a captain for it, Whaley Brittingham. With that acquisition he kept his version of his wedding night promise to Shirley.

One winter Brice and Shirley, along with Ann and John Dale took the *Shirley* down the inland waterway to Florida to have it available for the Florida fishing. As Ann explains it;

> Whaley had to work overtime keeping the generator working. Every time we stopped for the night, Shirley would start cooking on two hot plates and two electric frying pans. She'd cook enough food for everyone in all the boats at the dock whenever we overnighted, at Great Bridge [normally the first stop on a trip inside from Ocean City south.] and all the different places going south. She could feed an army with just two frying pans and a hot plate. A fun time. A super time.

Ann Showell tells of another memorable evening in New York about a month before Jeffrey's accident. They had all gone to New York to celebrate someone's birthday.

> Steve had a friend from college in New York who had told him about a great restaurant called the *Monk's Inn*. He'd told Brice and Shirley and they had made arrangements for our whole group to dine at this great restaurant. That was the first mistake.
>
> Everyone in the party was from the Eastern Shore, most appreciated a good sip of hard liquor before dinner. The *Monk's*

*Inn* didn't serve liquor and our men didn't drink wine in those days. The next mistake was that the menu was in French and the waiters didn't speak English, or wouldn't speak it. But we were saved from complete disaster. We thought. Harry and Bernice Murphy were with us and Harry said 'Not to worry, I speak French and I'll order the best dish in the house for all of us.' Last mistake. Before long everyone was served with Steak Tartar - uncooked hamburger with a raw egg on the top. Harry's days as an interpreter were over.

# CHAPTER FIFTY-SIX

## *Giving*

The most difficult part of accumulating information for the book was the main reason I wanted to write it in the first place, or perhaps I should say guide it, for it has mostly written itself. Everyone who knows any of the Phillips, but especially Brice and Shirley who have been around a little longer, also knows that 'giving back' is what they are about. Yes, they live well, they are wealthy. They travel, they give parties, go to parties. They live it up on occasion. Anyone who ever looks in Brice's eyes knows that.

But in the places of their origins, the Eastern Shore's book end islands - Hoopers Island to the west and Ocean City to the east, the social aspect of their lives is but a minor sideshow. They have been giving of their time and their energies, and yes their money, to a wide range of charitable, civic, educational and scientific causes all of their lives.

The difficult part of writing this particular chapter is that Shirley and Brice refused to help me on this issue. According to Shirley, "That's between me and God. He knows what we've done." And she simply refused at first to even let me mention the subject. Later, after a series of entreaties that the book would be incomplete without it, she said "If you can get it on your own, that's your business, but I'm not telling you. I'd feel like I was bragging." Steve agrees, "As to charity, Shirley's position is understandable. I have an old saying that 'a gift is not a gift if you call it a gift.' I like to keep a really low profile and I think my mother is probably right because I think pretty much the same way." All I could get him to directly say is, "We try to give." What I have found out about their charitable and civic activities has come from other sources first. Later they might confirm something but noone in the family would intentionally directly tell me of their charitable activities. Because of that, I have only scratched the surface with the information that follows.

Over a period of time I would see things, hear things, and I would go looking in other places as well. I didn't get the complete picture, no one ever will. But, I got enough of this particular aspect of their lives, along with the ways in which they have treated their employees, to at least sketch the picture of the giving nature of the Phillips family.

When you interview Brice and Shirley, they are compelled to feed you. They've been feeding people so long they can't help themselves. Besides, they're still Hoopers Islanders at heart. So, often our meetings began or ended in a dining room and frequently we'd be joined by their friends. Shirley or Brice would always be asking about how various friends of the old days were doing. If there was one not doing well, Shirley would excuse herself and unobtrusively write a personal check. She would return and quietly slip what looked like a check (and was a check) to someone at the table for delivery to whomever, someone they may not have seen for fifty years. It went on all the time. Shirley pretended that Brice didn't know about it, and he pretended he didn't, but he did.

I have learned that they keep a special account just for helping friends and other deserving people. And these were, and are, the types of gifts that are after-tax gifts. Personal gifts to individuals in need. Some of them I saw were substantial.

There were other public sources of information about their giving, and some private ones as well. I was one of the direct sources.

In the early nineties, I learned of a promising young high school senior who had a serious problem. He had saved up approximately $18,000 to pay for his first year's college tuition. About a week before his senior year was over his money was stolen. When I found out about it, I went over to the Crab House and met with Brice and Shirley. They suggested several other people for me to go see, and handed me a large check for the boy. Within 48 hours I was handing the boy a check replacing his stolen money, and, additionally, a four year, full scholarship to college. The young man now works on Wall Street.

But there are other sources. Sometimes their own records. Once Shirley and a friend met with Dr. Townsend and brow-beat him until he agreed to be the chairman of the fund drive for a new hospital. Later, Shirley stood up at the public kickoff for the fund-raising drive for the hospital and announced, "The Phillips family is giving seventy-five thousand dollars right now. Let's see who can match it." And it was matched, many times over by others, and again by themselves, and now that hospital sits in Powell Esham's old back pasture just outside of Berlin where his dogs chased me when I was a boy. Thirty minutes closer to Ocean City than the next nearest hospital. Over the years, untold lives have been saved by that thirty minutes.

There is the interview I had with Joyce Flowers, proudly of Fishing Creek/ Hoopers Island, who said, "Shirley was attending a function over here not too long ago. She asked me how I had made out in Isabel. I told her that I'd had some water damage. Before she left that day she handed me a thousand dollar check, a personal check, told me that she 'hoped it would help some.' Well it helped pay for the damage, helped my spirits, too." Ms. Flowers went on to note, "Shirley was never big in talking about what she does, but here on Hoopers Island we always knew when they were giving to a cause. The preachers would stand up in church and say, 'We got a big donation from Brice and Shirley Phillips this week. Everyone knows Shirley and Brice both keep their word."

Charlotte Sours notes,

> People looked up to Uncle Brice and knew of his soft heart___Long before they were rich they were giving money to others some of which I'm sure was never returned. But that didn't matter; they keep giving anyway, because that is who they are.

Every year since approximately 1968, at the end of the season, Brice and Shirley turned over the Beach Plaza to their church for a supper. The affair has gotten so big that it is now held in the Crab House. The church supplies the volunteer wait and hostess staff, Brice and Shirley, with some contributions from a few purveyors, provide all the rest. The hotel(or restaurant,) the food, the food preparation, the clean up, all comes from the Phillips. The supper has raised between ten and seventeen thousand dollars each year (seventeen thousand dollars last fall) - for 35 years - four to five hundred thousand dollars over the years.

In addition to helping their Ocean City church, they always participate in the activities of the Hoopers Island churches. Tom Flowers noted in our interview, "Brice and Shirley are consistent contributors to the Memorial Fund on Hoopers Island. They donate free weekends in Ocean City for almost any Hoopers Island church or civic fund raiser."

I have managed through various means to uncover numerous other contributions they have made in just the last three years. These are only some of their personal contributions, and the contributions of one of the corporations, a corporation in Ocean City. The figures do not include any contributions by those entities out west. There are at least ten other corporations, not counting what is probably the biggest of them all, Phillips Foods, whose charitable and civic contributions are not included in this computation, although the writer is aware of at least one additional contribution or grant made by Phillips Foods in the $400,000 dollar range within the same period of time.

According to written records in my possession, just some of Brice and Shirley's personal contributions, and the contributions from the one corporation in 2004 were at least $105,000. In 2003 they were at least $113,000, in 1002 at least $94,000. Additionally, through the first four months of 2005 the contributions of only the same single corporation amounted to over $13,000. I wasn't able to find any information on their personal contributions during this 2005 period. These are only contributions to entities with tax deductible status. They don't include gifts like those to the young student many years ago, the gifts to Joyce Flowers or any gifts to the many individuals back on Hoopers Island and in Ocean City who they help, constantly.

Additionally, there were the days when they led the restaurant industry with the creation of the profit sharing plan, the life insurance plan, the other employee benefit plans.

And these contributions, as I see it, are just the tip of the iceberg when it comes to donations make by the other corporations. Steve has carried the same philosophy overseas with Phillips Foods' operations.

Dr. Robbins first told me of this particular contribution, and only when I informed Steve that I knew of it, did he discuss it. During the early days of his time in the Philippines, Steve became aware that there seemed to be disproportionately large numbers of young girls with cleft lips or palates. On one of the islands where he had constructed a plant and was doing business, there were many of such girls. He met with island's elders and the parents of the girls. As Steve confirmed it,

> There were seventeen of these girls on the island. We found out that there was a American doctor team working temporarily on a nearby larger island. We made arrangements, took our seventeen girls by an hours long boat trip to the other island. There they had surgery. The girls and their mothers lived on the other island until the girls were mostly healed; then we returned them and their mothers to their home island. When we neared their home island word had gotten out and all six thousand residents of the island were there on the beaches waiting for us to come ashore. Many of them were crying.

What Steve declined to mention in the interview, was that Steve and Phillips Foods paid for everything. Just a continuation of what the Phillips had always been doing - giving back. I learned of another similar happening also from Dr. Robbins and only confirmed by Steve after he realized I knew of it.

After the operation on Bantayan Island had been underway for awhile, Steve began to notice that almost all of the children had bad teeth. He remembered a friend from his 'Hoot" days, the only dentist to keep on cooking as a fry cook out of loyalty. Dr. Geoffrey Robbins, a former 'Phillips Boy' tells this story.

> When Steve came home and we'd see each other, he'd keep talking about the Philippines. By that time the Bantayan Island operation was up and running.
>
> One day he came to me and began to discuss the health problems that his Philippines employees suffered, especially when it came to the employees' children and their teeth. He asked me to come over and help. Try to get what supplies I

could get donated from suppliers, and he'd pay for everything else. I agreed.

I first flew into Manila, then down to Cebu Island, and from there on a bush plane to Bantayan Island, landing on a dirt strip [after the Phillips Foods operation was under way the Philippine's government constructed a dirt air strip on Bantayan Island.] Steve first got me a room on the island's only hotel, a six room hotel. There was no air conditioning, and after a couple of nights I had to get out of there. Steve then put me up in a nipa hut. Three sides and a roof of thatch, a mosquito net over the front, no doors. It had a small rudimentary bed, and a burlap pillow case stuffed with chicken feathers. It was in the beach area and at least I had a sea breeze at night.

Steve had built cisterns to catch pure rainwater and channeled the rainwater into underground tanks for later use. And it rained a lot.

I had gone over there, in part anyway, because I thought it would be fun. But it ended up being the hardest dentistry I've done in my life. The island is divided into three provinces, and each province has eight villages. Steve drew employees from all over the island, from different areas. I would try to hit all villages in a province in a day. The only available ground transportation they had was an old motor scooter. They lent it to me and each day I'd load it up with supplies and equipment, including lots of bottles of distilled water to boil for sterilization purposes. By the end of my first trip, I'd carried so much water that the kids called me "The Water Man." A lot of what I was doing on the first trip was assessing need.

I was primarily concerned with the children of the workers on that first trip. I spent most of the time going from village to village on the motor scooter with water bottles every conceivable place. I'd arrive in a village, the elder, or an interpreter would line up the kids, and I'd go to work. When the children in one village were taken care of, it was on to the next village. I worked from sunup to sundown.

Everything, other than Dr. Robbins' time, was paid for by Steve.

Dr. Robbins also recalled that when he was there he realized that the well water wasn't very pure in many of the villages. Rain runoff would sometimes run from animal holding pens into some of the wells. When he suggested that, given the heavy rainfall, a cistern system could supply purer water to the villagers, Steve began to provide for them. Phillips Foods paid for everything.

Dr. Robbins, the former Phillips' fry cook, went back to Bantayan Island on another occasion and picked up where he left off the first time - addressing the dental needs of the people of the island. After he understood that I had the information about Dr. Robbins' trips to the Philippines, Steve confirmed it, but did so in his praise of Dr. Robbins.

> I've never seen anybody work as hard as Geoff did in my life. He would get up at five o'clock in the morning and go to one of the places or clinics where he was scheduled to be. I'd say to him, 'Geoff, you need to relax a little.' He'd say, 'No, no I have to help these people.' He would have fifty people lined up at five in the morning some of whom had been waiting since three o'clock, waiting for him to come. And he would sit there with the sweat running off him, off his face, all day long. I know he lost twenty pounds each trip. I swear I've never seen anything like it. He would start at five in the morning and around eight or nine in the evening I'd go down there, down to wherever he was working, and he'd still have thirty people lined up.
>
> He always had a local dentist working with him learning all the modern techniques that Geoff brought with him. . . .
>
> Geoff wouldn't even take a break. I'd say, 'You've got to eat something.' He'd answer, 'No, no, they're bringing me some food. I've got thirty people here.' I'd warn him that he was going to collapse. He was there for a week or ten days that first trip and if I hadn't pulled him away from there, he'd probably still be there. He really worked hard and all the people appreciated him for it. They could see how hard he was

working for them, what he was putting into the effort. They loved him.

Then there were the efforts of the Phillips' entities in the tsunami affected areas to bring relief, not only to its people, but to all the survivors. And there is still the ongoing program begun and led by the President of Phillips, Mark Snead, to restore boats to the affected fishermen of the villages devastated during the waves. An effort that will have produced a hundred or more boats by the time this book is in print.

Of course in discussing the ways in which Phillips Foods does business in Asia, Steve and others, not realizing that they were really talking about charitable endeavors, told of the volley-ball courts, the electrification of villages, the building of schools, the repair of churches, the building of Mosques. Business giving perhaps, but in the spirit of the Phillips.

Then there is the almost constant participation in civic and professional organizations by the family. Shirley serves, or has served, on the board of trustees, or the equivalent, of the University of Maryland, the University of Maryland Hospital, Washington College, Blue Cross/ Blue Shield, Maryland Historical Society, the Maryland Chamber of Commerce and on the Maryland Appellate Nomination Commission which is responsible for nomination of judicial candidates for Maryland's highest courts. She has received honorary Doctorate degrees from the University of Maryland - Eastern Shore and from the International Culinary School. She has been ranked in the top 100 of the Nations top 500 business women. In 2000 the Restaurant Association of Maryland established a Hospitality Hall of Honor and the Phillips family was inducted. She and Brice are also members of one of the major support groups of the Library of Congress. She and Brice have been honored by the Ocean City Art League as Patrons of the Arts (Shirley is, herself, an accomplished artist.) In 1986 they were named Restauranteurs of the Year, in 1996 they were named Maryland's Retail Entrepreneur of the Year. The magazine *Working Woman* named Shirley one of the nations's top 100 women. Additionally, the restaurants have won the Southern Living Reader's Award. The Maryland Senate issued a citation honoring Brice's service on the Chesapeake Bay Trust. The two of them have been named as "Ambassadors of Goodwill for Maryland" as a part of the Governor's Salute to Excellence. And there are many other recognitions they have received over the years.

Among other honors, Steve and the Phillips Foods company have been recognized by receiving the 2002 Emerging Company Award from the Association for Corporate Growth. In 2000 Steve was named the Ernst & Young Maryland Entrepreneur of the Year. Phillips Foods was named the fastest growing urban business in 2002 by *Inc. Magazines'* Inner City Top Businesses program, Steve was awarded the 2001 World Trade Center Institute's Maryland International Business Leadership Award, Phillips was a finalist in the National Restaurants Association's 'Restaurant Neighbor Award in 2001 in recognition of the firms contributions and support for the C.R.A.B. research project. The company was awarded the 2003 Innovator Award by the California Restaurant Association.

In 2001 Phillips Harborplace was ranked 13th in sales in the nation and the Washington restaurant was ranked 54th; in 2002 the two restaurants were ranked 11th and 42nd respectively; in 2003 11th and 63rd respectively. In 1981, the Steve-operated Phillips Harborplace Restaurant was ranked third in sales among American restaurants by *Restaurant Hospitality* magazine. Even today, with no or little expansion in the interim, it stays consistently in the top twenty grossing restaurants in the country.

Steve serves on the Chesapeake Bay Recovery Partnership Advisory Board, the Board of directors of the Philippine American Association. His Phillips Foods company has been placed 27th in the top 100 Inner-City businesses in the United States. And there have been many other awards to numerous to list here. And of course, he and Max have helped maintain the reputation of the Maryland sailing community with their national and world sailing titles.

And then there is Captain Happiness - Jeffrey Phillips. He and Janet are in the process of creating a "Nature Wilderness School," so that they can teach nature awareness and wilderness survival skills to children and adults where Jeffery's unconquerable spirit will no doubt show the way to surviving not only nature's obstacles, but man's as well. They note their purpose,

> No matter how large a business you create, or how much in material benefits you achieve, at some point you realize that your purpose in life is more than that. When that happens your ask yourself an important question. 'What next?' We answered the question by returning to nature in order to protect it and to teach others the skills to learn to appreciate the ultimate source of all existence.

In the living of his life to the fullness Jeffery, with his family's support, has redefined the meaning of happiness. The example he sets gives to each of us, every day we see him, a lesson teaching that life is a matter of spirit. He tells us that if you have it, if you have spirit, you will chose to be happy as he has done, and in choosing to be happy, seemingly insurmountable obstacles will be overcome - simply because you want it so.

There are several characteristics that mark the successes of this remarkable family: vision, structure, people, courage, *and giving back.*

# CHAPTER FIFTY-SEVEN

*Captain Ivy, Miss Lillie; Captain Ellie, Miss Leone*

*Captain Ivy: All I ever wanted was you. Swimming Tar Bay, laying in trenches in the Argonne Forest, all I could think of was you. I loved you then. Eventually the ivy blended with the Lillie and there were little flowers. I have loved you every day of your life - and since.*

*Wasn't it great fun taking the kids, Bernice, Shirley and Billy, out on the skipjack, over to Barren Island with the sails billowing in the wind. Sailing her over the waters I used to swim for you - back in the summers when I was but a boy and you but a girl. But so beautiful. You were so beautiful. Still so beautiful.*

*And we made her, made our Shirley. Who would ever have expected that the little girl we used to pay pennies to for picking lady bugs from the plants, who used to collect cow pies for your garden, would be the matriarch of a clan that would take Hoopers Islanders to the far corners of the world to find crab. Who would have thought that all of it would be done.*

*Miss Lillie: I thought it. When you came back to me, I knew there was a reason. I had lost two good men; never expected to find another. Then you returned, the little boy who used to swim to me, even in the fall when a chill was in the water. Swam to me. I'd never forgotten. And there you were again, loving me. And I loved you. I've never stopped the loving. Not even here.*

*You rescued me from my grief, brought me to living again. I knew then that we were to produce a line that would join with another and go out into the world and conquer it. And when our Shirley was born, I knew that great things would happen. She was so resolute even as a child. It seemed like she knew even then where it would all end up.*

*Then Brice showed up. He drove too fast, scared me some. But I knew he was the one. That he and our Shirley would be special travelers through life. And they have been. And they gave us special grandsons. Jeffrey and Steve sitting on the curb yelling 'customer coming!' Who could have asked for more than we have had?*

*Captain Ellie: Who would have thought that they would do what they did? Who would have thought it? How could we ever have known what we were starting in the aft cabin of the McCready on that very special night so long ago when the moon was shining through the porthole, as we passed off Hatteras Light? I knew I should have been on deck, that's where the Captain always is when rounding Hatteras. But, I felt that I was supposed to be with you; that it was time to start all this.*

*Miss Leone: I knew it from the beginning. I could feel it. A woman knows what a man can give her. A great life. A dynasty really. I saw it all in you. In us, even before you asked me to marry you and come live aboard your schooner. What great fun it was, sailing the coast, going south when the northwesters blew. Surfing the white combers with the wind astern, burying her nose in the waves ahead, spray in our hair, our clothes wet. Racing Uncle Warren. Beating him. What fun it was.*

*In the seasons of our youth.*

*And look at Steve still beating the Uncle Warrens of the sea - a Phillips through and through - like you. And Jeffrey of the indomitable spirit, surviving where most would not, teaching them, those back there, about happiness. No, you were where you should have been, with me, making Brice. Even Hatteras could understand. It let us by so that all that has come to pass - would start.*

*Captain Ellie: They know about Hoopers Islanders now. The world knows about them. The kids, Brice and Shirley and theirs, Steve and Jeffrey, the other Hoopers Islanders. All of them.*

*They found the Empires of the Crab.*